INTERNATIONAL

*A Portrait of the Artist
as a Young Man*

EDITED BY

Hans Walter Gabler WITH *Walter Hettche*

JAMES JOYCE

A Portrait of the Artist as a Young Man

VINTAGE INTERNATIONAL
VINTAGE BOOKS
A DIVISION OF RANDOM HOUSE, INC.
NEW YORK

FIRST VINTAGE INTERNATIONAL EDITION, FEBRUARY 1993

Library of Congress Cataloging-in-Publication Data
Joyce, James, 1882–1941.
A portrait of the artist as a young man / James Joyce. — 1st Vintage
international ed.
p. cm.
Includes bibliographical references (p.)
ISBN 0–679–73989–0 (pbk.)
I. Title.
PR6019.09P63 1992
823'.912—dc20   91–50715
CIP

BOOK DESIGN BY CATHRYN S. AISON

Electronically typeset by Wolfhard Steppe for pagina GmbH, Tübingen
Printed and bound in the United States of America
10   9   8   7   6   5   4   3   2   1

CONTENTS

A Portrait of the Artist as a Young Man

3

he Artist

Man

Et ignotas animum dimittit in artes.

Ovid, Metamorphoses. VIII.188.

I

Once upon a time and a very good time it was there was a moocow coming down along the road and this moocow that was coming down along the road met a nicens little boy named baby tuckoo .....

His father told him that story: his father looked at him through a glass: he had a hairy face.

He was baby tuckoo. The moocow came down the road where Betty Byrne lived: she sold lemon platt.

> O, the wild rose blossoms
> On the little green place.

He sang that song. That was his song.

> O, the geen wothe botheth.

When you wet the bed first it is warm then it gets cold. His mother put on the oilsheet. That had the queer smell.

His mother had a nicer smell than his father. She played on the piano the sailor's hornpipe for him to dance. He danced:

> Tralala lala
> Tralala tralaladdy
> Tralala lala
> Tralala lala.

Uncle Charles and Dante clapped. They were older than his father and mother but uncle Charles was older than Dante.

Dante had two brushes in her press. The brush with the maroon velvet back was for Michael Davitt and the brush with the green velvet back was for Parnell. Dante gave him a cachou every time he brought her a piece of tissue paper.

The Vances lived in number seven. They had a different father and mother. They were Eileen's father and mother. When they were grown up he was going to marry Eileen.

30 He hid under the table. His mother said:

— O, Stephen will apologise.

Dante said:

— O, if not, the eagles will come and pull out his eyes.

> *Pull out his eyes,*
> *Apologise,*
> *Apologise,*
> *Pull out his eyes.*
>
> *Apologise,*
> *Pull out his eyes,*
> 40 *Pull out his eyes,*
> *Apologise.*

◆ ◆ ◆

The wide playgrounds were swarming with boys. All were shouting and the prefects urged them on with strong cries. The evening air was pale and chilly and after every charge and thud of the footballers the greasy leather orb flew like a heavy bird through the grey light. He kept on the fringe of his line, out of sight of his prefect, out of the reach of the rude feet, feigning to run now and then. He felt his body small and weak amid the throng of players and his eyes were weak and watery. Rody 50 Kickham was not like that: he would be captain of the third line all the fellows said.

Rody Kickham was a decent fellow but Nasty Roche was a stink. Rody Kickham had greaves in his number and a hamper in the refectory. Nasty Roche had big hands. He called the Friday pudding dog-in-the-blanket. And one day he had asked:

— What is your name?

Stephen had answered:

— Stephen Dedalus.

Then Nasty Roche had said:

4

—What kind of a name is that?

And when Stephen had not been able to answer Nasty Roche had asked:

—What is your father?

Stephen had answered:

—A gentleman.

Then Nasty Roche had asked:

—Is he a magistrate?

He crept about from point to point on the fringe of his line, making little runs now and then. But his hands were bluish with cold. He kept his hands in the sidepockets of his belted grey suit. That was a belt round his jacket. And belt was also to give a fellow a belt. One day a fellow had said to Cantwell:

—I'd give you such a belt in a second.

Cantwell had answered:

—Go and fight your match. Give Cecil Thunder a belt. I'd like to see you. He'd give you a toe in the rump for yourself.

That was not a nice expression. His mother had told him not to speak with the rough boys in the college. Nice mother! The first day in the hall of the castle when she had said good= bye she had put up her veil double to her nose to kiss him: and her nose and eyes were red. But he had pretended not to see that she was going to cry. She was a nice mother but she was not so nice when she cried. And his father had given him two fiveshilling pieces for pocket money. And his father had told him if he wanted anything to write home to him and, whatever he did, never to peach on a fellow. Then at the door of the castle the rector had shaken hands with his father and mother, his soutane fluttering in the breeze, and the car had driven off with his father and mother on it. They had cried to him from the car, waving their hands:

—Goodbye, Stephen, goodbye!

—Goodbye, Stephen, goodbye!

He was caught in the whirl of a scrimmage and, fearful of the flashing eyes and muddy boots, bent down to look through the legs. The fellows were struggling and groaning and their legs were rubbing and kicking and stamping. Then Jack

Lawton's yellow boots dodged out the ball and all the other boots and legs ran after. He ran after them a little way and then stopped. It was useless to run on. Soon they would be going home for the holidays. After supper in the studyhall he would change the number pasted up inside his desk from seventyseven to seventysix.

It would be better to be in the studyhall than out there in the cold. The sky was pale and cold but there were lights in the castle. He wondered from which window Hamilton Rowan had thrown his hat on the haha and had there been flowerbeds at that time under the windows. One day when he had been called to the castle the butler had shown him the marks of the soldiers' slugs in the wood of the door and had given him a piece of shortbread that the community ate. It was nice and warm to see the lights in the castle. It was like something in a book. Perhaps Leicester Abbey was like that. And there were nice sentences in Doctor Cornwell's Spelling Book. They were like poetry but they were only sentences to learn the spelling from.

> *Wolsey died in Leicester Abbey*
> *Where the abbots buried him.*
> *Canker is a disease of plants,*
> *Cancer one of animals.*

It would be nice to lie on the hearthrug before the fire, leaning his head upon his hands, and think on those sentences. He shivered as if he had cold slimy water next his skin. That was mean of Wells to shoulder him into the square ditch because he would not swop his little snuffbox for Wells's seasoned hacking chestnut, the conqueror of forty. How cold and slimy the water had been! A fellow had once seen a big rat jump plop into the scum. He shivered and longed to cry. It would be so nice to be at home. Mother was sitting at the fire with Dante waiting for Brigid to bring in the tea. She had her feet on the fender and her jewelly slippers were so hot and they had such a lovely warm smell! Dante knew a lot of things. She had taught him where the Mozambique Channel was and what was the longest river in America and what was the name of the highest mountain in the moon. Father Arnall knew more than Dante because he was a priest but both his father and uncle Charles said that Dante was a clever woman and a wellread woman. And when Dante made that noise after dinner and then put up her hand to her mouth: that was heartburn.

A voice cried far out on the playground:

—All in!

Then other voices cried from the lower and third lines:

—All in! All in!

The players closed around, flushed and muddy, and he went among them, glad to go in. Rody Kickham held the ball by its greasy lace. A fellow asked him to give it one last: but he walked on without even answering the fellow. Simon Moonan told him not to because the prefect was looking. The fellow turned to Simon Moonan and said:

—We all know why you speak. You are McGlade's suck.

Suck was a queer word. The fellow called Simon Moonan that name because Simon Moonan used to tie the prefect's false sleeves behind his back and the prefect used to let on to be angry. But the sound was ugly. Once he had washed his hands in the lavatory of the Wicklow Hotel and his father pulled the stopper up by the chain after and the dirty water went down through the hole in the basin. And when it had all gone down slowly the hole in the basin had made a sound like that: suck. Only louder.

To remember that and the white look of the lavatory made him feel cold and then hot. There were two cocks that you turned and water came out: cold and hot. He felt cold and then a little hot: and he could see the names printed on the cocks. That was a very queer thing.

And the air in the corridor chilled him too. It was queer and wettish. But soon the gas would be lit and in burning it made a light noise like a little song. Always the same: and when the fellows stopped talking in the playroom you could hear it.

It was the hour for sums. Father Arnall wrote a hard sum on the board and then he said:

—Now then, who will win? Go ahead, York! Go ahead, Lan= caster!

Stephen tried his best but the sum was too hard and he felt confused. The little silk badge with the white rose on it that was pinned on the breast of his jacket began to flutter. He was no good at sums but he tried his best so that York might not lose. Father Arnall's face looked very black but he was not in a wax: he was laughing. Then Jack Lawton cracked his fingers and Father Arnall looked at his copybook and said:

—Right. Bravo Lancaster! The red rose wins. Come on now, York! Forge ahead!

Jack Lawton looked over from his side. The little silk badge with the red rose on it looked very rich because he had a blue sailor top on. Stephen felt his own face red too, thinking of all the bets about who would get first place in elements, Jack Lawton or he. Some weeks Jack Lawton got the card for first and some weeks he got the card for first. His white silk badge fluttered and fluttered as he worked at the next sum and heard Father Arnall's voice. Then all his eagerness passed away and he felt his face quite cool. He thought his face must be white because it felt so cool. He could not get out the answer for the sum but it did not matter. White roses and red roses: those were beautiful colours to think of. And the cards for first place and second place and third place were beautiful colours too: pink and cream and lavender. Lavender and cream and pink roses were beautiful to think of. Perhaps a wild rose might be like those colours: and he remembered the song about the wild rose blossoms on the little green place. But you could not have a green rose. But perhaps somewhere in the world you could.

The bell rang and then the classes began to file out of the rooms and along the corridors towards the refectory. He sat looking at the two prints of butter on his plate but could not eat the damp bread. The tablecloth was damp and limp. But he drank off the hot weak tea which the clumsy scullion, girt with a white apron, poured into his cup. He wondered whether the scullion's apron was damp too or whether all white things were cold and damp. Nasty Roche and Saurin drank cocoa that their people sent them in tins. They said they could not drink the tea; that it was hogwash. Their fathers were magistrates, the fel= lows said.

All the boys seemed to him very strange. They had all fa= thers and mothers and different clothes and voices. He longed to be at home and lay his head on his mother's lap. But he could not: and so he longed for the play and study and prayers to be over and to be in bed.

He drank another cup of hot tea and Fleming said:

—What's up? Have you a pain or what's up with you?

—I don't know, Stephen said.

—Sick in your breadbasket, Fleming said, because your face looks white. It will go away.

—O yes, Stephen said.

But he was not sick there. He thought that he was sick in his heart if you could be sick in that place. Fleming was very decent to ask him. He wanted to cry. He leaned his elbows on the table and shut and opened the flaps of his ears. Then he heard the noise of the refectory every time he opened the flaps of his ears. It made a roar like a train at night. And when he closed the flaps the roar was shut off like a train going into a tunnel. That night at Dalkey the train had roared like that and then, when it went into the tunnel, the roar stopped. He closed his eyes and the train went on, roaring and then stopping; roaring again, stopping. It was nice to hear it roar and stop and then roar out of the tunnel again and then stop.

Then the higher line fellows began to come down along the matting in the middle of the refectory, Paddy Rath and Jimmy Magee and the Spaniard who was allowed to smoke cigars and the little Portuguese who wore the woolly cap. And then the lower line tables and the tables of the third line. And every single fellow had a different way of walking.

He sat in a corner of the playroom pretending to watch a

240 game of dominos and once or twice he was able to hear for an instant the little song of the gas. The prefect was at the door with some boys and Simon Moonan was knotting his false sleeves. He was telling them something about Tullabeg.

Then he went away from the door and Wells came over to Stephen and said:

—Tell us, Dedalus, do you kiss your mother every night before you go to bed?

Stephen answered:

—I do.

250 Wells turned to the other fellows and said:

—O, I say, here's a fellow says he kisses his mother every night before he goes to bed.

The other fellows stopped their game and turned round, laughing. Stephen blushed under their eyes and said:

—I do not.

Wells said:

—O, I say, here's a fellow says he doesn't kiss his mother before he goes to bed.

They all laughed again. Stephen tried to laugh with them.
260 He felt his whole body hot and confused in a moment. What was the right answer to the question? He had given two and still Wells laughed. But Wells must know the right answer for he was in third of grammar. He tried to think of Wells's mother but he did not dare to raise his eyes to Wells's face. He did not like Wells's face. It was Wells who had shouldered him into the square ditch the day before because he would not swop his little snuffbox for Wells's seasoned hacking chestnut, the con= queror of forty. It was a mean thing to do; all the fellows said it was. And how cold and slimy the water had been! And a fellow
270 had once seen a big rat jump plop into the scum.

The cold slime of the ditch covered his whole body; and, when the bell rang for study and the lines filed out of the playrooms, he felt the cold air of the corridor and staircase inside his clothes. He still tried to think what was the right answer. Was it right to kiss his mother or wrong to kiss his mother? What did that mean, to kiss? You put your face up like that to say goodnight and then his mother put her face down. That was to kiss. His mother put her lips on his cheek; her lips were soft and they wetted his cheek; and they made a tiny little noise: kiss. Why did people do that with their two faces?

Sitting in the studyhall he opened the lid of his desk and changed the number pasted up inside from seventyseven to seventysix. But the Christmas vacation was very far away: but one time it would come because the earth moved round always.

There was a picture of the earth on the first page of his geography: a big ball in the middle of clouds. Fleming had a box of crayons and one night during free study he had coloured the earth green and the clouds maroon. That was like the two brushes in Dante's press, the brush with the green velvet back for Parnell and the brush with the maroon velvet back for Michael Davitt. But he had not told Fleming to colour them those colours. Fleming had done it himself.

He opened the geography to study the lesson; but he could not learn the names of places in America. Still they were all different places that had those different names. They were all in different countries and the countries were in continents and the continents were in the world and the world was in the universe.

He turned to the flyleaf of the geography and read what he had written there: himself, his name and where he was.

Stephen Dedalus
Class of Elements
Clongowes Wood College
Sallins
County Kildare
Ireland
Europe
The World
The Universe

That was in his writing: and Fleming one night for a cod had written on the opposite page:

Stephen Dedalus is my name,
Ireland is my nation.
Clongowes is my dwellingplace
And heaven my expectation.

He read the verses backwards but then they were not poetry. Then he read the flyleaf from the bottom to the top till he came to his own name. That was he: and he read down the page again. What was after the universe? Nothing. But was there anything round the universe to show where it stopped before the nothing place began? It could not be a wall but there could be a thin thin line there all round everything. It was very big to think about everything and everywhere. Only God could do that. He tried to think what a big thought that must be but he could think only of God. God was God's name just as his name was Stephen. *Dieu* was the French for God and that was God's name too; and when anyone prayed to God and said *Dieu* then God knew at once that it was a French person that was pray= ing. But though there were different names for God in all the different languages in the world and God understood what all the people who prayed said in their different languages still God remained always the same God and God's real name was God.

It made him very tired to think that way. It made him feel his head very big. He turned over the flyleaf and looked wearily at the green round earth in the middle of the maroon clouds. He wondered which was right, to be for the green or for the maroon, because Dante had ripped the green velvet back off the brush that was for Parnell one day with her scissors and had told him that Parnell was a bad man. He wondered if they were arguing at home about that. That was called politics. There were two sides in it: Dante was on one side and his father and Mr Casey were on the other side but his mother and uncle Charles were on no side. Every day there was something in the paper about it.

It pained him that he did not know well what politics meant and that he did not know where the universe ended. He felt small and weak. When would he be like the fellows in poetry and rhetoric? They had big voices and big boots and they studied trigonometry. That was very far away. First came the vacation and then the next term and then vacation again and then again another term and then again the vacation. It was like a train going in and out of tunnels and that was like the noise of the boys eating in the refectory when you opened and closed the flaps of the ears. Term, vacation; tunnel, out; noise, stop. How far away it was! It was better to go to bed to sleep. Only prayers in the chapel and then bed. He shivered and yawned. It would be lovely in bed after the sheets got a bit hot. First they were so cold to get into. He shivered to think how cold they were first. But then they got hot and then he could sleep. It was lovely to be tired. He yawned again. Night prayers and then bed: he shivered and wanted to yawn. It would be lovely in a few minutes. He felt a warm glow creeping up from the cold shivering sheets, warmer and warmer till he felt warm all over, ever so warm; ever so warm and yet he shivered a little and still wanted to yawn.

The bell rang for night prayers and he filed out of the study= hall after the others and down the staircase and along the corridors to the chapel. The corridors were darkly lit and the chapel was darkly lit. Soon all would be dark and sleeping. There was cold night air in the chapel and the marbles were the colour the sea was at night. The sea was cold day and night: but it was colder at night. It was cold and dark under the seawall beside his father's house. But the kettle would be on the hob to make punch.

The prefect of the chapel prayed above his head and his memory knew the responses:

> O Lord, open our lips
> And our mouth shall announce Thy praise.
> Incline unto our aid, O God!
> O Lord, make haste to help us!

There was a cold night smell in the chapel. But it was a holy smell. It was not like the smell of the old peasants who knelt at the back of the chapel at Sunday mass. That was a smell of air and rain and turf and corduroy. But they were very holy peas= ants. They breathed behind him on his neck and sighed as they prayed. They lived in Clane, a fellow said: there were little cottages there and he had seen a woman standing at the half= door of a cottage with a child in her arms as the cars had come past from Sallins. It would be lovely to sleep for one night in that cottage before the fire of smoking turf, in the dark lit by the fire, in the warm dark, breathing the smell of the peasants, air and rain and turf and corduroy. But, O, the road there between the trees was dark! You would be lost in the dark. It made him afraid to think of how it was.

He heard the voice of the prefect of the chapel saying the last prayer. He prayed it too against the dark outside under the trees.

> *Visit, we beseech Thee, O Lord, this habitation and drive away from it all the snares of the enemy. May Thy holy angels dwell herein to preserve us in peace and may Thy blessing be always upon us through Christ, Our Lord. Amen.*

His fingers trembled as he undressed himself in the dormi= tory. He told his fingers to hurry up. He had to undress and then kneel and say his own prayers and be in bed before the gas was lowered so that he might not go to hell when he died. He rolled his stockings off and put on his nightshirt quickly and knelt trembling at his bedside and repeated his prayers quickly quickly fearing that the gas would go down. He felt his shoul= ders shaking as he murmured:

> *God bless my father and my mother and spare them to me!*
> *God bless my little brothers and sisters and spare them to me!*
> *God bless Dante and uncle Charles and spare them to me!*

He blessed himself and climbed quickly into bed and, tuck=
ing the end of the nightshirt under his feet, curled himself to=
gether under the cold white sheets, shaking and trembling. But
he would not go to hell when he died; and the shaking would   420
stop. A voice bade the boys in the dormitory goodnight. He
peered out for an instant over the coverlet and saw the yellow
curtains round and before his bed that shut him off on all sides.
The light was lowered quietly.

The prefect's shoes went away. Where? Down the staircase
and along the corridors or to his room at the end? He saw the
dark. Was it true about the black dog that walked there at night
with eyes as big as carriagelamps? They said it was the ghost of
a murderer. A long shiver of fear flowed over his body. He saw
the dark entrance hall of the castle. Old servants in old dress   430
were in the ironingroom above the staircase. It was long ago.
The old servants were quiet. There was a fire there but the hall
was still dark. A figure came up the staircase from the hall. He
wore the white cloak of a marshal; his face was pale and
strange; he held his hand pressed to his side. He looked out of
strange eyes at the old servants. They looked at him and saw
their master's face and cloak and knew that he had received his
deathwound. But only the dark was where they looked: only
dark silent air. Their master had received his deathwound on
the battlefield of Prague far away over the sea. He was standing   440
on the field; his hand was pressed to his side; his face was pale
and strange and he wore the white cloak of a marshal.

O how cold and strange it was to think of that! All the dark
was cold and strange. There were pale strange faces there, great
eyes like carriagelamps. They were the ghosts of murderers, the
figures of marshals who had received their deathwound on
battlefields far away over the sea. What did they wish to say
that their faces were so strange?

*Visit, we beseech Thee, O Lord, this habitation and drive
away from it all*   450

Going home for the holidays! That would be lovely: the
fellows had told him. Getting up on the cars in the early wintry

morning outside the door of the castle. The cars were rolling on the gravel. Cheers for the rector!

Hurray! Hurray! Hurray!

The cars drove past the chapel and all caps were raised. They drove merrily along the country roads. The drivers pointed with their whips to Bodenstown. The fellows cheered. They passed the farmhouse of the Jolly Farmer. Cheer after cheer after cheer. Through Clane they drove, cheering and cheered. The peasant women stood at the halfdoors, the men stood here and there. The lovely smell there was in the wintry air: the smell of Clane: rain and wintry air and turf smouldering and corduroy.

The train was full of fellows: a long long chocolate train with cream facings. The guards went to and fro opening, closing, locking, unlocking the doors. They were men in dark blue and silver; they had silvery whistles and their keys made a quick music: click, click: click, click.

And the train raced on over the flat lands and past the Hill of Allen. The telegraphpoles were passing, passing. The train went on and on. It knew. There were coloured lanterns in the hall of his father's house and ropes of green branches. There were holly and ivy round the pierglass and holly and ivy, green and red, twined round the chandeliers. There were red holly and green ivy round the old portraits on the walls. Holly and ivy for him and for Christmas.

Lovely ......

All the people. Welcome home, Stephen! Noises of welcome. His mother kissed him. Was that right? His father was a marshal now: higher than a magistrate. Welcome home, Stephen!

Noises .....

There was a noise of curtainrings running back along the rods, of water being splashed in the basins. There was a noise of rising and dressing and washing in the dormitory: a noise of clapping of hands as the prefect went up and down telling the fellows to look sharp. A pale sunlight showed the yellow curtains drawn back, the tossed beds. His bed was very hot and his face and body were very hot.

He got up and sat on the side of his bed. He was weak. He   490
tried to pull on his stocking. It had a horrid rough feel. The
sunlight was queer and cold.

Fleming said:

—Are you not well?

He did not know; and Fleming said:

—Get back into bed. I'll tell McGlade you're not well.

—He's sick.

—Who is?

—Tell McGlade.

—Get back into bed.   500

—Is he sick?

A fellow held his arms while he loosened the stocking cling=
ing to his foot and climbed back into the hot bed.

He crouched down between the sheets, glad of their tepid
glow. He heard the fellows talk among themselves about him
as they dressed for mass. It was a mean thing to do, to shoulder
him into the square ditch, they were saying.

Then their voices ceased; they had gone. A voice at his bed
said:

—Dedalus, don't spy on us, sure you won't?   510

Wells's face was there. He looked at it and saw that Wells
was afraid.

—I didn't mean to. Sure you won't?

His father had told him, whatever he did, never to peach on
a fellow. He shook his head and answered no and felt glad.
Wells said:

—I didn't mean to, honour bright. It was only for cod. I'm
sorry.

The face and the voice went away. Sorry because he was
afraid. Afraid that it was some disease. Canker was a disease of   520
plants and cancer one of animals: or another different. That
was a long time ago then out on the playgrounds in the evening
light, creeping from point to point on the fringe of his line, a
heavy bird flying low through the grey light. Leicester Abbey lit
up. Wolsey died there. The abbots buried him themselves.

It was not Wells's face, it was the prefect's. He was not

foxing. No, no: he was sick really. He was not foxing. And he felt the prefect's hand on his forehead; and he felt his forehead warm and damp against the prefect's cold damp hand. That was the way a rat felt, slimy and damp and cold. Every rat had two eyes to look out of. Sleek slimy coats, little little feet tucked up to jump, black shiny eyes to look out of. They could understand how to jump. But the minds of rats could not understand trigonometry. When they were dead they lay on their sides. Their coats dried then. They were only dead things.

The prefect was there again and it was his voice that was saying that he was to get up, that Father Minister had said he was to get up and dress and go to the infirmary. And while he was dressing himself as quickly as he could the prefect said:

—We must pack off to Brother Michael because we have the collywobbles. Terrible thing to have the collywobbles! How we wobble when we have the collywobbles!

He was very decent to say that. That was all to make him laugh. But he could not laugh because his cheeks and lips were all shivery: and then the prefect had to laugh by himself.

The prefect cried:

—Quick march! Hayfoot! Strawfoot!

They went together down the staircase and along the corri=
dor and past the bath. As he passed the door he remembered with a vague fear the warm turfcoloured bogwater, the warm moist air, the noise of plunges, the smell of the towels, like medicine.

Brother Michael was standing at the door of the infirmary and from the door of the dark cabinet on his right came a smell like medicine. That came from the bottles on the shelves. The prefect spoke to Brother Michael and Brother Michael answered and called the prefect sir. He had reddish hair mixed with grey and a queer look. It was queer that he would always be a brother. It was queer too that you could not call him sir because he was a brother and had a different kind of look. Was he not holy enough or why could he not catch up on the others?

There were two beds in the room and in one bed there was a fellow: and when they went in he called out:

—Hello! It's young Dedalus! What's up?

—The sky is up, Brother Michael said.

He was a fellow out of third of grammar and, while Stephen was undressing, he asked Brother Michael to bring him a round of buttered toast.

—Ah, do! he said.

—Butter you up! said Brother Michael. You'll get your walking papers in the morning when the doctor comes.

—Will I? the fellow said. I'm not well yet.

Brother Michael repeated:

—You'll get your walking papers, I tell you.

He bent down to rake the fire. He had a long back like the long back of a tramhorse. He shook the poker gravely and nodded his head at the fellow out of third of grammar.

Then Brother Michael went away and after a while the fellow out of third of grammar turned in towards the wall and fell asleep.

That was the infirmary. He was sick then. Had they written home to tell his mother and father? But it would be quicker for one of the priests to go himself to tell them. Or he would write a letter for the priest to bring.

> Dear Mother
>   I am sick. I want to go home. Please come and take
>   me home. I am in the infirmary.
>   Your fond son,
>   Stephen

How far away they were! There was cold sunlight outside the window. He wondered if he would die. You could die just the same on a sunny day. He might die before his mother came. Then he would have a dead mass in the chapel like the way the fellows had told him it was when Little had died. All the fellows would be at the mass, dressed in black, all with sad faces. Wells too would be there but no fellow would look at him. The rector would be there in a cope of black and gold and there would be tall yellow candles on the altar and round the catafalque. And they would carry the coffin out of the chapel slowly and he would be buried in the little graveyard of the community off the main avenue of limes. And Wells would be sorry then for what he had done. And the bell would toll slowly.

He could hear the tolling. He said over to himself the song that Brigid had taught him.

> *Dingdong! The castle bell!*
> *Farewell, my mother!*
> *Bury me in the old churchyard*
> *Beside my eldest brother.*
> *My coffin shall be black,*
> *Six angels at my back,*
> *Two to sing and two to pray*
> *And two to carry my soul away.*

How beautiful and sad that was! How beautiful the words were where they said *Bury me in the old churchyard*! A tremor passed over his body. How sad and how beautiful! He wanted to cry quietly but not for himself: for the words, so beautiful and sad, like music. The bell! The bell! Farewell! O farewell!

The cold sunlight was weaker and Brother Michael was standing at his bedside with a bowl of beeftea. He was glad for his mouth was hot and dry. He could hear them playing on the playgrounds. It was after lunchtime. And the day was going on in the college just as if he were there.

Then Brother Michael was going away and the fellow out of third of grammar told him to be sure and come back and tell him all the news in the paper. He told Stephen that his name was Athy and that his father kept a lot of racehorses that were spiffing jumpers and that his father would give a good tip to Brother Michael any time he wanted it because Brother Michael was very decent and always told him the news out of the paper they got every day up in the castle. There was every kind of news in the paper: accidents, shipwrecks, sports and politics.

—Now it is all about politics in the paper, he said. Do your people talk about that too?

—Yes, Stephen said.

—Mine too, he said.

Then he thought for a moment and said:

—You have a queer name, Dedalus, and I have a queer name too, Athy. My name is the name of a town. Your name is like Latin.

Then he asked:

—Are you good at riddles?

Stephen answered:

—Not very good.

Then he said:

—Can you answer me this one? Why is the county Kildare like the leg of a fellow's breeches?

Stephen thought what could be the answer and then said:

—I give it up.

—Because there is a thigh in it, he said. Do you see the joke? Athy is the town in the county Kildare and a thigh is the other thigh.

—O, I see, Stephen said.

—That's an old riddle, he said.

After a moment he said:

—I say!

—What? asked Stephen.

—You know, he said, you can ask that riddle another way?

—Can you? said Stephen.

—The same riddle, he said. Do you know the other way to ask it?

—No, said Stephen.

—Can you not think of the other way? he said.

He looked at Stephen over the bedclothes as he spoke. Then he lay back on the pillow and said:

—There is another way but I won't tell you what it is.

Why did he not tell it? His father, who kept the racehorses, must be a magistrate too like Saurin's father and Nasty Roche's father. He thought of his own father, of how he sang songs while his mother played and of how he always gave him a shilling when he asked for sixpence and he felt sorry for him that he was not a magistrate like the other boys' fathers. Then why was he sent to that place with them? But his father had told him that he would be no stranger there because his grand= uncle had presented an address to the liberator there fifty years before. You could know the people of that time by their old dress. It seemed to him a solemn time: and he wondered if that was the time when the fellows in Clongowes wore blue coats with brass buttons and yellow waistcoats and caps of rabbit= skin and drank beer like grownup people and kept greyhounds of their own to course the hares with.

He looked at the window and saw that the daylight had grown weaker. There would be cloudy grey light over the play= grounds. There was no noise on the playgrounds. The class must be doing the themes or perhaps Father Arnall was reading a legend out of the book.

It was queer that they had not given him any medicine. Perhaps Brother Michael would bring it back when he came. They said you got stinking stuff to drink when you were in the infirmary. But he felt better now than before. It would be nice getting better slowly. You could get a book then. There was a book in the library about Holland. There were lovely foreign names in it and pictures of strangelooking cities and ships. It made you feel so happy.

How pale the light was at the window! But that was nice. The fire rose and fell on the wall. It was like waves. Someone had put coal on and he heard voices. They were talking. It was the noise of the waves. Or the waves were talking among them= selves as they rose and fell.

He saw the sea of waves, long dark waves rising and falling, dark under the moonless night. A tiny light twinkled at the pierhead where the ship was entering: and he saw a multitude of people gathered by the waters' edge to see the ship that was entering their harbour. A tall man stood on the deck, looking out towards the flat dark land: and by the light at the pierhead he saw his face, the sorrowful face of Brother Michael.

He saw him lift his hand towards the people and heard him say in a loud voice of sorrow over the waters:

—He is dead. We saw him lying upon the catafalque.

A wail of sorrow went up from the people.   710

—Parnell! Parnell! He is dead!

They fell upon their knees, moaning in sorrow.

And he saw Dante in a maroon velvet dress and with a green velvet mantle hanging from her shoulders walking proudly and silently past the people who knelt by the waters' edge.

◆　◆　◆

A great fire, banked high and red, flamed in the grate and under the ivytwined branches of the chandelier the Christmas table was spread. They had come home a little late and still dinner was not ready: but it would be ready in a jiffy, his mother had said. They were waiting for the door to open and   720 for the servants to come in, holding the big dishes covered with their heavy metal covers.

All were waiting: uncle Charles, who sat far away in the shadow of the window, Dante and Mr Casey, who sat in the easychairs at either side of the hearth, Stephen, seated on a chair between them, his feet resting on the toasted boss. Mr Dedalus looked at himself in the pierglass above the mantel= piece, waxed out his moustache ends and then, parting his coattails, stood with his back to the glowing fire: and still, from time to time, he withdrew a hand from his coattail to wax out   730 one of his moustache ends. Mr Casey leaned his head to one side and, smiling, tapped the gland of his neck with his fingers. And Stephen smiled too for he knew now that it was not true that Mr Casey had a purse of silver in his throat. He smiled to think how the silvery noise which Mr Casey used to make had deceived him. And when he had tried to open Mr Casey's hand to see if the purse of silver was hidden there he had seen that the fingers could not be straightened out: and Mr Casey had told him that he had got those three cramped fingers making a birthday present for Queen Victoria.   740

Mr Casey tapped the gland of his neck and smiled at Ste=
phen with sleepy eyes: and Mr Dedalus said to him:

— Yes. Well now, that's all right. O, we had a good walk,
hadn't we, John? Yes ...... I wonder if there's any likelihood of
dinner this evening. Yes ..... O, well now, we got a good breath
of ozone round the Head today. Ay, bedad.

He turned to Dante and said:

— You didn't stir out at all, Mrs Riordan?

Dante frowned and said shortly:

750 — No.

Mr Dedalus dropped his coattails and went over to the side=
board. He brought forth a great stone jar of whisky from the
locker and filled the decanter slowly, bending now and then to
see how much he had poured in. Then replacing the jar in the
locker he poured out a little of the whisky into two glasses,
added a little water and came with them back to the fireplace.

— A thimbleful, John, he said. Just to whet your appetite.

Mr Casey took the glass, drank, and placed it near him on
the mantelpiece. Then he said:

760 — Well, I can't help thinking of our friend Christopher manu=
facturing ....

He broke into a fit of laughter and coughing and added:

— ... manufacturing that champagne for those fellows.

Mr Dedalus laughed loudly.

— Is it Christy? he said. There's more cunning in one of those
warts on his bald head than in a pack of jack foxes.

He inclined his head, closed his eyes, and, licking his lips
profusely, began to speak with the voice of the hotel keeper.

— And he has such a soft mouth when he's speaking to you,

770 don't you know. He's very moist and watery about the dew=
laps, God bless him.

Mr Casey was still struggling through his fit of coughing and
laughter. Stephen, seeing and hearing the hotel keeper through
his father's face and voice, laughed.

Mr Dedalus put up his eyeglass and, staring down at him,
said quietly and kindly:

—What are you laughing at, you little puppy, you?

The servants entered and placed the dishes on the table. Mrs Dedalus followed and the places were arranged.

—Sit over, she said. 780

Mr Dedalus went to the end of the table and said:

—Now, Mrs Riordan, sit over. John, sit you down, my hearty.

He looked round to where uncle Charles sat and said:

—Now then, sir, there's a bird here waiting for you.

When all had taken their seats he laid his hand on the cover and then said quickly, withdrawing it:

—Now, Stephen.

Stephen stood up in his place to say the grace before meals:

*Bless us, O Lord, and these Thy gifts which through
Thy bounty we are about to receive through Christ* 790
Our Lord. Amen.

All blessed themselves and Mr Dedalus with a sigh of pleasure lifted from the dish the heavy cover pearled around the edge with glistening drops.

Stephen looked at the plump turkey which had lain, trussed and skewered, on the kitchen table. He knew that his father had paid a guinea for it in Dunn's of D'Olier Street and that the man had prodded it often at the breastbone to show how good it was: and he remembered the man's voice when he had said:

—Take that one, sir. That's the real Ally Daly. 800

Why did Mr Barrett in Clongowes call his pandybat a turkey? It was not like a turkey. But Clongowes was far away: and the warm heavy smell of turkey and ham and celery rose from the plates and dishes and the great fire was banked high and red in the grate and the green ivy and red holly made you feel so happy and when dinner was ended the big plumpudding would be carried in, studded with peeled almonds and sprigs of holly, with bluish fire running around it and a little green flag flying from the top.

It was his first Christmas dinner and he thought of his little 810 brothers and sisters who were waiting in the nursery, as he had often waited, till the pudding came. The deep low collar and the Eton jacket made him feel queer and oldish: and that morn= ing when his mother had brought him down to the parlour, dressed for mass, his father had cried. That was because he was thinking of his own father. And uncle Charles had said so too.

Mr Dedalus covered the dish and began to eat hungrily. Then he said:

—Poor old Christy, he's nearly lopsided now with roguery.

820 —Simon, said Mrs Dedalus, you haven't given Mrs Riordan any sauce.

Mr Dedalus seized the sauceboat.

—Haven't I? he cried. Mrs Riordan, pity the poor blind.

Dante covered her plate with her hands and said:

—No, thanks.

Mr Dedalus turned to uncle Charles.

—How are you off, sir?

—Right as the mail, Simon.

—You, John?

830 —I'm all right. Go on yourself.

—Mary? Here, Stephen, here's something to make your hair curl.

He poured sauce freely over Stephen's plate and set the boat again on the table. Then he asked uncle Charles was it tender. Uncle Charles could not speak because his mouth was full but he nodded that it was.

—That was a good answer our friend made to the canon. What? said Mr Dedalus.

—I didn't think he had that much in him, said Mr Casey.

840 —*I'll pay you your dues, father, when you cease turning the house of God into a pollingbooth.*

—A nice answer, said Dante, for any man calling himself a catholic to give to his priest.

—They have only themselves to blame, said Mr Dedalus suavely. If they took a fool's advice they would confine their attention to religion.

—It is religion, Dante said. They are doing their duty in warn= ing the people.

—We go to the house of God, Mr Casey said, in all humility to pray to our Maker and not to hear election addresses.

—It is religion, Dante said again. They are right. They must direct their flocks.

—And preach politics from the altar, is it? asked Mr Dedalus.

—Certainly, said Dante. It is a question of public morality. A priest would not be a priest if he did not tell his flock what is right and what is wrong.

Mrs Dedalus laid down her knife and fork, saying:

—For pity' sake and for pity' sake let us have no political discussion on this day of all days in the year.

—Quite right, ma'am, said uncle Charles. Now, Simon, that's quite enough now. Not another word now.

—Yes, yes, said Mr Dedalus quickly.

He uncovered the dish boldly and said:

—Now then, who's for more turkey?

Nobody answered. Dante said:

—Nice language for any catholic to use!

—Mrs Riordan, I appeal to you, said Mrs Dedalus, to let the matter drop now.

Dante turned on her and said:

—And am I to sit here and listen to the pastors of my church being flouted?

—Nobody is saying a word against them, said Mr Dedalus, so long as they don't meddle in politics.

—The bishops and priests of Ireland have spoken, said Dante, and they must be obeyed.

—Let them leave politics alone, said Mr Casey, or the people may leave their church alone.

—You hear? said Dante turning to Mrs Dedalus.

—Mr Casey! Simon! said Mrs Dedalus. Let it end now.

—Too bad! Too bad! said uncle Charles.

—What? cried Mr Dedalus. Were we to desert him at the bid= ding of the English people?

—He was no longer worthy to lead, said Dante. He was a public sinner.

—We are all sinners and black sinners, said Mr Casey coldly.

—*Woe be to the man by whom the scandal cometh!* said Mrs Riordan. *It would be better for him that a millstone were tied about his neck and that he were cast into the depths of the sea rather than that he should scandalise one of these, my least little ones.* That is the language of the Holy Ghost.

—And very bad language, if you ask me, said Mr Dedalus coolly.

—Simon! Simon! said uncle Charles. The boy.

—Yes, yes, said Mr Dedalus. I meant about the .... I was think= ing about the bad language of that railway porter. Well now, that's all right. Here, Stephen, show me your plate, old chap. Eat away now. Here.

He heaped up the food on Stephen's plate and served uncle Charles and Mr Casey to large pieces of turkey and splashes of sauce. Mrs Dedalus was eating little and Dante sat with her hands in her lap. She was red in the face. Mr Dedalus rooted with the carvers at the end of the dish and said:

—There's a tasty bit here we call the pope's nose. If any lady or gentleman .....

He held a piece of fowl up on the prong of the carvingfork. Nobody spoke. He put it on his own plate, saying:

—Well, you can't say but you were asked. I think I had better eat it myself because I'm not well in my health lately.

He winked at Stephen and, replacing the dishcover, began to eat again.

There was a silence while he ate. Then he said:

—Well now, the day kept up fine after all. There were plenty of strangers down too.

Nobody spoke. He said again:

—I think there were more strangers down than last Christmas.

He looked round at the others whose faces were bent to= wards their plates and, receiving no reply, waited for a moment and said bitterly:

—Well, my Christmas dinner has been spoiled anyhow.

—There could be neither luck nor grace, Dante said, in a house where there is no respect for the pastors of the church.

Mr Dedalus threw his knife and fork noisily on his plate.

—Respect! he said. Is it for Billy with the lip or for the tub of guts up in Armagh? Respect!

—Princes of the church, said Mr Casey with slow scorn.

—Lord Leitrim's coachman, yes, said Mr Dedalus.

—They are the Lord's anointed, Dante said. They are an hon= our to their country.

—Tub of guts, said Mr Dedalus coarsely. He has a handsome face, mind you, in repose. You should see that fellow lapping   930 up his bacon and cabbage of a cold winter's day. O Johnny!

He twisted his features into a grimace of heavy bestiality and made a lapping noise with his lips.

—Really, Simon, said Mrs Dedalus, you should not speak that way before Stephen. It's not right.

—O, he'll remember all this when he grows up, said Dante hotly, the language he heard against God and religion and priests in his own home.

—Let him remember too, cried Mr Casey to her from across the table, the language with which the priests and the priests'   940 pawns broke Parnell's heart and hounded him into his grave. Let him remember that too when he grows up.

—Sons of bitches! cried Mr Dedalus. When he was down they turned on him to betray him and rend him like rats in a sewer. Lowlived dogs! And they look it! By Christ, they look it!

—They behaved rightly, cried Dante. They obeyed their bishops and their priests. Honour to them!

—Well, it is perfectly dreadful to say that not even for one day of the year, said Mrs Dedalus, can we be free from these dread= ful disputes!   950

Uncle Charles raised his hands mildly and said:

—Come now, come now, come now! Can we not have our opinions whatever they are without this bad temper and this bad language? It is too bad surely.

Mrs Dedalus spoke to Dante in a low voice but Dante said loudly:

—I will not say nothing. I will defend my church and my religion when it is insulted and spit on by renegade catholics.

Mr Casey pushed his plate rudely into the middle of the

960 table and, resting his elbows before him, said in a harsh voice to his host:

— Tell me, did I tell you that story about a very famous spit?

— You did not, John, said Mr Dedalus.

— Why then, said Mr Casey, it is a most instructive story. It happened not long ago in the county Wicklow where we are now.

He broke off and, turning towards Dante, said with quiet indignation:

— And I may tell you, ma'am, that I, if you mean me, am no 970 renegade catholic. I am a catholic as my father was and his father before him and his father before him again when we gave up our lives rather than sell our faith.

— The more shame to you now, Dante said, to speak as you do.

— The story, John, said Mr Dedalus smiling. Let us have the story anyhow.

— Catholic indeed! repeated Dante ironically. The blackest protestant in the land would not speak the language I have heard this evening.

980 Mr Dedalus began to sway his head to and fro, crooning like a country singer.

— I am no protestant, I tell you again, said Mr Casey flushing.

Mr Dedalus, still crooning and swaying his head, began to sing in a grunting nasal tone:

> *O, come all you Roman catholics*
> *That never went to mass.*

He took up his knife and fork again in good humour and set to eating, saying to Mr Casey:

— Let us have the story, John. It will help us to digest.

990 Stephen looked with affection at Mr Casey's face which stared across the table over his joined hands. He liked to sit near him at the fire, looking up at his dark fierce face. But his dark eyes were never fierce and his slow voice was good to listen to. But why was he then against the priests? Because

Dante must be right then. But he had heard his father say that
she was a spoiled nun and that she had come out of the convent
in the Alleghanies when her brothers had got the money from
the savages for the trinkets and chainies. Perhaps that made her
severe against Parnell. And she did not like him to play with
Eileen because Eileen was a protestant and when she was
young she knew children that used to play with protestants and
the protestants used to make fun of the litany of the Blessed
Virgin. *Tower of Ivory*, they used to say, *House of Gold!* How
could a woman be a tower of ivory or a house of gold? Who
was right then? And he remembered the evening in the infirm=
ary in Clongowes, the dark waters, the light at the pierhead
and the moan of sorrow from the people when they had heard.

Eileen had long white hands. One evening when playing tig
she had put her hands over his eyes: long and white and thin
and cold and soft. That was ivory: a cold white thing. That
was the meaning of *Tower of Ivory*.

— The story is very short and sweet, Mr Casey said. It was one
day down in Arklow, a cold bitter day, not long before the
chief died. May God have mercy on him!

He closed his eyes wearily and paused. Mr Dedalus took a
bone from his plate and tore some meat from it with his teeth,
saying:

— Before he was killed, you mean.

Mr Casey opened his eyes, sighed and went on:

— It was down in Arklow one day. We were down there at a
meeting and after the meeting was over we had to make our
way to the railway station through the crowd. Such booing and
baaing, man, you never heard. They called us all the names in
the world. Well there was one old lady, and a drunken old
harridan she was surely, that paid all her attention to me. She
kept dancing along beside me in the mud bawling and scream=
ing into my face: *Priesthunter! The Paris Funds! Mr Fox! Kitty
O'Shea!*

— And what did you do, John? asked Mr Dedalus.

— I let her bawl away, said Mr Casey. It was a cold day and to keep up my heart I had (saving your presence, ma'am) a quid of Tullamore in my mouth and sure I couldn't say a word in any case because my mouth was full of tobacco juice.

—Well, John?

—Well. I let her bawl away to her heart's content *Kitty O'Shea* and the rest of it till at last she called that lady a name that I won't sully this Christmas board nor your ears, ma'am, nor my own lips by repeating.

He paused. Mr Dedalus, lifting his head from the bone, asked:

—And what did you do, John?

—Do! said Mr Casey. She stuck her ugly old face up at me when she said it and I had my mouth full of tobacco juice. I bent down to her and *Phth!* says I to her like that.

He turned aside and made the act of spitting.

—*Phth!* says I to her like that, right into her eye.

He clapped a hand to his eye and gave a hoarse scream of pain.

—*O Jesus, Mary and Joseph!* says she. *I'm blinded! I'm blinded and drownded!*

He stopped in a fit of coughing and laughter, repeating:

—*I'm blinded entirely!*

Mr Dedalus laughed loudly and lay back in his chair while uncle Charles swayed his head to and fro.

Dante looked terribly angry and repeated while they laughed:

—Very nice! Ha! Very nice!

It was not nice about the spit in the woman's eye. But what was the name the woman had called Kitty O'Shea that Mr Casey would not repeat? He thought of Mr Casey walking through the crowds of people and making speeches from a wagonette. That was what he had been in prison for and he remembered that one night Sergeant O'Neill had come to the house and had stood in the hall, talking in a low voice with his father and chewing nervously at the chinstrap of his cap. And that night Mr Casey had not gone to Dublin by train but a car

had come to the door and he had heard his father say some=
thing about the Cabinteely road.

He was for Ireland and Parnell and so was his father: and so
was Dante too for one night at the band on the esplanade she
had hit a gentleman on the head with her umbrella because he
had taken off his hat when the band played *God save the
Queen* at the end.

Mr Dedalus gave a snort of contempt.

—Ah, John, he said. It is true for them. We are an unfortunate
priestridden race and always were and always will be till the
end of the chapter.

Uncle Charles shook his head, saying:

—A bad business! A bad business!

Mr Dedalus repeated:

—A priestridden Godforsaken race!

He pointed to the portrait of his grandfather on the wall to
his right.

—Do you see that old chap up there, John? he said. He was a
good Irishman when there was no money in the job. He was
condemned to death as a whiteboy. But he had a saying about
our clerical friends, that he would never let one of them put his
two feet under his mahogany.

Dante broke in angrily:

—If we are a priestridden race we ought to be proud of it!
They are the apple of God's eye. *Touch them not,* says Christ,
for they are the apple of My eye.

—And can we not love our country then? asked Mr Casey. Are
we not to follow the man that was born to lead us?

—A traitor to his country! replied Dante. A traitor, an adul=
terer! The priests were right to abandon him. The priests were
always the true friends of Ireland.

—Were they, faith? said Mr Casey.

He threw his fist on the table and, frowning angrily, pro=
truded one finger after another.

—Didn't the bishops of Ireland betray us in the time of the
union when bishop Lanigan presented an address of loyalty to

the marquess Cornwallis? Didn't the bishops and priests sell the aspirations of this country in 1829 in return for catholic emancipation? Didn't they denounce the fenian movement from the pulpit and in the confession box? And didn't they dishonour the ashes of Terence Bellew MacManus?

His face was glowing with anger and Stephen felt the glow rise to his own cheek as the spoken words thrilled him. Mr Dedalus uttered a guffaw of coarse scorn.

—O, by God, he cried, I forgot little old Paul Cullen! Another apple of God's eye!

Dante bent across the table and cried to Mr Casey:

—Right! Right! They were always right! God and morality and religion come first.

Mrs Dedalus, seeing her excitement, said to her:

—Mrs Riordan, don't excite yourself answering them.

—God and religion before everything! Dante cried. God and religion before the world!

Mr Casey raised his clenched fist and brought it down on the table with a crash.

—Very well, then, he shouted hoarsely, if it comes to that, no God for Ireland!

—John! John! cried Mr Dedalus, seizing his guest by the coat sleeve.

Dante stared across the table, her cheeks shaking. Mr Casey struggled up from his chair and bent across the table towards her, scraping the air from before his eyes with one hand as though he were tearing aside a cobweb.

—No God for Ireland! he cried. We have had too much God in Ireland. Away with God!

—Blasphemer! Devil! screamed Dante, starting to her feet and almost spitting in his face.

Uncle Charles and Mr Dedalus pulled Mr Casey back into his chair again, talking to him from both sides reasonably. He stared before him out of his dark flaming eyes, repeating:

—Away with God, I say!

Dante shoved her chair violently aside and left the table, upsetting her napkinring which rolled slowly along the carpet

and came to rest against the foot of an easychair. Mrs Dedalus   1140
rose quickly and followed her towards the door. At the door
Dante turned round violently and shouted down the room, her
cheeks flushed and quivering with rage:

—Devil out of hell! We won! We crushed him to death! Fiend!

The door slammed behind her.

Mr Casey, freeing his arms from his holders, suddenly
bowed his head on his hands with a sob of pain.

—Poor Parnell! he cried loudly. My dead king!

He sobbed loudly and bitterly.

Stephen, raising his terrorstricken face, saw that his father's   1150
eyes were full of tears.

◆ ◆ ◆

The fellows talked together in little groups.

One fellow said:

—They were caught near the Hill of Lyons.

—Who caught them?

—Mr Gleeson and the minister. They were on a car.

The same fellow added:

—A fellow in the higher line told me.

Fleming asked:

—But why did they run away, tell us?   1160

—I know why, Cecil Thunder said. Because they had fecked
cash out of the rector's room.

—Who fecked it?

—Kickham's brother. And they all went shares in it.

But that was stealing. How could they have done that?

—A fat lot you know about it, Thunder! Wells said. I know
why they scut.

—Tell us why.

—I was told not to, Wells said.

—O, go on, Wells, all said. You might tell us. We won't let it   1170
out.

Stephen bent forward his head to hear. Wells looked round
to see if anyone was coming. Then he said secretly:

—You know the altar wine they keep in the press in the sac=
risty?

—Yes.

—Well, they drank that and it was found out who did it by the
smell. And that's why they ran away, if you want to know.

And the fellow who had spoken first said:

—Yes, that's what I heard too from the fellow in the higher
line.

The fellows were all silent. Stephen stood among them,
afraid to speak, listening. A faint sickness of awe made him feel
weak. How could they have done that? He thought of the dark
silent sacristy. There were dark wooden presses there where the
crimped surplices lay quietly folded. It was not the chapel but
still you had to speak under your breath. It was a holy place.
He remembered the summer evening he had been there to be
dressed as boatbearer, the evening of the procession to the little
altar in the wood. A strange and holy place. The boy that held
the censer had swung it gently to and fro near the door with the
silvery cap lifted by the middle chain to keep the coals lighting.
That was called charcoal: and it had burned quietly as the
fellow had swung it gently and had given off a weak sour smell.
And then when all were vested he had stood holding out the
boat to the rector and the rector had put a spoonful of incense
in and it had hissed on the red coals.

The fellows were talking together in little groups here and
there on the playground. The fellows seemed to him to have
grown smaller: that was because a sprinter had knocked him
down the day before, a fellow out of second of grammar. He
had been thrown by the fellow's machine lightly on the cinder=
path and his spectacles had been broken in three pieces and
some of the grit of the cinders had gone into his mouth.

That was why the fellows seemed to him smaller and farther
away and the goalposts so thin and far and the soft grey sky so
high up. But there was no play on the football grounds for
cricket was coming: and some said that Barnes would be the
prof and some said it would be Flowers. And all over the play=

grounds they were playing rounders and bowling twisters and   1210
lobs. And from here and from there came the sounds of the
cricket bats through the soft grey air. They said: pick, pack,
pock, puck: like drops of water in a fountain slowly falling in
the brimming bowl.

Athy, who had been silent, said quietly:

—You are all wrong.

All turned towards him eagerly.

—Why?

—Do you know?

—Who told you?   1220

—Tell us, Athy.

Athy pointed across the playground to where Simon
Moonan was walking by himself kicking a stone before him.

—Ask him, he said.

The fellows looked there and then said:

—Why him?

—Is he in it?

—Tell us, Athy. Go on. You might if you know.

Athy lowered his voice and said:

—Do you know why those fellows scut? I will tell you but you   1230
must not let on you know.

He paused for a moment and then said mysteriously:

—They were caught with Simon Moonan and Tusker Boyle in
the square one night.

The fellows looked at him and asked:

—Caught?

—What doing?

Athy said:

—Smugging.

All the fellows were silent: and Athy said: 1240

—And that's why.

Stephen looked at the faces of the fellows but they were all
looking across the playground. He wanted to ask somebody
about it. What did that mean about the smugging in the
square? Why did the five fellows out of the higher line run

away for that? It was a joke, he thought. Simon Moonan had nice clothes and one night he had shown him a ball of creamy sweets that the fellows of the football fifteen had rolled down to him along the carpet in the middle of the refectory when he was at the door. It was the night of the match against the Bective Rangers and the ball was made just like a red and green apple only it opened and it was full of the creamy sweets. And one day Boyle had said that an elephant had two tuskers instead of two tusks and that was why he was called Tusker Boyle but some fellows called him Lady Boyle because he was always at his nails, paring them.

Eileen had long thin cool white hands too because she was a girl. They were like ivory; only soft. That was the meaning of *Tower of Ivory* but protestants could not understand it and made fun of it. One day he had stood beside her looking into the hotel grounds. A waiter was running up a trail of bunting on the flagstaff and a fox terrier was scampering to and fro on the sunny lawn. She had put her hand into his pocket where his hand was and he had felt how cool and thin and soft her hand was. She had said that pockets were funny things to have: and then all of a sudden she had broken away and had run laughing down the sloping curve of the path. Her fair hair had streamed out behind her like gold in the sun. *Tower of Ivory. House of Gold.* By thinking about things you could understand them.

But why in the square? You went there when you wanted to do something. It was all thick slabs of slate and water trickled all day out of tiny pinholes and there was a queer smell of stale water there. And behind the door of one of the closets there was a drawing in red pencil of a bearded man in a Roman dress with a brick in each hand and underneath was the name of the drawing:

Balbus was building a wall.

Some fellow had drawn it there for a cod. It had a funny face but it was very like a man with a beard. And on the wall of another closet there was written in backhand in beautiful writing:

Julius Caesar wrote The Calico Belly.

Perhaps that was why they were there because it was a place where some fellows wrote things for cod. But all the same it was queer what Athy said and the way he said it. It was not a cod because they had run away. He looked with the others in silence across the playground and began to feel afraid.

At last Fleming said:

—And we are all to be punished for what other fellows did?

—I won't come back, see if I do, Cecil Thunder said. Three days' silence in the refectory and sending us up for six and eight every minute.

—Yes, said Wells. And old Barrett has a new way of twisting the note so that you can't open it and fold it again to see how many ferulae you are to get. I won't come back too.

—Yes, said Cecil Thunder, and the prefect of studies was in second of grammar this morning.

—Let us get up a rebellion, Fleming said. Will we?

All the fellows were silent. The air was very silent and you could hear the cricket bats but more slowly than before: pick, pock.

Wells asked:

—What is going to be done to them?

—Simon Moonan and Tusker are going to be flogged, Athy said, and the fellows in the higher line got their choice of flogging or being expelled.

—And which are they taking? asked the fellow who had spoken first.

—All are taking expulsion except Corrigan, Athy answered. He's going to be flogged by Mr Gleeson.

—Is it Corrigan that big fellow? said Fleming. Why, he'd be able for two of Gleeson!

—I know why, Cecil Thunder said. He is right and the other fellows are wrong because a flogging wears off after a bit but a fellow that has been expelled from college is known all his life on account of it. Besides Gleeson won't flog him hard.

—It's best of his play not to, Fleming said.

—I wouldn't like to be Simon Moonan and Tusker, Cecil Thunder said. But I don't believe they will be flogged. Perhaps they will be sent up for twice nine.

—No, no, said Athy. They'll both get it on the vital spot.

Wells rubbed himself and said in a crying voice:

—Please, sir, let me off!

Athy grinned and turned up the sleeves of his jacket, saying:

> It can't be helped;
> It must be done.
> So down with your breeches
> And out with your bum.

The fellows laughed; but he felt that they were a little afraid. In the silence of the soft grey air he heard the cricket bats from here and from there: pock. That was a sound to hear but if you were hit then you would feel a pain. The pandybat made a sound too but not like that. The fellows said it was made of whalebone and leather with lead inside: and he wondered what was the pain like. There were different kinds of pains for all the different kinds of sounds. A long thin cane would have a high whistling sound and he wondered what was that pain like. It made him shivery to think of it and cold: and what Athy said too. But what was there to laugh at in it? It made him shivery: but that was because you always felt like a shiver when you let down your trousers. It was the same in the bath when you undressed yourself. He wondered who had to let them down, the master or the boy himself. O how could they laugh about it that way?

He looked at Athy's rolledup sleeves and knuckly inky hands. He had rolled up his sleeves to show how Mr Gleeson would roll up his sleeves. But Mr Gleeson had round shiny cuffs and clean white wrists and fattish white hands and the nails of them were long and pointed. Perhaps he pared them too like Lady Boyle. But they were terribly long and pointed nails. So long and cruel they were though the white fattish hands were not cruel but gentle. And though he trembled with cold and fright to think of the cruel long nails and of the high whistling sound of the cane and of the chill you felt at the end of your shirt when you undressed yourself yet he felt a feeling of queer quiet pleasure inside him to think of the white fattish hands, clean and strong and gentle. And he thought of what Cecil Thunder had said: that Mr Gleeson would not flog Cor= rigan hard. And Fleming had said he would not because it was best of his play not to. But that was not why.   1360

A voice from far out on the playgrounds cried:

—All in!

And other voices cried:

—All in! All in!

During the writing lesson he sat with his arms folded, listen= ing to the slow scraping of the pens. Mr Harford went to and fro making little signs in red pencil and sometimes sitting beside the boy to show him how to hold the pen. He had tried to spell out the headline for himself though he knew already what it was for it was the last in the book. *Zeal without*   1370 *prudence is like a ship adrift.* But the lines of the letters were like fine invisible threads and it was only by closing his right eye tight tight and staring out of the left eye that he could make out the full curves of the capital.

But Mr Harford was very decent and never got into a wax. All the other masters got into dreadful waxes. But why were they to suffer for what fellows in the higher line did? Wells had said that they had drunk some of the altar wine out of the press in the sacristy and that it had been found out who had done it by the smell. Perhaps they had stolen a monstrance to run away   1380 with it and sell it somewhere. That must have been a terrible sin, to go in quietly there at night, to open the dark press and steal the flashing gold thing into which God was put on the altar in the middle of flowers and candles at benediction while the incense went up in clouds at both sides as the fellow swung the censer and Dominic Kelly sang the first part by himself in the choir. But God was not in it of course when they stole it. But still it was a strange and a great sin even to touch it. He thought of it with deep awe; a terrible and strange sin: it thrilled him to think of it in the silence when the pens scraped lightly. But to drink the altar wine out of the press and be found out by the smell was a sin too: but it was not terrible and strange. It only made you feel a little sickish on account of the smell of the wine. Because on the day when he had made his first holy communion in the chapel he had shut his eyes and opened his mouth and put out his tongue a little: and when the rector had stooped down to give him the holy com= munion he had smelt a faint winy smell off the rector's breath after the wine of the mass. The word was beautiful: wine. It made you think of dark purple because the grapes were dark purple that grew in Greece outside houses like white temples. But the faint smell off the rector's breath had made him feel a sick feeling on the morning of his first communion. The day of your first communion was the happiest day of your life. And once a lot of generals had asked Napoleon what was the happiest day of his life. They thought he would say the day he won some great battle or the day he was made an emperor. But he said:

—Gentlemen, the happiest day of my life was the day on which I made my first holy communion.

Father Arnall came in and the Latin lesson began and he remained still, leaning on the desk with his arms folded. Father Arnall gave out the themebooks and he said that they were scandalous and that they were all to be written out again with the corrections at once. But the worst of all was Fleming's theme because the pages were stuck together by a blot: and Father Arnall held it up by a corner and said it was an insult to any master to send him up such a theme. Then he asked Jack Lawton to decline the noun *mare* and Jack Lawton stopped at the ablative singular and could not go on with the plural.

—You should be ashamed of yourself, said Father Arnall sternly. You, the leader of the class!

Then he asked the next boy and the next and the next. Nobody knew. Father Arnall became very quiet, more and more quiet as each boy tried to answer and could not. But his face was blacklooking and his eyes were staring though his voice was so quiet. Then he asked Fleming and Fleming said that that word had no plural. Father Arnall suddenly shut the book and shouted at him:

—Kneel out there in the middle of the class. You are one of the idlest boys I ever met. Copy out your themes again the rest of you.

Fleming moved heavily out of his place and knelt between the two last benches. The other boys bent over their theme= books and began to write. A silence filled the classroom and Stephen, glancing timidly at Father Arnall's dark face, saw that it was a little red from the wax he was in.

Was that a sin for Father Arnall to be in a wax or was he allowed to get into a wax when the boys were idle because that made them study better or was he only letting on to be in a wax? It was because he was allowed because a priest would know what a sin was and would not do it. But if he did it one time by mistake what would he do to go to confession? Perhaps he would go to confession to the minister. And if the minister did it he would go to the rector: and the rector to the provin= cial: and the provincial to the general of the jesuits. That was called the order: and he had heard his father say that they were all clever men. They could all have become highup people in the world if they had not become jesuits. And he wondered what Father Arnall and Paddy Barrett would have become and what Mr McGlade and Mr Gleeson would have become if they had not become jesuits. It was hard to think what because you would have to think of them in a different way with different coloured coats and trousers and with beards and moustaches and different kinds of hats.

The door opened quietly and closed. A quick whisper ran through the class: the prefect of studies. There was an instant of dead silence and then the loud crack of a pandybat on the last desk. Stephen's heart leapt up in fear.

—Any boys want flogging here, Father Arnall? cried the pre= fect of studies. Any lazy idle loafers that want flogging in this class?

He came to the middle of the class and saw Fleming on his knees.

—Hoho! he cried. Who is this boy? Why is he on his knees? What is your name, boy?

—Fleming, sir.

—Hoho, Fleming! An idler of course. I can see it in your eye. Why is he on his knees, Father Arnall?

1470 —He wrote a bad Latin theme, Father Arnall said, and he missed all the questions in grammar.

—Of course he did! cried the prefect of studies. Of course he did! A born idler! I can see it in the corner of his eye.

He banged his pandybat down on the desk and cried:

—Up, Fleming! Up, my boy!

Fleming stood up slowly.

—Hold out! cried the prefect of studies.

Fleming held out his hand. The pandybat came down on it with a loud smacking sound: one, two, three, four, five, six.

1480 —Other hand!

The pandybat came down again in six loud quick smacks.

—Kneel down! cried the prefect of studies.

Fleming knelt down squeezing his hands under his armpits, his face contorted with pain, but Stephen knew how hard his hands were because Fleming was always rubbing rosin into them. But perhaps he was in great pain for the noise of the pandies was terrible. Stephen's heart was beating and fluttering.

—At your work, all of you! shouted the prefect of studies. We 1490 want no lazy idle loafers here, lazy idle little schemers. At your work, I tell you. Father Dolan will be in to see you every day. Father Dolan will be in tomorrow.

He poked one of the boys in the side with the pandybat, saying:

—You, boy! When will Father Dolan be in again?

—Tomorrow, sir, said Tom Furlong's voice.

—Tomorrow and tomorrow and tomorrow, said the prefect of studies. Make up your minds for that. Every day Father Dolan. Write away. You, boy, who are you?

Stephen's heart jumped suddenly.

—Dedalus, sir.

—Why are you not writing like the others?

—I ..... my ...

He could not speak with fright.

—Why is he not writing, Father Arnall?

—He broke his glasses, said Father Arnall, and I exempted him from work.

—Broke? What is this I hear? What is this your name is? said the prefect of studies.

—Dedalus, sir.

—Out here, Dedalus. Lazy little schemer. I see schemer in your face. Where did you break your glasses?

Stephen stumbled into the middle of the class, blinded by fear and haste.

—Where did you break your glasses? repeated the prefect of studies.

—The cinderpath, sir.

—Hoho! The cinderpath! cried the prefect of studies. I know that trick.

Stephen lifted his eyes in wonder and saw for a moment Father Dolan's whitegrey not young face, his baldy whitegrey head with fluff at the sides of it, the steel rims of his spectacles and his nocoloured eyes looking through the glasses. Why did he say that he knew that trick?

—Lazy idle little loafer! cried the prefect of studies. Broke my glasses! An old schoolboy trick! Out with your hand this mo=ment!

Stephen closed his eyes and held out in the air his trembling hand with the palm upwards. He felt the prefect of studies touch it for a moment at the fingers to straighten it and then the swish of the sleeve of the soutane as the pandybat was lifted to strike. A hot burning stinging tingling blow like the loud crack of a broken stick made his trembling hand crumple to=gether like a leaf in the fire: and at the sound and the pain scalding tears were driven into his eyes. His whole body was shaking with fright, his arm was shaking and his crumpled burning livid hand shook like a loose leaf in the air. A cry sprang to his lips, a prayer to be let off. But though the tears scalded his eyes and his limbs quivered with pain and fright he held back the hot tears and the cry that scalded his throat.

—Other hand! shouted the prefect of studies.

Stephen drew back his maimed and quivering right arm and held out his left hand. The soutane sleeve swished again as the pandybat was lifted and a loud crashing sound and a fierce maddening tingling burning pain made his hand shrink together with the palms and fingers in a livid quivering mass. The scalding water burst forth from his eyes and, burning with shame and agony and fear, he drew back his shaking arm in terror and burst out into a whine of pain. His body shook with a palsy of fright and in shame and rage he felt the scalding cry come from his throat and the scalding tears falling out of his eyes and down his flaming cheeks.

—Kneel down! cried the prefect of studies.

Stephen knelt down quickly pressing his beaten hands to his sides. To think of them beaten and swollen with pain all in a moment made him feel so sorry for them as if they were not his own but someone else's that he felt so sorry for. And as he knelt, calming the last sobs in his throat and feeling the burning tingling pain pressed in to his sides, he thought of the hands which he had held out in the air with the palms up and of the firm touch of the prefect of studies when he had steadied the shaking fingers and of the beaten swollen reddened mass of palm and fingers that shook helplessly in the air.

—Get at your work, all of you, cried the prefect of studies from the door. Father Dolan will be in every day to see if any boy, any lazy idle little loafer wants flogging. Every day. Every day.

The door closed behind him.

The hushed class continued to copy out the themes. Father Arnall rose from his seat and went among them, helping the boys with gentle words and telling them the mistakes they had made. His voice was very gentle and soft. Then he returned to his seat and said to Fleming and Stephen:

46

—You may return to your places, you two.

Fleming and Stephen rose and, walking to their seats, sat down. Stephen, scarlet with shame, opened a book quickly with one weak hand and bent down upon it, his face close to the page.

It was unfair and cruel: because the doctor had told him not to read without glasses and he had written home to his father that morning to send him a new pair. And Father Arnall had said that he need not study till the new glasses came. Then to be called a schemer before the class and to be pandied when he always got the card for first or second and was the leader of the Yorkists! How could the prefect of studies know that it was a trick? He felt the touch of the prefect's fingers as they had steadied his hand and at first he had thought that he was going to shake hands with him because the fingers were soft and firm: but then in an instant he had heard the swish of the soutane sleeve and the crash. It was cruel and unfair to make him kneel in the middle of the class then: and Father Arnall had told them both that they might return to their places without making any difference between them. He listened to Father Arnall's low and gentle voice as he corrected the themes. Perhaps he was sorry now and wanted to be decent. But it was unfair and cruel. The prefect of studies was a priest but that was cruel and unfair. And his whitegrey face and the nocoloured eyes behind the steelrimmed spectacles were cruel looking because he had steadied the hand first with his firm soft fingers and that was to hit it better and louder.

—It's a stinking mean thing, that's what it is, said Fleming in the corridor as the classes were passing out in file to the refec�= tory, to pandy a fellow for what is not his fault.

—You really broke your glasses by accident, didn't you? Nasty Roche asked.

Stephen felt his heart filled by Fleming's words and did not answer.

—Of course he did! said Fleming. I wouldn't stand it. I'd go up and tell the rector on him.

—Yes, said Cecil Thunder eagerly, and I saw him lift the

pandybat over his shoulder and he's not allowed to do that.

—Did they hurt much? Nasty Roche asked.

—Very much, Stephen said.

—I wouldn't stand it, Fleming repeated, from Baldyhead or any other Baldyhead. It's a stinking mean low trick, that's what it is. I'd go up straight up to the rector and tell him about it after dinner.

—Yes, do. Yes, do, said Cecil Thunder.

—Yes, do. Yes, go up and tell the rector on him, Dedalus, said Nasty Roche, because he said that he'd come in tomorrow again to pandy you.

—Yes, yes. Tell the rector, all said.

And there were some fellows out of second of grammar listening and one of them said:

—The senate and the Roman people declared that Dedalus had been wrongly punished.

It was wrong; it was unfair and cruel: and, as he sat in the refectory, he suffered time after time in memory the same humiliation until he began to wonder whether it might not really be that there was something in his face which made him look like a schemer and he wished he had a little mirror to see. But there could not be; and it was unjust and cruel and unfair.

He could not eat the blackish fish fritters they got on Wednesdays in lent and one of his potatoes had the mark of the spade in it. Yes, he would do what the fellows had told him. He would go up and tell the rector that he had been wrongly punished. A thing like that had been done before by somebody in history, by some great person whose head was in the books of history. And the rector would declare that he had been wrongly punished because the senate and the Roman people always declared that the man who did that had been wrongly punished. Those were the great men whose names were in Richmal Magnall's Questions. History was all about those men and what they did and that was what Peter Parley's Tales about Greece and Rome were all about. Peter Parley himself was on the first page in a picture. There was a road over a heath with

about it. No, it was best to forget all about it: and perhaps the prefect of studies had only said he would come in. No, it was best to hide out of the way because when you were small and young you could often escape that way.

The fellows at his table stood up. He stood up and passed out among them in the file. He had to decide. He was coming near the door. If he went on with the fellows he could never go up to the rector because he could not leave the playground for that. And if he went and was pandied all the same all the fellows would make fun and talk about young Dedalus going up to the rector to tell on the prefect of studies.

He was walking down along the matting and he saw the door before him. It was impossible: he could not. He thought of the baldy head of the prefect of studies with the cruel no=coloured eyes looking at him and he heard the voice of the prefect of studies asking him twice what his name was. Why could he not remember the name when he was told the first time? Was he not listening the first time or was it to make fun out of the name? The great men in the history had names like that and nobody made fun of them. It was his own name that he should have made fun of if he wanted to make fun. Dolan: it was like the name of a woman that washed clothes.

He had reached the door and, turning quickly to the right, walked up the stairs: and, before he could make up his mind to come back, he had entered the low dark narrow corridor that led to the castle. And as he crossed the threshold of the door of the corridor he saw, without turning his head to look, that all the fellows were looking after him as they went filing by.

He passed along the narrow dark corridor, passing little doors that were the doors of the rooms of the community. He peered in front of him and right and left through the gloom and thought that those must be portraits. It was dark and silent and his eyes were weak and tired with tears so that he could not see. But he thought they were the portraits of the saints and great men of the order who were looking down on him silently as he passed: saint Ignatius Loyola holding an open book and pointing to the words *Ad Majorem Dei Gloriam* in it, saint

Francis Xavier pointing to his chest, Lorenzo Ricci with his
berretta on his head like one of the prefects of the lines, the
three patrons of holy youth, saint Stanislaus Kostka, saint
Aloysius Gonzaga and blessed John Berchmans, all with young
faces because they died when they were young, and Father
Peter Kenny sitting in a chair wrapped in a big cloak.

He came out on the landing above the entrance hall and
looked about him. That was where Hamilton Rowan had
passed and the marks of the soldiers' slugs were there. And it
was there that the old servants had seen the ghost in the white
cloak of a marshal.

An old servant was sweeping at the end of the landing. He
asked him where was the rector's room and the old servant
pointed to the door at the far end and looked after him as he
went on to it and knocked.

There was no answer. He knocked again more loudly and
his heart jumped when he heard a muffled voice say:

— Come in!

He turned the handle and opened the door and fumbled for
the handle of the green baize door inside. He found it and
pushed it open and went in.

He saw the rector sitting at a desk writing. There was a skull
on the desk and a strange solemn smell in the room like the old
leather of chairs.

His heart was beating fast on account of the solemn place he
was in and the silence of the room: and he looked at the skull
and at the rector's kindlooking face.

— Well, my little man, said the rector. What is it?

Stephen swallowed down the thing in his throat and said:

— I broke my glasses, sir.

The rector opened his mouth and said:

— O!

Then he smiled and said:

— Well, if we broke our glasses we must write home for a new
pair.

— I wrote home, sir, said Stephen, and Father Arnall said I am
not to study till they come.

—Quite right! said the rector.

Stephen swallowed down the thing again and tried to keep his legs and his voice from shaking.

1760 —But, sir ....

—Yes?

—Father Dolan came in today and pandied me because I was not writing my theme.

The rector looked at him in silence and he could feel the blood rising to his face and the tears about to rise to his eyes.

The rector said:

—Your name is Dedalus, isn't it?

—Yes, sir.

—And where did you break your glasses?

1770 —On the cinderpath, sir. A fellow was coming out of the bicycle house and I fell and they got broken. I don't know the fellow's name.

The rector looked at him again in silence. Then he smiled and said:

—O, well, it was a mistake. I am sure Father Dolan did not know.

—But I told him I broke them, sir, and he pandied me.

—Did you tell him that you had written home for a new pair? the rector asked.

1780 —No, sir.

—O, well then, said the rector, Father Dolan did not under= stand. You can say that I excuse you from your lessons for a few days.

Stephen said quickly for fear his trembling would prevent him:

—Yes, sir, but Father Dolan said he will come in tomorrow to pandy me again for it.

—Very well, the rector said. It is a mistake and I shall speak to Father Dolan myself. Will that do now?

1790 Stephen felt the tears wetting his eyes and murmured:

—O yes, sir, thanks.

The rector held his hand across the side of the desk where

the skull was and Stephen, placing his hand in it for a moment, felt a cool moist palm.

—Good day now, said the rector, withdrawing his hand and bowing.

—Good day, sir, said Stephen.

He bowed and walked quietly out of the room, closing the doors carefully and slowly.

But when he had passed the old servant on the landing and was again in the low narrow dark corridor he began to walk faster and faster. Faster and faster he hurried on through the gloom, excitedly. He bumped his elbow against the door at the end and, hurrying down the staircase, walked quickly through the two corridors and out into the air.

He could hear the cries of the fellows on the playgrounds. He broke into a run and, running quicker and quicker, ran across the cinderpath and reached the third line playground, panting.

The fellows had seen him running. They closed round him in a ring, pushing one against another to hear.

—Tell us! Tell us!

—What did he say?

—Did you go in?

—What did he say?

—Tell us! Tell us!

He told them what he had said and what the rector had said and, when he had told them, all the fellows flung their caps spinning up into the air and cried:

—Hurroo!

They caught their caps and sent them up again spinning skyhigh and cried again:

—Hurroo! Hurroo!

They made a cradle of their locked hands and hoisted him up among them and carried him along till he struggled to get free. And when he had escaped from them they broke away in all directions, flinging their caps again into the air and whis= tling as they went spinning up and crying:

—Hurroo!

And they gave three groans for Baldyhead Dolan and three cheers for Conmee and they said he was the decentest rector that was ever in Clongowes.

The cheers died away in the soft grey air. He was alone. He was happy and free: but he would not be anyway proud with Father Dolan. He would be very quiet and obedient: and he wished that he could do something kind for him to show him that he was not proud.

The air was soft and grey and mild and evening was coming. There was the smell of evening in the air, the smell of the fields in the country where they digged up turnips to peel them and eat them when they went out for a walk to Major Barton's, the smell there was in the little wood beyond the pavilion where the gallnuts were.

The fellows were practising long shies and bowling lobs and slow twisters. In the soft grey silence he could hear the bump of the balls: and from here and from there through the quiet air the sound of the cricket bats: pick, pack, pock, puck: like drops of water in a fountain falling softly in the brimming bowl.

II

Uncle Charles smoked such black twist that at last his out=
spoken nephew suggested to him to enjoy his morning smoke
in a little outhouse at the end of the garden.
—Very good, Simon. All serene, Simon, said the old man tran=
quilly. Anywhere you like. The outhouse will do me nicely: it
will be more salubrious.
—Damn me, said Mr Dedalus frankly, if I know how you can
smoke such villainous awful tobacco. It's like gunpowder, by
God.
—It's very nice, Simon, replied the old man. Very cool and 10
mollifying.

Every morning, therefore, uncle Charles repaired to his out=
house but not before he had creased and brushed scrupulously
his back hair and brushed and put on his tall hat. While he
smoked the brim of his tall hat and the bowl of his pipe were
just visible beyond the jambs of the outhouse door. His arbour,
as he called the reeking outhouse which he shared with the cat
and the garden tools, served him also as a soundingbox: and
every morning he hummed contentedly one of his favourite
songs: O, twine me a bower or Blue eyes and golden hair or 20
The Groves of Blarney while the grey and blue coils of smoke
rose slowly from his pipe and vanished in the pure air.

During the first part of the summer in Blackrock uncle
Charles was Stephen's constant companion. Uncle Charles was
a hale old man with a well tanned skin, rugged features and
white side whiskers. On week days he did messages between
the house in Carysfort Avenue and those shops in the main
street of the town with which the family dealt. Stephen was
glad to go with him on these errands for uncle Charles helped

30 him very liberally to handfuls of whatever was exposed in open
boxes and barrels outside the counter. He would seize a hand=
ful of grapes and sawdust or three or four American apples and
thrust them generously into his grandnephew's hand while the
shopman smiled uneasily; and on Stephen's feigning reluctance
to take them, he would frown and say:
— Take them, sir. Do you hear me, sir? They're good for your
bowels.

When the order list had been booked the two would go on
to the park where an old friend of Stephen's father, Mike
40 Flynn, would be found seated on a bench, waiting for them.
Then would begin Stephen's run round the park. Mike Flynn
would stand at the gate near the railway station, watch in
hand, while Stephen ran round the track in the style Mike
Flynn favoured, his head high lifted, his knees well lifted and
his hands held straight down by his sides. When the morning
practice was over the trainer would make his comments and
sometimes illustrate them by shuffling along for a yard or so
comically in an old pair of blue canvas shoes. A small ring of
wonderstruck children and nursemaids would gather to watch
50 him and linger even when he and uncle Charles had sat down
again and were talking athletics and politics. Though he had
heard his father say that Mike Flynn had put some of the best
runners of modern times through his hands Stephen often
glanced with mistrust at his trainer's flabby stubblecovered
face, as it bent over the long stained fingers through which he
rolled his cigarette, and with pity at the mild lustreless blue
eyes which would look up suddenly from the task and gaze
vaguely into the bluer distance while the long swollen fingers
ceased their rolling and grains and fibres of tobacco fell back
60 into the pouch.

On the way home uncle Charles would often pay a visit to
the chapel and, as the font was above Stephen's reach, the old
man would dip his hand and then sprinkle the water briskly
about Stephen's clothes and on the floor of the porch. While he
prayed he knelt on his red handkerchief and read above his

breath from a thumbblackened prayerbook wherein catch=
words were printed at the foot of every page. Stephen knelt at
his side respecting, though he did not share, his piety. He often
wondered what his granduncle prayed for so seriously. Perhaps
he prayed for the souls in purgatory or for the grace of a happy   70
death: or perhaps he prayed that God might send him back a
part of the big fortune he had squandered in Cork.

On Sundays Stephen with his father and his granduncle took
their constitutional. The old man was a nimble walker in spite
of his corns and often ten or twelve miles of the road were
covered. The little village of Stillorgan was the parting of the
ways. Either they went to the left towards the Dublin moun=
tains or along the Goatstown road and thence into Dundrum,
coming home by Sandyford. Trudging along the road or
standing in some grimy wayside publichouse his elders spoke   80
constantly of the subjects nearest their hearts, of Irish politics,
of Munster and of the legends of their own family, to all of
which Stephen lent an avid ear. Words which he did not under=
stand he said over and over to himself till he had learned them
by heart: and through them he had glimpses of the real world
about him. The hour when he too would take his part in the
life of that world seemed drawing near and in secret he began
to make ready for the great part which he felt awaited him the
nature of which he only dimly apprehended.

His evenings were his own; and he pored over a ragged   90
translation of *The Count of Monte Cristo*. The figure of that
dark avenger stood forth in his mind for whatever he had heard
or divined in childhood of the strange and terrible. At night he
built up on the parlour table an image of the wonderful island
cave out of transfers and paper flowers and coloured tissue
paper and strips of the silver and golden paper in which choc=
olate is wrapped. When he had broken up this scenery, weary
of its tinsel, there would come to his mind the bright picture of
Marseilles, of sunny trellisses and of Mercedes. Outside Black=
rock, on the road that led to the mountains, stood a small   100
whitewashed house in the garden of which grew many rose=

bushes: and in this house, he told himself, another Mercedes lived. Both on the outward and on the homeward journey he measured distance by this landmark: and in his imagination he lived through a long train of adventures, marvellous as those in the book itself, towards the close of which there appeared an image of himself, grown older and sadder, standing in a moonlit garden with Mercedes who had so many years before slighted his love, and with a sadly proud gesture of refusal,
110 saying:

—Madam, I never eat muscatel grapes.

He became the ally of a boy named Aubrey Mills and founded with him a gang of adventurers in the avenue. Aubrey carried a whistle dangling from his buttonhole and a bicycle lamp attached to his belt while the others had short sticks thrust daggerwise through theirs. Stephen, who had read of Napoleon's plain style of dress, chose to remain unadorned and thereby heightened for himself the pleasure of taking counsel with his lieutenant before giving orders. The gang made forays
120 into the gardens of old maids or went down to the castle and fought a battle on the shaggy weedgrown rocks, coming home after it weary stragglers with the stale odours of the foreshore in their nostrils and the rank oils of the seawrack upon their hands and in their hair.

Aubrey and Stephen had a common milkman and often they drove out in the milkcar to Carrickmines where the cows were at grass. While the men were milking the boys would take turns in riding the tractable mare round the field. But when autumn came the cows were driven home from the grass: and the first
130 sight of the filthy cowyard at Stradbrook with its foul green puddles and clots of liquid dung and steaming brantroughs sickened Stephen's heart. The cattle which had seemed so beau= tiful in the country on sunny days revolted him and he could not even look at the milk they yielded.

The coming of September did not trouble him this year for he knew he was not to be sent back to Clongowes. The practice in the park came to an end when Mike Flynn went into hospi=

tal. Aubrey was at school and had only an hour or two free in the evening. The gang fell asunder and there were no more nightly forays or battles on the rocks. Stephen sometimes went round with the car which delivered the evening milk: and these chilly drives blew away his memory of the filth of the cowyard and he felt no repugnance at seeing the cowhairs and hayseeds on the milkman's coat. Whenever the car drew up before a house he waited to catch a glimpse of a well scrubbed kitchen or of a softly lighted hall and to see how the servant would hold the jug and how she would close the door. He thought it should be a pleasant life enough, driving along the roads every evening to deliver milk, if he had warm gloves and a fat bag of gingernuts in his pocket to eat from. But the same foreknowl= edge which had sickened his heart and made his limbs sag suddenly as he raced round the park, the same intuition which had made him glance with mistrust at his trainer's flabby stubblecovered face as it bent heavily over his long stained fingers, dissipated any vision of the future. In a vague way he understood that his father was in trouble and that this was the reason why he himself had not been sent back to Clongowes. For some time he had felt the slight changes in his house; and these changes in what he had deemed unchangeable were so many slight shocks to his boyish conception of the world. The ambition which he felt astir at times in the darkness of his soul sought no outlet. A dusk like that of the outer world obscured his mind as he heard the mare's hoofs clattering along the tramtrack on the Rock Road and the great can swaying and rattling behind him.

He returned to Mercedes and, as he brooded upon her im= age, a strange unrest crept into his blood. Sometimes a fever gathered within him and led him to rove alone in the evening along the quiet avenues. The peace of the gardens and the kindly lights in the windows poured a tender influence into his restless heart. The noise of children at play annoyed him and their silly voices made him feel, even more keenly than he had felt at Clongowes, that he was different from others. He did not want to play. He wanted to meet in the real world the unsubstantial image which his soul so constantly beheld. He did not know where to seek it or how: but a premonition which led him on told him that this image would, without any overt act of his, encounter him. They would meet quietly as if they had known each other and had made their tryst, perhaps at one of the gates or in some more secret place. They would be alone, surrounded by darkness and silence: and in that moment of supreme tenderness he would be transfigured. He would fade into something impalpable under her eyes and then, in a mo= ment, he would be transfigured. Weakness and timidity and inexperience would fall from him in that magic moment.

◆ ◆ ◆

Two great yellow caravans had halted one morning before the door and men had come tramping into the house to dis= mantle it. The furniture had been hustled out through the front garden which was strewn with wisps of straw and rope ends and into the huge vans at the gate. When all had been safely stowed the vans had set off noisily down the avenue: and from the window of the railway carriage, in which he had sat with his redeyed mother, Stephen had seen them lumbering heavily along the Merrion Road.

The parlour fire would not draw that evening and Mr Deda= lus rested the poker against the bars of the grate to attract the flame. Uncle Charles dozed in a corner of the half furnished uncarpeted room and near him the family portraits leaned against the wall. The lamp on the table shed a weak light over the boarded floor, muddied by the feet of the vanmen. Stephen sat on a footstool beside his father listening to a long and incoherent monologue. He understood little or nothing of it at first but he became slowly aware that his father had enemies and that some fight was going to take place. He felt, too, that he was being enlisted for the fight, that some duty was being laid upon his shoulders. The sudden flight from the comfort and revery of Blackrock, the passage through the gloomy foggy city, the thought of the bare cheerless house in which they were now to live made his heart heavy: and again an intuition or foreknowledge of the future came to him. He understood also why the servants had often whispered together in the hall and why his father had often stood on the hearthrug, with his back to the fire, talking loudly to uncle Charles who urged him to sit down and eat his dinner.

—There's a crack of the whip left in me yet, Stephen, old chap, said Mr Dedalus, poking at the dull fire with fierce energy. We're not dead yet, sonny. No, by the Lord Jesus (God forgive me) nor half dead.

Dublin was a new and complex sensation. Uncle Charles had grown so witless that he could no longer be sent out on errands and the disorder in settling in the new house left Ste=phen freer than he had been in Blackrock. In the beginning he contented himself with circling timidly round the neighbouring square or, at most, going half way down one of the side streets: but when he had made a skeleton map of the city in his mind he followed boldly one of its central lines until he reached the customhouse. He passed unchallenged among the docks and along the quays wondering at the multitude of corks that lay bobbing on the surface of the water in a thick yellow scum, at the crowds of quay porters and the rumbling carts and the illdressed bearded policeman. The vastness and strangeness of the life suggested to him by the bales of merchandise stacked along the walls or swung aloft out of the holds of steamers wakened again in him the unrest which had sent him wan=dering in the evening from garden to garden in search of Mercedes. And amid this new bustling life he might have fancied himself in another Marseilles but that he missed the bright sky and the sunwarmed trellisses of the wineshops. A vague dissatisfaction grew up within him as he looked on the quays and on the river and on the lowering skies and yet he continued to wander up and down day after day as if he really sought someone that eluded him.

He went once or twice with his mother to visit their rela=

tives: and, though they passed a jovial array of shops lit up and adorned for Christmas, his mood of embittered silence did not leave him. The causes of his embitterment were many, remote and near. He was angry with himself for being young and the prey of restless foolish impulses, angry also with the change of fortune which was reshaping the world about him into a vision of squalor and insincerity. Yet his anger lent nothing to the vision. He chronicled with patience what he saw, detaching himself from it and tasting its mortifying flavour in secret.

He was sitting on the backless chair in his aunt's kitchen. A lamp with a reflector hung on the japanned wall of the fire= place and by its light his aunt was reading the evening paper that lay on her knees. She looked a long time at a smiling picture that was set in it and said musingly:

—The beautiful Mabel Hunter!

A ringletted girl stood on tiptoe to peer at the picture and said softly:

—What is she in, mud?

—In the pantomime, love.

The child leaned her ringletted head against her mother's sleeve, gazing on the picture and murmured, as if fascinated:

—The beautiful Mabel Hunter!

As if fascinated, her eyes rested long upon those demurely taunting eyes and she murmured again devotedly:

—Isn't she an exquisite creature?

And the boy who came in from the street, stamping crook= edly under his stone of coal, heard her words. He dropped his load promptly on the floor and hurried to her side to see. But she did not raise her easeful head to let him see. He mauled the edges of the paper with his reddened and blackened hands, shouldering her aside and complaining that he could not see.

He was sitting in the narrow breakfast room high up in the old darkwindowed house. The firelight flickered on the wall and beyond the window a spectral dusk was gathering upon the river. Before the fire an old woman was busy making tea and, as she bustled at her task, she told in a low voice of what the priest and the doctor had said. She told too of certain changes that she had seen in her of late and of her odd ways and sayings. He sat listening to the words and following the ways of adventure that lay open in the coals, arches and vaults and winding galleries and jagged caverns.

Suddenly he became aware of something in the doorway. A skull appeared suspended in the gloom of the doorway. A feeble creature like a monkey was there, drawn thither by the sound of voices at the fire. A whining voice came from the door, asking:

—Is that Josephine?   290

The old bustling woman answered cheerily from the fire=place:

—No, Ellen. It's Stephen.

—O .... O, good evening, Stephen.

He answered the greeting and saw a silly smile break out over the face in the doorway.

—Do you want anything, Ellen? asked the old woman at the fire.

But she did not answer the question and said:

—I thought it was Josephine. I thought you were Josephine,   300 Stephen.

And, repeating this several times, she fell to laughing feebly.

He was sitting in the midst of a children's party at Harold's Cross. His silent watchful manner had grown upon him and he took little part in the games. The children, wearing the spoils of their crackers, danced and romped noisily and, though he tried to share their merriment, he felt himself a gloomy figure amid the gay cocked hats and sunbonnets.

But when he had sung his song and withdrawn into a snug corner of the room he began to taste the joy of his loneliness.   310 The mirth, which in the beginning of the evening had seemed to him false and trivial, was like a soothing air to him, passing gaily by his senses, hiding from other eyes the feverish agitation of his blood while through the circling of the dancers and amid the music and laughter her glances travelled to his corner, flattering, taunting, searching, exciting his heart.

In the hall the children who had stayed latest were putting

on their things: the party was over. She had thrown a shawl about her and, as they went together towards the tram, sprays of her fresh warm breath flew gaily above her cowled head and her shoes tapped blithely on the glassy road.

It was the last tram. The lank brown horses knew it and shook their bells to the clear night in admonition. The conductor talked with the driver, both nodding often in the green light of the lamp. On the empty seats of the tram were scattered a few coloured tickets. No sound of footsteps came up or down the road. No sound broke the peace of the night save when the lank brown horses rubbed their noses together and shook their bells.

They seemed to listen, he on the upper step and she on the lower. She came up to his step many times and went down to hers again between their phrases and once or twice stood close beside him for some moments on the upper step, forgetting to go down, and then went down. His heart danced upon her movements like a cork upon a tide. He heard what her eyes said to him from beneath their cowl and knew that in some dim past, whether in life or in revery, he had heard their tale before. He saw her urge her vanities, her fine dress and sash and long black stockings, and knew that he had yielded to them a thousand times. Yet a voice within him spoke above the noise of his dancing heart, asking him would he take her gift to which he had only to stretch out his hand. And he remembered the day when he and Eileen had stood looking into the hotel grounds, watching the waiters running up a trail of bunting on the flagstaff and the foxterrier scampering to and fro on the sunny lawn, and how, all of a sudden, she had broken out into a peal of laughter and had run down the sloping curve of the path. Now, as then, he stood listlessly in his place, seemingly a tranquil watcher of the scene before him.

—She too wants me to catch hold of her, he thought. That's why she came with me to the tram. I could easily catch hold of her when she comes up to my step: nobody is looking. I could hold her and kiss her.

But he did neither: and, when he was sitting alone in the deserted tram, he tore his ticket into shreds and stared gloomily at the corrugated footboard.

The next day he sat at his table in the bare upper room for many hours. Before him lay a new pen, a new bottle of ink and a new emerald exercise. From force of habit he had written at the top of the first page the initial letters of the jesuit motto: A. M. D. G. On the first line of the page appeared the title of the verses he was trying to write: To E— C—. He knew it was right to begin so for he had seen similar titles in the collected poems of Lord Byron. When he had written this title and drawn an ornamental line underneath he fell into a daydream and began to draw diagrams on the cover of the book. He saw himself sitting at his table in Bray the morning after the dis= cussion at the Christmas dinnertable, trying to write a poem about Parnell on the back of one of his father's second moiety notices. But his brain had then refused to grapple with the theme and, desisting, he had covered the page with the names and addresses of certain of his classmates:

Roderick Kickham
John Lawton
Anthony MacSwiney
Simon Moonan

Now it seemed as if he would fail again but, by dint of brooding on the incident, he thought himself into confidence. During this process all those elements which he deemed com= mon and insignificant fell out of the scene. There remained no trace of the tram itself nor of the trammen nor of the horses: nor did he and she appear vividly. The verses told only of the night and the balmy breeze and the maiden lustre of the moon. Some undefined sorrow was hidden in the hearts of the protag= onists as they stood in silence beneath the leafless trees and when the moment of farewell had come the kiss, which had been withheld by one, was given by both. After this the letters L. D. S. were written at the foot of the page and, having hidden

the book, he went into his mother's bedroom and gazed at his
face for a long time in the mirror of her dressingtable.

But his long spell of leisure and liberty was drawing to its
end. One evening his father came home full of news which kept
his tongue busy all through dinner. Stephen had been awaiting
his father's return for there had been mutton hash that day and
he knew that his father would make him dip his bread in the
gravy. But he did not relish the hash for the mention of Clon=
gowes had coated his palate with a scum of disgust.

—I walked bang into him, said Mr Dedalus for the fourth
time, just at the corner of the square.

—Then I suppose, said Mrs Dedalus, he will be able to arrange
it. I mean, about Belvedere.

—Of course he will, said Mr Dedalus. Don't I tell you he's
provincial of the order now?

—I never liked the idea of sending him to the christian brothers
myself, said Mrs Dedalus.

—Christian brothers be damned! said Mr Dedalus. Is it with
Paddy Stink and Mickey Mud? No, let him stick to the jesuits
in God's name since he began with them. They'll be of service
to him in after years. Those are the fellows that can get you a
position.

—And they're a very rich order, aren't they, Simon?

—Rather. They live well, I tell you. You saw their table at
Clongowes. Fed up, by God, like gamecocks.

Mr Dedalus pushed his plate over to Stephen and bade him
finish what was on it.

—Now then, Stephen, he said. You must put your shoulder to
the wheel, old chap. You've had a fine long holiday.

—O, I'm sure he'll work very hard now, said Mrs Dedalus.
Especially when he has Maurice with him.

—O, Holy Paul, I forgot about Maurice, said Mr Dedalus.
Here, Maurice! Come here, you thickheaded ruffian! Do you
know I'm going to send you to a college where they'll teach you
to spell c.a.t: cat. And I'll buy you a nice little penny handker=
chief to keep your nose dry. Won't that be grand fun?

Maurice grinned at his father and then at his brother. Mr Dedalus screwed his glass into his eye and stared hard at both his sons. Stephen mumbled his bread without answering his father's gaze.

—By the bye, said Mr Dedalus at length, the rector, or provin=
cial, rather, was telling me that story about you and Father 430
Dolan. You're an impudent thief, he said.

—O, he didn't, Simon!

—Not he! said Mr Dedalus. But he gave me a great account of the whole affair. We were chatting, you know, and one word borrowed another. And, by the way, who do you think he told me will get that job in the corporation? But I'll tell you that after. Well, as I was saying, we were chatting away quite friendly and he asked me did our friend here wear glasses still and then he told me the whole story.

—And was he annoyed, Simon? 440

—Annoyed! Not he! *Manly little chap!* he said.

Mr Dedalus imitated the mincing nasal tone of the provin=
cial.

—Father Dolan and I, when I told them all at dinner about it, Father Dolan and I had a great laugh over it. *You better mind yourself, Father Dolan*, said I, *or young Dedalus will send you up for twice nine*. We had a famous laugh together over it. Ha! Ha! Ha!

Mr Dedalus turned to his wife and interjected in his natural voice: 450

—Shows you the spirit in which they take the boys there. O, a jesuit for your life, for diplomacy!

He reassumed the provincial's voice and repeated:

—*I told them all at dinner about it and Father Dolan and I and all of us we all had a hearty laugh together over it. Ha! Ha! Ha!*

◆ ◆ ◆

The night of the Whitsuntide play had come and Stephen from the window of the dressingroom looked out on the small grassplot across which lines of Chinese lanterns were stretched.

He watched the visitors come down the steps from the house and pass into the theatre. Stewards in evening dress, old Belve= dereans, loitered in groups about the entrance to the theatre and ushered in the visitors with ceremony. Under the sudden glow of a lantern he could recognise the smiling face of a priest.

The Blessed Sacrament had been removed from the taber= nacle and the first benches had been driven back so as to leave the dais of the altar and the space before it free. Against the walls stood companies of barbells and Indian clubs; the dumb= bells were piled in one corner: and in the midst of countless hillocks of gymnasium shoes and sweaters and singlets in untidy brown parcels there stood the stout leatherjacketed vaulting horse waiting its turn to be carried up on to the stage. A large bronze shield, tipped with silver, leaned against the panel of the altar also waiting its turn to be carried up on to the stage and set in the middle of the winning team at the end of the gymnastic display.

Stephen, though in deference to his reputation for essay= writing he had been elected secretary to the gymnasium, had no part in the first section of the programme: but in the play which formed the second section he had the chief part, that of a farcical pedagogue. He had been cast for it on account of his stature and grave manners for he was now at the end of his second year at Belvedere and in number two.

A score of the younger boys in white knickers and singlets came pattering down from the stage, through the vestry and into the chapel. The vestry and chapel were peopled with eager masters and boys. The plump bald sergeantmajor was testing with his foot the springboard of the vaulting horse. The lean young man in a long overcoat, who was to give a special display of intricate club swinging, stood near watching with interest, his silvercoated clubs peeping out of his deep side= pockets. The hollow rattle of the wooden dumbbells was heard as another team made ready to go up on the stage: and in another moment the excited prefect was hustling the boys through the vestry like a flock of geese, flapping the wings of

his soutane nervously and crying to the laggards to make haste.
A little troop of Neapolitan peasants were practising their steps
at the end of the chapel, some arching their arms above their
heads, some swaying their baskets of paper violets and curtsey=
ing. In a dark corner of the chapel at the gospel side of the altar
a stout old lady knelt amid her copious black skirts. When she $\quad$ 500
stood up a pinkdressed figure, wearing a curly golden wig and
an oldfashioned straw sunbonnet, with black pencilled eye=
brows and cheeks delicately rouged and powdered, was dis=
covered. A low murmur of curiosity ran round the chapel at the
discovery of this girlish figure. One of the prefects, smiling and
nodding his head, approached the dark corner and, having
bowed to the stout old lady, said pleasantly:

— Is this a beautiful young lady or a doll that you have here,
Mrs Tallon?

Then, bending down to peer at the smiling painted face un= $\quad$ 510
der the leaf of the bonnet, he exclaimed:

— No! Upon my word I believe it's little Bertie Tallon after all!

Stephen at his post by the window heard the old lady and
the priest laugh together and heard the boys' murmur of ad=
miration behind him as they pressed forward to see the little
boy who had to dance the sunbonnet dance by himself. A
movement of impatience escaped him. He let the edge of the
blind fall and, stepping down from the bench on which he had
been standing, walked out of the chapel.

He passed out of the schoolhouse and halted under the shed $\quad$ 520
that flanked the garden. From the theatre opposite came the
muffled noise of the audience and sudden brazen clashes of the
soldiers' band. The light spread upwards from the glass roof
making the theatre seem a festive ark, anchored amid the hulks
of houses, her frail cables of lanterns looping her to her moor=
ings. A sidedoor of the theatre opened suddenly and a shaft of
light flew across the grassplots. A sudden burst of music issued
from the ark, the prelude of a waltz: and when the sidedoor
closed again the listener could hear the faint rhythm of the
music. The sentiment of the opening bars, their languor and $\quad$ 530

supple movement, evoked the incommunicable emotion which had been the cause of all his day's unrest and of his impatient movement of a moment before. His unrest issued from him like a wave of sound: and on the tide of flowing music the ark was journeying, trailing her cables of lanterns in her wake. Then a noise like dwarf artillery broke the movement. It was the clapping that greeted the entry of the dumbbell team on the stage.

At the far end of the shed near the street a speck of pink light showed in the darkness and as he walked towards it he became aware of a faint aromatic odour. Two boys were standing in the shelter of the doorway, smoking, and before he reached them he had recognised Heron by his voice.

—Here comes the noble Dedalus! cried a high throaty voice. Welcome to our trusty friend!

This welcome ended in a soft peal of mirthless laughter as Heron salaamed and then began to poke the ground with his cane.

—Here I am, said Stephen, halting and glancing from Heron to his friend.

The latter was a stranger to him but in the darkness, by the aid of the glowing cigarette tips, he could make out a pale dandyish face, over which a smile was travelling slowly, a tall overcoated figure and a hard hat. Heron did not trouble him= self about an introduction but said instead:

—I was just telling my friend Wallis what a lark it would be tonight if you took off the rector in the part of the school= master. It would be a ripping good joke.

Heron made a poor attempt to imitate for his friend Wallis the rector's pedantic bass and then, laughing at his failure, asked Stephen to do it.

—Go on, Dedalus, he urged. You can take him off rippingly. *He that will not hear the churcha let him be to theea as the heathena and the publicana.*

The imitation was prevented by a mild expression of anger from Wallis in whose mouthpiece the cigarette had become too tightly wedged.

—Damn this blankety blank holder, he said, taking it from his mouth and smiling and frowning upon it tolerantly. It's always getting stuck like that. Do you use a holder?

—I don't smoke, answered Stephen.

—No, said Heron, Dedalus is a model youth. He doesn't smoke and he doesn't go to bazaars and he doesn't flirt and he doesn't damn anything or damn all.

Stephen shook his head and smiled in his rival's flushed and mobile face, beaked like a bird's. He had often thought it strange that Vincent Heron had a bird's face as well as a bird's name. A shock of pale hair lay on the forehead like a ruffled crest: the forehead was narrow and bony and a thin hooked nose stood out between the closeset prominent eyes which were light and inexpressive. The rivals were school friends. They sat together in class, knelt together in the chapel, talked together after beads over their lunches. As the fellows in number one were undistinguished dullards Stephen and Heron had been during the year the virtual heads of the school. It was they who went up to the rector together to ask for a free day or to get a fellow off.

—O, by the way, said Heron suddenly, I saw your governor going in.

The smile waned on Stephen's face. Any allusion made to his father by a fellow or by a master put his calm to rout in a moment. He waited in timorous silence to hear what Heron might say next. Heron, however, nudged him expressively with his elbow and said:

—You're a sly dog, Dedalus!

—Why so? said Stephen.

—You'd think butter wouldn't melt in your mouth, said Heron. But I'm afraid you're a sly dog.

—Might I ask you what you are talking about? said Stephen urbanely.

—Indeed you might, answered Heron. We saw her, Wallis, didn't we? And deucedly pretty she is too. And so inquisitive! *And what part does Stephen take, Mr Dedalus? And will Stephen not sing, Mr Dedalus?* Your governor was staring at her through that eyeglass of his for all he was worth so that I think the old man has found you out too. I wouldn't care a bit, by Jove. She's ripping, isn't she, Wallis?

—Not half bad, answered Wallis quietly as he placed his holder once more in a corner of his mouth.

610   A shaft of momentary anger flew through Stephen's mind at these indelicate allusions in the hearing of a stranger. For him there was nothing amusing in a girl's interest and regard. All day he had thought of nothing but their leavetaking on the steps of the tram at Harold's Cross, the stream of moody emotions it had made to course through him and the poem he had written about it. All day he had imagined a new meeting with her for he knew that she was to come to the play. The old restless moodiness had again filled his heart as it had done on the night of the party but had not found an outlet in verse. The
620   growth and knowledge of two years of boyhood stood between then and now, forbidding such an outlet: and all day the stream of gloomy tenderness within him had started forth and re= turned upon itself in dark courses and eddies, wearying him in the end until the pleasantry of the prefect and the painted little boy had drawn from him a movement of impatience.

—So you may as well admit, Heron went on, that we've fairly found you out this time. You can't play the saint on me any more, that's one sure five.

A soft peal of mirthless laughter escaped from his lips and,
630   bending down as before, he struck Stephen lightly across the calf of the leg with his cane, as if in jesting reproof.

Stephen's moment of anger had already passed. He was nei= ther flattered nor confused but simply wished the banter to end. He scarcely resented what had seemed to him at first a silly indelicateness for he knew that the adventure in his mind stood in no danger from their words: and his face mirrored his rival's false smile.

—Admit! repeated Heron, striking him again with his cane across the calf of the leg.

640   The stroke was playful but not so lightly given as the first

one had been. Stephen felt the skin tingle and glow slightly and almost painlessly; and bowing submissively, as if to meet his companion's jesting mood, began to recite the *Confiteor*. The episode ended well for both Heron and Wallis laughed indul= gently at the irreverence.

The confession came only from Stephen's lips and, while they spoke the words, a sudden memory had carried him to another scene called up, as if by magic, at the moment when he had noted the faint cruel dimples at the corners of Heron's smiling lips and had felt the familiar stroke of the cane against his calf and had heard the familiar word of admonition:
— Admit!

It was towards the close of his first term in the college when he was in number six. His sensitive nature was still smarting under the lashes of an undivined and squalid way of life. His soul was still disquieted and cast down by the dull phenom= enon of Dublin. He had emerged from a two years' spell of revery to find himself in the midst of a new scene, every event and figure of which affected him intimately, disheartened him or allured him and, whether alluring or disheartening, filled him always with unrest and bitter thoughts. All the leisure that his school life left him was passed in the company of subversive writers whose gibes and violence of speech set up a ferment in his brain before they passed out of it into his crude writings.

The essay was for him the chief labour of his week and every Tuesday, as he marched from home to the school, he read his fate in the incidents of the way, pitting himself against some figure ahead of him and quickening his pace to outstrip it be= fore a certain goal was reached or planting his steps scrupu= lously in the spaces of the patchwork of the footpath and telling himself that he would be first and not first in the weekly essay.

On a certain Tuesday the course of his triumphs was rudely broken. Mr Tate, the English master, pointed his finger at him and said bluntly:
— This fellow has heresy in his essay.

A hush fell on the class. Mr Tate did not break it but dug with his hand between his crossed thighs while his heavily starched linen creaked about his neck and wrists. Stephen did not look up. It was a raw spring morning and his eyes were still smarting and weak. He was conscious of failure and of detec=tion, of the squalor of his own mind and home, and felt against his neck the raw edge of his turned and jagged collar.

A short loud laugh from Mr Tate set the class more at ease.
—Perhaps you didn't know that, he said.
—Where? asked Stephen.

Mr Tate withdrew his delving hand and spread out the es=say.
—Here. It's about the Creator and the soul. Rrm ... rrm ..... rrm ... Ah! *without a possibility of ever approaching nearer.* That's heresy.

Stephen murmured:
—I meant *without a possibility of ever reaching.*

It was a submission and Mr Tate, appeased, folded up the essay and passed it across to him, saying:
—O ... Ah! *ever reaching.* That's another story.

But the class was not so soon appeased. Though nobody spoke to him of the affair after class he could feel about him a vague general malignant joy.

A few nights after this public chiding he was walking with a letter along the Drumcondra Road when he heard a voice cry:
—Halt!

He turned and saw three boys of his own class coming to=wards him in the dusk. It was Heron who had called out and, as he marched forward between his two attendants, he cleft the air before him with a thin cane, in time to their steps. Boland, his friend, marched beside him, a large grin on his face, while Nash came on a few steps behind, blowing from the pace and wagging his great red head.

As soon as the boys had turned into Clonliffe Road together they began to speak about books and writers, saying what books they were reading and how many books there were in their fathers' bookcases at home. Stephen listened to them in some wonderment for Boland was the dunce and Nash the idler of the class. In fact after some talk about their favourite writers Nash declared for Captain Marryat who, he said, was the greatest writer.

—Fudge! said Heron. Ask Dedalus. Who is the greatest writer, Dedalus?

Stephen noted the mockery in the question and said: 720

—Of prose, do you mean?

—Yes.

—Newman, I think.

—Is it Cardinal Newman? asked Boland.

—Yes, answered Stephen.

The grin broadened on Nash's freckled face as he turned to Stephen and said:

—And do you like Cardinal Newman, Dedalus?

—O, many people say that Newman has the best prose style, Heron said to the other two in explanation. Of course, he's not 730 a poet.

—And who is the best poet, Heron? asked Boland.

—Lord Tennyson, of course, answered Heron.

—O, yes, Lord Tennyson, said Nash. We have all his poetry at home in a book.

At this Stephen forgot the silent vows he had been making and burst out:

—Tennyson a poet! Why, he's only a rhymester!

—O, get out! said Heron. Everyone knows that Tennyson is the greatest poet. 740

—And who do you think is the greatest poet? asked Boland, nudging his neighbour.

—Byron, of course, answered Stephen.

Heron gave the lead and all three joined in a scornful laugh.

—What are you laughing at? asked Stephen.

—You, said Heron. Byron the greatest poet! He's only a poet for uneducated people.

—He must be a fine poet! said Boland.

—You may keep your mouth shut, said Stephen, turning on him boldly. All you know about poetry is what you wrote up on the slates in the yard and were going to be sent to the loft for.

Boland, in fact, was said to have written on the slates in the yard a couplet about a classmate of his who often rode home from the college on a pony:

> *As Tyson was riding into Jerusalem*
> *He fell and hurt his Alec Kafoozelum.*

This thrust put the two lieutenants to silence but Heron went on:

—In any case Byron was a heretic and immoral too.

—I don't care what he was, cried Stephen hotly.

—You don't care whether he was a heretic or not? said Nash.

—What do you know about it? shouted Stephen. You never read a line of anything in your life except a trans or Boland either.

—I know that Byron was a bad man, said Boland.

—Here. Catch hold of this heretic, Heron called out.

In a moment Stephen was a prisoner.

—Tate made you buck up the other day, Heron went on, about the heresy in your essay.

—I'll tell him tomorrow, said Boland.

—Will you? said Stephen. You'd be afraid to open your lips.

—Afraid?

—Ay. Afraid of your life.

—Behave yourself! cried Heron, cutting at Stephen's legs with his cane.

It was the signal for their onset. Nash pinioned his arms behind while Boland seized a long cabbage stump which was lying in the gutter. Struggling and kicking under the cuts of the cane and the blows of the knotty stump Stephen was borne back against a barbed wire fence.

—Admit that Byron was no good.

—No.

—Admit.

—No.

—Admit.

—No. No.

At last after a fury of plunges he wrenched himself free. His tormentors set off towards Jones's Road, laughing and jeering at him, while he, half blinded with tears, stumbled on, clench= ing his fists madly and sobbing.   790

While he was still repeating the *Confiteor* amid the indul= gent laughter of his hearers and while the scenes of that malignant episode were still passing sharply and swiftly before his mind he wondered why he bore no malice now to those who had tormented him. He had not forgotten a whit of their cowardice and cruelty but the memory of it called forth no anger from him. All the descriptions of fierce love and hatred which he had met in books had seemed to him therefore unreal. Even that night as he stumbled homewards along Jones's Road   800 he had felt that some power was divesting him of that sudden= woven anger as easily as a fruit is divested of her soft ripe peel.

He remained standing with his two companions at the end of the shed, listening idly to their talk or to the bursts of applause in the theatre. She was sitting there among the others, perhaps waiting for him to appear. He tried to recall her ap= pearance but could not. He could remember only that she had worn a shawl about her head like a cowl and that her dark eyes had invited and unnerved him. He wondered had he been in her thoughts as she had been in his. Then in the dark and unseen   810 by the other two he rested the tips of the fingers of one hand upon the palm of the other hand, scarcely touching it and yet pressing upon it lightly. But the pressure of her fingers had been lighter and steadier: and suddenly the memory of their touch traversed his brain and body like an invisible warm wave.

A boy came towards them, running along under the shed. He was excited and breathless.

—O, Dedalus, he cried, Doyle is in a great bake about you.

820 You're to go in at once and get dressed for the play. Hurry up, you better.

—He's coming now, said Heron to the messenger with a haughty drawl, when he wants to.

The boy turned to Heron and repeated:

—But Doyle is in an awful bake.

—Will you tell Doyle with my best compliments that I damned his eyes? answered Heron.

—Well, I must go now, said Stephen who cared little for such points of honour.

830 —I wouldn't, said Heron, damn me if I would. That's no way to send for one of the senior boys. In a bake, indeed! I think it's quite enough that you're taking a part in his bally old play.

This spirit of quarrelsome comradeship which he had ob= served lately in his rival had not seduced Stephen from his habits of quiet obedience. He mistrusted the turbulence and doubted the sincerity of such comradeship which seemed to him a sorry anticipation of manhood. The question of honour here raised was, like all such questions, trivial to him. While his mind had been pursuing its intangible phantoms and turning in

840 irresolution from such pursuit he had heard about him the constant voices of his father and of his masters, urging him to be a gentleman above all things and urging him to be a good catholic above all things. These voices had now come to be hollowsounding in his ears. When the gymnasium had been opened he had heard another voice urging him to be strong and manly and healthy and when the movement towards national revival had begun to be felt in the college yet another voice had bidden him be true to his country and help to raise up her fallen language and tradition. In the profane world, as he

850 foresaw, a worldly voice would bid him raise up his father's fallen state by his labours and, meanwhile, the voice of his schoolcomrades urged him to be a decent fellow, to shield others from blame or to beg them off and to do his best to get free days for the school. And it was the din of all these hollow= sounding voices that made him halt irresolutely in the pursuit

of phantoms. He gave them ear only for a time but he was happy only when he was far from them, beyond their call, alone or in the company of phantasmal comrades.

In the vestry a plump freshfaced jesuit and an elderly man, in shabby blue clothes, were dabbling in a case of paints and chalks. The boys who had been painted walked about or stood still awkwardly, touching their faces in a gingerly fashion with their furtive fingertips. In the middle of the vestry a young jesuit, who was then on a visit to the college, stood rocking himself rhythmically from the tips of his toes to his heels and back again, his hands thrust well forward into his sidepockets. His small head set off with glossy red curls and his newly shaven face agreed well with the spotless decency of his soutane and with his spotless shoes.

As he watched this swaying form and tried to read for him= self the legend of the priest's mocking smile there came into Stephen's memory a saying which he had heard from his father before he had been sent to Clongowes, that you could always tell a jesuit by the style of his clothes. At the same moment he thought he saw a likeness between his father's mind and that of this smiling welldressed priest: and he was aware of some des= ecration of the priest's office or of the vestry itself, whose si= lence was now routed by loud talk and joking and its air pungent with the smells of the gasjets and the grease.

While his forehead was being wrinkled and his jaws painted black and blue by the elderly man he listened distractedly to the voice of the plump young jesuit which bade him speak up and make his points clearly. He could hear the band playing *The Lily of Killarney* and knew that in a few moments the curtain would go up. He felt no stage fright but the thought of the part he had to play humiliated him. A remembrance of some of his lines made a sudden flush rise to his painted cheeks. He saw her serious alluring eyes watching him from among the audience and their image at once swept away his scruples, leaving his will compact. Another nature seemed to have been lent him: the infection of the excitement and youth about him entered

860

870

880

890

into and transformed his moody mistrustfulness. For one rare moment he seemed to be clothed in the real apparel of boy=hood: and, as he stood in the wings among the other players, he shared the common mirth amid which the drop scene was hauled upwards by two ablebodied priests with violent jerks and all awry.

A few moments after he found himself on the stage amid the garish gas and the dim scenery, acting before the innumerable faces of the void. It surprised him to see that the play which he had known at rehearsals for a disjointed lifeless thing had suddenly assumed a life of its own. It seemed now to play itself, he and his fellow actors aiding it with their parts. When the curtain fell on the last scene he heard the void filled with applause and, through a rift in the side scene, saw the simple body before which he had acted magically deformed, the void of faces breaking at all points and falling asunder into busy groups.

He left the stage quickly and rid himself of his mummery and passed out through the chapel into the college garden. Now that the play was over his nerves cried for some further adventure. He hurried onwards as if to overtake it. The doors of the theatre were all open and the audience had emptied out. On the lines which he had fancied the moorings of an ark a few lanterns swung in the night breeze, flickering cheerlessly. He mounted the steps from the garden in haste, eager that some prey should not elude him, and forced his way through the crowd in the hall and past the two jesuits who stood watching the exodus and bowing and shaking hands with the visitors. He pushed onward nervously, feigning a still greater haste and faintly conscious of the smiles and stares and nudges which his powdered head left in its wake.

When he came out on the steps he saw his family waiting for him at the first lamp. In a glance he noted that every figure of the group was familiar and ran down the steps angrily.

—I have to leave a message down in George's Street, he said to his father quickly. I'll be home after you.

Without waiting for his father's questions he ran across the road and began to walk at breakneck speed down the hill. He hardly knew where he was walking. Pride and hope and desire like crushed herbs in his heart sent up vapours of maddening incense before the eyes of his mind. He strode down the hill amid the tumult of suddenrisen vapours of wounded pride and fallen hope and baffled desire. They streamed upwards before his anguished eyes in dense and maddening fumes and passed away above him till at last the air was clear and cold again.

A film still veiled his eyes but they burned no longer. A power, akin to that which had often made anger or resentment fall from him, brought his steps to rest. He stood still and gazed up at the sombre porch of the morgue and from that to the dark cobbled laneway at its side. He saw the word *Lotts* on the wall of the lane and breathed slowly the rank heavy air.

—That is horse piss and rotted straw, he thought. It is a good odour to breathe. It will calm my heart. My heart is quite calm now. I will go back.

◆ ◆ ◆

Stephen was once again seated beside his father in the corner of a railway carriage at Kingsbridge. He was travelling with his father by the night mail to Cork. As the train steamed out of the station he recalled his childish wonder of years before and every event of his first day in Clongowes. But he felt no wonder now. He saw the darkening lands slipping past him, the silent telegraphpoles passing his window swiftly every four seconds, the little glimmering stations, manned by a few silent sentries, flung by the mail behind her and twinkling for a moment in the darkness like fiery grains flung backwards by a runner.

He listened without sympathy to his father's evocation of Cork and of scenes of his youth, a tale broken by sighs or draughts from his pocket flask whenever the image of some dead friend appeared in it or whenever the evoker remembered suddenly the purpose of his actual visit. Stephen heard but could feel no pity. The images of the dead were all strange to him save that of uncle Charles, an image which had lately been fading out of memory. He knew, however, that his father's property was going to be sold by auction and in the manner of his own dispossession he felt the world give the lie rudely to his phantasy.

At Maryborough he fell asleep. When he awoke the train had passed out of Mallow and his father was stretched asleep on the other seat. The cold light of the dawn lay over the country, over the unpeopled fields and the closed cottages. The terror of sleep fascinated his mind as he watched the silent country or heard from time to time his father's deep breath or sudden sleepy movement. The neighbourhood of unseen sleepers filled him with strange dread as though they could harm him; and he prayed that the day might come quickly. His prayer, addressed neither to God nor saint, began with a shiver, as the chilly morning breeze crept through the chink of the carriage door to his feet, and ended in a trail of foolish words which he made to fit the insistent rhythm of the train: and silently, at intervals of four seconds, the telegraphpoles held the galloping notes of the music between punctual bars. This furi=ous music allayed his dread and, leaning against the window=ledge, he let his eyelids close again.

They drove in a jingle across Cork while it was still early morning and Stephen finished his sleep in a bedroom of the Victoria Hotel. The bright warm sunlight was streaming through the window and he could hear the din of traffic. His father was standing before the dressingtable, examining his hair and face and moustache with great care, craning his neck across the waterjug and drawing it back sideways to see the better. While he did so he sang softly to himself with quaint accent and phrasing:

> 'Tis youth and folly
> Makes young men marry,
> So here, my love, I'll
> No longer stay.

What can't be cured, sure,
Must be injured, sure,
So I'll go to
Amerikay.

My love she's handsome,
My love she's boney:
She's like good whisky
When it is new;
But when 'tis old
And growing cold
It fades and dies like
The mountain dew.

The consciousness of the warm sunny city outside his window and the tender tremors with which his father's voice festooned the strange sad happy air drove off all the mists of the night's ill humour from Stephen's brain. He got up quickly to dress and, when the song had ended, said:

—That's much prettier than any of your other *come-all-yous*.

—Do you think so? asked Mr Dedalus.

—I like it, said Stephen.

—It's a pretty old air, said Mr Dedalus, twirling the points of his moustache. Ah, but you should have heard Mick Lacy sing it! Poor Mick Lacy! He had little turns for it, grace notes he used to put in that I haven't got. That was the boy could sing a *come-all-you*, if you like.

Mr Dedalus had ordered drisheens for breakfast and during the meal he crossexamined the waiter for local news. For the most part they spoke at cross purposes when a name was mentioned, the waiter having in mind its present holder and Mr Dedalus his father or perhaps his grandfather.

—Well, I hope they haven't moved the Queen's College anyhow, said Mr Dedalus, for I want to show it to this youngster of mine.

Along the Mardyke the trees were in bloom. They entered the grounds of the college and were led by the garrulous porter across the quadrangle. But their progress across the gravel was brought to a halt after every dozen or so paces by some reply of the porter's.

—Ah, do you tell me so? And is poor Pottlebelly dead?

—Yes, sir. Dead, sir.

During these halts Stephen stood awkwardly behind the two men, weary of the subject and waiting restlessly for the slow march to begin again. By the time they had crossed the quad=
1040 rangle his restlessness had risen to fever. He wondered how his father, whom he knew for a shrewd suspicious man, could be duped by the servile manners of the porter: and the lively southern speech which had entertained him all the morning now irritated his ears.

They passed into the anatomy theatre where Mr Dedalus, the porter aiding him, searched the desks for his initials. Ste=
phen remained in the background, depressed more than ever by the darkness and silence of the theatre and by the air it wore of jaded and formal study. On the desk before him he read the
1050 word *Foetus* cut several times in the dark stained wood. The sudden legend startled his blood: he seemed to feel the absent students of the college about him and to shrink from their company. A vision of their life, which his father's words had been powerless to evoke, sprang up before him out of the word cut in the desk. A broadshouldered student with a moustache was cutting in the letters with a jackknife, seriously. Other students stood or sat near him laughing at his handiwork. One jogged his elbow. The big student turned on him, frowning. He was dressed in loose grey clothes and had tan boots.

1060 Stephen's name was called. He hurried down the steps of the theatre so as to be as far away from the vision as he could be and, peering closely at his father's initials, hid his flushed face.

But the word and the vision capered before his eyes as he walked back across the quadrangle and towards the college gate. It shocked him to find in the outer world a trace of what he had deemed till then a brutish and individual malady of his own mind. His recent monstrous reveries came thronging into his memory. They too had sprung up before him, suddenly and furiously, out of mere words. He had soon given in to them and allowed them to sweep across and abase his intellect, wonder= ing always where they came from, from what den of monstrous images, and always weak and humble towards others, restless and sickened of himself when they had swept over him. 1070

—Ay, bedad! And there's the Groceries sure enough! cried Mr Dedalus. You often heard me speak of the Groceries, didn't you, Stephen. Many's the time we went down there when our names had been marked, a crowd of us, Harry Peard and little Jack Mountain and Bob Dyas and Maurice Moriarty, the Frenchman, and Tom O'Grady and Mick Lacy that I told you of this morning and Joey Corbet and poor little goodhearted 1080 Johnny Keevers of the Tantiles.

The leaves of the trees along the Mardyke were astir and whispering in the sunlight. A team of cricketers passed, agile young men in flannels and blazers, one of them carrying the long green wicketbag. In a quiet bystreet a German band of five players in faded uniforms and with battered brass instruments was playing to an audience of street arabs and leisurely mess= enger boys. A maid in a white cap and apron was watering a box of plants on a sill which shone like a slab of limestone in the warm glare. From another window open to the air came the 1090 sound of a piano, scale after scale rising into the treble.

Stephen walked on at his father's side, listening to stories he had heard before, hearing again the names of the scattered and dead revellers who had been the companions of his father's youth. And a faint sickness sighed in his heart. He recalled his own equivocal position in Belvedere, a free boy, a leader afraid of his own authority, proud and sensitive and suspicious, bat= tling against the squalor of his life and against the riot of his mind. The letters cut in the stained wood of the desk stared upon him, mocking his bodily weakness and futile enthusiasms 1100 and making him loathe himself for his own mad and filthy orgies. The spittle in his throat grew bitter and foul to swallow and the faint sickness climbed to his brain so that for a moment he closed his eyes and walked on in darkness.

He could still hear his father's voice.

—When you kick out for yourself, Stephen, (as I daresay you will one of those days) remember, whatever you do, to mix with gentlemen. When I was a young fellow I tell you I enjoyed myself. I mixed with fine decent fellows. Everyone of us could do something. One fellow had a good voice, another fellow was a good actor, another could sing a good comic song, another was a good oarsman or a good racketplayer, another could tell a good story and so on. We kept the ball rolling anyhow and enjoyed ourselves and saw a bit of life and we were none the worse of it either. But we were all gentlemen, Stephen, (at least I hope we were) and bloody good honest Irishmen too. That's the kind of fellows I want you to associate with, fellows of the right kidney. I'm talking to you as a friend, Stephen. I don't believe in playing the stern father. I don't believe a son should be afraid of his father. No, I treat you as your grandfather treated me when I was a young chap. We were more like brothers than father and son. I'll never forget the first day he caught me smoking. I was standing at the end of the South Terrace one day with some maneens like myself and sure we thought we were grand fellows because we had pipes stuck in the corners of our mouths. Suddenly the governor passed. He didn't say a word or stop even. But the next day, Sunday, we were out for a walk together and when we were coming home he took out his cigar case and said: *By the bye, Simon, I didn't know you smoked:* or something like that. —Of course I tried to carry it off as best I could. *If you want a good smoke*, he said, *try one of these cigars. An American captain made me a present of them last night in Queenstown.*

Stephen heard his father's voice break into a laugh which was almost a sob.

—He was the handsomest man in Cork at that time, by God he was! The women used to stand to look after him in the street.

He heard the sob passing loudly down his father's throat and opened his eyes with a nervous impulse. The sunlight breaking suddenly on his sight turned the sky and clouds into a fantastic world of sombre masses with lakelike spaces of dark rosy light. His very brain was sick and powerless. He could scarcely interpret the letters of the signboards of the shops. By his monstrous way of life he seemed to have put himself be= yond the limits of reality. Nothing moved him or spoke to him from the real world unless he heard in it an echo of the infuriated cries within him. He could respond to no earthly or human appeal, dumb and insensible to the call of summer and gladness and companionship, wearied and dejected by his fa= ther's voice. He could scarcely recognise as his his own ¹¹⁵⁰ thoughts, and repeated slowly to himself:

—I am Stephen Dedalus. I am walking beside my father whose name is Simon Dedalus. We are in Cork, in Ireland. Cork is a city. Our room is in the Victoria Hotel. Victoria and Stephen and Simon. Simon and Stephen and Victoria. Names.

The memory of his childhood suddenly grew dim. He tried to call forth some of its vivid moments but could not. He recalled only names: Dante, Parnell, Clane, Clongowes. A little boy had been taught geography by an old woman who kept two brushes in her wardrobe. Then he had been sent away ¹¹⁶⁰ from home to a college. In the college he had made his first communion and eaten slim jim out of his cricket cap and watched the firelight leaping and dancing on the wall of a little bedroom in the infirmary and dreamed of being dead, of mass being said for him by the rector in a black and gold cope, of being buried then in the little graveyard of the community off the main avenue of limes. But he had not died then. Parnell had died. There had been no mass for the dead in the chapel and no procession. He had not died but he had faded out like a film in the sun. He had been lost or had wandered out of existence for ¹¹⁷⁰ he no longer existed. How strange to think of him passing out of existence in such a way, not by death but by fading out in the sun or by being lost and forgotten somewhere in the uni= verse! It was strange to see his small body appear again for a moment: a little boy in a grey belted suit. His hands were in his sidepockets and his trousers were tucked in at the knees by elastic bands.

On the evening of the day on which the property was sold Stephen followed his father meekly about the city from bar to bar. To the sellers in the market, to the barmen and barmaids, to the beggars who importuned him for a lob Mr Dedalus told the same tale, that he was an old Corkonian, that he had been trying for thirty years to get rid of his Cork accent up in Dublin and that Peter Pickackafox beside him was his eldest son but that he was only a Dublin jackeen.

They had set out early in the morning from Newcombe's coffeehouse where Mr Dedalus' cup had rattled noisily against its saucer and Stephen had tried to cover that shameful sign of his father's drinkingbout of the night before by moving his chair and coughing. One humiliation had succeeded another: the false smiles of the market sellers, the curvettings and oglings of the barmaids with whom his father flirted, the compliments and encouraging words of his father's friends. They had told him that he had a great look of his grandfather and Mr Dedalus had agreed that he was an ugly likeness. They had unearthed traces of a Cork accent in his speech and made him admit that the Lee was a much finer river than the Liffey. One of them in order to put his Latin to the proof had made him translate short passages from Dilectus and asked him whether it was correct to say: *Tempora mutantur nos et mutamur in illis* or *Tempora mutantur et nos mutamur in illis*. Another, a brisk old man, whom Mr Dedalus called Johnny Cashman, had covered him with confusion by asking him to say which were prettier, the Dublin girls or the Cork girls.

—He's not that way built, said Mr Dedalus. Leave him alone. He's a levelheaded thinking boy who doesn't bother his head about that kind of nonsense.

—Then he's not his father's son, said the little old man.

—I don't know, I'm sure, said Mr Dedalus, smiling complacently.

—Your father, said the little old man to Stephen, was the boldest flirt in the city of Cork in his day. Do you know that?

Stephen looked down and studied the tiled floor of the bar into which they had drifted.

II

—Now don't be putting ideas into his head, said Mr Dedalus. Leave him to his Maker.

—Yerra, sure I wouldn't put any ideas into his head. I'm old enough to be his grandfather. And I am a grandfather, said the little old man to Stephen. Do you know that?

—Are you? asked Stephen. 1220

—Bedad I am, said the little old man. I have two bouncing grandchildren out at Sunday's Well. Now then! What age do you think I am? And I remember seeing your grandfather in his red coat riding out to hounds. That was before you were born.

—Ay, or thought of, said Mr Dedalus.

—Bedad I did! repeated the little old man. And, more than that, I can remember even your greatgrandfather, old John Stephen Dedalus, and a fierce old fireeater he was. Now then! There's a memory for you!

—That's three generations—four generations, said another of 1230 the company. Why, Johnny Cashman, you must be nearing the century.

—Well, I'll tell you the truth, said the little old man. I'm just twentyseven years of age.

—We're as old as we feel, Johnny, said Mr Dedalus. And just finish what you have there and we'll have another. Here, Tim or Tom or whatever your name is, give us the same again here. By God, I don't feel more than eighteen myself. There's that son of mine there not half my age and I'm a better man than he is any day of the week. 1240

—Draw it mild now, Dedalus. I think it's about time for you to take a back seat, said the gentleman who had spoken before.

—No, by God! asserted Mr Dedalus. I'll sing a tenor song against him or I'll vault a fivebarred gate against him or I'll run with him after the hounds across the country as I did thirty years ago along with the Kerry Boy and the best man for it.

—But he'll beat you here, said the little old man, tapping his forehead and raising his glass to drain it.

—Well, I hope he'll be as good a man as his father. That's all I can say, said Mr Dedalus. 1250

—If he is, he'll do, said the little old man.

—And thanks be to God, Johnny, said Mr Dedalus, that we lived so long and did so little harm.

—But did so much good, Simon, said the little old man gravely. Thanks be to God we lived so long and did so much good.

Stephen watched the three glasses being raised from the counter as his father and his two cronies drank to the memory of their past. An abyss of fortune or of temperament sundered him from them. His mind seemed older than theirs: it shone coldly on their strifes and happiness and regrets like a moon upon a younger earth. No life or youth stirred in him as it had stirred in them. He had known neither the pleasure of compan= ionship with others nor the vigour of rude male health nor filial piety. Nothing stirred within his soul but a cold and cruel and loveless lust. His childhood was dead or lost and with it his soul capable of simple joys: and he was drifting amid life like the barren shell of the moon.

> *Art thou pale for weariness*
> *Of climbing heaven and gazing on the earth*
> *Wandering companionless ....?*

He repeated to himself the lines of Shelley's fragment. Its alternation of sad human ineffectiveness with vast inhuman cycles of activity chilled him: and he forgot his own human and ineffectual grieving.

◆   ◆   ◆

Stephen's mother and his brother and one of his cousins waited at the corner of quiet Foster Place while he and his father went up the steps and along the colonnade where the highland sentry was parading. When they had passed into the great hall and stood at the counter Stephen drew forth his orders on the governor of the bank of Ireland for thirty and three pounds; and these sums, the moneys of his exhibition and essay prize, were paid over to him rapidly by the teller in notes and in coin respectively. He bestowed them in his pockets with

feigned composure and suffered the friendly teller, to whom his
father chatted, to take his hand across the broad counter and
wish him a brilliant career in after life. He was impatient of
their voices and could not keep his feet at rest. But the teller
still deferred the serving of others to say that he was living in
changed times and that there was nothing like giving a boy the   1290
best education that money could buy. Mr Dedalus lingered in
the hall gazing about him and up at the roof and telling Ste=
phen, who urged him to come out, that they were standing in
the house of commons of the old Irish parliament.
—God help us! he said piously. To think of the men of those
times, Stephen, Hely Hutchinson and Flood and Henry Grattan
and Charles Kendal Bushe, and the noblemen we have now,
leaders of the Irish people at home and abroad. Why, by God,
they wouldn't be seen dead in a ten acre field with them. No,
Stephen, old chap, I'm sorry to say that they are only as I roved   1300
out one fine May morning in the merry month of sweet July.

A keen October wind was blowing round the bank. The
three figures standing at the edge of the muddy path had
pinched cheeks and watery eyes. Stephen looked at his thinly
clad mother and remembered that a few days before he had
seen a mantle priced at twenty guineas in the window of Bar=
nardo's.
—Well, that's done, said Mr Dedalus.
—We had better go to dinner, said Stephen. Where?
—Dinner? said Mr Dedalus. Well, I suppose we had better,   1310
what?
—Some place that's not too dear, said Mrs Dedalus.
—Underdone's?
—Yes. Some quiet place.
—Come along, said Stephen quickly. It doesn't matter about
the dearness.

He walked on before them with short nervous steps, smiling.
They tried to keep up with him, smiling also at his eagerness.
—Take it easy like a good young fellow, said his father. We're
not out for the half mile, are we?   1320

For a swift season of merrymaking the money of his prizes ran through Stephen's fingers. Great parcels of groceries and delicacies and dried fruits arrived from the city. Every day he drew up a bill of fare for the family and every night led a party of three or four to the theatre to see *Ingomar* or *The Lady of Lyons*. In his coat pockets he carried squares of Vienna choc= olate for his guests while his trousers' pockets bulged with masses of silver and copper coins. He bought presents for everyone, overhauled his room, wrote out resolutions, marshal= led his books up and down their shelves, pored upon all kinds of price lists, drew up a form of commonwealth for the household by which every member of it held some office, opened a loan bank for his family and pressed loans on willing borrowers so that he might have the pleasure of making out receipts and reckoning the interests on the sums lent. When he could do no more he drove up and down the city in trams. Then the season of pleasure came to an end. The pot of pink enamel paint gave out and the wainscot of his bedroom re= mained with its unfinished and illplastered coat.

His household returned to its usual way of life. His mother had no further occasion to upbraid him for squandering his money. He too returned to his old life at school and all his novel enterprises fell to pieces. The commonwealth fell, the loan bank closed its coffers and its books on a sensible loss, the rules of life which he had drawn about himself fell into desue= tude.

How foolish his aim had been! He had tried to build a breakwater of order and elegance against the sordid tide of life without him and to dam up, by rules of conduct and active interests and new filial relations, the powerful recurrence of the tides within him. Useless. From without as from within the waters had flowed over his barriers: their tides began once more to jostle fiercely above the crumbled mole.

He saw clearly too his own futile isolation. He had not gone one step nearer the lives he had sought to approach nor bridged the restless shame and rancour that divided him from father and mother and brother and sister. He felt that he was hardly of the one blood with them but stood to them rather in the mystical kinship of fosterage, fosterchild and fosterbrother.

He burned to appease the fierce longings of his heart before which everything else was idle and alien. He cared little that he was in mortal sin, that his life had grown to be a tissue of subterfuges and falsehood. Beside the savage desire within him to realise the enormities which he brooded on nothing was sacred. He bore cynically with the shameful details of his secret riots in which he exulted to defile with patience whatever image had attracted his eyes. By day and by night he moved among distorted images of the outer world. A figure that had seemed to him by day demure and innocent came towards him by night through the winding darkness of sleep, her face transfigured by a lecherous cunning, her eyes bright with brutish joy. Only the morning pained him with its dim memory of dark orgiastic riot, its keen and humiliating sense of transgression.

He returned to his wanderings. The veiled autumnal evenings led him from street to street as they had led him years before along the quiet avenues of Blackrock. But no vision of trim front gardens or of kindly lights in the windows poured a tender influence upon him now. Only at times, in the pauses of his desire, when the luxury that was wasting him gave room to a softer languor, the image of Mercedes traversed the background of his memory. He saw again the small white house and the garden of rosebushes on the road that led to the mountains and he remembered the sadly proud gesture of refusal which he was to make there, standing with her in the moonlit garden after years of estrangement and adventure. At those moments the soft speeches of Claude Melnotte rose to his lips and eased his unrest. A tender premonition touched him of the tryst he had then looked forward to and, in spite of the horrible reality which lay between his hope of then and now, of the holy encounter he had then imagined at which weakness and timidity and inexperience were to fall from him.

Such moments passed and the wasting fires of lust sprang up

again. The verses passed from his lips and the inarticulate cries and the unspoken brutal words rushed forth from his brain to force a passage. His blood was in revolt. He wandered up and down the dark slimy streets peering into the gloom of lanes and doorways, listening eagerly for any sound. He moaned to him= self like some baffled prowling beast. He wanted to sin with another of his kind, to force another being to sin with him and to exult with her in sin. He felt some dark presence moving irresistibly upon him from the darkness, a presence subtle and murmurous as a flood filling him wholly with itself. Its mur= mur besieged his ears like the murmur of some multitude in sleep; its subtle streams penetrated his being. His hands clenched convulsively and his teeth set together as he suffered the agony of its penetration. He stretched out his arms in the street to hold fast the frail swooning form that eluded him and incited him: and the cry that he had strangled for so long in his throat issued from his lips. It broke from him like a wail of despair from a hell of sufferers and died in a wail of furious entreaty, a cry for an iniquitous abandonment, a cry which was but the echo of an obscene scrawl which he had read on the oozing wall of a urinal.

He had wandered into a maze of narrow and dirty streets. From the foul laneways he heard bursts of hoarse riot and wrangling and the drawling of drunken singers. He walked onward, undismayed, wondering whether he had strayed into the quarter of the jews. Women and girls dressed in long vivid gowns traversed the street from house to house. They were leisurely and perfumed. A trembling seized him and his eyes grew dim. The yellow gasflames arose before his troubled vi= sion against the vapoury sky, burning as if before an altar. Before the doors and in the lighted halls groups were gathered, arrayed as for some rite. He was in another world: he had awakened from a slumber of centuries.

He stood still in the middle of the roadway, his heart clam= ouring against his bosom in a tumult. A young woman dressed in a long pink gown laid her hand on his arm to detain him and gazed into his face. She said gaily:

—Good night, Willie dear!

Her room was warm and lightsome. A huge doll sat with her
legs apart in the copious easychair beside the bed. He tried to
bid his tongue speak that he might seem at ease, watching her
as she undid her gown, noting the proud conscious movements
of her perfumed head.

As he stood silent in the middle of the room she came over
to him and embraced him gaily and gravely. Her round arms
held him firmly to her and he, seeing her face lifted to him in
serious calm and feeling the warm calm rise and fall of her
breast, all but burst into hysterical weeping. Tears of joy and
relief shone in his delighted eyes and his lips parted though they
would not speak.

She passed her tinkling hand through his hair, calling him a
little rascal.

—Give me a kiss, she said.

His lips would not bend to kiss her. He wanted to be held
firmly in her arms, to be caressed slowly, slowly, slowly. In her
arms he felt that he had suddenly become strong and fearless
and sure of himself. But his lips would not bend to kiss her.

With a sudden movement she bowed his head and joined her
lips to his and he read the meaning of her movements in her
frank uplifted eyes. It was too much for him. He closed his
eyes, surrendering himself to her, body and mind, conscious of
nothing in the world but the dark pressure of her softly parting
lips. They pressed upon his brain as upon his lips as though
they were the vehicle of a vague speech; and between them he
felt an unknown and timid pressure, darker than the swoon of
sin, softer than sound or odour.

III

The swift December dusk had come tumbling clownishly after its dull day and as he stared through the dull square of the window of the schoolroom he felt his belly crave for its food. He hoped there would be stew for dinner, turnips and carrots and bruised potatoes and fat mutton pieces to be ladled out in thick peppered flourfattened sauce. Stuff it into you, his belly counselled him.

It would be a gloomy secret night. After early nightfall the yellow lamps would light up here and there the squalid quarter of the brothels. He would follow a devious course up and down the streets, circling always nearer and nearer in a tremor of fear and joy, until his feet led him suddenly round a dark corner. The whores would be just coming out of their houses making ready for the night, yawning lazily after their sleep and settling the hairpins in their clusters of hair. He would pass by them calmly waiting for a sudden movement of his own will or a sudden call to his sinloving soul from their soft perfumed flesh. Yet as he prowled in quest of that call his senses, stultified only by his desire, would note keenly all that wounded and shamed them, his eyes a ring of porter froth on a clothless table or a photograph of two soldiers standing to attention or a gaudy playbill, his ears the drawling jargon of greeting:

—Hello, Bertie, any good in your mind?

—Is that you, pigeon?

—Number ten. Fresh Nelly is waiting on you.

—Good night, husband! Coming in to have a short time?

The equation on the page of his scribbler began to spread out a widening tail, eyed and starred like a peacock's: and when the eyes and stars of its indices had been eliminated be=

gan slowly to fold itself together again. The indices appearing
and disappearing were eyes opening and closing; the eyes
opening and closing were stars being born and being quenched.
The vast cycle of starry life bore his weary mind outward to its
verge and inward to its centre, a distant music accompanying
him outward and inward. What music? The music came nearer
and he recalled the words, the words of Shelley's fragment
upon the moon wandering companionless, pale for weariness.
The stars began to crumble and a cloud of fine stardust fell
through space.

The dull light fell more faintly upon the page whereon an=
other equation began to unfold itself slowly and to spread
abroad its widening tail. It was his own soul going forth to
experience, unfolding itself sin by sin, spreading abroad the
balefire of its burning stars and folding back upon itself, fading
slowly, quenching its own lights and fires. They were
quenched: and the cold darkness filled chaos.

A cold lucid indifference reigned in his soul. At his first
violent sin he had felt a wave of vitality pass out of him and
had feared to find his body or his soul maimed by the excess.
Instead the vital wave had carried him on its bosom out of
himself and back again when it receded: and no part of body or
soul had been maimed but a dark peace had been established
between them. The chaos in which his ardour extinguished
itself was a cold indifferent knowledge of himself. He had
sinned mortally not once but many times and he knew that,
while he stood in danger of eternal damnation for the first sin
alone, by every succeeding sin he multiplied his guilt and his
punishment. His days and works and thoughts could make no
atonement for him, the fountains of sanctifying grace having
ceased to refresh his soul. At most by an alms given to a
beggar, whose blessing he fled from, he might hope wearily to
win for himself some measure of actual grace. Devotion had
gone by the board. What did it avail to pray when he knew that
his soul lusted after its own destruction? A certain pride, a
certain awe, withheld him from offering to God even one

prayer at night though he knew it was in God's power to take away his life while he slept and hurl his soul hellward ere he could beg for mercy. His pride in his own sin, his loveless awe of God told him that his offence was too grievous to be atoned for in whole or in part by a false homage to the Allseeing and Allknowing.

— Well now, Ennis, I declare you have a head and so has my stick! Do you mean to say that you are not able to tell me what a surd is?

The blundering answer stirred the embers of his contempt of his fellows. Towards others he felt neither shame nor fear. On Sunday mornings as he passed the churchdoor he glanced coldly at the worshippers who stood bareheaded, four deep, outside the church, morally present at the mass which they could neither see nor hear. Their dull piety and the sickly smell of the cheap hairoil with which they had anointed their heads repelled him from the altar they prayed at. He stooped to the evil of hypocrisy with others, sceptical of their innocence which he could cajole so easily.

On the wall of his bedroom hung an illuminated scroll, the certificate of his prefecture in the college of the sodality of the Blessed Virgin Mary. On Saturday mornings when the sodality met in the chapel to recite the little office his place was a cushioned kneelingdesk at the right of the altar from which he led his wing of boys through the responses. The falsehood of his position did not pain him. If at moments he felt an impulse to rise from his post of honour and, confessing before them all his unworthiness, to leave the chapel, a glance at their faces restrained him. The imagery of the psalms of prophecy soothed his barren pride. The glories of Mary held his soul captive: spikenard and myrrh and frankincense, symbolising the preciousness of God's gifts to her soul, rich garments, symbol= ising her royal lineage, her emblems, the lateflowering plant and lateblossoming tree, symbolising the agelong gradual growth of her cultus among men. When it fell to him to read the lesson towards the close of the office he read it in a veiled voice, lulling his conscience to its music:

Quasi cedrus exaltata sum in Libanon et quasi cu=
pressus in monte Sion. Quasi palma exaltata sum in
Gades et quasi plantatio rosae in Jericho. Quasi uliva
speciosa in campis et quasi platanus exaltata sum juxta
aquam in plateis. Sicut cinnamomum et balsamum aro=
matizans odorem dedi et quasi myrrha electa dedi
suavitatem odoris.

His sin, which had covered him from the sight of God, had 110
led him nearer to the refuge of sinners. Her eyes seemed to
regard him with mild pity; her holiness, a strange light glowing
faintly upon her frail flesh, did not humiliate the sinner who
approached her. If ever he was impelled to cast sin from him
and to repent the impulse that moved him was the wish to be
her knight. If ever his soul, reentering her dwelling shyly after
the frenzy of his body's lust had spent itself, was turned to=
wards her whose emblem is the morning star, *bright and*
musical, telling of heaven and infusing peace, it was when her 120
names were murmured softly by lips whereon there still lin=
gered foul and shameful words, the savour itself of a lewd kiss.

That was strange. He tried to think how it could be but the
dusk, deepening in the schoolroom, covered over his thought.
The bell rang. The master marked the sums and cuts to be done
for the next lesson and went out. Heron, beside Stephen, began
to hum tunelessly:

My excellent friend Bombados.

Ennis, who had gone to the yard, came back, saying:
— The boy from the house is coming up for the rector.
A tall boy behind Stephen rubbed his hands and said: 130
— That's game ball. We can scut the whole hour. He won't be
in till after half two. Then you can ask him questions on the
catechism, Dedalus.
Stephen, leaning back and drawing idly on his scribbler,
listened to the talk about him which Heron checked from time
to time by saying:
— Shut up, will you. Don't make such a bally racket!

It was strange too that he found an arid pleasure in follow=
ing up to the end the rigid lines of the doctrines of the church
and penetrating into obscure silences only to hear and feel the
more deeply his own condemnation. The sentence of saint
James which says that he who offends against one command=
ment becomes guilty of all had seemed to him first a swollen
phrase until he had begun to grope in the darkness of his own
state. From the evil seed of lust all other deadly sins had sprung
forth: pride in himself and contempt of others, covetousness in
using money for the purchase of unlawful pleasure, envy of
those whose vices he could not reach to and calumnious
murmuring against the pious, gluttonous enjoyment of food,
the dull glowering anger amid which he brooded upon his
longing, the swamp of spiritual and bodily sloth in which his
whole being had sunk.

As he sat in his bench gazing calmly at the rector's shrewd
harsh face his mind wound itself in and out of the curious
questions proposed to it. If a man had stolen a pound in his
youth and had used that pound to amass a huge fortune how
much was he obliged to give back, the pound he had stolen
only or the pound together with the compound interest accru=
ing upon it or all his huge fortune? If a layman in giving
baptism pour the water before saying the words is the child
baptised? Is baptism with a mineral water valid? How comes it
that while the first beatitude promises the kingdom of heaven
to the poor of heart the second beatitude promises also to the
meek that they shall possess the land? Why was the sacrament
of the eucharist instituted under the two species of bread and
wine if Jesus Christ be present body and blood, soul and divin=
ity, in the bread alone and in the wine alone? Does a tiny
particle of the consecrated bread contain all the body and
blood of Jesus Christ or a part only of the body and blood? If
the wine change into vinegar and the host crumble into cor=
ruption after they have been consecrated is Jesus Christ still
present under their species as God and as man?
—Here he is! Here he is!

A boy from his post at the window had seen the rector come from the house. All the catechisms were opened and all heads bent upon them silently. The rector entered and took his seat on the dais. A gentle kick from the tall boy in the bench behind urged Stephen to ask a difficult question.

The rector did not ask for a catechism to hear the lesson from. He clasped his hands on the desk and said:
— The retreat will begin on Wednesday afternoon in honour of saint Francis Xavier whose feast day is Saturday. The retreat will go on from Wednesday to Friday. On Friday confessions will be heard all the afternoon after beads. If any boys have special confessors perhaps it will be better for them not to change. Mass will be on Saturday morning at nine o'clock and general communion for the whole college. Saturday will be a free day. Sunday of course. But Saturday and Sunday being free days some boys might be inclined to think that Monday is a free day also. Beware of making that mistake. I think you, Lawless, are likely to make that mistake.
— I, sir? Why, sir?

A little wave of quiet mirth broke forth over the class of boys from the rector's grim smile. Stephen's heart began slowly to fold and fade with fear like a withering flower.

The rector went on gravely:
— You are all familiar with the story of the life of saint Francis Xavier, I suppose, the patron of your college. He came of an old and illustrious Spanish family and you remember that he was one of the first followers of saint Ignatius. They met in Paris where Francis Xavier was professor of philosophy at the university. This young and brilliant nobleman and man of let= ters entered heart and soul into the ideas of our glorious founder and you know that he, at his own desire, was sent by saint Ignatius to preach to the Indians. He is called, as you know, the apostle of the Indies. He went from country to country in the east, from Africa to India, from India to Japan, baptising the people. He is said to have baptised as many as ten thousand idolaters in one month. It is said that his right arm

210 had grown powerless from having been raised so often over the heads of those whom he baptised. He wished then to go to China to win still more souls for God but he died of fever on the island of Sancian. A great saint, saint Francis Xavier! A great soldier of God!

The rector paused and then, shaking his clasped hands before him, went on:

—He had the faith in him that moves mountains. Ten thousand souls won for God in a single month! That is a true conqueror, true to the motto of our order *ad majorem Dei*

220 *gloriam*! A saint who has great power in heaven, remember: power to intercede for us in our grief, power to obtain whatever we pray for if it be for the good of our souls, power above all to obtain for us the grace to repent if we be in sin. A great saint, saint Francis Xavier! A great fisher of souls!

He ceased to shake his clasped hands and, resting them against his forehead, looked right and left of them keenly at his listeners out of his dark stern eyes.

In the silence their dark fire kindled the dusk into a tawny glow. Stephen's heart had withered up like a flower of the

230 desert that feels the simoom coming from afar.

◆ ◆ ◆

—*Remember only thy last things and thou shalt not sin for ever*—words taken, my dear little brothers in Christ, from the book of Ecclesiastes, seventh chapter, fortieth verse. In the name of the Father and of the Son and of the Holy Ghost. Amen.

Stephen sat in the front bench of the chapel. Father Arnall sat at a table to the left of the altar. He wore about his shoulders a heavy cloak; his pale face was drawn and his voice broken with rheum. The figure of his old master, so strangely

240 rearisen, brought back to Stephen's mind his life at Clongowes: the wide playgrounds, swarming with boys, the square ditch, the little cemetery off the main avenue of limes where he had dreamed of being buried, the firelight on the wall of the infirm=

ary where he lay sick, the sorrowful face of Brother Michael. His soul, as these memories came back to him, became again a child's soul.

—We are assembled here today, my dear little brothers in Christ, for one brief moment far away from the busy bustle of the outer world to celebrate and to honour one of the greatest of saints, the apostle of the Indies, the patron saint also of your college, saint Francis Xavier. Year after year for much longer than any of you, my dear little boys, can remember or than I can remember the boys of this college have met in this very chapel to make their annual retreat before the feast day of their patron saint. Time has gone on and brought with it its changes. Even in the last few years what changes can most of you not remember? Many of the boys who sat in those front benches a few short years ago are perhaps now in distant lands, in the burning tropics or immersed in professional duties or in sem= inaries or voyaging over the vast expanse of the deep or, it may be, already called by the great God to another life and to the rendering up of their stewardship. And still as the years roll by, bringing with them changes for good and bad, the memory of the great saint is honoured by the boys of his college who make every year their annual retreat on the days preceding the feast day set apart by our holy mother the church to transmit to all the ages the name and fame of one of the greatest sons of catholic Spain.

Now what is the meaning of this word *retreat* and why is it allowed on all hands to be a most salutary practice for all who desire to lead before God and in the eyes of men a truly chris= tian life? A retreat, my dear boys, signifies a withdrawal for a while from the cares of our life, the cares of this workaday world, in order to examine the state of our conscience, to reflect on the mysteries of holy religion and to understand better why we are here in this world. During these few days I intend to put before you some thoughts concerning the four last things. They are, as you know from your catechism, death, judgment, hell and heaven. We shall try to understand them

280 fully during these few days so that we may derive from the understanding of them a lasting benefit to our souls. And re= member, my dear boys, that we have been sent into this world for one thing and for one thing alone: to do God's holy will and to save our immortal souls. All else is worthless. One thing alone is needful, the salvation of one's soul. What doth it profit a man to gain the whole world if he suffer the loss of his immortal soul? Ah, my dear boys, believe me there is nothing in this wretched world that can make up for such a loss.

I will ask you therefore, my dear boys, to put away from
290 your minds during these few days all worldly thoughts, whether of study or pleasure or ambition, and to give all your attention to the state of your souls. I need hardly remind you that during the days of the retreat all boys are expected to preserve a quiet and pious demeanour and to shun all loud unseemly pleasure. The elder boys, of course, will see that this custom is not infringed and I look especially to the prefects and officers of the sodality of Our Blessed Lady and of the sodality of the holy angels to set a good example to their fellowstu= dents.

300 Let us try therefore to make this retreat in honour of saint Francis with our whole heart and our whole mind. God's bless= ing will then be upon all your year's studies. But, above and beyond all, let this retreat be one to which you can look back in after years when maybe you are far from this college and among very different surroundings, to which you can look back with joy and thankfulness and give thanks to God for having granted you this occasion of laying the first foundation of a pious honourable zealous christian life. And if, as may so happen, there be at this moment in these benches any poor soul
310 which has had the unutterable misfortune to lose God's holy grace and to fall into grievous sin I fervently trust and pray that this retreat may be the turningpoint in the life of that soul. I pray to God through the merits of His zealous servant Francis Xavier that such a soul may be led to sincere repentance and that the holy communion on saint Francis' day of this year may

be a lasting covenant between God and that soul. For just and unjust, for saint and sinner alike, may this retreat be a memorable one.

Help me, my dear little brothers in Christ. Help me by your pious attention, by your own devotion, by your outward demeanour. Banish from your minds all worldly thoughts and think only of the last things, death, judgment, hell and heaven. He who remembers these things, says Ecclesiastes, shall not sin for ever. He who remembers the last things will act and think with them always before his eyes. He will live a good life and die a good death, believing and knowing that, if he has sacrificed much in this earthly life, it will be given to him a hundredfold and a thousandfold more in the life to come, in the kingdom without end—a blessing, my dear boys, which I wish you from my heart; one and all, in the name of the Father and of the Son and of the Holy Ghost. Amen.

As he walked home with silent companions a thick fog seemed to compass his mind. He waited in stupor of mind till it should lift and reveal what it had hidden. He ate his dinner with surly appetite and, when the meal was over and the greasestrewn plates lay abandoned on the table, he rose and went to the window, clearing the thick scum from his mouth with his tongue and licking it from his lips. So he had sunk to the state of a beast that licks his chaps after meat. This was the end: and a faint glimmer of fear began to pierce the fog of his mind. He pressed his face against the pane of the window and gazed out into the darkening street. Forms passed this way and that way through the dull light. And that was life. The letters of the name of Dublin lay heavily upon his mind, pushing one another surlily hither and thither with slow boorish insistence. His soul was fattening and congealing into a gross grease, plunging ever deeper in its dull fear into a sombre threatening dusk, while the body that was his stood, listless and dishonoured, gazing out of darkened eyes, helpless, perturbed and human for a bovine god to stare upon.

The next day brought death and judgment, stirring his soul

slowly from its listless despair. The faint glimmer of fear be=
came a terror of spirit as the hoarse voice of the preacher blew
death into his soul. He suffered its agony. He felt the deathchill
touch the extremities and creep onward towards the heart, the
film of death veiling the eyes, the bright centres of the brain
extinguished one by one like lamps, the last sweat oozing upon
the skin, the powerlessness of the dying limbs, the speech
thickening and wandering and failing, the heart throbbing
360   faintly and more faintly, all but vanquished, the breath, the
poor timid breath, the poor helpless human spirit, sobbing and
sighing, gurgling and rattling in the throat. No help! No help!
He, he himself, his body to which he had yielded was dying.
Into the grave with it! Nail it down into a wooden box, the
corpse. Carry it out of the house on the shoulders of hirelings.
Thrust it out of men's sight into a long hole in the ground, into
the grave, to rot, to feed the mass of its creeping worms and to
be devoured by scuttling plumpbellied rats.

    And while the friends were still standing in tears by the
370   bedside the soul of the sinner was judged. At the last moment
of consciousness the whole earthly life passed before the vision
of the soul and, ere it had time to reflect, the body had died and
the soul stood terrified before the judgmentseat. God, who had
long been merciful, would then be just. He had long been
patient, pleading with the sinful soul, giving it time to repent,
sparing it yet awhile. But that time had gone. Time was to sin
and to enjoy, time was to scoff at God and at the warnings of
His holy church, time was to defy His majesty, to disobey His
commands, to hoodwink one's fellow men, to commit sin after
380   sin and sin after sin and to hide one's corruption from the sight
of men. But that time was over. Now it was God's turn: and He
was not to be hoodwinked or deceived. Every sin would then
come forth from its lurkingplace, the most rebellious against
the divine will and the most degrading to our poor corrupt
nature, the tiniest imperfection and the most heinous atrocity.
What did it avail then to have been a great emperor, a great
general, a marvellous inventor, the most learned of the learned?

All were as one before the judgmentseat of God. He would reward the good and punish the wicked. One single instant was enough for the trial of a man's soul. One single instant after the body's death, the soul had been weighed in the balance. The particular judgment was over and the soul had passed to the abode of bliss or to the prison of purgatory or had been hurled howling into hell.

Nor was that all. God's justice had still to be vindicated before men: after the particular there still remained the general judgment. The last day had come. The doomsday was at hand. The stars of heaven were falling upon the earth like the figs cast by the figtree which the wind has shaken. The sun, the great luminary of the universe, had become as sackcloth of hair. The moon was bloodred. The firmament was as a scroll rolled away. The archangel Michael, the prince of the heavenly host, appeared glorious and terrible against the sky. With one foot on the sea and one foot on the land he blew from the archangelical trumpet the brazen death of time. The three blasts of the angel filled all the universe. Time is, time was but time shall be no more. At the last blast the souls of universal humanity throng towards the valley of Jehoshaphat, rich and poor, gentle and simple, wise and foolish, good and wicked. The soul of every human being that has ever existed, the souls of all those who shall yet be born, all the sons and daughters of Adam, all are assembled on that supreme day. And lo the supreme judge is coming! No longer the lowly Lamb of God, no longer the meek Jesus of Nazareth, no longer the Man of Sorrows, no longer the Good Shepherd, He is seen now coming upon the clouds, in great power and majesty, attended by nine choirs of angels, angels and archangels, principalities, powers and virtues, thrones and dominations, cherubim and seraphim, God Omnipotent, God Everlasting. He speaks: and His voice is heard even at the farthest limits of space, even in the bottom= less abyss. Supreme Judge, from His sentence there will be and can be no appeal. He calls the just to His side bidding them enter into the kingdom, the eternity of bliss prepared for them.

The unjust He casts from Him, crying in His offended majesty: *Depart from me, ye cursed, into everlasting fire which was prepared for the devil and his angels.* O what agony then for the miserable sinners! Friend is torn apart from friend, children from their parents, husbands from their wives. The poor sinner holds out his arms to those who were dear and near to him in this earthly world, to those whose simple piety perhaps he made a mock of, to those who counselled him and tried to lead him on the right path, to a kind brother, to a loving sister, to the mother and father who loved him so dearly. But it is too late: the just turn away from the wretched damned souls which now appear before the eyes of all in their hideous and evil character. O you hypocrites, O you whited sepulchres, O you who present a smooth smiling face to the world while your soul within is a foul swamp of sin, how will it fare with you in that terrible day?

And this day will come, shall come, must come: the day of death and the day of judgment. It is appointed unto man to die and after death the judgment. Death is certain. The time and manner are uncertain, whether from long disease or from some unexpected accident: the Son of God cometh at an hour when you little expect Him. Be therefore ready every moment, seeing that you may die at any moment. Death is the end of us all. Death and judgment, brought into the world by the sin of our first parents, are the dark portals that close our earthly exist=ence, the portals that open into the unknown and the unseen, portals through which every soul must pass, alone, unaided save by its good works, without friend or brother or parents or master to help it, alone and trembling. Let that thought be ever before our minds and then we cannot sin. Death, a cause of terror to the sinner, is a blessed moment for him who has walked in the right path, fulfilling the duties of his station in life, attending to his morning and evening prayers, approaching the holy sacrament frequently and performing good and mer=ciful works. For the pious and believing catholic, for the just man, death is no cause of terror. Was it not Addison, the great

English writer, who, when on his deathbed, sent for the wicked   460
young earl of Warwick to let him see how a christian can meet
his end? He it is and he alone, the pious and believing christian,
who can say in his heart:

> O grave, where is thy victory?
> O death, where is thy sting?

Every word of it was for him. Against his sin, foul and
secret, the whole wrath of God was aimed. The preacher's
knife had probed deeply into his diseased conscience and he felt
now that his soul was festering in sin. Yes, the preacher was
right. God's turn had come. Like a beast in its lair his soul had   470
lain down in its own filth but the blasts of the angel's trumpet
had driven him forth from the darkness of sin into the light.
The words of doom cried by the angel shattered in an instant
his presumptuous peace. The wind of the last day blew through
his mind; his sins, the jeweleyed harlots of his imagination, fled
before the hurricane, squeaking like mice in their terror and
huddled under a mane of hair.

As he crossed the square, walking homeward, the light
laughter of a girl reached his burning ears. The frail gay sound
smote his heart more strongly than a trumpetblast, and, not   480
daring to lift his eyes, he turned aside and gazed, as he walked,
into the shadow of the tangled shrubs. Shame rose from his
smitten heart and flooded his whole being. The image of Emma
appeared before him and, under her eyes, the flood of shame
rushed forth anew from his heart. If she knew to what his mind
had subjected her or how his brutelike lust had torn and
trampled upon her innocence! Was that boyish love? Was that
chivalry? Was that poetry? The sordid details of his orgies stank
under his very nostrils: the sootcoated packet of pictures which
he had hidden in the flue of the fireplace and in the presence of   490
whose shameless or bashful wantonness he lay for hours sin=
ning in thought and deed: his monstrous dreams, peopled by
apelike creatures and by harlots with gleaming jewel eyes: the
foul long letters he had written in the joy of guilty confession

and carried secretly for days and days only to throw them
under cover of night among the grass in the corner of a field or
beneath some hingeless door or in some niche in the hedges
where a girl might come upon them as she walked by and read
them secretly. Mad! Mad! Was it possible he had done these
things? A cold sweat broke out upon his forehead as the foul
memories condensed within his brain.

When the agony of shame had passed from him he tried to
raise his soul from its abject powerlessness. God and the
Blessed Virgin were too far from him: God was too great and
stern and the Blessed Virgin too pure and holy. But he imagined
that he stood near Emma in a wide land and, humbly and in
tears, bent and kissed the elbow of her sleeve.

In a wide land under a tender lucid evening sky, a cloud
drifting westward amid a pale green sea of heaven, they stood
together, children that had erred. Their error had offended
deeply God's majesty, though it was the error of two children,
but it had not offended her whose beauty *is not like earthly
beauty, dangerous to look upon, but like the morning star
which is its emblem, bright and musical*. The eyes were not
offended which she turned upon them nor reproachful. She
placed their hands together, hand in hand, and said, speaking
to their hearts:
—Take hands, Stephen and Emma. It is a beautiful evening
now in heaven. You have erred but you are always my children.
It is one heart that loves another heart. Take hands together,
my dear children, and you will be happy together and your
hearts will love each other.

The chapel was flooded by the dull scarlet light that filtered
through the lowered blinds: and through the fissure between
the last blind and the sash a shaft of wan light entered like a
spear and touched the embossed brasses of the candlesticks
upon the altar that gleamed like the battleworn mail armour of
angels.

Rain was falling on the chapel, on the garden, on the college.
It would rain for ever, noiselessly. The water would rise inch
by inch, covering the grass and shrubs, covering the trees and

houses, covering the monuments and the mountain tops. All life would be choked off, noiselessly: birds, men, elephants, pigs, children: noiselessly floating corpses amid the litter of the wreckage of the world. Forty days and forty nights the rain would fall till the waters covered the face of the earth.

It might be. Why not?

— *Hell has enlarged its soul and opened its mouth without any limits* — words taken, my dear little brothers in Christ Jesus, from the book of Isaias, fifth chapter, fourteenth verse. In the name of the Father and of the Son and of the Holy Ghost. Amen.

540

The preacher took a chainless watch from a pocket within his soutane and, having considered its dial for a moment in silence, placed it silently before him on the table.

He began to speak in a quiet tone.

— Adam and Eve, my dear boys, were, as you know, our first parents and you will remember that they were created by God in order that the seats in heaven left vacant by the fall of Lucifer and his rebellious angels might be filled again. Lucifer, we are told, was a son of the morning, a radiant and mighty angel; yet he fell: he fell and there fell with him a third part of the host of heaven: he fell and was hurled with his rebellious angels into hell. What his sin was we cannot say. Theologians consider that it was the sin of pride, the sinful thought conceived in an instant: *non serviam: I will not serve.* That instant was his ruin. He offended the majesty of God by the sinful thought of one instant and God cast him out of heaven into hell for ever.

550

Adam and Eve were then created by God and placed in Eden, that lovely garden in the plain of Damascus resplendent with sunlight and colour, teeming with luxuriant vegetation. The fruitful earth gave them her bounty: beasts and birds were their willing servants: they knew not the ills our flesh is heir to, disease and poverty and death: all that a great and generous God could do for them was done. But there was one condition imposed on them by God: obedience to His word. They were not to eat of the fruit of the forbidden tree.

560

Alas, my dear little boys, they too fell. The devil, once a shining angel, a son of the morning, now a foul fiend came to them in the shape of a serpent, the subtlest of all the beasts of the field. He envied them. He, the fallen great one, could not bear to think that man, a being of clay, should possess the inheritance which he by his sin had forfeited for ever. He came to the woman, the weaker vessel, and poured the poison of his eloquence into her ear, promising her (O, the blasphemy of that promise!) that if she and Adam ate of the forbidden fruit they would become as gods, nay as God Himself. Eve yielded to the wiles of the archtempter. She ate the apple and gave it also to Adam who had not the moral courage to resist her. The poison tongue of Satan had done its work. They fell.

And then the voice of God was heard in that garden, calling His creature man to account: and Michael, prince of the heav= enly host, with a sword of flame in his hand appeared before the guilty pair and drove them forth from Eden into the world, the world of sickness and striving, of cruelty and disappoint= ment, of labour and hardship, to earn their bread in the sweat of their brow. But even then how merciful was God! He took pity on our poor degraded first parents and promised that in the fulness of time He would send down from heaven One who would redeem them, make them once more children of God and heirs to the kingdom of heaven: and that One, that Redeemer of fallen man, was to be God's onlybegotten Son, the Second Person of the Most Blessed Trinity, the Eternal Word.

He came. He was born of a virgin pure, Mary the virgin mother. He was born in a poor cowhouse in Judea and lived as a humble carpenter for thirty years until the hour of His mission had come. And then, filled with love for men, He went forth and called to men to hear the new gospel.

Did they listen? Yes, they listened but would not hear. He was seized and bound like a common criminal, mocked at as a fool, set aside to give place to a public robber, scourged with five thousand lashes, crowned with a crown of thorns, hustled through the streets by the jewish rabble and the Roman sol= diery, stripped of His garments and hanged upon a gibbet and

His side was pierced with a lance and from the wounded body of Our Lord water and blood issued continually.

Yet even then, in that hour of supreme agony, Our Merciful Redeemer had pity for mankind. Yet even there, on the hill of Calvary, He founded the holy catholic church against which, it is promised, the gates of hell shall not prevail. He founded it upon the rock of ages and endowed it with His grace, with sacraments and sacrifice, and promised that if men would obey the word of His church they would still enter into eternal life but if, after all that had been done for them, they still persisted in their wickedness there remained for them an eternity of torment: hell.

The preacher's voice sank. He paused, joined his palms for an instant, parted them. Then he resumed:

—Now let us try for a moment to realise, as far as we can, the nature of that abode of the damned which the justice of an offended God has called into existence for the eternal punish= ment of sinners. Hell is a strait and dark and foulsmelling prison, an abode of demons and lost souls, filled with fire and smoke. The straitness of this prison house is expressly designed by God to punish those who refused to be bound by His laws. In earthly prisons the poor captive has at least some liberty of movement, were it only within the four walls of his cell or in the gloomy yard of his prison. Not so in hell. There, by reason of the great number of the damned, the prisoners are heaped together in their awful prison the walls of which are said to be four thousand miles thick: and the damned are so utterly bound and helpless that, as a blessed saint, saint Anselm, writes in his book on similitudes, they are not even able to remove from the eye a worm that gnaws it.

They lie in exterior darkness. For, remember, the fire of hell gives forth no light. As, at the command of God, the fire of the Babylonian furnace lost its heat but not its light so, at the command of God, the fire of hell, while retaining the intensity of its heat, burns eternally in darkness. It is a neverending storm of darkness, dark flames and dark smoke of burning brimstone, amid which the bodies are heaped one upon another without even a glimpse of air. Of all the plagues with which the land of the Pharaohs was smitten one plague alone, that of darkness, was called horrible. What name, then, shall we give to the darkness of hell which is to last not for three days alone but for all eternity?

The horror of this strait and dark prison is increased by its awful stench. All the filth of the world, all the offal and scum of the world, we are told, shall run there as to a vast reeking sewer when the terrible conflagration of the last day has purged the world. The brimstone too which burns there in such pro= digious quantity fills all hell with its intolerable stench: and the bodies of the damned themselves exhale such a pestilential odour that, as saint Bonaventure says, one of them alone would suffice to infect the whole world. The very air of this world, that pure element, becomes foul and unbreathable when it has been long enclosed. Consider then what must be the foulness of the air of hell. Imagine some foul and putrid corpse that has lain rotting and decomposing in the grave, a jellylike mass of liquid corruption. Imagine such a corpse a prey to flames, devoured by the fire of burning brimstone and giving off dense choking fumes of nauseous loathsome decomposition. And then imagine this sickening stench, multiplied a millionfold and a millionfold again from the millions upon millions of fetid carcases massed together in the reeking darkness, a huge and rotting human fungus. Imagine all this and you will have some idea of the horror of the stench of hell.

But this stench is not, horrible though it is, the greatest physical torment to which the damned are subjected. The torment of fire is the greatest torment to which the tyrant has ever subjected his fellowcreatures. Place your finger for a mo= ment in the flame of a candle and you will feel the pain of fire. But our earthly fire was created by God for the benefit of man, to maintain in him the spark of life and to help him in the useful arts whereas the fire of hell is of another quality and was created by God to torture and punish the unrepentant sinner. Our earthly fire also consumes more or less rapidly according as the object which it attacks is more or less combustible so that human ingenuity has even succeeded in inventing chemical preparations to check or frustrate its action. But the sulphu= reous brimstone which burns in hell is a substance which is specially designed to burn for ever and for ever with unspeak= able fury. Moreover our earthly fire destroys at the same time as it burns so that the more intense it is the shorter is its dur= ation: but the fire of hell has this property that it preserves that which it burns and though it rages with incredible intensity it rages for ever.

Our earthly fire again, no matter how fierce or widespread it may be, is always of a limited extent: but the lake of fire in hell is boundless, shoreless and bottomless. It is on record that the devil himself, when asked the question by a certain soldier, was obliged to confess that if a whole mountain were thrown into the burning ocean of hell it would be burned up in an instant like a piece of wax. And this terrible fire will not afflict the bodies of the damned only from without but each lost soul will be a hell unto itself, the boundless fire raging in its very vitals. O, how terrible is the lot of those wretched beings! The blood seethes and boils in the veins, the brains are boiling in the skull, the heart in the breast glowing and bursting, the bowels a redhot mass of burning pulp, the tender eyes flaming like mol= ten balls.

And yet what I have said as to the strength and quality and boundlessness of this fire is as nothing when compared to its intensity, an intensity which it has as being the instrument chosen by divine design for the punishment of soul and body alike. It is a fire which proceeds directly from the ire of God, working not of its own activity but as an instrument of divine vengeance. As the waters of baptism cleanse the soul with the body so do the fires of punishment torture the spirit with the flesh. Every sense of the flesh is tortured and every faculty of the soul therewith: the eyes with impenetrable utter darkness, the nose with noisome odours, the ears with yells and howls and execrations, the taste with foul matter, leprous corruption, nameless suffocating filth, the touch with redhot goads and spikes, with cruel tongues of flame. And through the several torments of the senses the immortal soul is tortured eternally in its very essence amid the leagues upon leagues of glowing fires kindled in the abyss by the offended majesty of the Omnipotent God and fanned into everlasting and ever increasing fury by the breath of the anger of the Godhead.

Consider finally that the torment of this infernal prison is increased by the company of the damned themselves. Evil company on earth is so noxious that even the plants, as if by instinct, withdraw from the company of whatsoever is deadly or hurtful to them. In hell all laws are overturned: there is no thought of family or country, of ties or relationship. The damned howl and scream at one another, their torture and rage intensified by the presence of beings tortured and raging like themselves. All sense of humanity is forgotten. The yells of the suffering sinners fill the remotest corners of the vast abyss. The mouths of the damned are full of blasphemies against God and of hatred for their fellow sufferers and of curses against those souls which were their accomplices in sin. In olden times it was the custom to punish the parricide, the man who had raised his murderous hand against his father, by casting him into the depths of the sea in a sack in which were placed a cock, a monkey and a serpent. The intention of those lawgivers who framed such a law, which seems cruel in our times, was to punish the criminal by the company of hateful and hurtful beasts. But what is the fury of those dumb beasts compared with the fury of execration which bursts from the parched lips and aching throats of the damned in hell when they behold in their companions in misery those who aided and abetted them in sin, those whose words sowed the first seeds of evil thinking and evil living in their minds, those whose immodest sugges= tions led them on to sin, those whose eyes tempted and allured them from the path of virtue. They turn upon those accom= plices and upbraid them and curse them. But they are helpless and hopeless: it is too late now for repentance.

Last of all consider the frightful torment to those damned souls, tempters and tempted alike, of the company of the devils. These devils will afflict the damned in two ways, by their pres= ence and by their reproaches. We can have no idea of how horrible these devils are. Saint Catherine of Siena once saw a devil and she has written that, rather than look again for one single instant on such a frightful monster, she would prefer to walk until the end of her life along a track of red coals. These devils, who were once beautiful angels, have become as hideous and ugly as they once were beautiful. They mock and jeer at the lost souls whom they dragged down to ruin. It is they, the foul demons, who are made in hell the voices of conscience. Why did you sin? Why did you lend an ear to the temptings of fiends? Why did you turn aside from your pious practices and good works? Why did you not shun the occasions of sin? Why did you not leave that evil companion? Why did you not give up that lewd habit, that impure habit? Why did you not listen to the counsels of your confessor? Why did you not, even after you had fallen the first or the second or the third or the fourth or the hundredth time, repent of your evil ways and turn to God who only waited for your repentance to absolve you of your sins? Now the time for repentance has gone by. Time is, time was but time shall be no more! Time was to sin in secrecy, to indulge in that sloth and pride, to covet the unlawful, to yield to the promptings of your lower nature, to live like the beasts of the field, nay worse than the beasts of the field for they, at least, are but brutes and have not reason to guide them: time was but time shall be no more. God spoke to you by so many voices but you would not hear. You would not crush out that pride and anger in your heart, you would not restore those illgotten goods, you would not obey the precepts of your holy church nor attend to your religious duties, you would not abandon those wicked companions, you would not avoid those dangerous temptations. Such is the language of those fiendish tormentors, words of taunting and of reproach, of hatred and of disgust. Of disgust, yes! For even they, the very devils, when they sinned sinned by such a sin as alone was compatible with such angelical natures, a rebellion of the intellect: and they, even they, the foul devils must turn away, revolted and dis= gusted, from the contemplation of those unspeakable sins by which degraded man outrages and defiles the temple of the Holy Ghost, defiles and pollutes himself.

O, my dear little brothers in Christ, may it never be our lot to hear that language! May it never be our lot, I say! In the last day of terrible reckoning I pray fervently to God that not a single soul of those who are in this chapel today may be found among those miserable beings whom the Great Judge shall command to depart for ever from His sight, that not one of us may ever hear ringing in his ears the awful sentence of rejec= tion: *Depart from me, ye cursed, into everlasting fire which was prepared for the devil and his angels!*

He came down the aisle of the chapel, his legs shaking and the scalp of his head trembling as though it had been touched by ghostly fingers. He passed up the staircase and into the corridor along the walls of which the overcoats and water= proofs hung like gibbeted malefactors, headless and dripping and shapeless. And at every step he feared that he had already died, that his soul had been wrenched forth of the sheath of his body, that he was plunging headlong through space.

He could not grip the floor with his feet and sat heavily at his desk, opening one of his books at random and poring over it. Every word for him! It was true. God was almighty. God could call him now, call him as he sat at his desk, before he had time to be conscious of the summons. God had called him. Yes? What? Yes? His flesh shrank together as it felt the approach of the ravenous tongues of flames, dried up as it felt about it the swirl of stifling air. He had died. Yes. He was judged. A wave of fire swept through his body: the first. Again a wave. His brain began to glow. Another. His brain was simmering and bubbling within the cracking tenement of the skull. Flames burst forth from his skull like a corolla, shrieking like voices:

—Hell! Hell! Hell! Hell! Hell!

Voices spoke near him:

—On hell.

—I suppose he rubbed it into you well.

—You bet he did. He put us all into a blue funk.

—That's what you fellows want: and plenty of it to make you work.

He leaned back weakly in his desk. He had not died. God had spared him still. He was still in the familiar world of the school. Mr Tate and Vincent Heron stood at the window, talking, jesting, gazing out at the bleak rain, moving their heads.

—I wish it would clear up. I had arranged to go for a spin on the bike with some fellows out by Malahide. But the roads must be kneedeep.

—It might clear up, sir.

The voices that he knew so well, the common words, the quiet of the classroom when the voices paused and the silence was filled by the sound of softly browsing cattle as the other boys munched their lunches tranquilly, lulled his aching soul.

There was still time. O Mary, refuge of sinners, intercede for him! O Virgin Undefiled, save him from the gulf of death!

The English lesson began with the hearing of the history. Royal persons, favourites, intriguers, bishops passed like mute phantoms behind their veil of names. All had died: all had been judged. What did it profit a man to gain the whole world if he lost his soul? At last he had understood: and human life lay around him, a plain of peace whereon antlike men laboured in brotherhood, their dead sleeping under quiet mounds. The elbow of his companion touched him and his heart was touched: and when he spoke to answer a question of his master he heard his own voice full of the quietude of humility and contrition.

His soul sank back deeper into depths of contrite peace, no longer able to suffer the pain of dread and sending forth, as she sank, a faint prayer. Ah yes, he would still be spared; he would repent in his heart and be forgiven: and then those above, those in heaven, would see what he would do to make up for the past: a whole life, every hour of life. Only wait.

—All, God! All, all!

A messenger came to the door to say that confessions were being heard in the chapel. Four boys left the room; and he heard others passing down the corridor. A tremulous chill blew round his heart, no stronger than a little wind, and yet, listen= ing and suffering silently, he seemed to have laid an ear against the muscle of his own heart, feeling it close and quail, listening to the flutter of its ventricles.

No escape. He had to confess, to speak out in words what he had done and thought, sin after sin. How? How?

870 —Father, I ...

The thought slid like a cold shining rapier into his tender flesh: confession. But not there in the chapel of the college. He would confess all, every sin of deed and thought, sincerely: but not there among his school companions. Far away from there in some dark place he would murmur out his own shame: and he besought God humbly not to be offended with him if he did not dare to confess in the college chapel: and in utter abjection of spirit he craved forgiveness mutely of the boyish hearts about him.

880 Time passed.

He sat again in the front bench of the chapel. The daylight without was already failing and, as it fell slowly through the dull red blinds, it seemed that the sun of the last day was going down and that all souls were being gathered for the judgment.

—*I am cast away from the sight of Thine eyes:* words taken, my dear little brothers in Christ, from the Book of Psalms, thirtieth chapter, twentythird verse. In the name of the Father and of the Son and of the Holy Ghost. Amen.

The preacher began to speak in a quiet friendly tone. His

890 face was kind and he joined gently the fingers of each hand, forming a frail cage by the union of their tips.

—This morning we endeavoured, in our reflection upon hell, to make what our holy founder calls in his book of spiritual exercises, the composition of place. We endeavoured, that is, to imagine with the senses of the mind, in our imagination, the material character of that awful place and of the physical tor=

ments which all who are in hell endure. This evening we shall consider for a few moments the nature of the spiritual torments of hell.

Sin, remember, is a twofold enormity. It is a base consent to the promptings of our corrupt nature, to the lower instincts, to that which is gross and beastlike; and it is also a turning away from the counsel of our higher nature, from all that is pure and holy, from the Holy God Himself. For this reason mortal sin is punished in hell by two different forms of punishment, physical and spiritual.

Now of all these spiritual pains by far the greatest is the pain of loss, so great, in fact, that in itself it is a torment greater than all the others. Saint Thomas, the greatest doctor of the church, the angelic doctor, as he is called, says that the worst damnation consists in this that the understanding of man is totally deprived of divine light and his affection obstinately turned away from the goodness of God. God, remember, is a being infinitely good and therefore the loss of such a being must be a loss infinitely painful. In this life we have not a very clear idea of what such a loss must be but the damned in hell, for their greater torment, have a full understanding of that which they have lost and understand that they have lost it through their own sins and have lost it for ever. At the very instant of death the bonds of the flesh are broken asunder and the soul at once flies towards God. The soul tends towards God as towards the centre of her existence. Remember, my dear little boys, our souls long to be with God. We come from God, we live by God, we belong to God: we are His, inalien= ably His. God loves with a divine love every human soul and every human soul lives in that love. How could it be otherwise? Every breath that we draw, every thought of our brain, every instant of life proceed from God's inexhaustible goodness. And if it be pain for a mother to be parted from her child, for a man to be exiled from hearth and home, for friend to be sundered from friend, O think what pain, what anguish it must be for the poor soul to be spurned from the presence of the supremely

good and loving Creator Who has called that soul into exist=
ence from nothingness and sustained it in life and loved it with
an immeasurable love. This, then, to be separated for ever from
its greatest good, from God, and to feel the anguish of that
separation, knowing full well that it is unchangeable, this is the
greatest torment which the created soul is capable of bearing,
poena damni, the pain of loss.

940 The second pain which will afflict the souls of the damned in
hell is the pain of conscience. Just as in dead bodies worms are
engendered by putrefaction so in the souls of the lost there
arises a perpetual remorse from the putrefaction of sin, the
sting of conscience, the worm, as Pope Innocent the Third calls
it, of the triple sting. The first sting inflicted by this cruel worm
will be the memory of past pleasures. O what a dreadful mem=
ory will that be! In the lake of alldevouring flame the proud
king will remember the pomps of his court, the wise but wicked
man his libraries and instruments of research, the lover of ar=
950 tistic pleasures his marbles and pictures and other art treasures,
he who delighted in the pleasures of the table his gorgeous
feasts, his dishes prepared with such delicacy, his choice wines;
the miser will remember his hoard of gold, the robber his
illgotten wealth, the angry and revengeful and merciless mur=
derers their deeds of blood and violence in which they revelled,
the impure and adulterous the unspeakable and filthy pleasures
in which they delighted. They will remember all this and loathe
themselves and their sins. For how miserable will all those
pleasures seem to the soul condemned to suffer in hellfire for
960 ages and ages. How they will rage and fume to think that they
have lost the bliss of heaven for the dross of earth, for a few
pieces of metal, for vain honours, for bodily comforts, for a
tingling of the nerves. They will repent indeed: and this is the
second sting of the worm of conscience, a late and fruitless
sorrow for sins committed. Divine justice insists that the under=
standing of those miserable wretches be fixed continually on
the sins of which they were guilty and, moreover, as saint
Augustine points out, God will impart to them His own

knowledge of sin so that sin will appear to them in all its hideous malice as it appears to the eyes of God Himself. They will behold their sins in all their foulness and repent but it will be too late and then they will bewail the good occasions which they neglected. This is the last and deepest and most cruel sting of the worm of conscience. The conscience will say: You had time and opportunity to repent and would not. You were brought up religiously by your parents. You had the sacraments and graces and indulgences of the church to aid you. You had the minister of God to preach to you, to call you back when you had strayed, to forgive you your sins, no matter how many, how abominable, if only you had confessed and repented. No. You would not. You flouted the ministers of holy religion, you turned your back on the confessional, you wallowed deeper and deeper in the mire of sin. God appealed to you, threatened you, entreated you to return to Him. O what shame, what misery! The ruler of the universe entreated you, a creature of clay, to love Him Who made you and to keep His law. No. You would not. And now, though you were to flood all hell with your tears if you could still weep, all that sea of repentance would not gain for you what a single tear of true repentance shed during your mortal life would have gained for you. You implore now a moment of earthly life wherein to repent: in vain. That time is gone: gone for ever.

Such is the threefold sting of conscience, the viper which gnaws the very heart's core of the wretches in hell so that filled with hellish fury they curse themselves for their folly and curse the evil companions who have brought them to such ruin and curse the devils who tempted them in life and now mock them and torture them in eternity and even revile and curse the Supreme Being Whose goodness and patience they scorned and slighted but Whose justice and power they cannot evade.

The next spiritual pain to which the damned are subjected is the pain of extension. Man, in this earthly life, though he be capable of many evils, is not capable of them all at once inas= much as one evil corrects and counteracts another just as one poison frequently corrects another. In hell on the contrary one torment, instead of counteracting another, lends it still greater force: and moreover as the internal faculties are more perfect than the external senses so are they more capable of suffering. Just as every sense is afflicted with a fitting torment so is every spiritual faculty; the fancy with horrible images, the sensitive faculty with alternate longing and rage, the mind and under= standing with an interior darkness more terrible even than the exterior darkness which reigns in that dreadful prison. The malice, impotent though it be, which possesses these demon souls is an evil of boundless extension, of limitless duration, a frightful state of wickedness which we can scarcely realise unless we bear in mind the enormity of sin and the hatred God bears to it.

Opposed to this pain of extension and yet coexistent with it we have the pain of intensity. Hell is the centre of all evils and, as you know, things are more intense at their centres than at their remotest points. There are no contraries or admixtures of any kind to temper or soften in the least the pains of hell. Nay, things which are good in themselves become evil in hell. Com= pany, elsewhere a source of comfort to the afflicted, will be there a continual torment: knowledge, so much longed for as the chief good of the intellect, will there be hated worse than ignorance: light, so much coveted by all creatures from the lord of creation down to the humblest plant in the forest, will be loathed intensely. In this life our sorrows are either not very long or not very great because nature either overcomes them by habits or puts an end to them by sinking under their weight. But in hell the torments cannot be overcome by habit for while they are of terrible intensity they are at the same time of con= tinual variety, each pain, so to speak, taking fire from another and reendowing that which has enkindled it with a still fiercer flame. Nor can nature escape from these intense and various tortures by succumbing to them for the soul in hell is sustained and maintained in evil so that its suffering may be the greater. Boundless extension of torment, incredible intensity of suffer=

ing, unceasing variety of torture—this is what the divine majesty, so outraged by sinners, demands, this is what the holiness of heaven, slighted and set aside for the lustful and low pleasures of the corrupt flesh, requires, this is what the blood of the innocent Lamb of God, shed for the redemption of sinners, trampled upon by the vilest of the vile, insists upon.

Last and crowning torture of all the tortures of that awful place is the eternity of hell. Eternity! O dread and dire word. Eternity! What mind of man can understand it? And, remember, it is an eternity of pain. Even though the pains of hell were not so terrible as they are yet they would become infinite as they are destined to last for ever. But while they are everlasting they are at the same time, as you know, intolerably intense, unbearably extensive. To bear even the sting of an insect for all eternity would be a dreadful torment. What must it be then to bear the manifold tortures of hell for ever. For ever! For all eternity! Not for a year or for an age but for ever. Try to imagine the awful meaning of this. You have often seen the sand on the seashore. How fine are its tiny grains! And how many of those tiny little grains go to make up the small handful which a child grasps in its play. Now imagine a mountain of that sand, a million miles high, reaching from the earth to the farthest heavens, and a million miles broad, extending to remotest space, and a million miles in thickness: and imagine such an enormous mass of countless particles of sand multiplied as often as there are leaves in the forest, drops of water in the mighty ocean, feathers on birds, scales on fish, hairs on animals, atoms in the vast expanse of the air: and imagine that at the end of every million years a little bird came to that mountain and carried away in its beak a tiny grain of that sand. How many millions upon millions of centuries would pass before that bird had carried away even a square foot of that mountain, how many eons upon eons of ages before it had carried away all. Yet at the end of that immense stretch of time not even one instant of eternity could be said to have ended. At the end of all those billions and trillions of years eternity would

1050

1060

1070

have scarcely begun. And if that mountain rose again after it had been all carried away and if the bird came again and carried it all away again grain by grain: and if it so rose and sank as many times as there are stars in the sky, atoms in the air, drops of water in the sea, leaves on the trees, feathers upon birds, scales upon fish, hairs upon animals, at the end of all those innumerable risings and sinkings of that immeasurably vast mountain not one single instant of eternity could be said to have ended: even then, at the end of such a period, after that eon of time the mere thought of which makes our very brain reel dizzily, eternity would have scarcely begun.

A holy saint (one of our own fathers I believe it was) was once vouchsafed a vision of hell. It seemed to him that he stood in the midst of a great hall, dark and silent save for the ticking of a great clock. The ticking went on unceasingly; and it seemed to this saint that the sound of the ticking was the ceaseless repetition of the words: ever, never; ever, never. Ever to be in hell, never to be in heaven; ever to be shut off from the presence of God, never to enjoy the beatific vision; ever to be eaten with flames, gnawed by vermin, goaded with burning spikes, never to be free from those pains; ever to have the conscience upbraid one, the memory enrage, the mind filled with darkness and despair, never to escape; ever to curse and revile the foul demons who gloat fiendishly over the misery of their dupes, never to behold the shining raiment of the blessed spirits; ever to cry out of the abyss of fire to God for an instant, a single instant, of respite from such awful agony, never to receive, even for an instant, God's pardon; ever to suffer, never to enjoy; ever to be damned, never to be saved; ever, never; ever, never. O what a dreadful punishment! An eternity of endless agony, of endless bodily and spiritual torment, without one ray of hope, without one moment of cessation, of agony limitless in extent, limitless in intensity, of torment infinitely lasting, infinitely varied, of torture that sustains eternally that which it eternally devours, of anguish that everlastingly preys upon the spirit while it racks the flesh, an eternity, every instant of which is itself an eternity, and that eternity an eternity of woe. Such is the terrible punishment decreed for those who die in mortal sin by an almighty and a just God.

Yes, a just God! Men, reasoning always as men, are aston= ished that God should mete out an everlasting and infinite pun= ishment in the fires of hell for a single grievous sin. They reason thus because, blinded by the gross illusion of the flesh and the darkness of human understanding, they are unable to comprehend the hideous malice of mortal sin. They reason thus because they are unable to comprehend that even venial sin is of such a foul and hideous nature that even if the omnipotent Creator could end all the evil and misery in the world, the wars, the diseases, the robberies, the crimes, the deaths, the murders, on condition that He allowed a single venial sin to pass unpunished, a single venial sin, a lie, an angry look, a moment of wilful sloth, He, the great omnipotent God could not do so because sin, be it in thought or deed, is a trans= gression of His law and God would not be God if He did not punish the transgressor.

A sin, an instant of rebellious pride of the intellect, made Lucifer and a third part of the cohorts of angels fall from their glory. A sin, an instant of folly and weakness, drove Adam and Eve out of Eden and brought death and suffering into the world. To retrieve the consequences of that sin the onlybegot= ten Son of God came down to earth, lived and suffered and died a most painful death, hanging for three hours on the cross.

O, my dear little brethren in Christ Jesus, will we then offend that good Redeemer and provoke His anger? Will we trample again upon that torn and mangled corpse? Will we spit upon that face so full of sorrow and love? Will we too, like the cruel jews and the brutal soldiers, mock that gentle and com= passionate Saviour Who trod alone for our sakes the awful winepress of sorrow? Every word of sin is a wound in His tender side. Every sinful act is a thorn piercing His head. Every impure thought, deliberately yielded to, is a keen lance trans= fixing that sacred and loving heart. No, no. It is impossible for

1120

1130

1140

any human being to do that which offends so deeply the divine
majesty, that which is punished by an eternity of agony, that
which crucifies again the Son of God and makes a mockery of
Him.

I pray to God that my poor words may have availed today to
confirm in holiness those who are in a state of grace, to
strengthen the wavering, to lead back to the state of grace the
poor soul that has strayed if any such be among you. I pray to
God, and do you pray with me, that we may repent of our sins.
I will ask you now, all of you, to repeat after me the act of
contrition, kneeling here in this humble chapel in the presence
of God. He is there in the tabernacle burning with love for
mankind, ready to comfort the afflicted. Be not afraid. No
matter how many or how foul the sins if only you repent of
them they will be forgiven you. Let no worldly shame hold you
back. God is still the merciful Lord Who wishes not the eternal
death of the sinner but rather that he be converted and live.

He calls you to Him. You are His. He made you out of
nothing. He loved you as only a God can love. His arms are
open to receive you even though you have sinned against Him.
Come to Him, poor sinner, poor vain and erring sinner. Now is
the acceptable time. Now is the hour.

The priest rose and turning towards the altar knelt upon the
step before the tabernacle in the fallen gloom. He waited till all
in the chapel had knelt and every least noise was still. Then
raising his head he repeated the act of contrition, phrase by
phrase, with fervour. The boys answered him phrase by phrase.
Stephen, his tongue cleaving to his palate, bowed his head,
praying with his heart.

—*O my God!*—
—*O my God!*—
—*I am heartily sorry*—
—*I am heartily sorry*—
—*for having offended Thee*—
—*for having offended Thee*—

—and I detest my sins—
—and I detest my sins—
—above every other evil—
—above every other evil—
—because they displease Thee, my God—
—because they displease Thee, my God—
—Who art so deserving—   1190
—Who art so deserving—
—of all my love—
—of all my love—
—and I firmly purpose—
—and I firmly purpose—
—by Thy holy grace—
—by Thy holy grace—
—never more to offend Thee—
—never more to offend Thee—
—and to amend my life—   1200
—and to amend my life—

◆   ◆   ◆

He went up to his room after dinner in order to be alone with his soul: and at every step his soul seemed to sigh: at every step his soul mounted with his feet, sighing in the ascent, through a region of viscid gloom.

He halted on the landing before the door and then, grasping the porcelain knob, opened the door quickly. He waited in fear, his soul pining within him, praying silently that death might not touch his brow as he passed over the threshold, that the fiends that inhabit darkness might not be given power over   1210 him. He waited still at the threshold as at the entrance to some dark cave. Faces were there; eyes: they waited and watched.

—We knew perfectly well of course that though it was bound to come to the light he would find considerable difficulty in endeavouring to try to induce himself to try to endeavour to ascertain the spiritual plenipotentiary and so we knew of course perfectly well—

Murmuring faces waited and watched; murmurous voices filled the dark shell of the cave. He feared intensely in spirit and in flesh but, raising his head bravely, he strode into the room firmly. A doorway, a room, the same room, same win=dow. He told himself calmly that those words had absolutely no sense which had seemed to rise murmurously from the dark. He told himself that it was simply his room with the door open.

He closed the door and, walking swiftly to the bed, knelt beside it and covered his face with his hands. His hands were cold and damp and his limbs ached with chill. Bodily unrest and chill and weariness beset him, routing his thoughts. Why was he kneeling there like a child saying his evening prayers? To be alone with his soul, to examine his conscience, to meet his sins face to face, to recall their times and manners and circumstances, to weep over them. He could not weep. He could not summon them to his memory. He felt only an ache of soul and body, his whole being, memory, will, understanding, flesh, benumbed and weary.

That was the work of devils, to scatter his thoughts and overcloud his conscience, assailing him at the gates of the cow=ardly and sincorrupted flesh: and, praying God timidly to forgive him his weakness, he crawled up on to the bed and, wrapping the blankets closely about him, covered his face again with his hands. He had sinned. He had sinned so deeply against heaven and before God that he was not worthy to be called God's child.

Could it be that he, Stephen Dedalus, had done those things? His conscience sighed in answer. Yes, he had done them, se=cretly, filthily, time after time, and, hardened in sinful impeni=tence, he had dared to wear the mask of holiness before the tabernacle itself while his soul within was a living mass of corruption. How came it that God had not struck him dead? The leprous company of his sins closed about him, breathing upon him, bending over him from all sides. He strove to forget them in an act of prayer, huddling his limbs closer together and binding down his eyelids: but the senses of the soul would not be bound and, though his eyes were shut fast, he saw the places where he had sinned and, though his ears were tightly covered, he heard. He desired with all his will not to hear or see. He desired till his frame shook under the strain of his desire and until the senses of his soul closed. They closed for an instant and then opened. He saw. 1260

A field of stiff weeds and thistles and tufted nettlebunches. Thick among the tufts of rank stiff growth lay battered canis= ters and clots and coils of solid excrement. A faint marshlight struggled upwards from all the ordure through the bristling greygreen weeds. An evil smell, faint and foul as the light, curled upwards sluggishly out of the canisters and from the stale crusted dung.

Creatures were in the field; one, three, six: creatures were moving in the field, hither and thither. Goatish creatures with human faces, hornybrowed, lightly bearded and grey as india= 1270 rubber. The malice of evil glittered in their hard eyes, as they moved hither and thither, trailing their long tails behind them. A rictus of cruel malignity lit up greyly their old bony faces. One was clasping about his ribs a torn flannel waistcoat, an= other complained monotonously as his beard stuck in the tufted weeds. Soft language issued from their spittleless lips as they swished in slow circles round and round the field, winding hither and thither through the weeds, dragging their long tails amid the rattling canisters. They moved in slow circles, circling closer and closer, to enclose, to enclose, soft language issuing 1280 from their lips, their long swishing tails besmeared with stale shite, thrusting upwards their terrific faces .....

Help!

He flung the blankets from him madly to free his face and neck. That was his hell. God had allowed him to see the hell reserved for his sins: stinking, bestial, malignant, a hell of lech= erous goatish fiends. For him! For him!

He sprang from the bed, the reeking odour pouring down his throat, clogging and revolting his entrails. Air! The air of

1290 heaven! He stumbled towards the window, groaning and al=
most fainting with sickness. At the washstand a convulsion
seized him within: and, clasping his cold forehead wildly, he
vomited profusely in agony.

When the fit had spent itself he walked weakly to the win=
dow and, lifting the sash, sat in a corner of the embrasure and
leaned his elbow upon the sill. The rain had drawn off; and
amid the moving vapours from point to point of light the city
was spinning about herself a soft cocoon of yellowish haze.
Heaven was still and faintly luminous and the air sweet to
1300 breathe, as in a thicket drenched with showers: and amid peace
and shimmering lights and quiet fragrances he made a covenant
with his heart.

He prayed:

—*He once had meant to come on earth in heavenly glory but
we sinned: and then He could not safely visit us but with a
shrouded majesty and a bedimmed radiance for He was God.
So He came Himself in weakness not in power and He sent
thee, a creature in His stead, with a creature's comeliness and
lustre suited to our state. And now thy very face and form, dear*
1310 *mother, speak to us of the Eternal; not like earthly beauty,
dangerous to look upon, but like the morning star which is thy
emblem, bright and musical, breathing purity, telling of heaven
and infusing peace. O harbinger of day! O light of the pilgrim!
Lead us still as thou hast led. In the dark night, across the bleak
wilderness guide us on to our Lord Jesus, guide us home.*

His eyes were dimmed with tears and, looking humbly up to
heaven, he wept for the innocence he had lost.

When evening had fallen he left the house and the first touch
of the damp dark air and the noise of the door as it closed
1320 behind him made ache again his conscience, lulled by prayer
and tears. Confess! Confess! It was not enough to lull the con=
science with a tear and a prayer. He had to kneel before the
minister of the Holy Ghost and tell over his hidden sins truly
and repentantly. Before he heard again the footboard of the
housedoor trail over the threshold as it opened to let him in,

before he saw again the table in the kitchen set for supper he would have knelt and confessed. It was quite simple.

The ache of conscience ceased and he walked onward swiftly through the dark streets. There were so many flagstones on the footpath of that street and so many streets in that city and so many cities in the world. Yet eternity had no end. He was in mortal sin. Even once was a mortal sin. It could happen in an instant. But how so quickly? By seeing or by thinking of seeing. The eyes see the thing, without having wished first to see. Then in an instant it happens. But does that part of the body under= stand or what? The serpent, the most subtle beast of the field. It must understand when it desires in one instant and then prolongs its own desire instant after instant, sinfully. It feels and understands and desires. What a horrible thing! Who made it to be like that, a bestial part of the body able to understand bestially and desire bestially? Was that then he or an inhuman thing moved by a lower soul than his soul? His soul sickened at the thought of a torpid snaky life feeding itself out of the tender marrow of his life and fattening upon the slime of lust. O why was that so? O why?

He cowered in the shadow of the thought, abasing himself in the awe of God Who had made all things and all men. Mad= ness. Who could think such a thought? And, cowering in darkness and abject, he prayed mutely to his angel guardian to drive away with his sword the demon that was whispering to his brain.

The whisper ceased and he knew then clearly that his own soul had sinned in thought and word and deed wilfully through his own body. Confess! He had to confess every sin. How could he utter in words to the priest what he had done? Must, must. Or how could he explain without dying of shame? Or how could he have done such things without shame? A madman, a loathsome madman! Confess! O he would indeed to be free and sinless again! Perhaps the priest would know. O dear God!

He walked on and on through illlit streets, fearing to stand still for a moment lest it might seem that he held back from what awaited him, fearing to arrive at that towards which he still turned with longing. How beautiful must be a soul in the state of grace when God looked upon it with love!

Frowsy girls sat along the curbstones before their baskets. Their dank hair hung trailed over their brows. They were not beautiful to see as they crouched in the mire. But their souls were seen by God; and if their souls were in a state of grace they were radiant to see: and God loved them, seeing them.

A wasting breath of humiliation blew bleakly over his soul to think of how he had fallen, to feel that those souls were dearer to God than his. The wind blew over him and passed on to the myriads and myriads of other souls on whom God's favour shone now more and now less, stars now brighter and now dimmer, sustained and failing. And the glimmering souls passed away, sustained and failing, merged in a moving breath. One soul was lost; a tiny soul: his. It flickered once and went out, forgotten, lost. The end: black cold void waste.

Consciousness of place came ebbing back to him slowly over a vast tract of time unlit, unfelt, unlived. The squalid scene composed itself around him; the common accents, the burning gasjets in the shops, odours of fish and spirits and wet sawdust, moving men and women. An old woman was about to cross the street, an oilcan in her hand. He bent down and asked her was there a chapel near.

—A chapel, sir? Yes, sir. Church Street chapel.

—Church?

She shifted the can to her other hand and directed him: and, as she held out her reeking withered right hand under its fringe of shawl, he bent lower towards her, saddened and soothed by her voice.

—Thank you.

—You are quite welcome, sir.

The candles on the high altar had been extinguished but the fragrance of incense still floated down the dim nave. Bearded workmen with pious faces were guiding a canopy out through a sidedoor, the sacristan aiding them with quiet gestures and words. A few of the faithful still lingered, praying before one of the sidealtars or kneeling in the benches near the confessionals. He approached timidly and knelt at the last bench in the body, thankful for the peace and silence and fragrant shadow of the church. The board on which he knelt was narrow and worn and those who knelt near him were humble followers of Jesus. Jesus too had been born in poverty and had worked in the shop of a carpenter, cutting boards and planing them, and had first spoken of the kingdom of God to poor fishermen, teaching all men to be meek and humble of heart. 1400

He bowed his head upon his hands, bidding his heart be meek and humble that he might be like those who knelt beside him and his prayer as acceptable as theirs. He prayed beside them but it was hard. His soul was foul with sin and he dared not ask forgiveness with the simple trust of those whom Jesus, in the mysterious ways of God, had called first to His side, the carpenters, the fishermen, poor and simple people following a lowly trade, handling and shaping the wood of trees, mending their nets with patience. 1410

A tall figure came down the aisle and the penitents stirred: and, at the last moment glancing up swiftly, he saw a long grey beard and the brown habit of a capuchin. The priest entered the box and was hidden. Two penitents rose and entered the confessional at either side. The wooden slide was drawn back and the faint murmur of a voice troubled the silence. 1420

His blood began to murmur in his veins, murmuring like a sinful city summoned from its sleep to hear its doom. Little flakes of fire fell and powdery ashes fell softly, alighting on the houses of men. They stirred, waking from sleep, troubled by the heated air.

The slide was shot back. The penitent emerged from the side of the box. The farther slide was drawn. A woman entered quietly and deftly where the first penitent had knelt. The faint murmur began again. 1430

He could still leave the chapel. He could stand up, put one foot before the other and walk out softly and then run, run, run swiftly through the dark streets. He could still escape from the shame. O what shame! His face was burning with shame. Had it been any terrible crime but that one sin! Had it been murder! Little fiery flakes fell and touched him at all points, shameful thoughts, shameful words, shameful acts. Shame covered him wholly like fine glowing ashes falling continually. To say it in words! His soul, stifling and helpless, would cease to be.

The slide was shot back. A penitent emerged from the far= ther side of the box. The near slide was drawn. A penitent entered where the other penitent had come out. A soft whisper= ing noise floated in vaporous cloudlets out of the box. It was the woman: soft whispering cloudlets, soft whispering vapour, whispering and vanishing.

He beat his breast with his fist humbly, secretly under cover of the wooden armrest. He would be at one with others and with God. He would love his neighbour. He would love God Who had made and loved him. He would kneel and pray with others and be happy. God would look down on him and on them and would love them all.

It was easy to be good. God's yoke was sweet and light. It was better never to have sinned, to have remained always a child, for God loved little children and suffered them to come to Him. It was a terrible and a sad thing to sin. But God was merciful to poor sinners who were truly sorry. How true that was! That was indeed goodness.

The slide was shot to suddenly. The penitent came out. He was next. He stood up in terror and walked blindly into the box.

At last it had come. He knelt in the silent gloom and raised his eyes to the white crucifix suspended above him. God could see that he was sorry. He would tell all his sins. His confession would be long, long. Everybody in the chapel would know then what a sinner he had been. Let them know. It was true. But God had promised to forgive him if he was sorry. He was sorry. He clasped his hands and raised them towards the white form, praying with his darkened eyes, praying with all his

trembling body, swaying his head to and fro like a lost crea= 1470
ture, praying with whimpering lips.

—Sorry! Sorry! O sorry!

The slide clicked back and his heart bounded in his breast. The face of an old priest was at the grating, averted from him, leaning upon a hand. He made the sign of the cross and prayed of the priest to bless him for he had sinned. Then, bowing his head, he repeated the *Confiteor* in fright. At the words *my most grievous fault* he ceased, breathless.

—How long is it since your last confession, my child?

—A long time, father.   1480

—A month, my child?

—Longer, father.

—Three months, my child?

—Longer, father.

—Six months?

—Eight months, father.

He had begun. The priest asked:

—And what do you remember since that time?

He began to confess his sins: masses missed, prayers not said, lies.   1490

—Anything else, my child?

Sins of anger, envy of others, gluttony, vanity, disobedience.

—Anything else, my child?

Sloth.

—Anything else, my child?

There was no help. He murmured:

—I .... committed sins of impurity, father.

The priest did not turn his head.

—With yourself, my child?

—And ... with others.   1500

—With women, my child?

—Yes, father.

—Were they married women, my child?

He did not know. His sins trickled from his lips, one by one, trickled in shameful drops from his soul festering and oozing like a sore, a squalid stream of vice. The last sins oozed forth, sluggish, filthy. There was no more to tell. He bowed his head, overcome.

The priest was silent. Then he asked:

—How old are you, my child?

—Sixteen, father.

The priest passed his hand several times over his face. Then, resting his forehead against his hand, he leaned towards the grating and, with eyes still averted, spoke slowly. His voice was weary and old.

—You are very young, my child, he said, and let me implore of you to give up that sin. It is a terrible sin. It kills the body and it kills the soul. It is the cause of many crimes and misfortunes. Give it up, my child, for God' sake. It is dishonourable and unmanly. You cannot know where that wretched habit will lead you or where it will come against you. As long as you commit that sin, my poor child, you will never be worth one farthing to God. Pray to our mother Mary to help you. She will help you, my child. Pray to Our Blessed Lady when that sin comes into your mind. I am sure you will do that, will you not? You repent of all those sins. I am sure you do. And you will promise God now that by His holy grace you will never offend Him any more by that wicked sin. You will make that solemn promise to God, will you not?

—Yes, father.

The old and weary voice fell like sweet rain upon his quak= ing parching heart. How sweet and sad!

—Do so, my poor child. The devil has led you astray. Drive him back to hell when he tempts you to dishonour your body in that way—the foul spirit who hates Our Lord. Promise God now that you will give up that sin, that wretched wretched sin.

Blinded by his tears and by the light of God's mercifulness he bent his head and heard the grave words of absolution spoken and saw the priest's hand raised above him in token of forgiveness.

—God bless you, my child. Pray for me.

He knelt to say his penance, praying in a corner of the dark nave: and his prayers ascended to heaven from his purified heart like perfume streaming upwards from a heart of white rose.

The muddy streets were gay. He strode homeward, con= scious of an invisible grace pervading and making light his limbs. In spite of all he had done it. He had confessed and God had pardoned him. His soul was made fair and holy once more, holy and happy.

It would be beautiful to die if God so willed. It was beautiful to live if God so willed, to live in grace a life of peace and virtue and forbearance with others.

He sat by the fire in the kitchen, not daring to speak for happiness. Till that moment he had not known how beautiful and peaceful life could be. The green square of paper pinned round the lamp cast down a tender shade. On the dresser was a plate of sausages and white pudding and on the shelf there were eggs. They would be for the breakfast in the morning after the communion in the college chapel. White pudding and eggs and sausages and cups of tea. How simple and beautiful was life after all! And life lay all before him.

In a dream he fell asleep. In a dream he rose and saw that it was morning. In a waking dream he went through the quiet morning towards the college.

The boys were all there, kneeling in their places. He knelt among them, happy and shy. The altar was heaped with fra= grant masses of white flowers: and in the morning light the pale flames of the candles among the white flowers were clear and silent as his own soul.

He knelt before the altar with his classmates, holding the altar cloth with them over a living rail of hands. His hands were trembling: and his soul trembled as he heard the priest pass with the ciborium from communicant to communicant.

—*Corpus Domini nostri.*

Could it be? He knelt there sinless and timid: and he would hold upon his tongue the host and God would enter his purified body.

—*In vitam eternam. Amen.*

1550

1560

1570

1580   Another life! A life of grace and virtue and happiness! It was true. It was not a dream from which he would wake. The past was past.

—*Corpus Domini nostri.*

The ciborium had come to him.

IV

Sunday was dedicated to the mystery of the Holy Trinity, Monday to the Holy Ghost, Tuesday to the Guardian Angels, Wednesday to saint Joseph, Thursday to the Most Blessed Sacrament of the Altar, Friday to the Suffering Jesus, Saturday to the Blessed Virgin Mary.

Every morning he hallowed himself anew in the presence of some holy image or mystery. His day began with an heroic offering of its every moment of thought or action for the intentions of the sovereign pontiff and with an early mass. The raw morning air whetted his resolute piety; and often as he knelt among the few worshippers at the sidealtar, following with his interleaved prayerbook the murmur of the priest, he glanced up for an instant towards the vested figure standing in the gloom between the two candles which were the old and the new testaments and imagined that he was kneeling at mass in the catacombs.

His daily life was laid out in devotional areas. By means of ejaculations and prayers he stored up ungrudgingly for the souls in purgatory centuries of days and quarantines and years; yet the spiritual triumph which he felt in achieving with ease so many fabulous ages of canonical penances did not wholly reward his zeal of prayer since he could never know how much temporal punishment he had remitted by way of suffrage for the agonising souls: and, fearful lest in the midst of the purgatorial fire, which differed from the infernal only in that it was not everlasting, his penance might avail no more than a drop of moisture, he drove his soul daily through an increasing circle of works of supererogation.

Every part of his day, divided by what he regarded now as

30 the duties of his station in life, circled about its own centre of spiritual energy. His life seemed to have drawn near to eternity; every thought, word and deed, every instance of consciousness could be made to revibrate radiantly in heaven: and at times his sense of such immediate repercussion was so lively that he seemed to feel his soul in devotion pressing like fingers the keyboard of a great cash register and to see the amount of his purchase start forth immediately in heaven not as a number but as a frail column of incense or as a slender flower.

40 The rosaries too which he said constantly (for he carried his beads loose in his trousers' pockets that he might tell them as he walked the streets) transformed themselves into coronals of flowers of such vague unearthly texture that they seemed to him as hueless and odourless as they were nameless. He offered up each of his three daily chaplets that his soul might grow strong in each of the three theological virtues, in faith in the Father Who had created him, in hope in the Son Who had redeemed him and in love of the Holy Ghost Who had sanc= tified him: and this thrice triple prayer he offered to the Three Persons through Mary in the name of her joyful and sorrowful
50 and glorious mysteries.

On each of the seven days of the week he further prayed that one of the seven gifts of the Holy Ghost might descend upon his soul and drive out of it day by day the seven deadly sins which had defiled it in the past: and he prayed for each gift on its appointed day, confident that it would descend upon him, though it seemed to him strange at times that wisdom and understanding and knowledge were so distinct in their nature that each should be prayed for apart from the others. Yet he believed that at some future stage of his spiritual progress this
60 difficulty would be removed when his sinful soul had been raised up from its weakness and enlightened by the Third Per= son of the Most Blessed Trinity. He believed this all the more and with trepidation because of the divine gloom and silence wherein dwelt the unseen Paraclete, Whose symbols were a dove and a mighty wind, to sin against Whom was a sin be=

yond forgiveness, the eternal, mysterious, secret Being to Whom, as God, the priests offered up mass once a year, robed in the scarlet of the tongues of fire.

The imagery through which the nature and kinship of the Three Persons of the Trinity were darkly shadowed forth in the books of devotion which he read (the Father contemplating from all eternity as in a mirror His Divine Perfections and thereby begetting eternally the Eternal Son and the Holy Spirit proceeding out of Father and Son from all eternity) were easier of acceptance by his mind by reason of their august incomprehensibility than was the simple fact that God had loved his soul from all eternity, for ages before he had been born into the world, for ages before the world itself had existed. He had heard the names of the passions of love and hate pronounced solemnly on the stage and in the pulpit, had found them set forth solemnly in books, and had wondered why his soul was unable to harbour them for any time or to force his lips to utter their names with conviction. A brief anger had often invested him but he had never been able to make it an abiding passion and had always felt himself passing out of it as if his very body were being divested with ease of some outer skin or peel. He had felt a subtle, dark and murmurous presence penetrate his being and fire him with a brief iniquitous lust: it too had slipped beyond his grasp leaving his mind lucid and indifferent. This, it seemed, was the only love and that the only hate his soul would harbour.

But he could no longer disbelieve in the reality of love since God Himself had loved his individual soul with divine love from all eternity. Gradually, as his soul was enriched with spiritual knowledge, he saw the whole world forming one vast symmetrical expression of God's power and love. Life became a divine gift for every moment and sensation of which, were it even the sight of a single leaf hanging on the twig of a tree, his soul should praise and thank the Giver. The world for all its solid substance and complexity no longer existed for his soul save as a theorem of divine power and love and universality. So entire and unquestionable was this sense of the divine meaning in all nature granted to his soul that he could scarcely under= stand why it was in any way necessary that he should continue to live. Yet that also was part of the divine purpose and he dared not question its use, he above all others who had sinned so deeply and so foully against the divine purpose. Meek and abased by this consciousness of the one eternal omnipresent perfect reality his soul took up again her burden of pieties, masses and prayers and sacraments and mortifications: and only then for the first time since he had brooded on the great mystery of love did he feel within him a warm movement like that of some newly born life or virtue of the soul itself. The attitude of rapture in sacred art, the raised and parted hands, the parted lips and eyes as of one about to swoon, became for him an image of the soul in prayer, humiliated and faint before her Creator.

But he had been forewarned of the dangers of spiritual exal= tation and did not allow himself to desist from even the least or lowliest devotion, striving also by constant mortification to undo the sinful past rather than to achieve a saintliness fraught with peril. Each of his senses was brought under a rigorous discipline. In order to mortify the sense of sight he made it his rule to walk in the street with downcast eyes, glancing neither to right nor left and never behind him. His eyes shunned every encounter with the eyes of women. From time to time also he balked them by a sudden effort of the will, as by lifting them suddenly in the middle of an unfinished sentence and closing the book. To mortify his hearing he exerted no control over his voice which was then breaking, neither sang nor whistled and made no attempt to flee from noises which caused him painful nervous irritation such as the sharpening of knives on the knifeboard, the gathering of cinders on the fireshovel and the twigging of the carpet. To mortify his smell was more difficult as he found in himself no instinctive repugnance to bad odours, whether they were the odours of the outdoor world such as those of dung and tar or the odours of his own person among which he had made many curious comparisons and experi= ments. He found in the end that the only odour against which his sense of smell revolted was a certain stale fishy stink like that of longstanding urine: and whenever it was possible he subjected himself to this unpleasant odour. To mortify the taste he practised strict habits at table, observed to the letter all the fasts of the church and sought by distraction to divert his mind from the savours of different foods. But it was to the mortifi= cation of touch that he brought the most assiduous ingenuity of inventiveness. He never consciously changed his position in bed, sat in the most uncomfortable positions, suffered patiently every itch and pain, kept away from the fire, remained on his knees all through the mass except at the gospels, left parts of his neck and face undried so that the air might sting them and, whenever he was not saying his beads, carried his arms stiffly at his sides like a runner and never in his pockets or clasped behind him.

He had no temptations to sin mortally. It surprised him however to find that at the end of his course of intricate piety and selfrestraint he was so easily at the mercy of childish and unworthy imperfections. His prayers and fasts availed him little for the suppression of anger at hearing his mother sneeze or at being disturbed in his devotions. It needed an immense effort of his will to master the impulse which urged him to give outlet to such irritation. Images of the outbursts of trivial anger which he had often noted among his masters, their twitching mouths, closeshut lips and flushed cheeks, recurred to his memory, dis= couraging him, for all his practice of humility, by the compari= son. To merge his life in the common tide of other lives was harder for him than any fasting or prayer and it was his constant failure to do this to his own satisfaction which caused in his soul at last a sensation of spiritual dryness together with a growth of doubts and scruples. His soul traversed a period of desolation in which the sacraments themselves seemed to have turned into dried up sources. His confession became a channel for the escape of scrupulous and unrepented imperfections. His actual reception of the eucharist did not bring him the same dissolving moments of virginal selfsurrender as did those spiri= tual communions made by him sometimes at the close of some visit to the Blessed Sacrament. The book which he used for these visits was an old neglected book written by saint Alphon= sus Liguori with fading characters and sere foxpapered leaves. A faded world of fervent love and virginal responses seemed to be evoked for his soul by the reading of its pages in which the imagery of the canticles was interwoven with the communi= cant's prayers. An inaudible voice seemed to caress the soul, telling her names and glories, bidding her arise as for espousal and come away, bidding her look forth, a spouse, from Amana and from the mountains of the leopards; and the soul seemed to answer with the same inaudible voice, surrendering herself:

Inter ubera mea commorabitur.

This idea of surrender had a perilous attraction for his mind now that he felt his soul beset once again by the insistent voices of the flesh which began to murmur to him again during his prayers and meditations. It gave him an intense sense of power to know that he could, by a single act of consent, in a moment of thought, undo all that he had done. He seemed to feel a flood slowly advancing towards his naked feet and to be wait= ing for the first faint timid noiseless wavelet to touch his fevered skin. Then, almost at the instant of that touch, almost at the verge of sinful consent, he found himself standing far away from the flood upon a dry shore, saved by a sudden act of the will or a sudden ejaculation: and, seeing the silver line of the flood far away and beginning again its slow advance to= wards his feet, a new thrill of power and satisfaction shook his soul to know that he had not yielded nor undone all.

When he had eluded the flood of temptation many times in this way he grew troubled and wondered whether the grace which he had refused to lose was not being filched from him little by little. The clear certitude of his own immunity grew dim and to it succeeded a vague fear that his soul had really fallen unawares. It was with difficulty that he won back his old consciousness of his state of grace by telling himself that he had prayed to God at every temptation and that the grace which he had prayed for must have been given to him inasmuch as God was obliged to give it. The very frequency and violence of temptations showed him at last the truth of what he had heard about the trials of the saints. Frequent and violent temptations were a proof that the citadel of the soul had not fallen and that the devil raged to make it fall.

Often when he had confessed his doubts and scruples, some momentary inattention at prayer, a movement of trivial anger in his soul or a subtle wilfulness in speech or act, he was bidden by his confessor to name some sin of his past life before absolution was given him. He named it with humility and shame and repented of it once more. It humiliated and shamed him to think that he would never be freed from it wholly, however holily he might live or whatever virtues or perfections he might attain. A restless feeling of guilt would always be present with him: he would confess and repent and be absolved, confess and repent again and be absolved again, fruitlessly. Perhaps that first hasty confession wrung from him by the fear of hell had not been good? Perhaps, concerned only for his imminent doom, he had not had sincere sorrow for his sin? But the surest sign that his confession had been good and that he had had sincere sorrow for his sin was, he knew, the amendment of his life.

—I have amended my life, have I not? he asked himself.

◆　◆　◆

The director stood in the embrasure of the window, his back to the light, leaning an elbow on the brown crossblind and, as he spoke and smiled, slowly dangling and looping the cord of the other blind. Stephen stood before him, following for a moment with his eyes the waning of the long summer daylight above the roofs or the slow deft movements of the priestly fingers. The priest's face was in total shadow but the waning daylight from behind him touched the deeply grooved temples and the curves of the skull. Stephen followed also with his ears the accents and intervals of the priest's voice as he spoke gravely and cordially of indifferent themes, the vacation which had just ended, the colleges of the order abroad, the transfer= ence of masters. The grave and cordial voice went on easily with its tale and in the pauses Stephen felt bound to set it on again with respectful questions. He knew that the tale was a prelude and his mind waited for the sequel. Ever since the message of summons had come for him from the director his mind had struggled to find the meaning of the message: and during the long restless time he had sat in the college parlour waiting for the director to come in his eyes had wandered from one sober picture to another around the walls and his mind had wandered from one guess to another until the meaning of the summons had almost become clear. Then just as he was wish= ing that some unforeseen cause might prevent the director from coming he had heard the handle of the door turning and the swish of a soutane.

The director had begun to speak of the dominican and fran= ciscan orders and of the friendship between saint Thomas and saint Bonaventure. The capuchin dress, he thought, was rather too ....

Stephen's face gave back the priest's indulgent smile and, not being anxious to give an opinion, he made a slight dubitative movement with his lips.

—I believe, continued the director, that there is some talk now among the capuchins themselves of doing away with it and following the example of the other franciscans.

—I suppose they would retain it in the cloister, said Stephen.

—O certainly, said the director. For the cloister it is all right but for the street I really think it would be better to do away with it, don't you?

—It must be troublesome, I imagine.

—Of course it is: of course. Just imagine, when I was in Bel= gium I used to see them out cycling in all kinds of weather with this thing up about their knees! It was really ridiculous. *Les jupes*, they call them in Belgium.   280

The vowel was so modified as to be indistinct.

—What do they call them?

—*Les jupes.*

—O.

Stephen smiled again in answer to the smile which he could not see on the priest's shadowed face, its image or spectre only passing rapidly across his mind as the low discreet accent fell upon his ear. He gazed calmly before him at the waning sky, glad of the cool of the evening and of the faint yellow glow which hid the tiny flame kindling upon his cheek.   290

The names of articles of dress worn by women or of certain soft and delicate stuffs used in their making brought always to his mind a delicate and sinful perfume. As a boy he had imag= ined the reins by which horses are driven as slender silken bands and it had shocked him to feel at Stradbrooke the greasy leather of harness. It had shocked him too when he had felt for the first time beneath his tremulous fingers the brittle texture of a woman's stocking for, retaining nothing of all he read save that which seemed to him an echo or a prophecy of his own state, it was only amid softworded phrases or within rosesoft   300 stuffs that he dared to conceive of the soul or body of a woman moving with tender life.

But the phrase on the priest's lips was disingenuous for he knew that a priest should not speak lightly on that theme. The phrase had been spoken lightly with design and he felt that his face was being searched by the eyes in the shadow. Whatever he had heard or read of the craft of jesuits he had put aside frankly as not borne out by his own experience. His masters, even when they had not attracted him, had seemed to him always intelligent and serious priests, athletic and highspirited   310 prefects. He thought of them as men who washed their bodies briskly with cold water and wore clean cold linen. During all the years he had lived among them in Clongowes and in Bel= vedere he had received only two pandies and, though these had been dealt him in the wrong, he knew that he had often escaped punishment. During all those years he had never heard from any of his masters a flippant word: it was they who had taught him christian doctrine and urged him to live a good life and, when he had fallen into grievous sin, it was they who had led him back to grace. Their presence had made him diffident of himself when he was a muff in Clongowes and it had made him diffident of himself also while he had held his equivocal position in Belvedere. A constant sense of this had remained with him up to the last year of his school life. He had never once disobeyed or allowed turbulent companions to seduce him from his habit of quiet obedience: and, even when he doubted some statement of a master, he had never presumed to doubt openly. Lately some of their judgments had sounded a little childish in his ears and had made him feel a regret and pity as though he were slowly passing out of an accustomed world and were hearing its language for the last time. One day when some boys had gathered round a priest under the shed near the chapel he had heard the priest say:

—I believe that Lord Macaulay was a man who probably never committed a mortal sin in his life, that is to say, a deliberate mortal sin.

Some of the boys had then asked the priest if Victor Hugo were not the greatest French writer. The priest had answered that Victor Hugo had never written half so well when he had turned against the church as he had written when he was a catholic.

—But there are many eminent French critics, said the priest, who consider that even Victor Hugo, great as he certainly was, had not so pure a French style as Louis Veuillot.

The tiny flame which the priest's allusion had kindled upon Stephen's cheek had sunk down again and his eyes were still fixed calmly on the colourless sky. But an unresting doubt flew hither and thither before his mind. Masked memories passed quickly before him: he recognised scenes and persons yet he was conscious that he had failed to perceive some vital circum= stance in them. He saw himself walking about the grounds watching the sports in Clongowes and eating slim jim out of his cricketcap. Some jesuits were walking round the cycletrack in the company of ladies. The echoes of certain expressions used in Clongowes sounded in remote caves of his mind.

His ears were listening to these distant echoes amid the si= lence of the parlour when he became aware that the priest was addressing him in a different voice.

—I sent for you today, Stephen, because I wished to speak to you on a very important subject.

—Yes, sir.

—Have you ever felt that you had a vocation?

Stephen parted his lips to answer yes and then withheld the word suddenly. The priest waited for the answer and added:

—I mean have you ever felt within yourself, in your soul, a desire to join the order. Think.

—I have sometimes thought of it, said Stephen.

The priest let the blindcord fall to one side and, uniting his hands, leaned his chin gravely upon them, communing with himself.

—In a college like this, he said at length, there is one boy or perhaps two or three boys whom God calls to the religious life. Such a boy is marked off from his companions by his piety, by the good example he shows to others. He is looked up to by them; he is chosen perhaps as prefect by his fellow sodalists. And you, Stephen, have been such a boy in this college, prefect of Our Blessed Lady's sodality. Perhaps you are the boy in this college whom God designs to call to Himself.

A strong note of pride reinforcing the gravity of the priest's voice made Stephen's heart quicken in response.

—To receive that call, Stephen, said the priest, is the greatest honour that the Almighty God can bestow upon a man. No king or emperor on this earth has the power of the priest of God. No angel or archangel in heaven, no saint, not even the Blessed Virgin herself has the power of a priest of God: the power of the keys, the power to bind and to loose from sin, the power of exorcism, the power to cast out from the creatures of God the evil spirits that have power over them, the power, the

authority, to make the great God of Heaven come down upon
the altar and take the form of bread and wine. What an awful
power, Stephen!

A flame began to flutter again on Stephen's cheek as he
heard in this proud address an echo of his own proud musings.
How often had he seen himself as a priest wielding calmly and
humbly the awful power of which angels and saints stood in
reverence! His soul had loved to muse in secret on this desire.
He had seen himself, a young and silentmannered priest, en=
tering a confessional swiftly, ascending the altarsteps, in=
censing, genuflecting, accomplishing the vague acts of the
priesthood which pleased him by reason of their semblance of
reality and of their distance from it. In that dim life which he
had lived through in his musings he had assumed the voices and
gestures which he had noted with various priests. He had bent
his knee sideways like such a one, he had shaken the thurible
only slightly like such a one, his chasuble had swung open like
that of such another as he had turned to the altar again after
having blessed the people. And above all it had pleased him to
fill the second place in those dim scenes of his imagining. He
shrank from the dignity of celebrant because it displeased him
to imagine that all the vague pomp should end in his own
person or that the ritual should assign to him so clear and final
an office. He longed for the minor sacred offices, to be vested
with the tunicle of subdeacon at high mass, to stand aloof from
the altar, forgotten by the people, his shoulders covered with a
humeral veil, holding the paten within its folds, or when the
sacrifice had been accomplished, to stand as deacon in a dal=
matic of cloth of gold on the step below the celebrant, his
hands joined and his face towards the people, and sing the
chant *Ite, missa est.* If ever he had seen himself celebrant it was
as in the pictures of the mass in his child's massbook, in a
church without worshippers, save for the angel of the sacrifice,
at a bare altar and served by an acolyte scarcely more boyish
than himself. In vague sacrificial or sacramental acts alone his
will seemed drawn to go forth to encounter reality: and it was
partly the absence of an appointed rite which had always con=

strained him to inaction whether he had allowed silence to cover his anger or pride or had suffered only an embrace he longed to give.

He listened in reverent silence now to the priest's appeal and through the words he heard even more distinctly a voice bid= 430 ding him approach, offering him secret knowledge and secret power. He would know then what was the sin of Simon Magus and what the sin against the Holy Ghost for which there was no forgiveness. He would know obscure things, hidden from others, from those who were conceived and born children of wrath. He would know the sins, the sinful longings and sinful thoughts and sinful acts, of others, hearing them murmured into his ear in the confessional under the shame of a darkened chapel by the lips of women and of girls: but rendered immune mysteriously at his ordination by the imposition of hands his 440 soul would pass again uncontaminated to the white peace of the altar. No touch of sin would linger upon the hands with which he would elevate and break the host; no touch of sin would linger on his lips in prayer to make him eat and drink damnation to himself, not discerning the body of the Lord. He would hold his secret knowledge and secret power, being as sinless as the innocent: and he would be a priest for ever according to the order of Melchisedech.

—I will offer up my mass tomorrow morning, said the direc= tor, that Almighty God may reveal to you His holy will. And 450 let you, Stephen, make a novena to your patron saint, the first martyr, who is very powerful with God, that God may en= lighten your mind. But you must be quite sure, Stephen, that you have a vocation because it would be terrible if you found afterwards that you had none. Once a priest always a priest, remember. Your catechism tells you that the sacrament of Holy Orders is one of those which can be received only once because it imprints on the soul an indelible spiritual mark which can never be effaced. It is before you must weigh well, not after. It is a solemn question, Stephen, because on it may depend the 460 salvation of your eternal soul. But we will pray to God to= gether.

He held open the heavy halldoor and gave his hand as if already to a companion in the spiritual life. Stephen passed out on to the wide platform above the steps and was conscious of the caress of mild evening air. Towards Findlater's church a quartet of young men were striding along with linked arms, swaying their heads and stepping to the agile melody of their leader's concertina. The music passed in an instant, as the first bars of sudden music always did, over the fantastic fabrics of his mind, dissolving them painlessly and noiselessly as a sudden wave dissolves the sandbuilt turrets of children. Smiling at the trivial air he raised his eyes to the priest's face and, seeing in it a mirthless reflection of the sunken day, detached his hand slowly which had acquiesced faintly in that companionship.

As he descended the steps the impression which effaced his troubled selfcommunion was that of a mirthless mask reflecting a sunken day from the threshold of the college. The shadow, then, of the life of the college passed gravely over his conscious= ness. It was a grave and ordered and passionless life that awaited him, a life without material cares. He wondered how he would pass the first night in the novitiate and with what dismay he would wake the first morning in the dormitory. The troubling odour of the long corridors of Clongowes came back to him and he heard the discreet murmur of the burning gasflames. At once from every part of his being unrest began to irradiate. A feverish quickening of his pulses followed and a din of meaningless words drove his reasoned thoughts hither and thither confusedly. His lungs dilated and sank as if he were inhaling a warm moist unsustaining air and he smelt again the warm moist air which hung in the bath in Clongowes above the sluggish turfcoloured water.

Some instinct, waking at these memories, stronger than edu= cation or piety, quickened within him at every near approach to that life, an instinct subtle and hostile, and armed him against acquiescence. The chill and order of the life repelled him. He saw himself rising in the cold of the morning and filing down with the others to early mass and trying vainly to struggle with his prayers against the fainting sickness of his

stomach. He saw himself sitting at dinner with the community 500
of a college. What then had come of that deeprooted shyness of
his which had made him loth to eat or drink under a strange
roof? What had come of the pride of his spirit which had
always made him conceive himself as a being apart in every
order?

The Reverend Stephen Dedalus, S. J.

His name in that new life leaped into characters before his
eyes and to it there followed a mental sensation of an unde=
fined face or colour of a face. The colour faded and became
strong like a changing glow of pallid brick red. Was it the raw 510
reddish glow he had so often seen on wintry mornings on the
shaven gills of the priests? The face was eyeless and sourfa=
voured and devout, shot with pink tinges of suffocated anger.
Was it not a mental spectre of the face of one of the jesuits
whom some of the boys called Lantern Jaws and others Foxy
Campbell?

He was passing at that moment before the jesuit house in
Gardiner Street and wondered vaguely which window would
be his if he ever joined the order. Then he wondered at the
vagueness of his wonder, at the remoteness of his own soul 520
from what he had hitherto imagined her sanctuary, at the frail
hold which so many years of order and obedience had of him
when once a definite and irrevocable act of his threatened to
end for ever, in time and in eternity, his freedom. The voice of
the director urging upon him the proud claims of the church
and the mystery and power of the priestly office repeated itself
idly in his memory. His soul was not there to hear and greet it
and he knew now that the exhortation he had listened to had
already fallen into an idle formal tale. He would never swing
the thurible before the tabernacle as priest. His destiny was to 530
be elusive of social or religious orders. The wisdom of the
priest's appeal did not touch him to the quick. He was destined
to learn his own wisdom apart from others or to learn the
wisdom of others himself wandering among the snares of the
world.

The snares of the world were its ways of sin. He would fall.

He had not yet fallen but he would fall silently, in an instant. Not to fall was too hard, too hard: and he felt the silent lapse of his soul, as it would be at some instant to come, falling, falling but not yet fallen, still unfallen but about to fall.

He crossed the bridge over the stream of the Tolka and turned his eyes coldly for an instant towards the faded blue shrine of the Blessed Virgin which stood fowlwise on a pole in the middle of a hamshaped encampment of poor cottages. Then, bending to the left, he followed the lane which led up to his house. The faint sour stink of rotted cabbages came to= wards him from the kitchen gardens on the rising ground above the river. He smiled to think that it was this disorder, the misrule and confusion of his father's house and the stagnation of vegetable life, which was to win the day in his soul. Then a short laugh broke from his lips as he thought of that solitary farmhand in the kitchen gardens behind their house whom they had nicknamed the man with the hat. A second laugh, taking rise from the first after a pause, broke from him involuntarily as he thought of how the man with the hat worked, considering in turn the four points of the sky and then regretfully plunging his spade in the earth.

He pushed open the latchless door of the porch and passed through the naked hallway into the kitchen. A group of his brothers and sisters was sitting round the table. Tea was nearly over and only the last of the second watered tea remained in the bottoms of the small glassjars and jampots which did ser= vice for teacups. Discarded crusts and lumps of sugared bread, turned brown by the tea which had been poured over them, lay scattered on the table. Little wells of tea lay here and there on the board and a knife with a broken ivory handle was stuck through the pith of a ravaged turnover.

The sad quiet greyblue glow of the dying day came through the window and the open door, covering over and allaying quietly a sudden instinct of remorse in Stephen's heart. All that had been denied them had been freely given to him, the eldest: but the quiet glow of evening showed him in their faces no sign of rancour.

He sat near them at the table and asked where his father and mother were. One answered:

—Goneboro toboro lookboro atboro aboro houseboro.

Still another removal! A boy named Fallon in Belvedere had often asked him with a silly laugh why they moved so often. A frown of scorn darkened quickly his forehead as he heard again the silly laugh of the questioner.

He asked:

—Why are we on the move again, if it's a fair question?

The same sister answered:

—Becauseboro theboro landboro lordboro willboro putboro usboro outboro.

The voice of his youngest brother from the farther side of the fireplace began to sing the air *Oft in the Stilly Night*. One by one the others took up the air until a full choir of voices was singing. They would sing so for hours, melody after melody, glee after glee, till the last pale light died down on the horizon, till the first dark nightclouds came forth and night fell.

He waited for some moments, listening, before he too took up the air with them. He was listening with pain of spirit to the overtone of weariness behind their frail fresh innocent voices. Even before they set out on life's journey they seemed weary already of the way.

He heard the choir of voices in the kitchen echoed and multiplied through an endless reverberation of the choirs of endless generations of children: and heard in all the echoes an echo also of the recurring note of weariness and pain. All seemed weary of life even before entering upon it. And he remembered that Newman had heard this note also in the broken lines of Virgil *giving utterance, like the voice of Nature herself, to that pain and weariness yet hope of better things which has been the experience of her children in every time.*

◆ ◆ ◆

He could wait no longer.

From the door of Byron's publichouse to the gate of Clontarf chapel, from the gate of Clontarf chapel to the door of

Byron's publichouse and then back again to the chapel and
then back again to the publichouse he had paced slowly at first
planting his steps scrupulously in the spaces of the patchwork
of the footpath, then timing their fall to the fall of verses. A full
hour had passed since his father had gone in with Dan Crosby,
the tutor, to find out from him something about the university.
For a full hour he had paced up and down, waiting: but he
could wait no longer.

He set off abruptly for the Bull, walking rapidly lest his
father's shrill whistle might call him back; and in a few mo=
ments he had rounded the curve at the police barrack and was
safe.

Yes, his mother was hostile to the idea as he had read from
her listless silence. Yet her mistrust pricked him more keenly
than his father's pride and he thought coldly how he had
watched the faith which was fading down in his soul aging and
strengthening in her eyes. A dim antagonism gathered force
within him and darkened his mind as a cloud against her dis=
loyalty: and when it passed cloudlike leaving his mind serene
and dutiful towards her again he was made aware dimly and
without regret of a first noiseless sundering of their lives.

The university! So he had passed beyond the challenge of the
sentries who had stood as guardians of his boyhood and had
sought to keep him among them, that he might be subject to
them and serve their ends. Pride after satisfaction uplifted him
like long slow waves. The end he had been born to serve yet
did not see had led him to escape by an unseen path: and now it
beckoned to him once more and a new adventure was about to
be opened to him. It seemed to him that he heard notes of fitful
music leaping upwards a tone and downwards a diminished
fourth, upwards a tone and downwards a major third, like
triplebranching flames leaping fitfully, flame after flame, out of
a midnight wood. It was an elfin prelude, endless and formless:
and, as it grew wilder and faster, the flames leaping out of
time, he seemed to hear from under the boughs and grasses
wild creatures racing, their feet pattering like rain upon the

leaves. Their feet passed in pattering tumult over his mind, the feet of hares and rabbits, the feet of harts and hinds and ante= lopes, until he heard them no more and remembered only a proud cadence from Newman: *Whose feet are as the feet of harts and underneath the everlasting arms.*

The pride of that dim image brought back to his mind the 650 dignity of the office he had refused. All through his boyhood he had mused upon that which he had so often thought to be his destiny and when the moment had come for him to obey the call he had turned aside, obeying a wayward instinct. Now time lay between: the oils of ordination would never anoint his body. He had refused. Why?

He turned seaward from the road at Dollymount and as he passed on to the thin wooden bridge he felt the planks shaking with the tramp of heavily shod feet. A squad of christian brothers was on its way back from the Bull and had begun to 660 pass, two by two, across the bridge. Soon the whole bridge was trembling and resounding. The uncouth faces passed him two by two, stained yellow or red or livid by the sea and, as he strove to look at them with ease and indifference, a faint stain of personal shame and commiseration rose to his own face. Angry with himself he tried to hide his face from their eyes by gazing down sideways into the shallow swirling water under the bridge but he still saw a reflection therein of their topheavy silk hats and humble tapelike collars and loosely hanging cleri= cal clothes. 670
—Brother Hickey.

Brother Quaid.

Brother MacArdle.

Brother Keogh.

Their piety would be like their names, like their faces, like their clothes: and it was idle for him to tell himself that their humble and contrite hearts, it might be, paid a far richer tribute of devotion than his had ever been, a gift tenfold more accept= able than his elaborate adoration. It was idle for him to move himself to be generous towards them, to tell himself that if he 680 ever came to their gates, stripped of his pride, beaten and in beggar's weeds, that they would be generous towards him, loving him as themselves. Idle and embittering, finally, to ar= gue, against his own dispassionate certitude, that the com= mandment of love bade us not to love our neighbour as ourselves with the same amount and intensity of love but to love him as ourselves with the same kind of love.

He drew forth a phrase from his treasure and spoke it softly to himself:

690   —A day of dappled seaborne clouds.

The phrase and the day and the scene harmonised in a chord. Words. Was it their colours? He allowed them to glow and fade, hue after hue: sunrise gold, the russet and green of apple orchards, azure of waves, the greyfringed fleece of clouds. No, it was not their colours: it was the poise and balance of the period itself. Did he then love the rhythmic rise and fall of words better than their associations of legend and colour? Or was it that, being as weak of sight as he was shy of mind, he drew less pleasure from the reflection of the glowing

700   sensible world through the prism of a language manycoloured and richly storied than from the contemplation of an inner world of individual emotions mirrored perfectly in a lucid supple periodic prose?

He passed from the trembling bridge on to firm land again. At that instant, as it seemed to him, the air was chilled; and looking askance towards the water he saw a flying squall dark= ening and crisping suddenly the tide. A faint click at his heart, a faint throb in his throat told him once more of how his flesh dreaded the cold infrahuman odour of the sea: yet he did not

710   strike across the downs on his left but held straight on along the spine of rocks that pointed against the river's mouth.

A veiled sunlight lit up faintly the grey sheet of water where the river was embayed. In the distance along the course of the slowflowing Liffey slender masts flecked the sky and, more distant still, the dim fabric of the city lay prone in haze. Like a scene on some vague arras, old as man's weariness, the image of the seventh city of christendom was visible to him across the

timeless air, no older nor more weary nor less patient of subjec=
tion than in the days of the thingmote.

Disheartened, he raised his eyes towards the slowdrifting   720
clouds, dappled and seaborne. They were voyaging across the
deserts of the sky, a host of nomads on the march, voyaging
high over Ireland, westward bound. The Europe they had come
from lay out there beyond the Irish Sea, Europe of strange
tongues and valleyed and woodbegirt and citadelled and of
entrenched and marshalled races. He heard a confused music
within him as of memories and names which he was almost
conscious of but could not capture even for an instant; then the
music seemed to recede, to recede, to recede: and from each
receding trail of nebulous music there fell always one long=   730
drawn calling note, piercing like a star the dusk of silence.
Again! Again! Again! Again! A voice from beyond the world
was calling.
—Hello, Stephanos!
—Here comes The Dedalus!
—Ao! ... Eh, give it over, Dwyer, I'm telling you or I'll give you
a stuff in the kisser for yourself .... Ao!
—Good man, Towser! Duck him!
—Come along, Dedalus! Bous Stephanoumenos! Bous Steph=
aneforos!   740
—Duck him! Guzzle him now, Towser!
—Help! Help! ... Ao!

He recognised their speech collectively before he distin=
guished their faces. The mere sight of that medley of wet
nakedness chilled him to the bone. Their bodies, corpsewhite
or suffused with a pallid golden light or rawly tanned by the
sun, gleamed with the wet of the sea. Their divingstone, poised
on its rude supports and rocking under their plunges, and the
roughhewn stones of the sloping breakwater over which they
scrambled in their horseplay gleamed with cold wet lustre. The   750
towels with which they smacked their bodies were heavy with
cold seawater: and drenched with cold brine was their matted
hair.

He stood still in deference to their calls and parried their banter with easy words. How characterless they looked: Shuley without his deep unbuttoned collar, Ennis without his scarlet belt with the snaky clasp and Connolly without his Norfolk coat with the flapless sidepockets! It was a pain to see them and a swordlike pain to see the signs of adolescence that made repellent their pitiable nakedness. Perhaps they had taken ref= uge in number and noise from the secret dread in their souls. But he, apart from them and in silence, remembered in what dread he stood of the mystery of his own body.

—Stephanos Dedalos! Bous Stephanoumenos! Bous Stephane= foros!

Their banter was not new to him and now, as always, it flattered his mild proud sovereignty. Now, as never before, his strange name seemed to him a prophecy. So timeless seemed the grey warm air, so fluid and impersonal his own mood, that all ages were as one to him. A moment before the ghost of the ancient kingdom of the Danes had looked forth through the vesture of the hazewrapped city. Now, at the name of the fabulous artificer, he seemed to hear the noise of dim waves and to see a winged form flying above the waves and slowly climbing the air. What did it mean? Was it a quaint device opening a page of some medieval book of prophecies and sym= bols, a hawklike man flying sunward above the sea, a prophecy of the end he had been born to serve and had been following through the mists of childhood and boyhood, a symbol of the artist forging anew in his workshop out of the sluggish matter of the earth a new soaring impalpable imperishable being?

His heart trembled; his breath came faster and a wild spirit passed over his limbs as though he were soaring sunward. His heart trembled in an ecstasy of fear and his soul was in flight. His soul was soaring in an air beyond the world and the body he knew was purified in a breath and delivered of incertitude and made radiant and commingled with the element of the spirit. An ecstasy of flight made radiant his eyes and wild his breath and tremulous and wild and radiant his windswept limbs.

—One! Two! ... Look out!

—O, Cripes, I'm drownded!

—One! Two! Three and away!

—Me next! Me next!

—One! ... Uk!

—Stephaneforos!

His throat ached with a desire to cry aloud, the cry of a hawk or eagle on high, to cry piercingly of his deliverance to the winds. This was the call of life to his soul not the dull gross voice of the world of duties and despair, not the inhuman voice that had called him to the pale service of the altar. An instant of wild flight had delivered him and the cry of triumph which his lips withheld cleft his brain.

—Stephaneforos!

What were they now but cerements shaken from the body of death—the fear he had walked in night and day, the incertitude that had ringed him round, the shame that had abased him within and without—cerements, the linens of the grave?

His soul had arisen from the grave of boyhood, spurning her graveclothes. Yes! Yes! Yes! He would create proudly out of the freedom and power of his soul, as the great artificer whose name he bore, a living thing, new and soaring and beautiful, impalpable, imperishable.

He started up nervously from the stoneblock for he could no longer quench the flame in his blood. He felt his cheeks aflame and his throat throbbing with song. There was a lust of wan= dering in his feet that burned to set out for the ends of the earth. On! On! his heart seemed to cry. Evening would deepen above the sea, night fall upon the plains, dawn glimmer before the wanderer and show him strange fields and hills and faces. Where?

He looked northward towards Howth. The sea had fallen below the line of seawrack on the shallow side of the break= water and already the tide was running out fast along the foreshore. Already one long oval bank of sand lay warm and dry amid the wavelets. Here and there warm isles of sand gleamed above the shallow tide: and about the isles and around the long bank and amid the shallow currents of the beach were lightclad gayclad figures wading and delving.

830   In a few moments he was barefoot, his stockings folded in his pockets and his canvas shoes dangling by their knotted laces over his shoulders: and, picking a pointed salteaten stick out of the jetsam among the rocks, he clambered down the slope of the breakwater.

    There was a long rivulet in the strand: and, as he waded slowly up its course, he wondered at the endless drift of sea=weed. Emerald and black and russet and olive, it moved beneath the current, swaying and turning. The water of the rivulet was dark with endless drift and mirrored the highdrift=
840 ing clouds. The clouds were drifting above him silently and silently the seatangle was drifting below him; and the grey warm air was still: and a new wild life was singing in his veins.

    Where was his boyhood now? Where was the soul that had hung back from her destiny, to brood alone upon the shame of her wounds and in her house of squalor and subterfuge to queen it in faded cerements and in wreaths that withered at the touch? Or where was he?

    He was alone. He was unheeded, happy and near to the wild heart of life. He was alone and young and wilful and wild=
850 hearted, alone amid a waste of wild air and brackish waters and the seaharvest of shells and tangle and veiled grey sunlight and gayclad lightclad figures of children and girls and voices childish and girlish in the air.

    A girl stood before him in midstream: alone and still, gazing out to sea. She seemed like one whom magic had changed into the likeness of a strange and beautiful seabird. Her long slender bare legs were delicate as a crane's and pure save where an emerald trail of seaweed had fashioned itself as a sign upon the flesh. Her thighs, fuller and softhued as ivory, were bared al=
860 most to the hips where the white fringes of her drawers were like featherings of soft white down. Her slateblue skirts were kilted boldly about her waist and dovetailed behind her. Her bosom was as a bird's, soft and slight; slight and soft as the

breast of some darkplumaged dove. But her long fair hair was girlish; and girlish, and touched with the wonder of mortal beauty, her face.

She was alone and still, gazing out to sea; and when she felt his presence and the worship of his eyes her eyes turned to him in quiet sufferance of his gaze, without shame or wantonness. Long, long she suffered his gaze and then quietly withdrew her eyes from his and bent them towards the stream, gently stirring the water with her foot hither and thither. The first faint noise of gently moving water broke the silence, low and faint and whispering, faint as the bells of sleep; hither and thither, hither and thither: and a faint flame trembled on her cheek.

—Heavenly God! cried Stephen's soul in an outburst of pro= fane joy.

He turned away from her suddenly and set off across the strand. His cheeks were aflame; his body was aglow; his limbs were trembling. On and on and on and on he strode, far out over the sands, singing wildly to the sea, crying to greet the advent of the life that had cried to him.

Her image had passed into his soul for ever and no word had broken the holy silence of his ecstasy. Her eyes had called him and his soul had leaped at the call. To live, to err, to fall, to triumph, to recreate life out of life! A wild angel had appeared to him, the angel of mortal youth and beauty, an envoy from the fair courts of life, to throw open before him in an instant of ecstasy the gates of all the ways of error and glory. On and on and on and on!

He halted suddenly and heard his heart in the silence. How far had he walked? What hour was it?

There was no human figure near him nor any sound borne to him over the air. But the tide was near the turn and already the day was on the wane. He turned landward and ran towards the shore and, running up the sloping beach, reckless of the sharp shingle, found a sandy nook amid a ring of tufted sand= knolls and lay down there that the peace and silence of the evening might still the riot of his blood.

He felt above him the vast indifferent dome and the calm

870

880

890

900

processes of the heavenly bodies: and the earth beneath him, the earth that had borne him, had taken him to her breast.

He closed his eyes in the languor of sleep. His eyelids trembled as if they felt the vast cyclic movement of the earth and her watchers, trembled as if they felt the strange light of some new world. His soul was swooning into some new world, fantastic, dim, uncertain as under sea, traversed by cloudy shapes and beings. A world, a glimmer or a flower? Glimmering and trembling, trembling and unfolding, a breaking light, an opening flower, it spread in endless succession to itself, breaking in full crimson and unfolding and fading to palest rose, leaf by leaf and wave of light by wave of light, flooding all the heavens with its soft flushes, every flush deeper than other.

Evening had fallen when he woke and the sand and arid grasses of his bed glowed no longer. He rose slowly and, recalling the rapture of his sleep, sighed at its joy.

He climbed to the crest of the sandhill and gazed about him. Evening had fallen. A rim of the young moon cleft the pale waste of sky like the rim of a silver hoop embedded in grey sand: and the tide was flowing in fast to the land with a low whisper of her waves, islanding a few last figures in distant pools.

V

He drained his third cup of watery tea to the dregs and set to chewing the crusts of fried bread that were scattered near him, staring into the dark pool of the jar. The yellow dripping had been scooped out like a boghole and the pool under it brought back to his memory the dark turfcoloured water of the bath in Clongowes. The box of pawntickets at his elbow had just been rifled and he took up idly one after another in his greasy fingers the blue and white dockets, scrawled and sanded and creased and bearing the name of the pledger as Daly or MacEvoy.

—1 Pair Buskins
  1 D. Coat
  3 Articles and White
  1 Man's Pants

Then he put them aside and gazed thoughtfully at the lid of the box, speckled with lousemarks, and asked vaguely:

—How much is the clock fast now?

His mother straightened the battered alarmclock that was lying on its side in the middle of the kitchen mantelpiece until its dial showed a quarter to twelve and then laid it once more on its side.

—An hour and twentyfive minutes, she said. The right time now is twenty past ten. The dear knows you might try to be in time for your lectures.

—Fill out the place for me to wash, said Stephen.

—Katey, fill out the place for Stephen to wash.

—Boody, fill out the place for Stephen to wash.

—I can't. I'm going for blue. Fill it out, you, Maggie.

When the enamelled basin had been fitted into the well of the sink and the old washingglove flung on the side of it he

30 allowed his mother to scrub his neck and root into the folds of his ears and into the interstices at the wings of his nose.

—Well, it's a poor case, she said, when a university student is so dirty that his mother has to wash him.

—But it gives you pleasure, said Stephen calmly.

An earsplitting whistle was heard from upstairs and his mother thrust a damp overall into his hands, saying:

—Dry yourself and hurry out for the love of goodness.

A second shrill whistle, prolonged angrily, brought one of the girls to the foot of the staircase.

40 —Yes, father?

—Is your lazy bitch of a brother gone out yet?

—Yes, father.

—Sure?

—Yes, father.

—Hm!

The girl came back making signs to him to be quick and go out quietly by the back. Stephen laughed and said:

—He has a curious idea of genders if he thinks a bitch is masculine.

50 —Ah, it's a scandalous shame for you, Stephen, said his mother, and you'll live to rue the day you set your foot in that place. I know how it has changed you.

—Good morning, everybody, said Stephen smiling and kissing the tips of his fingers in adieu.

The lane behind the terrace was waterlogged and as he went down it slowly, choosing his steps amid heaps of wet rubbish, he heard a mad nun screeching in the nuns' madhouse beyond the wall:

—Jesus! O Jesus! Jesus!

60 He shook the sound out of his ears by an angry toss of his head and hurried on, stumbling through the mouldering offal, his heart already bitten by an ache of loathing and bitterness. His father's whistle, his mother's mutterings, the screech of an unseen maniac were to him now so many voices offending and threatening to humble the pride of his youth. He drove their

echoes even out of his heart with an execration: but as he walked down the avenue and felt the grey morning light falling about him through the dripping trees and smelt the strange wild smell of the wet leaves and bark his soul was loosed of her miseries.

The rainladen trees of the avenue evoked in him, as always, memories of the girls and women in the plays of Gerhart Hauptmann: and the memory of their pale sorrows and the fragrance falling from the wet branches mingled in a mood of quiet joy. His morning walk across the city had begun: and he foreknew that as he passed the sloblands of Fairview he would think of the cloistral silverveined prose of Newman, that as he walked along the North Strand Road, glancing idly at the win= dows of the provision shops, he would recall the dark humour of Guido Cavalcanti and smile, that as he went by Baird's stonecutting works in Talbot Place the spirit of Ibsen would blow through him like a keen wind, a spirit of wayward boyish beauty, and that passing a grimy marine dealer's shop beyond the Liffey he would repeat the song by Ben Jonson which begins:

I was not wearier where I lay.

His mind when wearied of its search for the essence of beauty amid the spectral words of Aristotle or Aquinas turned often for its pleasure to the dainty songs of the Elizabethans. His mind, in the vesture of a doubting monk, stood often in shadow under the windows of that age, to hear the grave and mocking music of the lutenists or the frank laughter of waist= coateers until a laugh too low, a phrase, tarnished by time, of chambering and false honour stung his monkish pride and drove him on from his lurkingplace.

The lore which he was believed to pass his days brooding upon so that it had rapt him from the companionships of youth was only a garner of slender sentences from Aristotle's poetics and psychology and a *Synopsis Philosophiae Scholasticae ad mentem divi Thomae.* His thinking was a dusk of doubt and selfmistrust lit up at moments by the lightnings of intuition, but lightnings of so clear a splendour that in those moments the world perished about his feet as if it had been fireconsumed: and thereafter his tongue grew heavy and he met the eyes of others with unanswering eyes for he felt that the spirit of beauty had folded him round like a mantle and that in revery at least he had been acquainted with nobility. But when this brief pride of silence upheld him no longer he was glad to find him= self still in the midst of common lives, passing on his way amid the squalor and noise and sloth of the city fearlessly and with a light heart.

Near the hoardings on the canal he met the consumptive man with the doll's face and the brimless hat coming towards him down the slope of the bridge with little steps, tightly but= toned into his chocolate overcoat and holding his furled um= brella a span or two from him like a diviningrod. It must be eleven, he thought, and peered into a dairy to see the time. The clock in the dairy told him that it was five minutes to five but, as he turned away, he heard a clock somewhere near him but unseen beating eleven strokes in swift precision. He laughed as he heard it for it made him think of MacCann; and he saw him a squat figure in a shooting jacket and breeches and with a fair goatee standing in the wind at Hopkins' corner and heard him say:

—Dedalus, you're an antisocial being, wrapped up in yourself. I'm not. I'm a democrat: and I'll work and act for social liberty and equality among all classes and sexes in the United States of the Europe of the future.

Eleven! Then he was late for that lecture too. What day of the week was it? He stopped at a newsagent's to read the headline of a placard. Thursday. Ten to eleven; English: eleven to twelve; French: twelve to one; physics. He fancied to himself the English lecture and felt, even at that distance, restless and helpless. He saw the heads of his classmates meekly bent as they wrote in their notebooks the points they were bidden to note, nominal definitions, essential definitions and examples or dates of birth and death, chief works, a favourable and an unfavourable criticism side by side. His own head was unbent for his thoughts wandered abroad and whether he looked around the little class of students or out of the window across the desolate gardens of the green an odour assailed him of cheerless cellardamp and decay. Another head than his, right before him in the first benches, was poised squarely above its bending fellows like the head of a priest appealing without humility to the tabernacle for the humble worshippers about him. Why was it that when he thought of Cranly he could never raise before his mind the entire image of his body but only the image of the head and face? Even now against the grey curtain of the morning he saw it before him like the phantom of a dream, the face of a severed head or deathmask, crowned on the brows by its stiff black upright hair as by an iron crown. It was a priestlike face, priestlike in its pallor, in the wide= winged nose, in the shadowings below the eyes and along the jaws, priestlike in the lips that were long and bloodless and faintly smiling: and Stephen, remembering swiftly how he had told Cranly of all the tumults and unrest and longings in his soul, day after day and night by night only to be answered by his friend's listening silence, would have told himself that it was the face of a guilty priest who heard confessions of those whom he had not power to absolve but that he felt again in memory the gaze of its dark womanish eyes.

Through this image he had a glimpse of a strange dark cavern of speculation but at once turned away from it feeling that it was not yet the hour to enter it. But the nightshade of his friend's listlessness seemed to be diffusing in the air around him a tenuous and deadly exhalation: and he found himself glancing from one casual word to another on his right or left in stolid wonder that they had been so silently emptied of instan= taneous sense until every mean shop legend bound his mind like the words of a spell and his soul shrivelled up sighing with age as he walked on in a lane among heaps of dead language. His own consciousness of language was ebbing from his brain and trickling into the very words themselves which set to band and disband themselves in wayward rhythms:

> *The ivy whines upon the wall*
> *And whines and twines upon the wall*
> *The ivy whines upon the wall*
> *The yellow ivy on the wall*
> *Ivy, ivy up the wall.*

180   Did any one ever hear such drivel? Lord Almighty! Who ever heard of ivy whining on a wall? Yellow ivy: that was all right. Yellow ivory also. And what about ivory ivy?

The word now shone in his brain, clearer and brighter than any ivory sawn from the mottled tusks of elephants. *Ivory, ivoire, avorio, ebur.* One of the first examples that he had learnt in Latin had run: *India mittit ebur*: and he recalled the shrewd northern face of the rector who had taught him to construe the Metamorphoses of Ovid in a courtly English, made whimsical by the mention of porkers and potsherds and
190   chines of bacon. He had learnt what little he knew of the laws of Latin verse from a ragged book written by a Portuguese priest:

> *Contrahit orator, variant in carmine vates.*

The crises and victories and secessions in Roman history were handed on to him in the trite words *in tanto discrimine* and he had tried to peer into the social life of the city of cities through the words *implere ollam denariorum* which the rector had rendered sonorously as the filling of a pot with denaries. The pages of his timeworn Horace never felt cold to the touch
200   even when his own fingers were cold: they were human pages: and fifty years before they had been turned by the human fingers of John Duncan Inverarity and by his brother William Malcolm Inverarity. Yes, those were noble names on the dusky flyleaf and, even for so poor a Latinist as he, the dusky verses were as fragrant as though they had lain all those years in myrtle and lavender and vervain: but yet it wounded him to

think that he would never be but a shy guest at the feast of the world's culture and that the monkish learning, in terms of which he was striving to forge out an esthetic philosophy, was held no higher by the age he lived in than the subtle and curious jargons of heraldry and falconry.

210

The grey block of Trinity on his left, set heavily in the city's ignorance like a great dull stone set in a cumbrous ring, pulled his mind downward: and while he was striving this way and that to free his feet from the fetters of the reformed conscience he came upon the droll statue of the national poet of Ireland.

He looked at it without anger: for, though sloth of the body and of the soul crept over it like unseen vermin, over the shuffling feet and up the folds of the cloak and around the servile head, it seemed humbly conscious of its indignity. It was a Firbolg in the borrowed cloak of a Milesian; and he thought of his friend Davin, the peasant student. It was a jesting name between them but the young peasant bore with it lightly, saying:

220

—Go on, Stevie. I have a hard head, you tell me. Call me what you will.

The homely version of his christian name on the lips of his friend had touched Stephen pleasantly when first heard for he was as formal in speech with others as they were with him. Often, as he sat in Davin's rooms in Grantham Street, wondering at his friend's wellmade boots that flanked the wall pair by pair and repeating for his friend's simple ear the verses and cadences of others which were the veils of his own longing and dejection, the rude Firbolg mind of his listener had drawn his mind towards it and flung it back again, drawing it by a quiet inbred courtesy of attention or by a quaint turn of old English speech or by the force of its delight in rude bodily skill (for Davin had sat at the feet of Michael Cusack, the Gael), repelling swiftly and suddenly by a grossness of intelligence or by a bluntness of feeling or by a dull stare of terror in the eyes the terror of soul of a starving Irish village in which the curfew was still a nightly fear.

230

240

Side by side with his memory of the deeds of prowess of his uncle Mat Davin, the athlete, the young peasant worshipped the sorrowful legend of Ireland. The gossip of his fellowstu=dents which strove to render the flat life of the college signifi=cant at any cost loved to think of him as a young fenian. His nurse had taught him Irish and shaped the rude imagination by the broken lights of Irish myth. He stood towards this myth
250 upon which no individual mind had ever drawn out a line of beauty and to its unwieldy tales that divided against themselves as they moved down the cycles in the same attitude as towards the Roman catholic religion, the attitude of a dullwitted loyal serf. Whatsoever of thought or of feeling came to him from England or by way of English culture his mind stood armed against in obedience to a password: and of the world that lay beyond England he knew only the foreign legion of France in which he spoke of serving.

Coupling this ambition with the young man's diffident hu=
260 mour Stephen had often called him one of the tame geese: and there was even a point of irritation in the name pointed against that very reluctance of speech and deed in his friend which seemed so often to stand between Stephen's mind, eager of speculation, and the hidden ways of Irish life.

One night the young peasant, his spirit stung by the violent or luxurious language in which Stephen escaped from the cold silence of intellectual revolt, had called up before Stephen's mind a strange vision. The two were walking slowly towards Davin's rooms through the dark narrow streets of the poorer
270 jews.

—A thing happened to myself, Stevie, last autumn coming on winter and I never told it to a living soul and you are the first person now I ever told it to. I disremember if it was October or November. It was October because it was before I came up here to join the matriculation class.

Stephen had turned his smiling eyes towards his friend's face, flattered by his confidence and won over to sympathy by the speaker's simple accent.

—I was away all that day from my own place, over in Butte= 280
vant (I don't know if you know where that is) at a hurling
match between the Croke's Own Boys and the Fearless Thurles
and by God, Stevie, that was the hard fight. My first cousin
Fonsy Davin was stripped to his buff that day minding cool for
the Limericks but he was up with the forwards half the time
and shouting like mad. I never will forget that day. One of the
Crokes made a woful wipe at him one time with his camaun
and I declare to God he was within an aim's ace of getting it at
the side of the temple. O, honest to God, if the crook of it
caught him that time he was done for.
—I am glad he escaped, Stephen had said with a laugh, but 290
surely that's not the strange thing that happened you?
—Well, I suppose that doesn't interest you but leastways there
was such noise after the match that I missed the train home and
I couldn't get any kind of a yoke to give me a lift for, as luck
would have it, there was a mass meeting that same day over in
Castletownroche and all the cars in the country were there. So
there was nothing for it only to stay the night or to foot it out.
Well, I started to walk and on I went and it was coming on
night when I got into the Ballyhoura hills, that's better than ten
miles from Kilmallock and there's a long lonely road after that. 300
You wouldn't see the sign of a christian house along the road or
hear a sound. It was pitch dark almost. Once or twice I stopped
by the way under a bush to redden my pipe and only for the
dew was thick I'd have stretched out there and slept. At last
after a bend of the road I spied a little cottage with a light in
the window. I went up and knocked at the door. A voice asked
who was there and I answered I was over at the match in
Buttevant and was walking back and that I'd be thankful for a
glass of water. After a while a young woman opened the door
and brought me out a big mug of milk. She was half undressed 310
as if she was going to bed when I knocked and she had her hair
hanging: and I thought by her figure and by something in the
look of her eyes that she must be carrying a child. She kept me
in talk a long while at the door and I thought it strange because

her breast and her shoulders were bare. She asked me was I
tired and would I like to stop the night there. She said she was
all alone in the house and that her husband had gone that
morning to Queenstown with his sister to see her off. And all
the time she was talking, Stevie, she had her eyes fixed on my
320 face and she stood so close to me I could hear her breathing.
When I handed her back the mug at last she took my hand to
draw me in over the threshold and said: *Come in and stay the
night here. You've no call to be frightened. There's no-one in it
but ourselves* .... I didn't go in, Stevie. I thanked her and
went on my way again, all in a fever. At the first bend of the
road I looked back and she was standing in the door.

The last words of Davin's story sang in his memory and the
figure of the woman in the story stood forth reflected in other
figures of the peasant women whom he had seen standing in
330 the doorways at Clane as the college cars drove by, as a type of
her race and his own, a batlike soul waking to the conscious=
ness of itself in darkness and secrecy and loneliness and,
through the eyes and voice and gesture of a woman without
guile, calling the stranger to her bed.

A hand was laid on his arm and a young voice cried:

—Ah, gentleman, your own girl, sir! The first handsel today,
gentleman. Buy that lovely bunch. Will you, gentleman?

The blue flowers which she lifted towards him and her
young blue eyes seemed to him at that instant images of guile=
340 lessness: and he halted till the image had vanished and he saw
only her ragged dress and damp coarse hair and hoydenish
face.

—Do, gentleman! Don't forget your own girl, sir!

—I have no money, said Stephen.

—Buy them lovely ones, will you, sir? Only a penny.

—Did you hear what I said? asked Stephen, bending towards
her. I told you I had no money. I tell you again now.

—Well, sure, you will some day, sir, please God, the girl
answered after an instant.

350 —Possibly, said Stephen, but I don't think it likely.

He left her quickly, fearing that her intimacy might turn to gibing and wishing to be out of the way before she offered her ware to another, a tourist from England or a student of Trinity. Grafton Street along which he walked prolonged that moment of discouraged poverty. In the roadway at the head of the street a slab was set to the memory of Wolfe Tone and he remem= bered having been present with his father at its laying. He re= membered with bitterness that scene of tawdry tribute. There were four French delegates in a brake and one, a plump smiling young man, held, wedged on a stick, a card on which were printed the words: *Vive l'Irlande!*

But the trees in Stephen's Green were fragrant of rain and the rainsodden earth gave forth its mortal odour, a faint in= cense rising upward through the mould from many hearts. The soul of the gallant venal city which his elders had told him of had shrunk with time to a faint mortal odour rising from the earth and he knew that in a moment when he entered the sombre college he would be conscious of a corruption other than that of Buck Egan and Burnchapel Whaley.

It was too late to go upstairs to the French class. He crossed the hall and took the corridor to the left which led to the physics theatre. The corridor was dark and silent but not un= watchful. Why did he feel that it was not unwatchful? Was it because he had heard that in Buck Whaley's time there was a secret staircase there? Or was the jesuit house extraterritorial and was he walking among aliens? The Ireland of Tone and of Parnell seemed to have receded in space.

He opened the door of the theatre and halted in the chilly grey light that struggled through the dusty windows. A figure was crouching before the large grate and by its leanness and greyness he knew that it was the dean of studies lighting the fire. Stephen closed the door quietly and approached the fire= place.

—Good morning, sir! Can I help you?

The priest looked up quickly and said:

—One moment now, Mr Dedalus, and you will see. There is an art in lighting a fire. We have the liberal arts and we have the useful arts. This is one of the useful arts.

—I will try to learn it, said Stephen.

390 —Not too much coal, said the dean, working briskly at his task, that is one of the secrets.

He produced four candle butts from the sidepockets of his soutane and placed them deftly among the coals and twisted papers. Stephen watched him in silence. Kneeling thus on the flagstone to kindle the fire and busied with the disposition of his wisps of paper and candle butts he seemed more than ever a humble server making ready the place of sacrifice in an empty temple, a levite of the Lord. Like a levite's robe of plain linen the faded worn soutane draped the kneeling figure of one 400 whom the canonicals or the bellbordered ephod would irk and trouble. His very body had waxed old in lowly service of the Lord—in tending the fire upon the altar, in bearing tidings se=cretly, in waiting upon worldlings, in striking swiftly when bidden—and yet had remained ungraced by aught of saintly or of prelatic beauty. Nay, his very soul had waxed old in that service without growing towards light and beauty or spreading abroad a sweet odour of her sanctity—a mortified will no more responsive to the thrill of its obedience than was to the thrill of love or combat his aging body, spare and sinewy, greyed with a 410 silverpointed down.

The dean rested back on his hunkers and watched the sticks catch. Stephen, to fill the silence, said:

—I am sure I could not light a fire.

—You are an artist, are you not, Mr Dedalus? said the dean, glancing up and blinking his pale eyes. The object of the artist is the creation of the beautiful. What the beautiful is is another question.

He rubbed his hands slowly and drily over the difficulty.

—Can you solve that question now? he asked.

420 —Aquinas, answered Stephen, says *Pulcra sunt quae visa placent.*

—This fire before us, said the dean, will be pleasing to the eye. Will it therefore be beautiful?

—In so far as it is apprehended by the sight, which I suppose means here esthetic intellection, it will be beautiful. But Aqui=

nas also says *Bonum est in quod tendit appetitus.* In so far as it satisfies the animal craving for warmth fire is a good. In hell however it is an evil.

—Quite so, said the dean, you have certainly hit the nail on the head.

He rose nimbly and went towards the door, set it ajar and said:

—A draught is said to be a help in these matters.

As he came back to the hearth, limping slightly but with a brisk step, Stephen saw the silent soul of a jesuit look out at him from the pale loveless eyes. Like Ignatius he was lame but in his eyes burned no spark of Ignatius' enthusiasm. Even the legendary craft of the company, a craft subtler and more secret than its fabled books of secret subtle wisdom, had not fired his soul with the energy of apostleship. It seemed as if he used the shifts and lore and cunning of the world, as bidden to do, for the greater glory of God, without joy in their handling or hatred of that in them which was evil but turning them, with a firm gesture of obedience, back upon themselves: and for all this silent service it seemed as if he loved not at all the master and little, if at all, the ends he served. *Similiter atque senis baculus,* he was, as the founder would have had him, like a staff in an old man's hand, to be left in a corner, to be leaned on in the road at nightfall or in stress of weather, to lie with a lady's nosegay on a garden seat, to be raised in menace.

The dean returned to the hearth and began to stroke his chin.

—When may we expect to have something from you on the esthetic question? he asked.

—From me! said Stephen in astonishment. I stumble on an idea once a fortnight if I am lucky.

—These questions are very profound, Mr Dedalus, said the dean. It is like looking down from the cliffs of Moher into the depths. Many go down into the depths and never come up. Only the trained diver can go down into those depths and explore them and come to the surface again.

—If you mean speculation, sir, said Stephen, I also am sure

that there is no such thing as free thinking inasmuch as all thinking must be bound by its own laws.

—Ha!

—For my purpose I can work on at present by the light of one or two ideas of Aristotle and Aquinas.

—I see. I quite see your point.

—I need them only for my own use and guidance until I have done something for myself by their light. If the lamp smokes or smells I shall try to trim it. If it does not give light enough I shall sell it and buy or borrow another.

—Epictetus also had a lamp, said the dean, which was sold for a fancy price after his death. It was the lamp he wrote his philosophical dissertations by. You know Epictetus?

—An old gentleman, said Stephen coarsely, who said that the soul is very like a bucketful of water.

—He tells us in his homely way, the dean went on, that he put an iron lamp before a statue of one of the gods and that a thief stole the lamp. What did the philosopher do? He reflected that it was in the character of a thief to steal and determined to buy an earthen lamp next day instead of the iron lamp.

A smell of molten tallow came up from the dean's candle butts and fused itself in Stephen's consciousness with the jingle of the words, bucket and lamp and lamp and bucket. The priest's voice too had a hard jingling tone. Stephen's mind halted by instinct, checked by the strange tone and the imagery and by the priest's face which seemed like an unlit lamp or a reflector hung in a false focus. What lay behind it or within it? A dull torpor of the soul or the dullness of the thundercloud, charged with intellection and capable of the gloom of God?

—I meant a different kind of lamp, sir, said Stephen.

—Undoubtedly, said the dean.

—One difficulty, said Stephen, in esthetic discussion is to know whether words are being used according to the literary tradition or according to the tradition of the marketplace. I remember a sentence of Newman's in which he says of the Blessed Virgin that she was detained in the full company of the

saints. The use of the word in the marketplace is quite differ=
ent. *I hope I am not detaining you.*   500
—Not in the least, said the dean politely.
—No, no, said Stephen smiling, I mean ....
—Yes, yes: I see, said the dean quickly, I quite catch the point:
detain.

He thrust forward his under jaw and uttered a dry short
cough.
—To return to the lamp, he said, the feeding of it is also a nice
problem. You must choose the pure oil and you must be careful
when you pour it in not to overflow it, not to pour in more
than the funnel can hold.   510
—What funnel? asked Stephen.
—The funnel through which you pour the oil into your lamp.
—That? said Stephen. Is that called a funnel? Is it not a tun=
dish?
—What is a tundish?
—That. The ... the funnel.
—Is that called a tundish in Ireland? asked the dean. I never
heard the word in my life.
—It is called a tundish in Lower Drumcondra, said Stephen
laughing, where they speak the best English.   520
—A tundish! said the dean reflectively. That is a most interest=
ing word. I must look that word up. Upon my word I must.

His courtesy of manner rang a little false and Stephen looked
at the English convert with the same eyes as the elder brother in
the parable may have turned on the prodigal. A humble fol=
lower in the wake of clamorous conversions, a poor English=
man in Ireland, he seemed to have entered on the stage of jesuit
history when that strange play of intrigue and suffering and
envy and struggle and indignity had been all but given through
—a latecomer, a tardy spirit. From what had he set out? Per=   530
haps he had been born and bred among serious dissenters,
seeing salvation in Jesus only and abhorring the vain pomps of
the establishment. Had he felt the need of an implicit faith
amid the welter of sectarianism and the jargon of its turbulent

schisms, six principle men, peculiar people, seed and snake baptists, supralapsarian dogmatists? Had he found the true church all of a sudden in winding up to the end like a reel of cotton some finespun line of reasoning upon insufflation or the imposition of hands or the procession of the Holy Ghost? Or had Lord Christ touched him and bidden him follow, like that disciple who had sat at the receipt of custom, as he sat by the door of some zincroofed chapel, yawning and telling over his church pence?

The dean repeated the word yet again.

—Tundish! Well now, that is interesting!

—The question you asked me a moment ago seems to me more interesting. What is that beauty which the artist struggles to express from lumps of earth, said Stephen coldly.

The little word seemed to have turned a rapier point of his sensitiveness against this courteous and vigilant foe. He felt with a smart of dejection that the man to whom he was speak=ing was a countryman of Ben Jonson. He thought:

—The language in which we are speaking is his before it is mine. How different are the words *home, Christ, ale, master* on his lips and on mine! I cannot speak or write these words with=out unrest of spirit. His language, so familiar and so foreign, will always be for me an acquired speech. I have not made or accepted its words. My voice holds them at bay. My soul frets in the shadow of his language.

—And to distinguish between the beautiful and the sublime, the dean added. To distinguish between moral beauty and ma=terial beauty. And to inquire what kind of beauty is proper to each of the various arts. These are some interesting points we might take up.

Stephen, disheartened suddenly by the dean's firm dry tone, was silent. The dean also was silent: and through the silence a distant noise of many boots and confused voices came up the staircase.

—In pursuing these speculations, said the dean conclusively, there is however the danger of perishing of inanition. First you must take your degree. Set that before you as your first aim. Then, little by little, you will see your way. I mean in every sense, your way in life and in thinking. It may be uphill pedal= ling at first. Take Mr Moonan. He was a long time before he got to the top. But he got there.

—I may not have his talent, said Stephen quietly.

—You never know, said the dean brightly. We never can say what is in us. I most certainly should not be despondent. *Per aspera ad astra.*

He left the hearth quickly and went towards the landing to oversee the arrival of the first arts' class. 580

Leaning against the fireplace Stephen heard him greet briskly and impartially every student of the class and could almost see the frank smiles of the coarser students. A desolating pity be= gan to fall like a dew upon his easily embittered heart for this faithful servingman of the knightly Loyola, for this halfbrother of the clergy, more venal than they in speech, more steadfast of soul than they, one whom he would never call his ghostly fa= ther: and he thought how this man and his companions had earned the name of worldlings at the hands not of the un= 590 worldly only but of the worldly also for having pleaded, during all their history, at the bar of God's justice for the souls of the lax and the lukewarm and the prudent.

The entry of the professor was signalled by a few rounds of Kentish fire from the heavy boots of those students who sat on the highest tier of the gloomy theatre under the grey cob= webbed windows. The calling of the roll began and the re= sponses to the names were given out in all tones until the name of Peter Byrne was reached.

—Here! 600

A deep bass note in response came from the upper tier, followed by coughs of protest along the other benches.

The professor paused in his reading and called the next name:

—Cranly!

No answer.

—Mr Cranly!

A smile flew across Stephen's face as he thought of his friend's studies.

610 —Try Leopardstown! said a voice from the bench behind.

Stephen glanced up quickly but Moynihan's snoutish face outlined on the grey light was impassive. A formula was given out. Amid the rustling of the notebooks Stephen turned back again and said:

—Give me some paper for God' sake.

—Are you as bad as that? asked Moynihan with a broad grin.

He tore a sheet from his scribbler and passed it down, whis= pering:

—In case of necessity any layman or woman can do it.

620 The formula which he wrote obediently on the sheet of paper, the coiling and uncoiling calculations of the professor, the spectrelike symbols of force and velocity fascinated and jaded Stephen's mind. He had heard some say that the old professor was an atheist freemason. O the grey dull day! It seemed a limbo of painless patient consciousness through which souls of mathematicians might wander, projecting long slender fabrics from plane to plane of ever rarer and paler twilight, radiating swift eddies to the last verges of a universe ever vaster, farther and more impalpable.

630 —So we must distinguish between elliptical and ellipsoidal. Perhaps some of you gentlemen may be familiar with the works of Mr W. S. Gilbert. In one of his songs he speaks of the billiard sharp who is condemned to play:

> *On a cloth untrue*
> *With a twisted cue*
> *And elliptical billiard balls.*

He means a ball having the form of the ellipsoid of the princi= pal axes of which I spoke a moment ago.

Moynihan leaned down towards Stephen's ear and mur=
640 mured:

—What price ellipsoidal balls! Chase me, ladies, I'm in the cavalry!

His fellowstudent's rude humour ran like a gust through the cloister of Stephen's mind, shaking into gay life limp priestly vestments that hung upon the walls, setting them to sway and caper in a sabbath of misrule. The forms of the community emerged from the gustblown vestments, the dean of studies, the portly florid bursar with his cap of grey hair, the president, the little priest with feathery hair who wrote devout verses, the squat peasant form of the professor of economics, the tall form of the young professor of mental science discussing on the landing a case of conscience with his class like a giraffe crop= ping high leafage among a herd of antelopes, the grave troubled prefect of the sodality, the plump roundheaded professor of Italian with his rogue's eyes. They came ambling and stum= bling, tumbling and capering, kilting their gowns for leap frog, holding one another back, shaken with deep false laughter, smacking one another behind and laughing at their rude mal= ice, calling to one another by familiar nicknames, protesting with sudden dignity at some rough usage, whispering two and two behind their hands.

The professor had gone to the glass cases on the sidewall from a shelf of which he took down a set of coils, blew away the dust from many points and, bearing it carefully to the table, held a finger on it while he proceeded with his lecture. He explained that the wires in modern coils were of a compound called platinoid lately discovered by F. W. Martino.

He spoke clearly the initials and surname of the discoverer. Moynihan whispered from behind:

—Good old Fresh Water Martin!

—Ask him, Stephen whispered back with weary humour, if he wants a subject for electrocution. He can have me.

Moynihan, seeing the professor bend over the coils, rose in his bench and, clacking noiselessly the fingers of his right hand, began to call with the voice of a slobbering urchin:

—Please, teacher! Please, teacher! This boy is after saying a bad word, teacher.

—Platinoid, the professor said solemnly, is preferred to Ger= man silver because it has a lower coefficient of resistance

650

660

670

680 variation by changes of temperature. The platinoid wire is in=
sulated and the covering of silk that insulates it is wound
double on the ebonite bobbins just where my finger is. If it
were wound single an extra current would be induced in the
coils. The bobbins are saturated in hot paraffinwax ...

A sharp Ulster voice said from the bench below Stephen:
—Are we likely to be asked questions on applied science?

The professor began to juggle gravely with the terms pure
science and applied science. A heavybuilt student wearing gold
spectacles stared with some wonder at the questioner. Moyni=
690 han murmured from behind in his natural voice:
—Isn't MacAlister a devil for his pound of flesh?

Stephen looked down coldly on the oblong skull beneath
him overgrown with tangled twinecoloured hair. The voice, the
accent, the mind of the questioner offended him and he allowed
the offence to carry him towards wilful unkindness, bidding his
mind think that the student's father would have done better
had he sent his son to Belfast to study and have saved some=
thing on the trainfare by so doing.

The oblong skull beneath did not turn to meet this shaft of
700 thought and yet the shaft came back to its bowstring: for he
saw in a moment the student's wheypale face.
—That thought is not mine, he said to himself quickly. It came
from the comic Irishman in the bench behind. Patience. Can
you say with certitude by whom the soul of your race was
bartered and its elect betrayed—by the questioner or by the
mocker? Patience. Remember Epictetus. It is probably in his
character to ask such a question at such a moment in such a
tone and to pronounce the word *science* as a monosyllable.

The droning voice of the professor continued to wind itself
710 slowly round and round the coils it spoke of, doubling,
trebling, quadrupling its somnolent energy as the coil multi=
plied its ohms of resistance.

Moynihan's voice called from behind in echo to a distant
bell:
—Closing time, gents!

The entrance hall was crowded and loud with talk. On a table near the door were two photographs in frames and between them a long roll of paper bearing an irregular tail of signatures. MacCann went briskly to and fro among the students, talking rapidly, answering rebuffs and leading one after another to the table. In the inner hall the dean of studies stood talking to a young professor, stroking his chin gravely and nodding his head.

Stephen, checked by the crowd at the door, halted irresolutely. From under the wide falling leaf of a soft hat Cranly's dark eyes were watching him.

— Have you signed? Stephen asked.

Cranly closed his long thinlipped mouth, communed with himself an instant and answered:

— *Ego habeo.*

— What is it for?

— *Quod?*

— What is it for?

Cranly turned his pale face to Stephen and said blandly and bitterly:

— *Per pax universalis.*

Stephen pointed to the Czar's photograph and said:

— He has the face of a besotted Christ.

The scorn and anger in his voice brought Cranly's eyes back from a calm survey of the walls of the hall.

— Are you annoyed? he asked.

— No, answered Stephen.

— Are you in bad humour?

— No.

— *Credo ut vos sanguinarius mendax estis*, said Cranly, *quia facies vostra monstrat ut vos in damno malo humore estis.*

Moynihan, on his way to the table, said in Stephen's ear:

— MacCann is in tiptop form. Ready to shed the last drop. Brandnew world. No stimulants and votes for the bitches.

Stephen smiled at the manner of this confidence and, when Moynihan had passed, turned again to meet Cranly's eyes.

—Perhaps you can tell me, he said, why he pours his soul so freely into my ear. Can you?

A dull scowl appeared on Cranly's forehead. He stared at the table where Moynihan had bent to write his name on the roll, and then said flatly:

—A sugar!

—*Quis est in malo humore*, said Stephen, *ego aut vos?*

Cranly did not take up the taunt. He brooded sourly on his judgment and repeated with the same flat force:

—A flaming bloody sugar, that's what he is!

It was his epitaph for all dead friendships and Stephen wondered whether it would ever be spoken in the same tone over his memory. The heavy lumpish phrase sank slowly out of hearing like a stone through a quagmire. Stephen saw it sink as he had seen many an other, feeling its heaviness depress his heart. Cranly's speech, unlike that of Davin, had neither rare phrases of Elizabethan English nor quaintly turned versions of Irish idioms. Its drawl was an echo of the quays of Dublin given back by a bleak decaying seaport, its energy an echo of the sacred eloquence of Dublin given back flatly by a Wicklow pulpit.

The heavy scowl faded from Cranly's face as MacCann marched briskly towards them from the other side of the hall.

—Here you are! said MacCann cheerily.

—Here I am! said Stephen.

—Late as usual. Can you not combine the progressive tendency with a respect for punctuality?

—That question is out of order, said Stephen. Next business.

His smiling eyes were fixed on a silverwrapped tablet of milk chocolate which peeped out of the propagandist's breastpocket. A little ring of listeners closed round to hear the war of wits. A lean student with olive skin and lank black hair thrust his face between the two, glancing from one to the other at each phrase and seeming to try to catch each flying phrase in his open moist mouth. Cranly took a small grey handball from his pocket and began to examine it closely, turning it over and over.

—Next business? said MacCann. Hom!

He gave a loud cough of laughter, smiled broadly and tugged twice at the strawcoloured goatee which hung from his blunt chin.   790

—The next business is to sign the testimonial.

—Will you pay me anything if I sign? asked Stephen.

—I thought you were an idealist, said MacCann.

The gipsylike student looked about him and addressed the onlookers in an indistinct bleating voice.

—By hell, that's a queer notion. I consider that notion to be a mercenary notion.

His voice faded into silence. No heed was paid to his words. He turned his olive face, equine in expression, towards Ste=   800 phen, inviting him to speak again.

MacCann began to speak with fluent energy of the Czar's rescript, of Stead, of general disarmament, arbitration in cases of international disputes, of the signs of the times, of the new humanity and the new gospel of life which would make it the business of the community to secure as cheaply as possible the greatest possible happiness of the greatest possible number.

The gipsy student responded to the close of the period by crying:

—Three cheers for universal brotherhood!   810

—Go on, Temple, said a stout ruddy student near him. I'll stand you a pint after.

—I'm a believer in universal brotherhood, said Temple, glancing about him out of his dark oval eyes. Marx is only a bloody cod.

Cranly gripped his arm tightly to check his tongue, smiling uneasily, and repeated:

—Easy, easy, easy!

Temple struggled to free his arm but continued, his mouth flecked by a thin foam: 820

—Socialism was founded by an Irishman and the first man in Europe who preached the freedom of thought was Collins. Two hundred years ago. He denounced priestcraft. The philosopher of Middlesex. Three cheers for John Anthony Collins!

A thin voice from the verge of the ring replied:

—Pip! pip!

Moynihan murmured beside Stephen's ear:

—And what about John Anthony's poor little sister:

> *Lottie Collins lost her drawers;*
> *Won't you kindly lend her yours?*

Stephen laughed and Moynihan, pleased with the result, murmured again:

—We'll have five bob each way on John Anthony Collins.

—I am waiting for your answer, said MacCann briefly.

—The affair doesn't interest me in the least, said Stephen wearily. You knew that well. Why do you make a scene about it?

—Good! said MacCann, smacking his lips. You are a reaction= ary then?

—Do you think you impress me, Stephen asked, when you flourish your wooden sword?

—Metaphors! said MacCann bluntly. Come to facts.

Stephen blushed and turned aside. MacCann stood his ground and said with hostile humour:

—Minor poets, I suppose, are above such trivial questions as the question of universal peace.

Cranly raised his head and held the handball between the two students by way of a peaceoffering, saying:

—*Pax super totum sanguinarium globum.*

Stephen, moving away the bystanders, jerked his shoulder angrily in the direction of the Czar's image, saying:

—Keep your icon. If we must have a Jesus let us have a legit= imate Jesus.

—By hell, that's a good one! said the gipsy student to those about him. That's a fine expression. I like that expression immensely.

He gulped down the spittle in his throat as if he were gulp= ing down the phrase and, fumbling at the peak of his tweed cap, turned to Stephen, saying:

—Excuse me, sir, what do you mean by that expression you   860
uttered just now?

Feeling himself jostled by the students near him, he said to
them:

—I am curious to know now what he meant by that ex=
pression.

He turned again to Stephen and said in a whisper:

—Do you believe in Jesus? I believe in man. Of course, I don't
know if you believe in man. I admire you, sir. I admire the
mind of man independent of all religions. Is that your opinion
about the mind of Jesus?   870

—Go on, Temple, said the stout ruddy student returning, as
was his wont, to his first idea, that pint is waiting for you.

—He thinks I'm an imbecile, Temple explained to Stephen,
because I'm a believer in the power of mind.

Cranly linked his arms into those of Stephen and his admirer
and said:

—*Nos ad manum ballum jocabimus.*

Stephen, in the act of being led away, caught sight of
MacCann's flushed bluntfeatured face.

—My signature is of no account, he said politely. You are right   880
to go your way. Leave me to go mine.

—Dedalus, said MacCann crisply, I believe you're a good fel=
low but you have yet to learn the dignity of altruism and the
responsibility of the human individual.

A voice said:

—Intellectual crankery is better out of this movement than in
it.

Stephen, recognising the harsh tone of MacAlister's voice,
did not turn in the direction of the voice. Cranly pushed sol=
emnly through the throng of students, linking Stephen and   890
Temple like a celebrant attended by his ministers on his way to
the altar.

Temple bent eagerly across Cranly's breast and said:

—Did you hear MacAlister what he said? That youth is jealous
of you. Did you see that? I bet Cranly didn't see that. By hell, I
saw that at once.

As they crossed the inner hall the dean of studies was in the act of escaping from the student with whom he had been conversing. He stood at the foot of the staircase, a foot on the lowest step, his threadbare soutane gathered about him for the ascent with womanish care, nodding his head often and repeating:

—Not a doubt of it, Mr Hackett! Very true! Not a doubt of it!

In the middle of the hall the prefect of the college sodality was speaking earnestly, in a soft querulous voice, with a boarder. As he spoke he wrinkled a little his freckled brow and bit, between his phrases, at a tiny bone pencil.

—I hope the matric men will all come. The first arts men are pretty sure. Second arts too. We must make sure of the newcomers.

Temple bent again across Cranly, as they were passing through the doorway, and said in a swift whisper:

—Do you know that he is a married man? He was a married man before they converted him. He has a wife and children somewhere. By hell, I think that's the queerest notion I ever heard! Eh?

His whisper trailed off into sly cackling laughter. The moment they were through the doorway Cranly seized him rudely by the neck and shook him, saying:

—You flaming floundering fool! I'll take my dying bible there isn't a bigger bloody ape, do you know, than you in the whole flaming bloody world!

Temple wriggled in his grip, laughing still with sly content, while Cranly repeated flatly at every rude shake:

—A flaming flaring bloody idiot!

They crossed the weedy garden together. The president, wrapped in a heavy loose cloak, was coming towards them along one of the walks, reading his office. At the end of the walk he halted before turning and raised his eyes. The students saluted, Temple fumbling as before at the peak of his cap. They walked forward in silence. As they neared the alley Stephen could hear the thuds of the players' hands and the wet smacks of the ball and Davin's voice crying out excitedly at each stroke.

The three students halted round the box on which Davin sat to follow the game. Temple, after a few moments, sidled across to Stephen and said:

—Excuse me, I wanted to ask you do you believe that Jean Jacques Rousseau was a sincere man?

Stephen laughed outright. Cranly, picking up the broken stave of a cask from the grass at his foot, turned swiftly and said sternly:

—Temple, I declare to the living God if you say another word, do you know, to anybody on any subject I'll kill you *super spottum.*

—He was like you, I fancy, said Stephen, an emotional man.

—Blast him, curse him! said Cranly broadly. Don't talk to him at all. Sure you might as well be talking, do you know, to a flaming chamberpot as talking to Temple. Go home, Temple. For God' sake go home.

—I don't care a damn about you, Cranly, answered Temple, moving out of reach of the uplifted stave and pointing at Stephen. He's the only man I see in this institution that has an individual mind.

—Institution! Individual! cried Cranly. Go home, blast you, for you're a hopeless bloody man.

—I'm an emotional man, said Temple. That's quite rightly expressed. And I'm proud that I'm an emotionalist.

He sidled out of the alley, smiling slily. Cranly watched him with a blank expressionless face.

—Look at him! he said. Did you ever see such a go-by-the-wall?

His phrase was greeted by a strange laugh from a student who lounged against the wall, his peaked cap down on his eyes. The laugh, pitched in a high key and coming from a so muscular frame, seemed like the whinny of an elephant. The student's body shook all over and, to ease his mirth, he rubbed both his hands delightedly over his groins.

—Lynch is awake, said Cranly.

Lynch, for answer, straightened himself and thrust forward his chest.

—Lynch puts out his chest, said Stephen, as a criticism of life.

Lynch smote himself sonorously on the chest and said:

—Who has anything to say about my girth?

Cranly took him at the word and the two began to tussle. When their faces had flushed with the struggle they drew apart, panting. Stephen bent down towards Davin who, intent on the game, had paid no heed to the talk of the others.

—And how is my little tame goose? he asked. Did he sign too?

Davin nodded and said:

—And you, Stevie?

Stephen shook his head.

—You're a terrible man, Stevie, said Davin, taking the short pipe from his mouth. Always alone.

—Now that you have signed the petition for universal peace, said Stephen, I suppose you will burn that little copybook I saw in your room.

As Davin did not answer Stephen began to quote:

—Long pace, fianna! Right incline, fianna! Fianna, by num=bers, salute, one, two!

—That's a different question, said Davin. I'm an Irish nation=alist, first and foremost. But that's you all out. You're a born sneerer, Stevie.

—When you make the next rebellion with hurleysticks, said Stephen, and want the indispensable informer, tell me. I can find you a few in this college.

—I can't understand you, said Davin. One time I hear you talk against English literature. Now you talk against the Irish in=formers. What with your name and your ideas .... Are you Irish at all?

—Come with me now to the office of arms and I will show you the tree of my family, said Stephen.

—Then be one of us, said Davin. Why don't you learn Irish? Why did you drop out of the league class after the first lesson?

—You know one reason why, answered Stephen.

Davin tossed his head and laughed.

—O, come now, he said. Is it on account of that certain young lady and Father Moran? But that's all in your own mind, Stevie. They were only talking and laughing.

Stephen paused and laid a friendly hand upon Davin's shoulder.

—Do you remember, he said, when we knew each other first. The first morning we met you asked me to show you the way to the matriculation class, putting a very strong stress on the first syllable. You remember? Then you used to address the jesuits as father, you remember? I ask myself about you: *Is he as innocent as his speech?*

—I'm a simple person, said Davin. You know that. When you told me that night in Harcourt Street those things about your private life, honest to God, Stevie, I was not able to eat my dinner. I was quite bad. I was awake a long time that night. Why did you tell me those things?

—Thanks, said Stephen. You mean I am a monster.

—No, said Davin, but I wish you had not told me.

A tide began to surge beneath the calm surface of Stephen's friendliness.

—This race and this country and this life produced me, he said. I shall express myself as I am.

—Try to be one of us, repeated Davin. In your heart you are an Irishman but your pride is too powerful.

—My ancestors threw off their language and took on another, Stephen said. They allowed a handful of foreigners to subject them. Do you fancy I am going to pay in my own life and person debts they made? What for?

—For our freedom, said Davin.

—No honourable and sincere man, said Stephen, has given up to you his life and his youth and his affections from the days of Tone to those of Parnell but you sold him to the enemy or failed him in need or reviled him and left him for another. And you invite me to be one of you. I'd see you damned first.

—They died for their ideals, Stevie, said Davin. Our day will come yet, believe me.

Stephen, following his own thought, was silent for an in= stant.

—The soul is born, he said vaguely, first in those moments I told you of. It has a slow and dark birth, more mysterious than the birth of the body. When the soul of a man is born in this country there are nets flung at it to hold it back from flight. You talk to me of nationality, language, religion. I shall try to fly by those nets.

Davin knocked the ashes from his pipe.

—Too deep for me, Stevie, he said. But a man's country comes first. Ireland first, Stevie. You can be a poet or a mystic after.

—Do you know what Ireland is? asked Stephen with cold violence. Ireland is the old sow that eats her farrow.

Davin rose from his box and went towards the players, shaking his head sadly. But in a moment his sadness left him and he was hotly disputing with Cranly and the two players who had finished their game. A match of four was arranged, Cranly insisting, however, that his ball should be used. He let it rebound twice or thrice to his hand and then struck it strongly and swiftly towards the base of the alley, exclaiming in answer to its thud:

—Your soul!

Stephen stood with Lynch till the score began to rise. Then he plucked him by the sleeve to come away. Lynch obeyed, saying:

—Let us eke go, as Cranly has it.

Stephen smiled at this sidethrust. They passed back through the garden and out through the hall where the doddering porter was pinning up a notice in the frame. At the foot of the steps they halted and Stephen took a packet of cigarettes from his pocket and offered it to his companion.

—I know you are poor, he said.

—Damn your yellow insolence, answered Lynch.

This second proof of Lynch's culture made Stephen smile again.

—It was a great day for European culture, he said, when you made up your mind to swear in yellow.

They lit their cigarettes and turned to the right. After a pause Stephen began: 1080

—Aristotle has not defined pity and terror. I have. I say ...

Lynch halted and said bluntly:

—Stop! I won't listen! I am sick. I was out last night on a yellow drunk with Horan and Goggins.

Stephen went on:

—Pity is the feeling which arrests the mind in the presence of whatsoever is grave and constant in human sufferings and unites it with the human sufferer. Terror is the feeling which arrests the mind in the presence of whatsoever is grave and 1090 constant in human sufferings and unites it with the secret cause.

—Repeat, said Lynch.

Stephen repeated the definitions slowly.

—A girl got into a hansom a few days ago, he went on, in London. She was on her way to meet her mother whom she had not seen for many years. At the corner of a street the shaft of a lorry shivered the window of the hansom in the shape of a star. A long fine needle of the shivered glass pierced her heart. She died on the instant. The reporter called it a tragic death. It 1100 is not. It is remote from terror and pity according to the terms of my definitions.

The tragic emotion, in fact, is a face looking two ways, towards terror and towards pity, both of which are phases of it. You see I use the word *arrest*. I mean that the tragic emotion is static. Or rather the dramatic emotion is. The feelings excited by improper art are kinetic, desire or loathing. Desire urges us to possess, to go to something, loathing urges us to abandon, to go from something. These are kinetic emotions. The arts which excite them, pornographical or didactic, are 1110 therefore improper arts. The esthetic emotion (I use the general term) is therefore static. The mind is arrested and raised above desire and loathing.

—You say that art must not excite desire, said Lynch. I told you that one day I wrote my name in pencil on the backside of the Venus of Praxiteles in the Museum. Was that not desire?

—I speak of normal natures, said Stephen. You also told me that when you were a boy in that charming carmelite school you ate pieces of dried cowdung.

Lynch broke again into a whinny of laughter and again rubbed both his hands over his groins but without taking them from his pockets.

—O, I did! I did! he cried.

Stephen turned towards his companion and looked at him for a moment boldly in the eyes. Lynch, recovering from his laughter, answered his look from his humbled eyes. The long slender flattened skull beneath the long pointed cap brought before Stephen's mind the image of a hooded reptile. The eyes, too, were reptilelike in glint and gaze. Yet at that instant, humbled and alert in their look, they were lit by one tiny human point, the window of a shrivelled soul, poignant and selfembittered.

—As for that, Stephen said in polite parenthesis, we are all animals. I also am an animal.

—You are, said Lynch.

—But we are just now in a mental world, Stephen continued. The desire and loathing excited by improper esthetic means are really not esthetic emotions not only because they are kinetic in character but also because they are not more than physical. Our flesh shrinks from what it dreads and responds to the stimulus of what it desires by a purely reflex action of the nerv= ous system. Our eyelid closes before we are aware that the fly is about to enter our eye.

—Not always, said Lynch critically.

—In the same way, said Stephen, your flesh responded to the stimulus of a naked statue but it was, I say, simply a reflex action of the nerves. Beauty expressed by the artist cannot awaken in us an emotion which is kinetic or a sensation which is purely physical. It awakens, or ought to awaken, or induces, or ought to induce, an esthetic stasis, an ideal pity or an ideal terror, a stasis called forth, prolonged and at last dissolved by what I call the rhythm of beauty.

—What is that exactly? asked Lynch.

—Rhythm, said Stephen, is the first formal esthetic relation of part to part in any esthetic whole or of an esthetic whole to its part or parts or of any part to the esthetic whole of which it is a part.

—If that is rhythm, said Lynch, let me hear what you call beauty: and, please remember, though I did eat a cake of cow= dung once, that I admire only beauty. ₁₁₆₀

Stephen raised his cap as if in greeting. Then, blushing slightly, he laid his hand on Lynch's thick tweed sleeve.

—We are right, he said, and the others are wrong. To speak of these things and to try to understand their nature and, having understood it, to try slowly and humbly and constantly to express, to press out again, from the gross earth or what it brings forth, from sound and shape and colour which are the prison gates of our soul, an image of the beauty we have come to understand—that is art.

They had reached the canal bridge and, turning from their ₁₁₇₀ course, went on by the trees. A crude grey light, mirrored in the sluggish water, and a smell of wet branches over their heads seemed to war against the course of Stephen's thought.

—But you have not answered my question, said Lynch. What is art? What is the beauty it expresses?

—That was the first definition I gave you, you sleepyheaded wretch, said Stephen, when I began to try to think out the matter for myself. Do you remember the night? Cranly lost his temper and began to talk about Wicklow bacon.

—I remember, said Lynch. He told us about them flaming fat ₁₁₈₀ devils of pigs.

—Art, said Stephen, is the human disposition of sensible or intelligible matter for an esthetic end. You remember the pigs and forget that. You are a distressing pair, you and Cranly.

Lynch made a grimace at the raw grey sky and said:

—If I am to listen to your esthetic philosophy give me at least another cigarette. I don't care about it. I don't even care about women. Damn you and damn everything. I want a job of five hundred a year. You can't get me one.

Stephen handed him the packet of cigarettes. Lynch took the last one that remained, saying simply:

—Proceed!

—Aquinas, said Stephen, says that is beautiful the apprehen= sion of which pleases.

Lynch nodded.

—I remember that, he said. *Pulcra sunt quae visa placent.*

—He uses the word *visa*, said Stephen, to cover esthetic appre= hension of all kinds, whether through sight or hearing or through any other avenue of apprehension. This word, though it is vague, is clear enough to keep away good and evil which excite desire and loathing. It means certainly a stasis and not a kinesis. How about the true? It produces also a stasis of the mind. You would not write your name in pencil across the hypothenuse of a rightangled triangle.

—No, said Lynch. Give me the hypothenuse of the Venus of Praxiteles.

—Static therefore, said Stephen. Plato, I believe, said that beauty is the splendour of truth. I don't think that it has a meaning but the true and the beautiful are akin. Truth is beheld by the intellect which is appeased by the most satisfying relations of the intelligible: beauty is beheld by the imagination which is appeased by the most satisfying relations of the sen= sible. The first step in the direction of truth is to understand the frame and scope of the intellect itself, to comprehend the act itself of intellection. Aristotle's entire system of philosophy rests upon his book of psychology and that, I think, rests on his statement that the same attribute cannot at the same time and in the same connection belong to and not belong to the same subject. The first step in the direction of beauty is to under= stand the frame and scope of the imagination, to comprehend the act itself of esthetic apprehension. Is that clear?

—But what is beauty? asked Lynch impatiently. Out with an=

other definition. Something we see and like! Is that the best you and Aquinas can do?

—Let us take woman, said Stephen.

—Let us take her! said Lynch fervently.

—The Greek, the Turk, the Chinese, the Copt, the Hottentot, said Stephen, all admire a different type of female beauty. That seems to be a maze out of which we cannot escape. I see however two ways out. One is this hypothesis: that every physi= 1230 cal quality admired by men in women is in direct connection with the manifold functions of women for the propagation of the species. It may be so. The world, it seems, is drearier than even you, Lynch, imagined. For my part I dislike that way out. It leads to eugenics rather than to esthetic. It leads you out of the maze into a new gaudy lectureroom where MacCann, with one hand on *The Origin of Species* and the other hand on the new testament, tells you that you admired the great flanks of Venus because you felt that she would bear you burly offspring and admired her great breasts because you felt that she would 1240 give good milk to her children and yours.

—Then MacCann is a sulphuryellow liar, said Lynch energeti= cally.

—There remains another way out, said Stephen laughing.

—To wit? said Lynch.

—This hypothesis, Stephen began.

A long dray laden with old iron came round the corner of sir Patrick Dun's hospital covering the end of Stephen's speech with the harsh roar of jangled and rattling metal. Lynch closed his ears and gave out oath after oath till the dray had passed. 1250 Then he turned on his heel rudely. Stephen turned also and waited for a few moments till his companion's illhumour had had its vent.

—This hypothesis, Stephen repeated, is the other way out: that, though the same object may not seem beautiful to all people, all people who admire a beautiful object find in it certain relations which satisfy and coincide with the stages themselves of all esthetic apprehension. These relations of the

sensible, visible to you through one form and to me through
another, must be therefore the necessary qualities of beauty.
Now, we can return to our old friend saint Thomas for another
pennyworth of wisdom.

Lynch laughed.

—It amuses me vastly, he said, to hear you quoting him time
after time like a jolly round friar. Are you laughing in your
sleeve?

—MacAlister, answered Stephen, would call my esthetic theory applied Aquinas. So far as this side of esthetic philosophy
extends Aquinas will carry me all along the line. When we
come to the phenomenon of artistic conception, artistic gestation and artistic reproduction I require a new terminology and
a new personal experience.

—Of course, said Lynch. After all Aquinas, in spite of his
intellect, was exactly a good round friar. But you will tell me
about the new personal experience and new terminology some
other day. Hurry up and finish the first part.

—Who knows? said Stephen smiling. Perhaps Aquinas would
understand me better than you. He was a poet himself. He
wrote a hymn for Maundy Thursday. It begins with the words
Pange lingua gloriosi. They say it is the highest glory of the
hymnal. It is an intricate and soothing hymn. I like it: but there
is no hymn that can be put beside that mournful and majestic
processional song, the *Vexilla Regis* of Venantius Fortunatus.

Lynch began to sing softly and solemnly in a deep bass
voice:

> *Impleta sunt quae concinit*
> *David fideli carmine*
> *Dicendo nationibus*
> *Regnavit a ligno Deus.*

—That's great! he said, well pleased. Great music!

They turned into Lower Mount Street. A few steps from the
corner a fat young man, wearing a silk neckcloth, saluted them
and stopped.

—Did you hear the results of the exams? he asked. Griffin was plucked. Halpin and O'Flynn are through the home civil. Moonan got fifth place in the Indian. O'Shaughenessy got four= teenth. The Irish fellows in Clarke's gave them a feed last night. They all ate curry.

His pallid bloated face expressed benevolent malice and, as he had advanced through his tidings of success, his small fatencircled eyes vanished out of sight and his weak wheezing voice out of hearing. 1300

In reply to a question of Stephen's his eyes and his voice came forth again from their lurkingplaces.

—Yes. MacCullagh and I, he said. He's taking pure mathemat= ics and I'm taking constitutional history. There are twenty subjects. I'm taking botany too. You know I'm a member of the field club.

He drew back from the other two in a stately fashion and placed a plump woollengloved hand on his breast from which 1310 muttered wheezing laughter at once broke forth.

—Bring us a few turnips and onions the next time you go out said Stephen drily, to make a stew.

The fat student laughed indulgently and said:

—We are all highly respectable people in the field club. Last Saturday we went out to Glenmalure, seven of us.

—With women, Donovan? said Lynch.

Donovan again laid his hand on his chest and said:

—Our end is the acquisition of knowledge.

Then he said quickly: 1320

—I hear you are writing some essay about esthetics.

Stephen made a vague gesture of denial.

—Goethe and Lessing, said Donovan, have written a lot on that subject, the classical school and the romantic school and all that. The *Laocoon* interested me very much when I read it. Of course it is idealistic, German, ultraprofound.

Neither of the others spoke. Donovan took leave of them urbanely.

—I must go, he said softly and benevolently. I have a strong

1330 suspicion, amounting almost to a conviction, that my sister intended to make pancakes today for the dinner of the Don= ovan family.

—Goodbye, Stephen said in his wake. Don't forget the turnips for me and my mate.

Lynch gazed after him, his lip curling in slow scorn till his face resembled a devil's mask:

—To think that that yellow pancakeeating excrement can get a good job, he said at length, and I have to smoke cheap ciga= rettes!

1340 They turned their faces towards Merrion Square and went on for a little in silence.

—To finish what I was saying about beauty, said Stephen, the most satisfying relations of the sensible must therefore corre= spond to the necessary phases of artistic apprehension. Find these and you find the qualities of universal beauty. Aquinas says: *ad pulcritudinem tria requiruntur, integritas, consonantia, claritas.* I translate it so: *Three things are needed for beauty, wholeness, harmony and radiance.* Do these correspond to the phases of apprehension? Are you following?

1350 —Of course, I am, said Lynch. If you think I have an excre= mentitious intelligence run after Donovan and ask him to listen to you.

Stephen pointed to a basket which a butcher's boy had slung inverted on his head.

—Look at that basket, he said.

—I see it, said Lynch.

—In order to see that basket, said Stephen, your mind first of all separates the basket from the rest of the visible universe which is not the basket. The first phase of apprehension is a
1360 bounding line drawn about the object to be apprehended. An esthetic image is presented to us either in space or in time. What is audible is presented in time, what is visible is presented in space. But temporal or spatial the esthetic image is first luminously apprehended as selfbounded and selfcontained upon the immeasurable background of space or time which is

not it. You apprehend it as *one* thing. You see it as one whole.
You apprehend its wholeness. That is *integritas*.

—Bull's eye! said Lynch laughing. Go on.

—Then, said Stephen, you pass from point to point, led by its
formal lines; you apprehend it as balanced part against part   1370
within its limits; you feel the rhythm of its structure. In other
words the synthesis of immediate perception is followed by the
analysis of apprehension. Having first felt that it is *one* thing
you feel now that it is a *thing*. You apprehend it as complex,
multiple, divisible, separable, made up of its parts, the result of
its parts and their sum, harmonious. That is *consonantia*.

—Bull's eye again! said Lynch wittily. Tell me now what is
claritas and you win the cigar.

—The connotation of the word, Stephen said, is rather vague.
Aquinas uses a term which seems to be inexact. It baffled me   1380
for a long time. It would lead you to believe that he had in
mind symbolism or idealism, the supreme quality of beauty
being a light from some other world, the idea of which the
matter is but the shadow, the reality of which it is but the
symbol. I thought he might mean that *claritas* is the artistic
discovery and representation of the divine purpose in anything
or a force of generalisation which would make the esthetic
image a universal one, make it outshine its proper conditions.
But that is literary talk. I understand it so. When you have
apprehended that basket as one thing and have then analysed it   1390
according to its form and apprehended it as a thing you make
the only synthesis which is logically and esthetically permiss=
ible. You see that it is that thing which it is and no other thing.
The radiance of which he speaks is the scholastic *quidditas*, the
whatness of a thing. This supreme quality is felt by the artist
when the esthetic image is first conceived in his imagination.
The mind in that mysterious instant Shelley likened beautifully
to a fading coal. The instant wherein that supreme quality of
beauty, the clear radiance of the esthetic image, is apprehended
luminously by the mind which has been arrested by its whole=   1400
ness and fascinated by its harmony is the luminous silent stasis

of esthetic pleasure, a spiritual state very like to that cardiac condition which the Italian physiologist Luigi Galvani, using a phrase almost as beautiful as Shelley's, called the enchantment of the heart.

Stephen paused and, though his companion did not speak, felt that his words had called up around them a thoughten= chanted silence.

1410 —What I have said, he began again, refers to beauty in the wider sense of the word, in the sense which the word has in the literary tradition. In the marketplace it has another sense. When we speak of beauty in the second sense of the term our judgment is influenced in the first place by the art itself and by the form of that art. The image, it is clear, must be set between the mind or senses of the artist himself and the mind or senses of others. If you bear this in memory you will see that art necessarily divides itself into three forms progressing from one to the next. These forms are: the lyrical form, the form wherein the artist presents his image in immediate relation to himself; 1420 the epical form, the form wherein he presents his image in mediate relation to himself and to others; the dramatic form, the form wherein he presents his image in immediate relation to others.

—That you told me a few nights ago, said Lynch, and we began the famous discussion.

—I have a book at home, said Stephen, in which I have written down questions which are more amusing than yours were. In finding the answers to them I found the theory of esthetic which I am trying to explain. Here are some questions I set 1430 myself: *Is a chair finely made tragic or comic? Is the portrait of Mona Lisa good if I desire to see it? Is the bust of sir Philip Crampton lyrical, epical or dramatic? Can excrement or a child or a louse be a work of art? If not, why not?*

—Why not, indeed? said Lynch laughing.

—*If a man hacking in fury at a block of wood*, Stephen con= tinued, *make there an image of a cow is that image a work of art? If not, why not?*

—That's a lovely one, said Lynch laughing again. That has the true scholastic stink.

—Lessing, said Stephen, should not have taken a group of statues to write of. The art, being inferior, does not present the forms I spoke of distinguished clearly one from another. Even in literature, the highest and most spiritual art, the forms are often confused. The lyrical form is in fact the simplest verbal vesture of an instant of emotion, a rhythmical cry such as ages ago cheered on the man who pulled at the oar or dragged stones up a slope. He who utters it is more conscious of the instant of emotion than of himself as feeling emotion. The simplest epical form is seen emerging out of lyrical literature when the artist prolongs and broods upon himself as the centre of an epical event and this form progresses till the centre of emotional gravity is equidistant from the artist himself and from others. The narrative is no longer purely personal. The personality of the artist passes into the narration itself, flowing round and round the persons and the action like a vital sea. This progress you will see easily in that old English ballad *Turpin Hero* which begins in the first person and ends in the third person. The dramatic form is reached when the vitality which has flowed and eddied round each person fills every person with such vital force that he or she assumes a proper and intangible esthetic life. The personality of the artist at first a cry or a cadence or a mood and then a fluid and lambent narrative finally refines itself out of existence, impersonalises itself, so to speak. The esthetic image in the dramatic form is life purified in and reprojected from the human imagination. The mystery of esthetic like that of material creation is accom= plished. The artist, like the God of the creation, remains within or behind or beyond or above his handiwork, invisible, refined out of existence, indifferent, paring his fingernails.

—Trying to refine them also out of existence, said Lynch.

A fine rain began to fall from the high veiled sky and they turned into the duke's lawn to reach the national library before the shower came.

—What do you mean, Lynch asked surlily, by prating about beauty and the imagination in this miserable Godforsaken is= land? No wonder the artist retired within or behind his handi= work after having perpetrated this country.

The rain fell faster. When they passed through the passage beside Kildare house they found many students sheltering un= der the arcade of the library. Cranly leaning against a pillar was picking his teeth with a sharpened match, listening to some companions. Some girls stood near the entrance door. Lynch whispered to Stephen:

—Your beloved is here.

Stephen took his place silently on the step below the group of students, heedless of the rain which fell fast, turning his eyes towards her from time to time. She too stood silently among her companions. She has no priest to flirt with, he thought with conscious bitterness, remembering how he had seen her last. Lynch was right. His mind, emptied of theory and courage, lapsed back into a listless peace.

He heard the students talking among themselves. They spoke of two friends who had passed the final medical exam= ination, of the chances of getting places on ocean liners, of poor and rich practices.

—That's all a bubble. An Irish country practice is better.

—Hynes was two years in Liverpool and he says the same. A frightful hole he said it was. Nothing but midwifery cases. Half a crown cases.

—Do you mean to say it is better to have a job here in the country than in a rich city like that? I know a fellow ....

—Hynes has no brains. He got through by stewing, pure stewing.

—Don't mind him. There's plenty of money to be made in a big commercial city.

—Depends on the practice.

—*Ego credo ut vita pauperum est simpliciter atrox, simpliciter sanguinarius atrox, in Liverpoolio.*

Their voices reached his ears as if from a distance in inter=

rupted pulsation. She was preparing to go away with her companions.

The quick light shower had drawn off, tarrying in clusters of diamonds among the shrubs of the quadrangle where an exha=lation was breathed forth by the blackened earth. Their trim boots prattled as they stood on the steps of the colonnade talking quietly and gaily, glancing at the clouds, holding their umbrellas at cunning angles against the few last raindrops, closing them again, holding their skirts demurely.

And if he had judged her harshly? If her life were a simple rosary of hours, her life simple and strange as a bird's life, gay in the morning, restless all day, tired at sundown? Her heart simple and wilful as a bird's heart?

◆   ◆   ◆

Towards dawn he awoke. O what sweet music! His soul was all dewy wet. Over his limbs in sleep pale cool waves of light had passed. He lay still, as if his soul lay amid cool waters, conscious of faint sweet music. His mind was waking slowly to a tremulous morning knowledge, a morning inspiration. A spirit filled him, pure as the purest water, sweet as dew, moving as music. But how faintly it was inbreathed, how passionlessly as if the seraphim themselves were breathing upon him! His soul was waking slowly, fearing to awake wholly. It was that windless hour of dawn when madness wakes and strange plants open to the light and the moth flies forth silently.

An enchantment of the heart! The night had been enchanted. In dream or vision he had known the ecstasy of seraphic life. Was it an instant of enchantment only or long hours and days and years and ages?

The instant of inspiration seemed now to be reflected from all sides at once from a multitude of cloudy circumstance of what had happened or of what might have happened. The in= stant flashed forth like a point of light and now from cloud on cloud of vague circumstance confused form was veiling softly its afterglow. O! In the virgin womb of the imagination the word was made flesh. Gabriel the seraph had come to the virgin's chamber. An afterglow deepened within his spirit, whence the white flame had passed, deepening to a rose and ardent light. That rose and ardent light was her strange wilful heart, strange that no man had known or would know, wilful from before the beginning of the world: and lured by that ardent roselike glow the choirs of the seraphim were falling from heaven.

> Are you not weary of ardent ways,
> Lure of the fallen seraphim?
> Tell no more of enchanted days.

The verses passed from his mind to his lips and, murmuring them over, he felt the rhythmic movement of a villanelle pass through them. The roselike glow sent forth its rays of rhyme; ways, days, blaze, praise, raise. Its rays burned up the world, consumed the hearts of men and angels: the rays from the rose that was her wilful heart.

> Your eyes have set man's heart ablaze
> And you have had your will of him.
> Are you not weary of ardent ways?

And then? The rhythm died away, ceased, began again to move and beat. And then? Smoke, incense ascending from the altar of the world.

> Above the flame the smoke of praise
> Goes up from ocean rim to rim.
> Tell no more of enchanted days.

Smoke went up from the whole earth, from the vapoury oceans, smoke of her praise. The earth was like a swinging swaying smoking censer, a ball of incense, an ellipsoidal ball. The rhythm died out at once; the cry of his heart was broken. His lips began to murmur the first verses over and over; then went on stumbling through half verses, stammering and baffled; then stopped. The heart's cry was broken.

The veiled windless hour had passed and behind the panes

of the naked window the morning light was gathering. A bell beat faintly very far away. A bird twittered; two birds, three. The bell and the birds ceased: and the dull white light spread itself east and west, covering the world, covering the roselight in his heart.   1580

Fearing to lose all he raised himself suddenly on his elbow to look for paper and pencil. There was neither on the table; only the soup plate he had eaten the rice from for supper and the candlestick with its tendrils of tallow and its paper socket, singed by the last flame. He stretched his arm wearily towards the foot of the bed, groping with his hand in the pockets of the coat that hung there. His fingers found a pencil and then a cigarette packet. He lay back and, tearing open the packet,   1590 placed the last cigarette on the window ledge and began to write out the stanzas of the villanelle in small neat letters on the rough cardboard surface.

Having written them out he lay back on the lumpy pillow, murmuring them again. The lumps of knotted flock under his head reminded him of the lumps of knotted horsehair in the sofa of her parlour on which he used to sit, smiling or serious, asking himself why he had come, displeased with her and with himself, confounded by the print of the Sacred Heart above the untenanted sideboard. He saw her approach him in a lull of the   1600 talk and beg him to sing one of his curious songs. Then he saw himself sitting at the old piano, striking chords softly from its speckled keys and singing, amid the talk which had risen again in the room, to her who leaned beside the mantelpiece a dainty song of the Elizabethans, a sad and sweet loth to depart, the victory chant of Agincourt, the happy air of Greensleeves. While he sang and she listened, or feigned to listen, his heart was at rest but when the quaint old songs had ended and he heard again the voices in the room he remembered his own sarcasm: the house where young men are called by their chris=   1610 tian names a little too soon.

At certain instants her eyes seemed about to trust him but he had waited in vain. She passed now dancing lightly across his memory as she had been that night at the carnival ball. Her

white dress a little lifted, a white spray nodding in her hair. She
danced lightly in the round. She was dancing towards him and,
as she came, her eyes were a little averted and a faint glow was
on her cheek. At the pause in the chain of hands her hand had
lain in his an instant, a soft merchandise.

1620 — You are a great stranger now.

— Yes. I was born to be a monk.

— I am afraid you are a heretic.

— Are you much afraid?

For answer she had danced away from him along the chain
of hands, dancing lightly and discreetly, giving herself to none.
The white spray nodded to her dancing and when she was in
shadow the glow was deeper on her cheek.

A monk! His own image started forth a profaner of the
cloister, a heretic franciscan, willing and willing not to serve,
1630 spinning like Gherardino da Borgo San Donnino a lithe web of
sophistry and whispering in her ear.

No, it was not his image. It was the image of the young
priest in whose company he had seen her last, looking at him
out of dove's eyes, toying with the pages of her Irish phrase=
book.

— Yes, yes, the ladies are coming round to us. I can see it every
day. The ladies are with us. The best helpers the language has.

— And the church, Father Moran?

— The church too. Coming round too. The work is going
1640 ahead there too. Don't fret about the church.

Bah! he had done well to leave the room in disdain. He had
done well not to salute her on the steps of the library. He had
done well to leave her to flirt with her priest, to toy with a
church which was the scullerymaid of christendom.

Rude brutal anger routed the last lingering instant of ecstasy
from his soul. It broke up violently her fair image and flung the
fragments on all sides. On all sides distorted reflections of her
image started from his memory: the flowergirl in the ragged
dress with damp coarse hair and a hoyden's face who had
1650 called herself his own girl and begged his handsel, the kitchen=

girl in the next house who sang over the clatter of her plates with the drawl of a country singer the first bars of *By Killarney's Lakes and Fells*, a girl who had laughed gaily to see him stumble when the iron grating in the footpath near Cork Hill had caught the broken sole of his shoe, a girl he had glanced at, attracted by her small ripe mouth as she passed out of Jacob's biscuit factory, who had cried to him over her shoulder:

—Do you like what you seen of me, straight hair and curly eyebrows?

1660

And yet he felt that, however he might revile and mock her image, his anger was also a form of homage. He had left the classroom in disdain that was not wholly sincere, feeling that perhaps the secret of her race lay behind those dark eyes upon which her long lashes flung a quick shadow. He had told himself bitterly as he walked through the streets that she was a figure of the womanhood of her country, a batlike soul waking to the consciousness of itself in darkness and secrecy and loneliness, tarrying a while, loveless and sinless, with her mild lover and leaving him to whisper of innocent transgressions in the 1670 latticed ear of a priest. His anger against her found vent in coarse railing at her paramour, whose name and voice and features offended his baffled pride: a priested peasant, with a brother a policeman in Dublin and a brother a potboy in Moycullen. To him she would unveil her soul's shy nakedness, to one who was but schooled in the discharging of a formal rite rather than to him, a priest of the eternal imagination, transmuting the daily bread of experience into the radiant body of everliving life.

The radiant image of the eucharist united again in an instant 1680 his bitter and despairing thoughts, their cries arising unbroken in a hymn of thanksgiving.

> *Our broken cries and mournful lays*
> *Rise in one eucharistic hymn.*
> *Are you not weary of ardent ways?*

While sacrificing hands upraise
The chalice flowing to the brim.
Tell no more of enchanted days.

He spoke the verses aloud from the first lines till the music and rhythm suffused his mind, turning it to quiet indulgence; then copied them painfully to feel them the better by seeing them; then lay back on his bolster.

The full morning light had come. No sound was to be heard: but he knew that all around him life was about to awaken in common noises, hoarse voices, sleepy prayers. Shrinking from that life he turned towards the wall, making a cowl of the blanket and staring at the great overblown scarlet flowers of the tattered wallpaper. He tried to warm his perishing joy in their scarlet glow, imagining a roseway from where he lay upwards to heaven all strewn with scarlet flowers. Weary! Weary! He too was weary of ardent ways.

A gradual warmth, a languorous weariness passed over him descending along his spine from his closely cowled head. He felt it descend and, seeing himself as he lay, smiled. Soon he would sleep.

He had written verses for her again after ten years. Ten years before she had worn her shawl cowlwise about her head, send= ing sprays of her warm breath into the night air, tapping her foot upon the glassy road. It was the last tram; the lank brown horses knew it and shook their bells to the clear night in admonition. The conductor talked with the driver, both nod= ding often in the green light of the lamp. They stood on the steps of the tram, he on the upper, she on the lower. She came up to his step many times between their phrases and went down again and once or twice remained beside him forgetting to go down and then went down. Let be! Let be!

Ten years from that wisdom of children to his folly. If he sent her the verses? They would be read out at breakfast amid the tapping of eggshells. Folly indeed! The brothers would laugh and try to wrest the page from each other with their strong hard fingers. The suave priest, her uncle, seated in his armchair, would hold the page at arm's length, read it smiling and approve of the literary form.

No, no: that was folly. Even if he sent her the verses she would not show them to others. No, no: she could not.

He began to feel that he had wronged her. A sense of her innocence moved him almost to pity her, an innocence he had never understood till he had come to the knowledge of it through sin, an innocence which she too had not understood while she was innocent or before the strange humiliation of her nature had first come upon her. Then first her soul had begun to live as his soul had when he had first sinned: and a tender compassion filled his heart as he remembered her frail pallor and her eyes, humbled and saddened by the dark shame of womanhood.

While his soul had passed from ecstasy to languor where had she been? Might it be, in the mysterious ways of spiritual life, that her soul at those same moments had been conscious of his homage? It might be.

A glow of desire kindled again his soul and fired and ful=filled all his body. Conscious of his desire she was waking from odorous sleep, the temptress of his villanelle. Her eyes, dark and with a look of languor, were opening to his eyes. Her nakedness yielded to him, radiant, warm, odorous and lavish=limbed, enfolded him like a shining cloud, enfolded him like water with a liquid life: and like a cloud of vapour or like waters circumfluent in space the liquid letters of speech, sym=bols of the element of mystery, flowed forth over his brain.

> *Are you not weary of ardent ways?*
> *Lure of the fallen seraphim.*
> *Tell no more of enchanted days.*
>
> *Your eyes have set man's heart ablaze*
> *And you have had your will of him.*
> *Are you not weary of ardent ways?*

1730

1740

1750

Above the flame the smoke of praise
Goes up from ocean rim to rim.
Tell no more of enchanted days.

Our broken cries and mournful lays
Rise in one eucharistic hymn.
Are you not weary of ardent ways?

While sacrificing hands upraise
The chalice flowing to the brim.
Tell no more of enchanted days.

And still you hold our longing gaze
With languorous look and lavish limb.
Are you not weary of ardent ways?
Tell no more of enchanted days.

◆ ◆ ◆

What birds were they?

He stood on the steps of the library to look at them, leaning
wearily on his ashplant. They flew round and round the jutting
shoulder of a house in Molesworth Street. The air of the late
March evening made clear their flight, their dark darting
quivering bodies flying clearly against the sky as against a
limphung cloth of smoky tenuous blue.

He watched their flight: bird after bird: a dark flash, a
swerve, a flash again, a dart aside, a curve, a flutter of wings.
He tried to count them before all their darting quivering bodies
passed: six, ten, eleven: and wondered were they odd or even in
number. Twelve, thirteen: for two came wheeling down from
the upper sky. They were flying high and low but ever round
and round in straight and curving lines and ever flying from left
to right, circling about a temple of air.

He listened to their cries: like the squeak of mice behind the
wainscot: a shrill twofold note. But the notes were long and
shrill and whirring, unlike the cry of vermin, falling a third or a
fourth and trilled as the flying beaks clove the air. Their cry

was shrill and clear and fine and falling like threads of silken light unwound from whirring spools.

The inhuman clamour soothed his ears in which his mother's sobs and reproaches murmured insistently and the dark frail quivering bodies wheeling and fluttering and swerv= ing round an airy temple of the tenuous sky soothed his eyes which still saw the image of his mother's face. 1790

Why was he gazing upwards from the steps of the porch, hearing their shrill twofold cry, watching their flight? For an augury of good or evil? A phrase of Cornelius Agrippa flew through his mind and then there flew hither and thither shape= less thoughts from Swedenborg on the correspondence of birds to things of the intellect and of how the creatures of the air have their knowledge and know their times and seasons be= cause they, unlike man, are in the order of their life and have not perverted that order by reason. 1800

And for ages men had gazed upward as he was gazing at birds in flight. The colonnade above him made him think vaguely of an ancient temple and the ashplant on which he leaned wearily of the curved stick of an augur. A sense of fear of the unknown moved in the heart of his weariness, a fear of symbols and portents, of the hawklike man whose name he bore soaring out of his captivity on osierwoven wings, of Thoth, the god of writers, writing with a reed upon a tablet and bearing on his narrow ibis head the cusped moon. 1810

He smiled as he thought of the god's image for it made him think of a bottlenosed judge in a wig, putting commas into a document which he held at arm's length and he knew that he would not have remembered the god's name but that it was like an Irish oath. It was folly. But was it for this folly that he was about to leave for ever the house of prayer and prudence into which he had been born and the order of life out of which he had come?

They came back with shrill cries over the jutting shoulder of the house, flying darkly against the fading air. What birds were they? He thought that they must be swallows who had come 1820 back from the south. Then he was to go away? for they were birds ever going and coming, building ever an unlasting home under the eaves of men's houses and ever leaving the homes they had built to wander.

> *Bend down your faces, Oona and Aleel.*
> *I gaze upon them as the swallow gazes*
> *Upon the nest under the eave before*
> *He wander the loud waters.*

A soft liquid joy like the noise of many waters flowed over his memory and he felt in his heart the soft peace of silent spaces of fading tenuous sky above the waters, of oceanic si= lence, of swallows flying through the seadusk over the flowing waters.

A soft liquid joy flowed through the words where the soft long vowels hurtled noiselessly and fell away, lapping and flowing back and ever shaking the white bells of their waves in mute chime and mute peal and soft low swooning cry: and he felt that the augury he had sought in the wheeling darting birds and in the pale space of sky above him had come forth from his heart like a bird from a turret quietly and swiftly.

Symbol of departure or of loneliness? The verses crooned in the ear of his memory composed slowly before his remember= ing eyes the scene of the hall on the night of the opening of the national theatre. He was alone at the side of the balcony, looking out of jaded eyes at the culture of Dublin in the stalls and at the tawdry scenecloths and human dolls framed by the garish lamps of the stage. A burly policeman sweated behind him and seemed at every moment about to act. The catcalls and hisses and mocking cries ran in rude gusts round the hall from his scattered fellowstudents.

—A libel on Ireland!

—Made in Germany!

—Blasphemy!

—We never sold our faith!

—No Irish woman ever did it!

—We want no amateur atheists.

—We want no budding buddhists.

A sudden soft hiss fell from the windows above him and he knew that the electric lamps had been switched on in the readers' room. He turned into the pillared hall, now calmly lit, went up the staircase and passed in through the clicking turn=stile.

Cranly was sitting over near the dictionaries. A thick book, opened at the frontispiece, lay before him on the wooden rest. He leaned back in his chair, inclining his ear like that of a confessor to the face of the medical student who was reading to him a problem from the chess page of a journal. Stephen sat down at his right and the priest at the other side of the table closed his copy of *The Tablet* with an angry snap and stood up.

Cranly gazed after him blandly and vaguely. The medical student went on in a softer voice:

—Pawn to king's fourth.

—We had better go, Dixon, said Stephen in warning. He has gone to complain.

Dixon folded the journal and rose with dignity, saying:

—Our men retired in good order.

—With guns and cattle, added Stephen, pointing to the title=page of Cranly's book on which was printed *Diseases of the Ox*.

As they passed through a lane of the tables Stephen said:

—Cranly, I want to speak to you.

Cranly did not answer or turn. He laid his book on the counter and passed out, his wellshod feet sounding flatly on the floor. On the staircase he paused and gazing absently at Dixon repeated:

—Pawn to king's bloody fourth.

—Put it that way if you like, Dixon said.

He had a quiet toneless voice and urbane manners and on a finger of his plump clean hand he displayed at moments a signet ring.

As they crossed the hall a man of dwarfish stature came

towards them. Under the dome of his tiny hat his unshaven face began to smile with pleasure and he was heard to murmur. The eyes were melancholy as those of a monkey.

—Good evening, captain, said Cranly, halting.

—Good evening, gentlemen, said the stubblegrown monkeyish face.

—Warm weather for March, said Cranly. They have the windows open upstairs.

Dixon smiled and turned his ring. The blackish monkeypuckered face pursed its human mouth with gentle pleasure and its voice purred:

—Delightful weather for March. Simply delightful.

—There are two nice young ladies upstairs, captain, tired of waiting, Dixon said.

Cranly smiled and said kindly:

—The captain has only one love: sir Walter Scott. Isn't that so, captain?

—What are you reading now, captain? Dixon asked. *The Bride of Lammermoor?*

—I love old Scott, the flexible lips said. I think he writes something lovely. There is no writer can touch sir Walter Scott.

He moved a thin shrunken brown hand gently in the air in time to his praise and his thin quick eyelids beat often over his sad eyes.

Sadder to Stephen's ear was his speech: a genteel accent, low and moist, marred by errors: and listening to it he wondered was the story true and was the thin blood that flowed in his shrunken frame noble and come of an incestuous love?

The park trees were heavy with rain and rain fell still and ever in the lake, lying grey like a shield. A game of swans flew there and the water and the shore beneath were fouled with their greenwhite slime. They embraced softly impelled by the grey rainy light, the wet silent trees, the shieldlike witnessing lake, the swans. They embraced without joy or passion, his arm about his sister's neck. A grey woollen cloak was wrapped athwart from her shoulder to her waist: and her fair head was

bent in willing shame. He had loose redbrown hair and tender 1930
shapely strong freckled hands. Face? There was no face seen.
The brother's face was bent upon her fair rainfragrant hair.
The hand freckled and strong and shapely and caressing was
Davin's hand.

He frowned angrily upon his thought and on the shrivelled
mannikin who had called it forth. His father's gibes at the
Bantry gang leaped out of his memory. He held them at a
distance and brooded uneasily on his own thought again. Why
were they not Cranly's hands? Had Davin's simplicity and in= 1940
nocence stung him more secretly?

He walked on across the hall with Dixon, leaving Cranly to
take leave elaborately of the dwarf.

Under the colonnade Temple was standing in the midst of a
little group of students. One of them cried:

—Dixon, come over till you hear. Temple is in grand form.

Temple turned on him his dark gipsy eyes.

—You're a hypocrite, O'Keeffe, he said. And Dixon's a smiler.
By hell, I think that's a good literary expression.

He laughed slily, looking in Stephen's face, repeating:

—By hell, I'm delighted with that name. A smiler. 1950

A stout student who stood below them on the steps said:

—Come back to the mistress, Temple. We want to hear about
that.

—He had, faith, Temple said. And he was a married man too.
And all the priests used to be dining there. By hell, I think they
all had a touch.

—We shall call it riding a hack to spare the hunter, said Dixon.

—Tell us, Temple, O'Keeffe said. How many quarts of porter
have you in you?

—All your intellectual soul is in that phrase, O'Keeffe, said 1960
Temple with open scorn.

He moved with a shambling gait round the group and spoke
to Stephen.

—Did you know that the Forsters are the kings of Belgium? he
asked.

Cranly came out through the door of the entrance hall, his hat thrust back on the nape of his neck and picking his teeth with care.

—And here's the wiseacre, said Temple. Do you know that about the Forsters?

He paused for an answer. Cranly dislodged a figseed from his teeth on the point of his rude toothpick and gazed at it intently.

—The Forster family, Temple said, is descended from Baldwin the First, king of Flanders. He was called the Forester. Forester and Forster are the same name. A descendant of Baldwin the First, captain Francis Forster, settled in Ireland and married the daughter of the last chieftain of Clanbrassil. Then there are the Blake Forsters. That's a different branch.

—From Baldhead, king of Flanders, Cranly repeated, rooting again deliberately at his gleaming uncovered teeth.

—Where did you pick up all that history? O'Keeffe asked.

—I know all the history of your family too, Temple said, turning to Stephen. Do you know what Giraldus Cambrensis says about your family?

—Is he descended from Baldwin too? asked a tall consumptive student with dark eyes.

—Baldhead, Cranly repeated, sucking at a crevice in his teeth.

—*Pernobilis et pervetusta familia*, Temple said to Stephen.

The stout student who stood below them on the steps farted briefly. Dixon turned towards him saying in a soft voice:

—Did an angel speak?

Cranly turned also and said vehemently but without anger:

—Goggins, you're the flamingest dirty devil I ever met, do you know.

—I had it on my mind to say that, Goggins answered firmly. It did no-one any harm, did it?

—We hope, Dixon said suavely, that it was not of the kind known to science as a *paulo post futurum*.

—Didn't I tell you he was a smiler? said Temple, turning right and left. Didn't I give him that name?

— You did. We're not deaf, said the tall consumptive.

Cranly still frowned at the stout student below him. Then, with a snort of disgust, he shoved him violently down the steps.

— Go away from here, he said rudely. Go away, you stinkpot. And you are a stinkpot.

Goggins skipped down on to the gravel and at once returned to his place with good humour. Temple turned back to Stephen and asked:

— Do you believe in the law of heredity?

— Are you drunk or what are you or what are you trying to say? asked Cranly, facing round on him with an expression of wonder.

— The most profound sentence ever written, Temple said with enthusiasm, is the sentence at the end of the zoology. Repro= duction is the beginning of death.

He touched Stephen timidly at the elbow and said eagerly:

— Do you feel how profound that is because you are a poet?

Cranly pointed his long forefinger.

— Look at him! he said with scorn to the others. Look at Ireland's hope!

They laughed at his words and gesture. Temple turned on him bravely, saying:

— Cranly, you're always sneering at me. I can see that. But I am as good as you are any day. Do you know what I think about you now as compared with myself?

— My dear man, said Cranly urbanely, you are incapable, do you know, absolutely incapable of thinking.

— But do you know, Temple went on, what I think of you and of myself compared together?

— Out with it, Temple! the stout student cried from the steps. Get it out in bits!

Temple turned right and left, making sudden feeble gestures as he spoke.

— I'm a ballocks, he said, shaking his head in despair. I am. And I know I am. And I admit it that I am.

Dixon patted him lightly on the shoulder and said mildly:

—And it does you every credit, Temple.

—But he, Temple said, pointing to Cranly. He is a ballocks too
like me. Only he doesn't know it. And that's the only difference
I see.

A burst of laughter covered his words. But he turned again
to Stephen and said with a sudden eagerness:

—That word is a most interesting word. That's the only Eng=
lish dual number. Did you know?

—Is it? Stephen said vaguely.

He was watching Cranly's firmfeatured suffering face, lit up
now by a smile of false patience. The gross name had passed
over it like foul water poured over an old stone image, patient
of injuries: and, as he watched him, he saw him raise his hat in
salute and uncover the black hair that stood up stiffly from his
forehead like an iron crown.

She passed out from the porch of the library and bowed
across Stephen in reply to Cranly's greeting. He also? Was there
not a slight flush on Cranly's cheek? Or had it come forth at
Temple's words? The light had waned. He could not see.

Did that explain his friend's listless silence, his harsh com=
ments, the sudden intrusions of rude speech with which he had
shattered so often Stephen's ardent wayward confessions? Ste=
phen had forgiven freely for he had found this rudeness also in
himself towards himself. And he remembered an evening when
he had dismounted from a borrowed creaking bicycle to pray
to God in a wood near Malahide. He had lifted up his arms
and spoken in ecstasy to the sombre nave of the trees, knowing
that he stood on holy ground and in a holy hour. And when
two constabularymen had come into sight round a bend in the
gloomy road he had broken off his prayer to whistle loudly an
air from the last pantomime.

He began to beat the frayed end of his ashplant against the
base of a pillar. Had Cranly not heard him? Yet he could wait.
The talk about him ceased for a moment: and a soft hiss fell
again from a window above. But no other sound was in the air
and the swallows whose flight he had followed with idle eyes
were sleeping.

She had passed through the dusk. And therefore the air was silent save for one soft hiss that fell. And therefore the tongues about him had ceased their babble. Darkness was falling.

Darkness falls from the air.

A trembling joy, lambent as a faint light, played like a fairy host around him. But why? Her passage through the darkening air or the verse with its black vowels and its opening sound, rich and lutelike?

He walked away slowly towards the deeper shadows at the end of the colonnade, beating the stone softly with his stick to hide his revery from the students whom he had left: and allowed his mind to summon back to itself the age of Dowland and Byrd and Nash.

Eyes, opening from the darkness of desire, eyes that dimmed the breaking east. What was their languid grace but the softness of chambering? And what was their shimmer but the shimmer of the scum that mantled the cesspool of the court of a slobbering Stuart. And he tasted in the language of memory ambered wines, dying fallings of sweet airs, the proud pavan: and saw with the eyes of memory kind gentlewomen in Covent Garden wooing from their balconies with sucking mouths and the poxfouled wenchers of the taverns and young wives that, gaily yielding to their ravishers, clipped and clipped again.

The images he had summoned gave him no pleasure. They were secret and enflaming but her image was not entangled by them. That was not the way to think of her. It was not even the way in which he thought of her. Could his mind then not trust itself? Old phrases, sweet only with a disinterred sweetness like the figseeds Cranly rooted out of his gleaming teeth.

It was not thought nor vision though he knew vaguely that her figure was passing homeward through the city. Vaguely first and then more sharply he smelt her body. A conscious unrest seethed in his blood. Yes, it was her body that he smelt: a wild and languid smell: the tepid limbs over which his music had flowed desirously and the secret soft linen upon which her flesh distilled odour and a dew.

A louse crawled over the nape of his neck and, putting his thumb and forefinger deftly beneath his loose collar, he caught it. He rolled its body, tender yet brittle as a grain of rice, be= tween thumb and finger for an instant before he let it fall from him and wondered would it live or die. There came to his mind a curious phrase from Cornelius a Lapide which said that the lice born of human sweat were not created by God with the other animals on the sixth day. But the tickling of the skin of his neck made his mind raw and red. The life of his body, illclad, illfed, louseeaten, made him close his eyelids in a sud= den spasm of despair: and in the darkness he saw the brittle bright bodies of lice falling from the air and turning often as they fell. Yes: and it was not darkness that fell from the air. It was brightness.

Brightness falls from the air.

He had not even remembered rightly Nash's line. All the images it had awakened were false. His mind bred vermin. His thoughts were lice born of the sweat of sloth.

He came back quickly along the colonnade towards the group of students. Well then let her go and be damned to her. She could love some clean athlete who washed himself every morning to the waist and had black hair on his chest. Let her.

Cranly had taken another dried fig from the supply in his pocket and was eating it slowly and noisily. Temple sat on the pediment of a pillar, leaning back, his cap pulled down on his sleepy eyes. A squat young man came out of the porch, a leather portfolio tucked under his armpit. He marched towards the group, striking the flags with the heels of his boots and with the ferrule of his heavy umbrella. Then, raising the um= brella in salute, he said to all:

—Good evening, sirs.

He struck the flags again and tittered while his head trembled with a slight nervous movement. The tall consump= tive student and Dixon and O'Keeffe were speaking in Irish and did not answer him. Then, turning to Cranly, he said:

—Good evening, particularly to you.

He moved the umbrella in indication and tittered again. Cranly, who was still chewing the fig, answered with loud movements of his jaws.

—Good? Yes. It is a good evening. 2150

The squat student looked at him seriously and shook his umbrella gently and reprovingly.

—I can see, he said, that you are about to make obvious remarks.

—Um, Cranly answered, holding out what remained of the halfchewed fig and jerking it towards the squat student's mouth in sign that he should eat.

The squat student did not eat it but, indulging his special humour, said gravely, still tittering and prodding his phrase with his umbrella: 2160

—Do you intend that ...

He broke off, pointed bluntly to the munched pulp of the fig and said loudly:

—I allude to that.

—Um, Cranly said as before.

—Do you intend that now, the squat student said, as *ipso facto* or, let us say, as so to speak?

Dixon turned aside from his group, saying:

—Goggins was waiting for you, Glynn. He has gone round to the Adelphi to look for you and Moynihan. What have you 2170 there? he asked, tapping the portfolio under Glynn's arm.

—Examination papers, Glynn answered. I give them monthly examinations to see that they are profiting by my tuition.

He also tapped the portfolio and coughed gently and smiled.

—Tuition! said Cranly rudely. I suppose you mean the bare= footed children that are taught by a bloody ape like you. God help them!

He bit off the rest of the fig and flung away the butt.

—I suffer little children to come unto me, Glynn said amiably.

—A bloody ape, Cranly repeated with emphasis, and a blas= 2180 phemous bloody ape!

Temple stood up and, pushing past Cranly, addressed Glynn:

—That phrase you said now, he said, is from the new testa=
ment about suffer the children to come to me.

—Go to sleep again, Temple, said O'Keeffe.

—Very well, then, Temple continued, still addressing Glynn,
and if Jesus suffered the children to come why does the church
send them all to hell if they die unbaptised? Why is that?

2190 —Were you baptised yourself, Temple? the consumptive stu=
dent asked.

—But why are they sent to hell if Jesus said they were all to
come? Temple said, his eyes searching in Glynn's eyes.

Glynn coughed and said gently, holding back with difficulty
the nervous titter in his voice and moving his umbrella at every
word:

—And, as you remark, if it is thus I ask emphatically whence
comes this thusness.

—Because the church is cruel like all old sinners, Temple said.

2200 —Are you quite orthodox on that point, Temple? Dixon said
suavely.

—Saint Augustine says that about unbaptised children going to
hell, Temple answered, because he was a cruel old sinner too.

—I bow to you, Dixon said, but I had the impression that
limbo existed for such cases.

—Don't argue with him, Dixon, Cranly said brutally. Don't
talk to him or look at him. Lead him home with a sugan the
way you'd lead a bleating goat.

—Limbo! Temple cried. That's a fine invention too. Like hell.

2210 —But with the unpleasantness left out, Dixon said.

He turned smiling to the others and said:

—I think I am voicing the opinions of all present in saying so
much.

—You are, Glynn said in a firm tone. On that point Ireland is
united.

He struck the ferrule of his umbrella on the stone floor of
the colonnade.

—Hell, Temple said. I can respect that invention of the grey spouse of Satan. Hell is Roman, like the walls of the Romans, strong and ugly. But what is limbo?

—Put him back into the perambulator, Cranly, O'Keeffe called out.

Cranly made a swift step towards Temple, halted, stamping his foot and crying as if to a fowl:

—Hoosh!

Temple moved away nimbly.

—Do you know what limbo is? he cried. Do you know what we call a notion like that in Roscommon?

—Hoosh! Blast you! Cranly cried, clapping his hands.

—Neither my arse nor my elbow! Temple cried out scornfully. And that's what I call limbo.

—Give us that stick here, Cranly said.

He snatched the ashplant roughly from Stephen's hand and sprang down the steps: but Temple, hearing him move in pur=suit, fled through the dusk like a wild creature, nimble and fleetfooted. Cranly's heavy boots were heard loudly charging across the quadrangle and then returning heavily, foiled and spurning the gravel at each step.

His step was angry and with an angry abrupt gesture he thrust the stick back into Stephen's hand. Stephen felt that his anger had another cause but, feigning patience, touched his arm slightly and said quietly:

—Cranly, I told you I wanted to speak to you. Come away.

Cranly looked at him for a few moments and asked:

—Now?

—Yes, now, Stephen said. We can't speak here. Come away.

They crossed the quadrangle together without speaking. The birdcall from *Siegfried* whistled softly followed them from the steps of the porch. Cranly turned: and Dixon, who had whistled, called out:

—Where are you fellows off to? What about that game, Cranly?

They parleyed in shouts across the still air about a game of billiards to be played in the Adelphi hotel. Stephen walked on alone and out into the quiet of Kildare Street. Opposite Maple's hotel he stood to wait, patient again. The name of the hotel, a colourless polished wood, and its colourless quiet front stung him like a glance of polite disdain. He stared angrily back at the softly lit drawingroom of the hotel in which he imagined the sleek lives of the patricians of Ireland housed in calm. They thought of army commissions and land agents: peasants greeted them along the roads in the country: they knew the names of certain French dishes and gave orders to jarvies in highpitched provincial voices which pierced through their skintight accents.

How could he hit their conscience or how cast his shadow over the imagination of their daughters, before their squires begat upon them, that they might breed a race less ignoble than their own? And under the deepened dusk he felt the thoughts and desires of the race to which he belonged flitting like bats across the dark country lanes, under trees by the edges of streams and near the poolmottled bogs. A woman had waited in the doorway as Davin had passed by at night and, offering him a cup of milk, had all but wooed him to her bed: for Davin had the mild eyes of one that could be secret. But him no woman's eyes had wooed.

His arm was taken in a strong grip and Cranly's voice said:
—Let us eke go.

They walked southward in silence. Then Cranly said:
—That blithering idiot Temple! I swear to Moses, do you know, that I'll be the death of that fellow one time.

But his voice was no longer angry and Stephen wondered was he thinking of her greeting to him under the porch.

They turned to the left and walked on as before. When they had gone on so for some time Stephen said:
—Cranly, I had an unpleasant quarrel this evening.
—With your people? Cranly asked.
—With my mother.
—About religion?
—Yes, Stephen answered.

After a pause Cranly asked:

—What age is your mother?

—Not old, Stephen said. She wishes me to make my easter duty.

—And will you?

—I will not, Stephen said.

—Why not? Cranly said.

—I will not serve, answered Stephen.

—That remark was made before, Cranly said calmly.

—It is made behind now, said Stephen hotly.

Cranly pressed Stephen's arm, saying: 2300

—Go easy, my dear man. You're an excitable bloody man, do you know.

He laughed nervously as he spoke and, looking up into Ste=phen's face with moved and friendly eyes, said:

—Do you know that you are an excitable man?

—I daresay I am, said Stephen, laughing also.

Their minds, lately estranged, seemed suddenly to have been drawn closer, one to the other.

—Do you believe in the eucharist? Cranly asked.

—I do not, Stephen said. 2310

—Do you disbelieve then?

—I neither believe in it nor disbelieve in it, Stephen answered.

—Many persons have doubts, even religious persons, yet they overcome them or put them aside, Cranly said. Are your doubts on that point too strong?

—I do not wish to overcome them, Stephen answered.

Cranly, embarrassed for a moment, took another fig from his pocket and was about to eat it when Stephen said:

—Don't, please. You cannot discuss this question with your mouth full of chewed fig. 2320

Cranly examined the fig by the light of a lamp under which he halted. Then he smelt it with both nostrils, bit a tiny piece, spat it out and threw the fig rudely into the gutter. Addressing it as it lay, he said:

—Depart from me, ye cursed, into everlasting fire!

Taking Stephen's arm he went on again and said:

—Do you not fear that those words may be spoken to you on the day of judgment?

—What is offered me on the other hand? Stephen asked. An eternity of bliss in the company of the dean of studies?

—Remember, Cranly said, that he would be glorified.

—Ay, Stephen said somewhat bitterly. Bright, agile, impassible and, above all, subtle.

—It is a curious thing, do you know, Cranly said dispassion= ately, how your mind is supersaturated with the religion in which you say you disbelieve. Did you believe in it when you were at school? I bet you did.

—I did, Stephen answered.

—And were you happier then? Cranly asked softly. Happier than you are now, for instance?

—Often happy, Stephen said, and often unhappy. I was some= one else then.

—How someone else? What do you mean by that statement?

—I mean, said Stephen, that I was not myself as I am now, as I had to become.

—Not as you are now, not as you had to become, Cranly repeated. Let me ask you a question. Do you love your mother?

Stephen shook his head slowly.

—I don't know what your words mean, he said simply.

—Have you never loved anyone? Cranly asked.

—Do you mean women?

—I am not speaking of that, Cranly said in a colder tone. I ask you if you ever felt love towards anyone or anything.

Stephen walked on beside his friend, staring gloomily at the footpath.

—I tried to love God, he said at length. It seems now I failed. It is very difficult. I tried to unite my will with the will of God instant by instant. In that I did not always fail. I could perhaps do that still .....

Cranly cut him short by asking:

—Has your mother had a happy life?

—How do I know? Stephen said.

—How many children had she?

—Nine or ten, Stephen answered. Some died.

—Was your father .... Cranly interrupted himself for an in=
stant: and then said: I don't want to pry into your family
affairs. But was your father what is called well-to-do? I mean
when you were growing up?

—Yes, Stephen said.

—What was he? Cranly asked after a pause.   2370

Stephen began to enumerate glibly his father's attributes.

—A medical student, an oarsman, a tenor, an amateur actor, a
shouting politician, a small landlord, a small investor, a
drinker, a good fellow, a storyteller, somebody's secretary,
something in a distillery, a taxgatherer, a bankrupt and at
present a praiser of his own past.

Cranly laughed, tightening his grip on Stephen's arm, and
said:

—The distillery is damn good.

—Is there anything else you want to know? Stephen asked.   2380

—Are you in good circumstances at present?

—Do I look it? Stephen asked bluntly.

—So then, Cranly went on musingly, you were born in the lap
of luxury.

He used the phrase broadly and loudly as he often used
technical expressions as if he wished his hearer to understand
that they were used by him without conviction.

—Your mother must have gone through a good deal of suffer=
ing, he said then. Would you not try to save her from suffering
more even if .... or would you?   2390

—If I could, Stephen said. That would cost me very little.

—Then do so, Cranly said. Do as she wishes you to do. What
is it for you? You disbelieve in it. It is a form: nothing else. And
you will set her mind at rest.

He ceased and, as Stephen did not reply, remained silent.
Then, as if giving utterance to the process of his own thought,
he said:

—Whatever else is unsure in this stinking dunghill of a world a mother's love is not. Your mother brings you into the world, carries you first in her body. What do we know about what she feels? But whatever she feels, it, at least, must be real. It must be. What are our ideas or ambitions? Play. Ideas! Why, that bloody bleating goat Temple has ideas. MacCann has ideas too. Every jackass going the roads thinks he has ideas.

Stephen, who had been listening to the unspoken speech behind the words, said with assumed carelessness:

—Pascal, if I remember rightly, would not suffer his mother to kiss him as he feared the contact of her sex.

—Pascal was a pig, said Cranly.

—Aloysius Gonzaga, I think, was of the same mind, Stephen said.

—And he was another pig then, said Cranly.

—The church calls him a saint, Stephen objected.

—I don't care a flaming damn what anyone calls him, Cranly said rudely and flatly. I call him a pig.

Stephen, preparing the words neatly in his mind, continued:

—Jesus too seems to have treated his mother with scant courtesy in public but Suarez, a jesuit theologian and Spanish gentleman, has apologised for him.

—Did the idea ever occur to you, Cranly asked, that Jesus was not what he pretended to be?

—The first person to whom that idea occurred, Stephen answered, was Jesus himself.

—I mean, Cranly said, hardening in his speech, did the idea ever occur to you that he was himself a conscious hypocrite, what he called the jews of his time, a whited sepulchre? Or, to put it more plainly, that he was a blackguard?

—That idea never occurred to me, Stephen answered. But I am curious to know are you trying to make a convert of me or a pervert of yourself?

He turned towards his friend's face and saw there a raw smile which some force of will strove to make finely significant.

Cranly asked suddenly in a plain sensible tone:

—Tell me the truth. Were you at all shocked by what I said?

—Somewhat, Stephen said.

—And why were you shocked, Cranly pressed on in the same
tone, if you feel sure that our religion is false and that Jesus
was not the son of God?

—I am not at all sure of it, Stephen said. He is more like a son
of God than a son of Mary.   2440

—And is that why you will not communicate, Cranly asked,
because you are not sure of that too, because you feel that the
host too may be the body and blood of the son of God and not
a wafer of bread? And because you fear that it may be?

—Yes, Stephen said quietly. I feel that and I also fear it.

—I see, Cranly said.

Stephen, struck by his tone of closure, reopened the dis=
cussion at once by saying:

—I fear many things: dogs, horses, firearms, the sea, thunder=
storms, machinery, the country roads at night.   2450

—But why do you fear a bit of bread?

—I imagine, Stephen said, that there is a malevolent reality
behind those things I say I fear.

—Do you fear then, Cranly asked, that the God of the Roman
catholics would strike you dead and damn you if you made a
sacrilegious communion?

—The God of the Roman catholics could do that now, Stephen
said. I fear more than that the chemical action which would be
set up in my soul by a false homage to a symbol behind which
are massed twenty centuries of authority and veneration.   2460

—Would you, Cranly asked, in extreme danger commit that
particular sacrilege? For instance, if you lived in the penal days?

—I cannot answer for the past, Stephen replied. Possibly not.

—Then, said Cranly, you do not intend to become a protes=
tant?

—I said that I had lost the faith, Stephen answered, but not
that I had lost selfrespect. What kind of liberation would that
be to forsake an absurdity which is logical and coherent and to
embrace one which is illogical and incoherent?

They had walked on towards the township of Pembroke and   2470
now, as they went on slowly along the avenues, the trees and

the scattered lights in the villas soothed their minds. The air of wealth and repose diffused about them seemed to comfort their neediness. Behind a hedge of laurel a light glimmered in the window of a kitchen and the voice of a servant was heard singing as she sharpened knives. She sang in short broken bars *Rosie O'Grady*.

Cranly stopped to listen, saying:

— *Mulier cantat.*

2480   The soft beauty of the Latin word touched with an enchant= ing touch the dark of the evening, with a touch fainter and more persuading than the touch of music or of a woman's hand. The strife of their minds was quelled. The figure of woman as she appears in the liturgy of the church passed si= lently through the darkness: a whiterobed figure, small and slender as a boy and with a falling girdle. Her voice, frail and high as a boy's, was heard intoning from a distant choir the first words of a woman which pierce the gloom and clamour of the first chanting of the passion:

2490   — *Et tu cum Jesu Galilaeo eras.*

And all hearts were touched and turned to her voice, shining like a young star, shining clearer as the voice intoned the pro= paroxyton and more faintly as the cadence died.

The singing ceased. They went on together, Cranly repeating in strongly stressed rhythm the end of the refrain:

> *And when we are married*
> *O, how happy we'll be*
> *For I love sweet Rosie O'Grady*
> *And Rosie O'Grady loves me.*

2500   — There's real poetry for you, he said. There's real love.

He glanced sideways at Stephen with a strange smile and said:

— Do you consider that poetry? Or do you know what the words mean?

— I want to see Rosie first, said Stephen.

— She's easy to find, Cranly said.

His hat had come down on his forehead. He shoved it back:

and in the shadow of the trees Stephen saw his pale face, framed by the dark, and his large dark eyes. Yes. His face was handsome: and his body was strong and hard. He had spoken of a mother's love. He felt then the sufferings of women, the weaknesses of their bodies and souls: and would shield them with a strong and resolute arm and bow his mind to them.

Away then: it is time to go. A voice spoke softly to Stephen's lonely heart, bidding him go and telling him that his friendship was coming to an end. Yes: he would go. He could not strive against another. He knew his part.

—Probably I shall go away, he said.

—Where? Cranly asked.

—Where I can, Stephen said.

—Yes, Cranly said. It might be difficult for you to live here now. But is it that that makes you go?

—I have to go, Stephen answered.

—Because, Cranly continued, you need not look upon yourself as driven away if you do not wish to go or as a heretic or an outlaw. There are many good believers who think as you do. Would that surprise you? The church is not the stone building nor even the clergy and their dogmas. It is the whole mass of those born into it. I don't know what you wish to do in life. Is it what you told me the night we were standing outside Har= court Street station?

—Yes, Stephen said, smiling in spite of himself at Cranly's way of remembering thoughts in connection with places. The night you spent half an hour wrangling with Doherty about the shortest way from Sallygap to Larras.

—Pothead! Cranly said with calm contempt. What does he know about the way from Sallygap to Larras? Or what does he know about anything for that matter? And the big slobbering washingpot head of him!

He broke out into a loud long laugh.

—Well? Stephen said. Do you remember the rest?

—What you said, is it? Cranly asked. Yes, I remember it. To discover the mode of life or of art whereby your spirit could express itself in unfettered freedom.

Stephen raised his hat in acknowledgment.

—Freedom! Cranly repeated. But you are not free enough yet to commit a sacrilege. Tell me, would you rob?

—I would beg first, Stephen said.

—And if you got nothing would you rob?

2550 —You wish me to say, Stephen answered, that the rights of property are provisional and that in certain circumstances it is not unlawful to rob. Everyone would act in that belief. So I will not make you that answer. Apply to the jesuit theologian Juan Mariana de Talavera who will also explain to you in what circumstances you may lawfully kill your king and whether you had better hand him his poison in a goblet or smear it for him upon his robe or his saddlebow. Ask me rather would I suffer others to rob me or, if they did, would I call down upon them what I believe is called the chastisement of the secular arm.

2560 —And would you?

—I think, Stephen said, it would pain me as much to do so as to be robbed.

—I see, Cranly said.

He produced his match and began to clean the crevice be= tween two teeth. Then he said carelessly:

—Tell me, for example, would you deflower a virgin?

—Excuse me, Stephen said politely. Is that not the ambition of most young gentlemen?

—What then is your point of view? Cranly asked.

2570 His last phrase, soursmelling as the smoke of charcoal and disheartening, excited Stephen's brain over which its fumes seemed to brood.

—Look here, Cranly, he said. You have asked me what I would do and what I would not do. I will tell you what I will do and what I will not do. I will not serve that in which I no longer believe whether it call itself my home, my fatherland or my church: and I will try to express myself in some mode of life or art as freely as I can and as wholly as I can, using for my defence the only arms I allow myself to use, silence, exile and 2580 cunning.

Cranly seized his arm and steered him round so as to lead

him back towards Leeson Park. He laughed almost slily and pressed Stephen's arm with an elder's affection.

—Cunning indeed! he said. Is it you? You poor poet, you!

—And you made me confess to you, Stephen said, thrilled by his touch, as I have confessed to you so many other things, have I not?

—Yes, my child, Cranly said, still gaily.

—You made me confess the fears that I have. But I will tell you also what I do not fear. I do not fear to be alone or to be spurned for another or to leave whatever I have to leave. And I am not afraid to make a mistake, even a great mistake, a lifelong mistake and perhaps as long as eternity too.

Cranly, now grave again, slowed his pace and said:

—Alone, quite alone. You have no fear of that. And you know what that word means? Not only to be separate from all others but to have not even one friend.

—I will take the risk, said Stephen.

—And not to have any one person, Cranly said, who would be more than a friend, more even than the noblest and truest friend a man ever had.

His words seemed to have struck some deep chord in his own nature. Had he spoken of himself, of himself as he was or wished to be? Stephen watched his face for some moments in silence. A cold sadness was there. He had spoken of himself, of his own loneliness which he feared.

—Of whom are you speaking? Stephen asked at length.

Cranly did not answer.

◆ ◆ ◆

20 March: Long talk with Cranly on the subject of my re= volt. He had his grand manner on. I supple and suave. Attacked me on the score of love for one's mother. Tried to imagine his mother: cannot. Told me once, in a moment of thoughtlessness, his father was sixtyone when he was born. Can see him. Strong farmer type. Pepper and salt suit. Square feet. Unkempt grizzled beard. Probably attends coursing matches. Pays his dues regularly but not plentifully to Father Dwyer of Larras.

Sometimes talks to girls after nightfall. But his mother? Very young or very old? Hardly the first. If so, Cranly would not have spoken as he did. Old then. Probably: and neglected. Hence Cranly's despair of soul: the child of exhausted loins.

21 March, morning: Thought this in bed last night but was too lazy and free to add it. Free, yes. The exhausted loins are those of Elizabeth and Zachary. Then is he the precursor. Item: he eats chiefly belly bacon and dried figs. Read locusts and wild honey. Also, when thinking of him, saw always a stern severed head or deathmask as if outlined on a grey curtain or veronica. Decollation they call it in the fold. Puzzled for the moment by saint John at the Latin gate. What do I see? A decollated precursor trying to pick the lock.

21 March, night: Free. Soulfree and fancyfree. Let the dead bury the dead. Ay. And let the dead marry the dead.

22 March: In company with Lynch followed a sizable hospital nurse. Lynch's idea. Dislike it. Two lean hungry greyhounds walking after a heifer.

23 March: Have not seen her since that night. Unwell? Sits at the fire perhaps with mamma's shawl on her shoulders. But not peevish. A nice bowl of gruel? Won't you now?

24 March: Began with a discussion with my mother. Subject: B. V. M. Handicapped by my sex and youth. To escape held up relations between Jesus and Papa against those between Mary and her son. Said religion is not a lying-in hospital. Mother indulgent. Said I have a queer mind and have read too much. Not true. Have read little and understood less. Then she said I would come back to faith because I had a restless mind. This means to leave church by backdoor of sin and reenter through the skylight of repentance. Cannot repent. Told her so and asked for sixpence. Got threepence.

Then went to college. Other wrangle with little roundhead rogue's eye Ghezzi. This time about Bruno the Nolan. Began in Italian and ended in pidgin English. He said Bruno was a terrible heretic. I said he was terribly burned. He agreed to this with some sorrow. Then gave me recipe for what he calls *risotto alla bergamasca.* When he pronounces a soft *o* he pro=

trudes his full carnal lips as if he kissed the vowel. Has he? And could he repent? Yes, he could: and cry two round rogue's tears, one from each eye.

Crossing Stephen's, that is, my green, remembered that his countrymen and not mine had invented what Cranly the other night called our religion. A quartet of them, soldiers of the ninetyseventh infantry regiment, sat at the foot of the cross and tossed up dice for the overcoat of the crucified.

Went to library. Tried to read three reviews. Useless. She is not out yet. Am I alarmed? About what? That she will never be out again. Blake wrote:

> I wonder if William Bond will die.
> For assuredly he is very ill.

Alas, poor William!

I was once at a diorama in Rotunda. At the end were pic= tures of big nobs. Among them William Ewart Gladstone, just then dead. Orchestra played O Willie, we have missed you.

A race of clodhoppers.

25 March, morning: A troubled night of dreams. Want to get them off my chest.

A long curving gallery. From the floor ascend pillars of dark vapours. It is peopled by the images of fabulous kings, set in stone. Their hands are folded upon their knees in token of weariness and their eyes are darkened for the errors of men go up before them for ever as dark vapours.

Strange figures advance from a cave. They are not as tall as men. One does not seem to stand quite apart from another. Their faces are phosphorescent, with darker streaks. They peer at me and their eyes seem to ask me something. They do not speak.

30 March: This evening Cranly was in the porch of the library, proposing a problem to Dixon and her brother. A mother let her child fall into the Nile. Still harping on the mother. A crocodile seized the child. Mother asked it back. Crocodile said all right if she told him what he was going to do with the child, eat it or not eat it.

2690 This mentality, Lepidus would say, is indeed bred out of your mud by the operation of your sun.

And mine? Is it not too? Then into Nilemud with it!

1 April: Disapprove of this last phrase.

2 April: Saw her drinking tea and eating cakes in Johnston, Mooney and O'Brien's. Rather, lynxeyed Lynch saw her as we passed. He tells me Cranly was invited there by brother. Did he bring his crocodile? Is he the shining light now? Well, I dis= covered him. I protest I did. Shining quietly behind a bushel of Wicklow bran.

2700 *3 April:* Met Davin at the cigar shop opposite Findlater's church. He was in a black sweater and had a hurleystick. Asked me was it true I was going away and why. Told him the shortest way to Tara was via Holyhead. Just then my father came up. Introduction. Father polite and observant. Asked Davin if he might offer him some refreshment. Davin could not, was going to a meeting. When we came away father told me he had a good honest eye. Asked me why I did not join a rowing club. I pretended to think it over. Told me then how he broke Pennyfeather's heart. Wants me to read law. Says I was 2710 cut out for that. More mud, more crocodiles.

5 April: Wild spring. Scudding clouds. O life! Dark stream of swirling bogwater on which appletrees have cast down their delicate flowers. Eyes of girls among the leaves. Girls demure and romping. All fair or auburn: no dark ones. They blush better. Houp-la!

6 April: Certainly she remembers the past. Lynch says all women do. Then she remembers the time of her childhood— and mine if I was ever a child. The past is consumed in the present and the present is living only because it brings forth the 2720 future. Statues of women, if Lynch be right, should always be fully draped, one hand of the woman feeling regretfully her own hinder parts.

6 April: later: Michael Robartes remembers forgotten beauty and, when his arms wrap her round, he presses in his arms the loveliness which has long faded from the world. Not this. Not at all. I desire to press in my arms the loveliness which has not yet come into the world.

10 April: Faintly, under the heavy night, through the silence of the city which has turned from dreams to dreamless sleep as a weary lover whom no caresses move, the sound of hoofs upon the road. Not so faintly now as they come near the bridge; and in a moment as they pass the darkened windows the silence is cloven by alarm as by an arrow. They are heard now far away, hoofs that shine amid the heavy night as gems, hurrying beyond the sleeping fields to what journey's end— what heart?—bearing what tidings?

11 April: Read what I wrote last night. Vague words for a vague emotion. Would she like it? I think so. Then I should have to like it also.

13 April: That tundish has been on my mind for a long time. I looked it up and find it is English and good old blunt English too. Damn the dean of studies and his funnel! What did he come here for to teach us his own language or to learn it from us. Damn him one way or the other!

14 April: John Alphonsus Mulrennan has just returned from the west of Ireland (European and Asiatic papers please copy). He told us he met an old man there in a mountain cabin. Old man had red eyes and short pipe. Old man spoke Irish. Mulrennan spoke Irish. Then old man and Mulrennan spoke English. Mulrennan spoke to him about universe and stars. Old man sat, listened, smoked, spat. Then said:

—Ah, there must be terrible queer creatures at the latter end of the world.

I fear him. I fear his redrimmed horny eyes. It is with him I must struggle all through this night till day come, till he or I lie dead, gripping him by the sinewy throat till .... Till what? Till he yield to me? No. I mean him no harm.

15 April: Met her today pointblank in Grafton Street. The crowd brought us together. We both stopped. She asked me why I never came, said she had heard all sorts of stories about me. This was only to gain time. Asked me was I writing poems.

243

About whom? I asked her. This confused her more and I felt sorry and mean. Turned off that valve at once and opened the spiritual-heroic refrigerating apparatus, invented and patented in all countries by Dante Alighieri. Talked rapidly of myself and my plans. In the midst of it unluckily I made a sudden gesture of a revolutionary nature. I must have looked like a fellow throwing a handful of peas up into the air. People began to look at us. She shook hands a moment after and, in going away, said she hoped I would do what I said.

Now I call that friendly, don't you?

Yes. I liked her today. A little or much? Don't know. I liked her—and it seems a new feeling to me. Then, in that case, all the rest, all that I thought I thought and all that I felt I felt, all the rest before now, in fact ...... O, give it up, old chap! Sleep it off!

16 April: Away! Away!

The spell of arms and voices: the white arms of roads, their promise of close embraces and the black arms of tall ships that stand against the moon, their tale of distant nations. They are held out to say: We are alone. Come. And the voices say with them: We are your kinsmen. And the air is thick with their company as they call to me, their kinsman, making ready to go, shaking the wings of their exultant and terrible youth.

26 April: Mother is putting my new secondhand clothes in order. She prays now, she says, that I may learn in my own life and away from home and friends what the heart is and what it feels. Amen. So be it. Welcome, O life! I go to encounter for the millionth time the reality of experience and to forge in the smithy of my soul the uncreated conscience of my race.

27 April: Old father, old artificer, stand me now and ever in good stead.

Dublin 1904
Trieste 1914

A NOTE ON THE TEXT

AFTERWORD

SELECT BIBLIOGRAPHY

A NOTE ON THE TEXT

This edition is a copy-text edition of *A Portrait of the Artist as a Young Man*. Its copy-text is the text in James Joyce's faircopy holograph, preserved in the original in the National Library of Ireland and photographically reprinted in the *James Joyce Archive*.[1] To establish the critical text, the surviving fragments of the typescript, the serialization in *The Egoist* (London, 1914–15), the first edition (B. W. Huebsch, New York, 1916), the second edition (The Egoist Ltd., London, 1918), and the third edition (Jonathan Cape, London, 1924) have been collated against the fair copy. Marked-up *Egoist* tearsheets, surviving separate lists of corrections, the marked-up printer's copy for the 1918 British edition and published and unpublished correspondence itemizing textual changes have been checked.

From the textual materials so collated and assembled, the edited text has been constituted. Apart from emending obvious slips of the pen and authorial copying errors, it maintains the wording, spelling and punctuation of the copy-text. Yet onto this have been grafted: first, the author's revisions, few in number, effected successively in the typescript, the serialization, and the book editions of 1916, 1918, and 1924; second, the authorial, or authorially instigated, restyling of capitals and compounds without hyphens (i.e., in one word or two words) achieved successively in the book editions; third, the styling of dialogue with opening flush-left dialogue dashes only, as realized by authorial direction in the Jonathan Cape edition of 1924. By the definitions and rules of copy-text editing, the text in this edition is thus a critically eclectic text.

The rules of copy-text editing stipulate that, from the transmission, the text in one document—or "copy"—be selected as edition base text. By conventionalized operations of critical editing, the base text—that is, the copy-text—is then transformed into the edited text. Transforming the copy-text means emending it, and emendation in copy-text editing is double-natured. In one respect, emendation removes the copy-text's imperfections and transmissional corruption. It corrects (or may correct) authorial misspellings or restores words accidentally dropped from the manuscript copy; or corrects copying, typing or printer's errors, or undoes house-styling and other effects of the text's fashioning by the printers or publisher's editor. In another respect, emendation replaces good and authentic readings of the copy-text by their respective authorial revisions—equally good and authentic, but superseding the copy-text readings by authorial intervention and change—as found in authoritative document texts other than the copy-text. In other words, the copy-text–edited text is not definable as the text of any one historical document. It is an eclectic text, constituted by grafting authentic (succeeding) textual revisions onto the authentic (preceding) substratum of the copy-text.

Copy-text editing thus telescopes a textual development into one text, the edited text, conceived of as an ideal text. The ideal text is commonly justified by the claim that, as eclectically edited, it fulfills the author's (final) intentions. But this means putting an ideological perspective on the procedural solution of a pragmatic task. From the outset, an editor faces the situation that the author's intentions may be considered fulfilled in a general way in each manifest historical documentation of the text—say, an accomplished draft, a fair copy, the printer's copy, the first edition, or each authorially revised edition. The document texts provide the editor with an historical series of intentional moments. Copy-text editing is recognized as a way of reconciling these successive moments. It observes authorial intention and invokes it as a superior consideration in each instance of adjudicating authenticity in variant readings among the documented states of the text. Yet the legitimacy is moot of claiming final authorial intention for the resulting editorial product. At the most, the edited text may claim to represent a text of composite authenticity. This is a claim which the textual situation for *A Portrait of the Artist as a Young Man* permits.

On the textual surface, the edition here offered closely realizes my proposals for a copy-text edition of *A Portrait of the Artist as a Young Man* of 1974.[2] But my thinking about the copy-text method has since developed. The new rationale is set out in the Introduction to the full critical edition—to which the present edition is the text-only companion volume—simultaneously published by Garland Publishing, Inc. The established text may be assessed by the critical apparatus of the Garland edition.

Typographically, the text of this edition broadly observes the standards and conventions of modern professional printing and publishing, yet endeavors at the same time to maintain the character of a scholarly edited text in preserving essential features of irregularity in the authorial writing of the copy-text. Word forms and word-division, spellings, capitalization and punctuation have been neither normalized nor modernized, nor have typographical matters such as abbreviations or ellipses been standardized. End-of-line hyphenation in the edited text occurs in two modes. The sign "=" marks a division for mere typographical reasons. Words so printed should always be cited as one undivided word. The regular hyphen indicates an authentic Joycean hyphen. The through line numbering for each chapter independent of the pagination is identical in the Vintage and Garland editions. ("5.1854" means line 1854 in the fifth chapter; and "2.796–799," lines 796 to 799 in chapter II.)

The present text and that of Chester G. Anderson's Viking edition of 1964 do not drastically differ. Anderson was the first carefully to explore the Dublin holograph of *A Portrait*. Yet for his 1964 edition he was forced into textual compromises. These our edition eschews when merging in its edited text the words and punctuation of Joyce's fair copy with the changes in wording and restyling of capitalization and compound formation of his later revisions for *A Portrait of the Artist as a Young Man*.

Hans Walter Gabler

1. James Joyce, *A Portrait of the Artist as a Young Man*, MSS 920 and 921 in the holdings of the National Library of Ireland.
   James Joyce, *A Portrait of the Artist as a Young Man. A Facsimile of the Final Holograph Manuscript*. Prefaced and Arranged by Hans Walter Gabler. 2 vols. New York & London, Garland Publishing, Inc., 1977. (=Vols. [9] and [10] of the *James Joyce Archive*, 63 vols., Gen. Ed. Michael Groden.)
2. Hans Walter Gabler, "Towards a Critical Text of James Joyce's *A Portrait of the Artist as a Young Man*." *Studies in Bibliography* 27 (1974), 1–53.

AFTERWORD

Joyce's *A Portrait of the Artist as a Young Man* is neither the kind of "portrait" nor a portrait of the kind of "artist" that its title might at first lead the reader to assume. Leaving aside, for the moment, the stylistic terms in which its portrayal of the young Stephen Dedalus revolutionized the potential for modern literary portraiture, we might pause to consider the kind of "artist" Stephen himself is shown to be. He is not, for instance, like Paul Morel in Lawrence's near-contemporary *Sons and Lovers*, interested primarily in the visual arts. Nor does he produce much in the way of literary art beyond an intricate and repetitive poem that, despite or because of its technical cleverness, many readers find rather feeble.

Of course there is a sense in which the title represents the conundrum of a self-fulfilling prophecy: that the novel is an autobiographical portrait of the novelist who produced it and indeed that the "young man" (Stephen) may have become the "artist" (Joyce) by the very act of painting his own "portrait." But Joyce's "artist," as he is seen in the novel, is a reader as much as he is a writer, a consumer as much as he is a producer of art; and among what he does produce, in the final chapter of the novel, is a kind of literary theory which he calls his "esthetic." In this, he forms a bridge between the ordinary experiences of the reader and the exceptional experience of the artistic producer. The reader may in a direct way seem engaged in the process of portrayal, which may in turn make him or her into a kind of "artist," too.

Nor is the aesthetic, as it is presented both inside and beyond Stephen's own "esthetic" theory, a narrow, specialized or elitist activity. Stephen's experience of and thoughts about art are intimately bound up with the portrayal of his childhood and adolescence, and of his emerging male sexuality, and they are situated within the pressing ideological conflicts of emerging Irish nationhood. The sphere of the aesthetic is posed not just as some escapist alternative to these experiences and ideologies, to the religion or to the modes of knowledge by which Stephen's brutal education structures, controls, and punishes him, but seems to be put forward as a potential new synthesis and redefinition of them. Stephen's striving for an aesthetic serves as little less than a medium in which both the psychodrama of his selfhood and the intellectual drama of the century can be played out.

Among the aspects of contemporary social change in terms of which we may read the artistic codes of *A Portrait of the Artist as a Young Man* we may list the advent of a new suburban, consumer, "liberal" society which followed the collapse of the old empires at the time of World War I; the exposure and overthrow of Victorian moralities; the emergence of Ireland as a nation-state; the political enfranchisement of women; the growth of mass literacy and education; and the emergence of the new technological cultural media of the age.

And we should not forget, among these, within the expanding educational institutions, the birth and prolific expansion of subjects like English and Literary Studies, in whose curricula Joyce's books have played such an important part. These subjects of study have their origins in high Victorian debates about the value of studying traditions of vernacular literature in relation to culture and humanity, conducted by writers like Carlyle, Arnold, and Newman, who are also the writers whose influence is so profoundly felt in *A Portrait*. The institutions that attempted to put these ideas into practice established English as an academic subject during the early years of Joyce's life. Joyce was born in 1882 and the first Chair of English at Oxford set up in 1884, though the subject was already well established in the newer universities of London and Dublin by then. The subject became especially popular both with the new mass audience for education and literacy among the lower-middle and working classes and in the colonies.

Joyce's own education—among the first generations of students of the new Catholic University in Ireland, which had been set up under the rectorship of Cardinal Newman himself—may be thought a typical or exemplary one, as is that of his protagonist Stephen, who is shown studying in that same university. Stephen's curriculum is mixed: "Thursday. Ten to eleven; English: eleven to twelve; French: twelve to one; physics" and the formal English part of it a disappointingly drab mixture: "nominal definitions, essential definitions and examples or dates of birth and death, chief works, a favourable and an unfavourable criticism side by side." And yet it is precisely the theorizing of literature that becomes his primary mode of self-expression. "English"—the study of literary art in the English language—is often the subject within *A Portrait*, just as *A Portrait* has often been and quite rightly should be the subject within the "English" curriculum. To put it more simply: the subject of *A Portrait of the Artist as a Young Man* is the subject of English itself.

That both Stephen and Joyce's "English" may be thought to be ambiguous because of their respective upbringings in Ireland is neither a disadvantage nor any definitive advantage in this. It is not just, as Stephen jokes, that "they speak the best English" in Lower Drumcondra or only that his sense of the English language, as he explains it in his discussion with the Dean, is that of a colonized subject, that it "will always be for me an acquired speech." Stephen's Irishness is as ambiguous as his English. In pre-Independence Ireland he has as much in common with the inhabitant of any other provincial British city as with the post-Independence American, Indian, or Australasian citizen. Either experience (not to mention the declining economic fortunes of his family and his feeling of distance from the objects of his sexual desire) may underpin the sense of detachment, exile and self-consciousness which predates his flight into exile at the end of the novel and shows itself from the beginning most of all in his extraordinary sensitivity to the material of words.

The intellectual experience of the novel's final chapter might be hard to anticipate from its opening, which is sensational in more than one sense of the word. Little could be more startling than the accomplished pastiche of childish language that greets the reader on the first page of the book and draws a conceptual map of the consciousness of the young Stephen. The device instantly universalizes the experiments made with linguistic pastiche as a means of literary representation by one of Joyce's great literary exemplars, Flaubert. In Joyce's own earliest attempt at an autobiographical sketch or essay, already called *A Portrait of the Artist*, written in

1904 in Dublin, he begins by arguing that events in the past, when they happened, were not experienced as past but as present and that a narrative should therefore try to recapture the "fluid succession of presents" that this implies. The final version of the novel, finished a decade later in Trieste, makes this a basic principle of its tightly episodic structure of five chapters or nineteen episodes, each containing one or more vividly represented "present." The technique is almost like cinematic montage but it is also highly attentive to its linguistic medium, being written in a "fluid succession" of prose styles appropriate to the boy's maturing consciousness.

The opening section imagines the small boy's experience in a prerational, almost prelinguistic state where his thoughts are feelings: "His mother had a nicer smell than his father." This continues into the second section, where his experiences as a nine-year-old schoolboy in a succession of typical school scenes are narrated in a similarly naive style of simple observations and sensations: "His mother put her lips on his cheek; her lips were soft and they wetted his cheek; and they made a tiny noise: kiss." Typically his fascination is with the sensation of the word as well as with the sensation it describes. An intriguing mixture of thoughts and feelings make up his experience. He thinks about naming, identity, the nature of the universe, God, and politics but the first school scene is soured by the bullying he suffers from the older and richer boys. He is pushed into the school's "square ditch," bringing on a bout of fever and an early return home.

In the meantime the political world which has begun to impinge on his naive consciousness has also invaded the domestic arena. Told through his naive eyes, the family Christmas dinner scene which follows shows the growing tensions in the contemporary political scene with great immediacy and not a little hint of what Joyce called in a 1912 essay the "exaggeration" of Dickensian comedy. The young Stephen's hopes, like those of Parliamentary Irish nationalism, were pinned on the consensus represented by Charles Stewart Parnell, but that consensus collapsed when Parnell's affair with Kitty O'Shea became public knowledge and the Irish priesthood came out against him on moral grounds. From that moment, insurrectionary violence became the most likely future for Irish politics and Joyce's best hopes for personal and artistic freedom lay in exile.

In the Dedalus household Stephen's father and his radical nationalist friend Mr Casey (who has evidently been in prison for his views) both support Parnell and lament his fall, but the children's governess, Dante Riordan, will not be shaken from her loyalty to the orthodox Catholic Church position and she argues with an increasing fury for her views: "Devil out of hell! We won! We crushed him to death! Fiend!" Only Stephen's mother stands outside the battle, though the fact that she seems to sympathize with Dante Riordan ensures that national politics are significantly complicated by the sexual politics of the household.

The final section of the chapter returns Stephen to Clongowes, where politics is still at issue. Stephen has been wrongly punished by one of the more sadistic prefects but has the courage to complain and becomes a short-lived popular hero among his schoolfellows. He seems almost another Parnell himself, a symbol of justice restored over force and violence in the community. But it is a community from which he is evidently just about to be withdrawn because of the declining fortunes of his family. So we infer from his school-free roaming at the beginning of the second chapter. It is typical of the novel's episodic structure for there to be gaps between the incidents narrated, which invite or require the reader to puzzle out the connections for him or herself.

Stephen's sexuality is the main theme of this second chapter, which takes us in a few strides from his prepubescent schoolboy experience to his precocious, if not untypical, sexual initiation at the hands of a Dublin prostitute. A number of incidents prepare us for what is both an erotically muted and a psychologically profound scene. First are his outings with his father's uncle Charles, who lives with the family in the Dublin suburb of Blackrock. A masculine environment flavored with the slightly perverse combination of tobacco smoke and athletic training greets Stephen here and he forms a "gang" with a male friend, Aubrey Mills. But he soon learns that his father is "in trouble" and it may be that his inability to retain a confidence in the security of the paternal leads him to alternate in his sense of gender loyalties. In the next incident it is the female environment of his mother's relatives where he is a visitor and, in a curious scene, he is himself mistaken by the old lady of the house for his Aunt Josephine.

At this point we hear for the first time of Stephen's fondness for

a girl who is here named only by her initials E— C— and of the
fact that he has written a poem about a failed or insubstantial
romantic encounter with her. Stephen's psychology is a material
force in the novel, traceable in its components, even at this early
stage, to his maternal affections, to his fascinations with the figure
of the Virgin Mary, and to strong feelings of guilt brought on by
the punitive moral atmosphere represented by both Dante and the
beatings characteristic of his boarding school. Such a combination
of influences leaves him powerfully desiring some physical contact
with E— C— but with no means of fulfilling or even legitimating
such desires. His feelings remain at the level of velleities and
translate themselves into a poem of wish-fulfilment in which "the
kiss, which had been withheld by one, was given by both." There
is some pathos in the "force of habit" which makes him begin and
end his putatively Byronic poem of sexual adventure with the
Jesuit mottos A.M.D.G. and L.D.S.

Indeed, the fact that Byron and his education (now in the
Dublin day school Belvedere) might be in radical conflict with
each other is reinforced by the next scene. In another incident
Stephen (once again the victim of schoolboy bullying) is ragged by
his schoolfellows for having incorporated an unintentionally heretical phrase in a school essay and for daring to call Byron a great
poet while, according to their reductionist and hardly literate
morality, he is a "heretic." The Whitsuntide Play scene further
problematizes questions of gender for Stephen, with its atmosphere of theatrical cross-dressing and the inevitable schoolboy
teasing that accompanies it. E— C— is present in the audience
but Stephen is unable to make contact with her and she seems
content with his father's company rather than his own.

Stephen is eventually going to find writing a means of express-
ing his masculinity and his identity, not a means of escape from
either or both; but he must emerge from beneath the authorities
that constrain him in order for this self-expression to be achieved.
The trip to Cork which he makes with his father has been rightly
seen by critics as an important stage in this process. The first
words of the novel are a fragment of a story to which the child
listens, a story told him by his father and a story in which he
himself appears as "baby tuckoo." Stephen's voluble father is still
telling stories on their train trip to Cork but Stephen can no longer

hear them with sympathy. He is more concerned with the present
circumstances of economic disaster which have caused them to go
to Cork to sell off property. It is not until they reach the anatomy
theatre of his father's old college that the word *Foetus*, scratched
on a school desk, calls a vivid and fertile stream of images and
associations into Stephen's mind.

For some critics this represents another image of his shy or
guilty temperament but for others it represents a radical change in
his thinking, asserting his own "narrative" over that provided for
him by his father or even implying a victory of the maternal,
"foetal" loyalty over the paternal one in his mind. It seems
especially significant that the incident should take place in a theatre of "anatomy," since it is precisely the imperatives of Stephen's
physical body which have been most obscured and inhibited by the
excessively abstract morality imposed on him by punishment at
school. By the end of the incident he has achieved some critical
distance on the weakness of his father and his father's friends:
"His mind seemed older than theirs."

Curiously it is his "heretical" art of writing critical essays
rather than his piously dedicated poetry which wins Stephen his
first rewards. Since they are apparently quite substantial financial
rewards, they give him his first sense of a place in society and they
further help to free him from dependence both on his father and
on his mother and the rest of his family to whom he now becomes,
at least in his own imagination, a surrogate breadwinner.

But passionate desires are also burning within him and the
drifting or wandering condition in which he finds himself hungers
for some fixity or definition in the presence of an other. His
wanderings take him to the flourishing red light district of contemporary Dublin, where the sexual experience of the prostitute who
welcomes him is clearly represented as supplying an important
lack in his own experiences and awareness up to this point. The
language in which the encounter with the girl is described deserves
close attention. Stephen's imagination runs wild with a range of
extravagant and hellish fantasies that the "proud conscious movements" of the girl help to dispel and replace with phenomenolog-
ical reality. For all the linguistic skills implied by his school prize
victory he is only beginning to be able to read the language of her
body "darker than the swoon of sin, softer than sound or odour."

Terms like "sin," "soul," and "transgression" frequently occur in the prose and Stephen's sexual initiation is presented as a necessary transgression. Indeed, in the essay Joyce himself wrote for a Triestine paper on the Irish writer Oscar Wilde at the time he was composing *A Portrait*, he argues that an element of "sin" or transgression was necessary in Wilde's and, by implication, in all forms of creative art.

If terms like "sin" and "soul" take on a seductive Baudelairean tinge in these contexts, they are seized back for moral authority in the next chapter. The postmodern reader, who is likely to find Stephen's sexual "sins" more affecting than shocking, is just as likely to be very deeply shocked by the psychological terrorism to which he is subjected in the name of morality in these next pages. Just as his visits to the red light district are becoming habitual, Stephen and his classmates are subjected to a retreat in celebration of the founder of the School's Jesuit order, Francis Xavier, and during this retreat they are mercilessly lectured on death, judgment, heaven, and hell by Father Arnall.

The sermons take Joyce's experimentation with pastiche to its furthest extreme in *A Portrait*, with page after page given over to an exact transcription of their words, which are themselves very closely based on the general pattern of Ignatius Loyola's Counter-Reformation *Spiritual Exercises* and in much detail on the work of a seventeenth-century Italian Jesuit, Giovanni Pinamonti, which had been translated and published in Dublin in 1868 under the curiously ambiguous title *Hell Opened to Christians*.

The first sermons deal with death and judgment and already provoke a strong reaction from Stephen, who feels their general message to apply to him in particular. Moreover, though sexual sins are not stressed by Arnall, Stephen's sense of sin focuses on sex. In his guilt-ridden thoughts the visits to prostitutes do not figure as prominently as we might expect. He lists "the jeweleyed harlots of his imagination," his sexual fantasies about Emma, masturbation with a "sootcoated packet of pictures which he had hidden in the flue of the fireplace," and "foul long letters he had written in the joy of guilty confession and carried secretly for days and days." This last memory is an especially interesting one since Joyce himself had composed a sequence of extravagantly coprophiliac and masochistic love letters to his common-law wife, Nora, during a visit to Dublin some five years before the publication of *A Portrait*. Though personal in intention, the writing of such letters must have contributed greatly to Joyce's development as the writer of the mature published fictions, and their extraordinary prose of extreme bodily sensations helps to mark the distance between the maturing author Joyce and the guilty feelings his naive hero Stephen must escape in order to find himself as a writer. They were written in 1909, midway between the 1904 and 1914 noted at the novel's close.

Stephen's guilty reverie is short-lived. Arnall's sermons resume with a terrifyingly detailed and extended depiction of hell: not the human tragic hell of Dante's *Inferno* so much as a Sadeian catalogue of extreme pains and tortures to which the damned will be subjected. It is little wonder that the sensitive and impressionable Stephen reacts to this with an act of contrition whose very repetitions reflect the numbed and traumatized condition of his mind. In what is structurally the midpoint of the novel, he escapes to his room only to encounter there a jumble of mysterious overheard voices which he translates into his own vivid nightmare of a hell peopled with goatish creatures.

It is at this midpoint in the narrative that he makes a confession of his sins: a confession whose importance as a liturgical symbol should not obscure from the reader its interest in relation to Stephen's development as a secular literary writer. The act of confession represents a linguistic as well as a spiritual problem for Stephen and an alarming survival of the way that sexual guilt had been mobilized during the nineteenth century as a means of social control. To confess he must put into words the bodily actions for which language—or at any rate the sanctified languages he has learned in school—has no terms. To put such actions into language itself seems to him to be potentially sinful: "To say it in words! His soul, stifling and helpless, would cease to be." The confession "trickles" and "oozes" from him almost like a bodily fluid. The sensual immediacy and sense of freedom in the experiences is obscured by the official moralistic language of the confessional that attempts to contain or deny.

Other aspects of Stephen's temporary conversion also deserve comment. The idea of eternal time put over by Arnall in his lectures is a mystical one of a perpetual present tense ("Time is, time was but time shall be no more"), but it is far from spiritually liberating for Stephen, whose mental freedom up to this point has been based on his ability to remember and imagine times past and future. After his conversion he orders his life according to a super-strict organization of his time into a daily routine of actions and devotions which is at first clarifying for him but prevents the imaginative associations which we have come to expect of him from developing.

Along with this tyrannical reification of his time comes a new mathematical frame of reference for ordering his life. While still enjoying his brothel visits, Stephen experiences a curious hallucination in front of his schoolbooks: the vision of a mathematical problem spreading and expanding in front of his eyes like the patterns of a peacock's tail. On one level such patterns may seem to provide an analogy for Stephen's "fall" into "sin" but they are at the same time experienced as beautiful and seem analogous to the patterns generated by recent fractal geometry in its theorizing of chaos. At any rate they contrast dramatically with the crassly commercial arithmetic that characterizes his new obsession: "his soul in devotion pressing like fingers the keyboard of a great cash register." Father Arnall, who gives the sermons at the retreat, was, we might remember, the teacher in Stephen's previous school who set the boys "hard sums."

Nothing less than a conflict between two modes of knowledge seems to be at stake here and it is a conflict which may at once take us back to the linguistic origins of the aesthetic as a concept or category and more deeply into the final chapters of Joyce's novel. In its ancient Greek roots (and as it was adopted by philosophers in the eighteenth century) the aesthetic did not imply a separate territory of art as opposed to life. *Aisthesis* denoted those things which can be experienced by the body and through the feelings and emotions, as opposed to *physis* which denoted those things that can be understood only abstractly, by the reason alone.

The fact that Stephen's priests and teachers, with their abstract and arithmetical morality, seem to be lined up on the side of *physis* as opposed to *aisthesis* helps to explain the choice of vocation which he makes during the course of Chapter Four of the novel. Stephen is taken aside by Conmee, the Director of Belvedere, and offered the possibility of a priestly career. He is clearly very tempted by the idea and fascinated by the secret languages and rituals of the Church, but the irreducibly human blush with which he responds to the offer shows us that he will eventually decline it, apparently out of a moral scrupulousness and austerity which goes far beyond that of the ordinary aspirant to priestly orders. He feels that to be a priest would leave him in an impossibly compromised and hypocritical position.

Readers who feel that Stephen's ultimate choice of a career in writing and exile is self-centered, aloof, or politically redundant would do well to study the passage at the end of this interview in the middle section of Chapter Four, where Stephen makes his way back home to a family environment which has by now collapsed into poverty and overpopulated anarchy. His brothers and sisters, grouped around the "glassjars and jampots which did service for teacups" are an image of the society in whose terms Stephen must make his choice. As he ponders they break into the communal activity of singing a popular secular song of Thomas Moore, *Oft in the Stilly Night*. The phrase from Newman that Stephen remembers poignantly and inspiringly connects this "choir of voices" with the kind of idealism and optimism, the "hope of better things" that Newman's ideal of spreading secular education must have represented at the time.

In the lyrical climax that follows, Stephen is shown progressing towards a resolution or synthesis of these conflicting loyalties and aspirations: between "Clontarf Chapel" and "Byron's public-house." It is the prospect of studying at the University that so excites him, though he is actually portrayed on a symbolic walk that takes him out of the mean streets of urban Dublin towards the extended horizons of its inspiring sea coast. A startling modern musical melody fills his mind, as does an almost nonsensically rich piece of Newman's prose rhetoric about the "feet of harts" that, in its original context, celebrates the infinitely renewable power of the Christian Church, but in Stephen's mind surely implies the contradictions and excitements of his own bodily desires.

The image in which all these contradictions are to be resolved, apparently in some sense replacing the traditional role of a re-

solving transcendent deity in Stephen's psychology, is the image of
the wading bird/girl that closes the chapter. "Heavenly God!" he,
not insignificantly, shouts out inwardly when he sees her half-
naked body on the beach and his blushing cheeks, indeed his
whole body, confirm the message. Little remains in *A Portrait*
from Joyce's 1904 "Portrait" essay, but the description of this
figure as an "envoy from the fair courts of life" is one phrase that
does. As a deity the bird/girl is an undoubted improvement on the
"cash register" God whom he has most recently been worship-
ping. To him she represents "some new world, fantastic, dim,
uncertain as under sea, traversed by cloudy shapes and beings. A
world, a glimmer or a flower?" In the powerful labial imagery of
his ecstasy the new world or new age which she promises is
described as "an opening flower, it spread in endless succession to
itself, breaking in full crimson and unfolding and fading to palest
rose, leaf by leaf and wave of light by wave of light, flooding all
the heavens with its soft flushes, every flush deeper than other."

As a representation of a woman, however, she is incorporeal,
refracted like so much else in the novel through the lens of Stephen's desires. Rather than attempting artificially to foreground
his women characters in *A Portrait*, or even to develop the New
Woman figure who is potentially present in the Emma of his early
draft, *Stephen Hero*, Joyce responded to the changing status of
and attitudes towards women at the time with a heightened self-
consciousness towards his male protagonist's masculine psychology, thereby challenging many contemporary stereotypes and as-
sumptions about gender.

As a sexual object the bird/girl remains dangerously idealized
and mystified and the same might be said of her function as a
symbol of the new age and new world of secular knowledge that
Stephen hopes to find in the University as an alternative to priestly
vocation and religious belief. As a result of this purely ideal climax
Stephen falls asleep in a kind of swoon or trance. At the start of
the final chapter we see him commuting between the realistic
kitchen-sink world of his impoverished family and the new-age
idealism represented in his mind by the "cloistral silverveined
prose of Newman" and the "wayward boyish beauty" of Ibsen.

As for Joyce's contemporary Eliot (who celebrated the Elizabethan dramatists and the Metaphysical poets in his critical

essays) it is the Elizabethan writers who fascinate Stephen more than the disappointingly factual studies in his official curriculum. We may note that the only lecture he actually attends takes place in the physics theatre (to some student heckling), providing a marked contrast with Stephen's more fruitful researches in the anatomy theatre in Cork in Chapter Two.

Against this "physics" he attempts to establish his aesthetic theory, responding not only to the dynamic of his own intellectual development but also providing for the deep-seated needs felt by both the student of literature and by the noninstitutional reader of such a pleasurably literary novel to explore abstract questions of literary theory. Indeed, the chapter responds to these needs and curiosities more than much study of the subject of literature as it still takes place in schools and colleges today. The fragments of theoretical insight which he delivers in minilectures to his reluctant college friends have a certain validity. We need look no further than Eliot's essay "The Three Voices of Poetry" to see the relevance of Stephen's distinction between lyrical, epical, and dramatic voices. Subsequent theories of modern narrative and authority from Wayne Booth to Bakhtin or Barthes confirm the importance of his description of the impersonalized or indifferent artistic stance.

However, much of the theory is far too locked within Aristotelian and Aquinan terms of reference, which value abstract classical order and symmetry over experiential and exploratory forms of literary disruption, to be of much use as a defense of *A Portrait* itself. One of the great literary encounters that Joyce himself had made before completing the final version of *A Portrait* was with Shakespeare, on whom he lectured in Trieste in 1911, but whose nonclassical example of literary brilliance he denies to Stephen until his next incarnation in Joyce's next great novel-encyclopedia, *Ulysses*.

In relation to Joyce's view of Shakespeare (which we can in part reconstruct from his lecture notes, from Stephen's theory of Shakespeare in *Ulysses*, and elsewhere), in relation to Joyce's 1909 letters to Nora, and in relation to the concept of *aisthesis* towards which the novel as a whole may be said to be implicitly moving, Stephen's theory is only a fragment and an ascetic fragment at that. It is, he himself admits, as yet only a theory of "apprehension" or of artistic consumption. The bodily direction needed to accomplish any further development of it is implied both in his half-completed comparison of artistic beauty to the beauty of the female body and in his stated need for a new terminology of what he calls "artistic conception, artistic gestation and artistic reproduction."

No more complete by the end of the novel is his attempt to be a poet. The villanelle which he composes emerges straight out of his unfulfilled erotic desires, undercutting the ascetic strain in his theory of the "static" nature of art. However, its repetitiveness may recall to us the repetitions of his earlier "act of contrition," implying that the vision of the bird/girl on the beach has turned into a rather morbid and paralyzing pre-Raphaelite woman-worship from which reality is in danger of being excluded.

The development of Stephen's heterosexuality is also left teasingly incomplete at the end of the novel. All his relationships have become soured by a sense of betrayal—not least his putative relationship with E— C—, whom he has worshipped from afar, suspected of disloyalty to him in distant glances and gestures before any agreement has passed between them, and reluctantly abandoned at the level of fantasy before even trying to get to know her in reality. At the end of the novel he is capable of no more than a ridiculous gesture in front of her which "must have looked like a fellow throwing a handful of peas up into the air." Unlike Joyce himself, who left Ireland in 1904 to "live in sin" with Nora Barnacle, Stephen, we feel, is in danger of taking the boat to Holyhead on his own.

The final chapter places Stephen's literary theorizing in the context of the increasingly divergent political ideologies of contemporary Dublin. The maturity and distance that resulted from Joyce having written articles for the Trieste papers on Irish literature and politics contribute much to *A Portrait*. Davin, with his Gaelic League enthusiasm for Irish nationalism by means of myth and Irish field sports, is one force; MacCann, with his struggle for "social liberty and equality" by means of signing petitions, is another. The Dean's fear that Stephen's speculations are dangerous "like looking down from the cliffs of Moher into the depths" may to some extent be echoed by Stephen's best friend Cranly, and Lynch, who listens to him, is presented as little more than a joker and cynic. We are given a brief glimpse of the new national theatre which did so much to establish Irish cultural identity and to expand the repertoire of European drama, but Stephen is more impressed by the moral narrowness of its audience than by its potential for a new Irish art. Against these programs Stephen offers his famous austere and heroic catchwords of cultural resistance and autonomy: "silence, exile and cunning."

A Portrait of the Artist as a Young Man does not end with some heroic or tragic scene that might resolve its action but rather with a section of Stephen's supposed diary. The diary is to some readers a preeminently solipsistic type of writing, self-centered and formless, proof of the incompleteness or even futility of Stephen's hopes. But it provides just the right note for the conclusion of this novel. It is, on one level, another style in the succession of stylistic pastiches that have echoed Stephen's progress throughout. During the final chapter the reader may have noticed a process of relaxation, almost dissipation, both in Stephen's thoughts and in the narrative structure by comparison with the tight order of Chapter Three or the climax of Chapter Four. Stephen himself experiences a sense of disremembering or decline in the piece of self-confessed poetic drivel he produces, beginning "The ivy whines upon the wall," or in his misremembering of a line from the Elizabethan writer Nashe that he associates with a louse crawling over his neck, in a potently ugly image of animal and mental decay. The diary, with its brilliant flashes and fragments of observation, implies a necessary deconstruction of those oppressive ideological orders Stephen has been striving to escape, but also an intimation that such fragmentariness or forgetfulness of human memory, such deconstruction, may be the intellectual mode appropriate to such a radical apostasy as that which Stephen proposes.

This and other doublenesses underpin the novel's much-quoted concluding diary entries. The penultimate one announces an existential "welcome" to "life" and a determination to "encounter for the millionth time the reality of experience and to forge in the smithy of my soul the uncreated conscience of my race." Whether Stephen means the Irish "race" he is leaving or the new "race" of cosmopolitan aestheticism which he is hoping to find, is not clear. The final entry contrasts such exuberance with a more sober appeal to Stephen's mythic namesake or secular-mystical "father,"

Daedalus, that (since it apparently identifies him with Daedalus's unfortunate son Icarus) some read as a premonition of his fall. Implicit in the former entry is the belief that the writer can and must create something entirely new; in the latter, identity is predetermined by language and name. To encounter these and other contradictions and to accept them where no simple resolution can be achieved may be the role towards which Stephen is progressing, a stage of which this diary form can best represent.

Stephen achieves at least some measured form of self-possession and self-expression at the end of the novel, but he is left in a position of dangerous isolation both from his own and from any other as-yet-existing community. He may, as another recent Irish writer has put it, be left with an audience but with no constituency. Joyce himself, massively successful though his artistic achievement has been, may be a paradoxical victim of this kind of fate. The face of W. B. Yeats, like that of Shakespeare, appears on his country's banknotes, but it may be harder for us to imagine the nation or economic community on whose currency Joyce's face might appear.

Though not completed until his early thirties, the novel, which had been begun in Dublin at the time of the events it narrates, was the first work of Joyce's artistic maturity to be published. When it first appeared in serial form in 1914, the *Dubliners* stories that had been rejected by publishers for the past ten years were also finally brought out. The novel, published in book form in 1916, gradually won Joyce the wide recognition and respect he deserved and it frequently still provides readers with their first introduction to his work.

Many of the early debates that colored critical writing about the book (whether Stephen is or is not Joyce himself; whether his presentation is "heroic" or "ironic"; whether or not he is successful as an artist; to what type or genre the novel should be assigned; whether he or Joyce is for or against political positions nationalistic, feministic, socialistic, and so on) can probably now be taken onto a different level. According to one of its most perceptive early critics, Kenneth Burke, *A Portrait* can be defined as an "angelic" text: that is, a work that is complete unto itself and unique. Indeed, for Burke, Joyce's texts inaugurated a new literary activity of joyful punning and associative interpretation to which he referred as "Joycing" or "to Joyce."

Mixing material from his own life with portraits of the lives of other artists, Joyce's novel charts out the new territory of secular imaginative writing and culture that the high Victorians were proposing as an alternative means of social cohesion and self-discovery to that traditionally supplied by established religion. That Stephen's own thinking and his experiences both proceed with this extraordinary goal and show up several of its potential pitfalls figures not least among its achievements. It describes and defines for us the new subject of English Literature, can still help us to shape the academic subject to the genuine needs and desires of those who study it, and is assured a place wherever English Literature is read or taught.

Richard Brown

SELECT BIBLIOGRAPHY

Books on Joyce are now so numerous that only those which are devoted mainly or exclusively to *A Portrait of the Artist as a Young Man* can be included here. What follows is a brief selection of material on the novel, with priority given to those critical books and articles to which the Afterword is most indebted. Readers requiring more complete bibliographical information on Joyce's other works and the very extensive secondary literature on Joyce are referred to the descriptive bibliography by Thomas Jackson Rice, *James Joyce: A Guide to Research*, Garland, New York, 1982.

The standard biography of Joyce is, of course, by Richard Ellmann, revised for Oxford University Press in 1982. The most easily available volume of Joyce's letters was also edited by Ellmann, under the title *Selected Letters of James Joyce*, Viking, New York, and Faber, London, 1975.

Textual materials for *A Portrait* have been published in the *James Joyce Archive*, ed. Michael Groden, Garland, New York, 1978, as have the 1904 *Portrait* essay and Joyce's intermediary version of the novel entitled *Stephen Hero* (*Archive* volumes [7]–[10], volumes editor Hans Walter Gabler). *Stephen Hero* has also been published separately by New Directions and Jonathan Cape in 1944, and in revised editions in 1959/1956.

Useful annotated editions of *A Portrait* for the student are the Heinemann edition of 1964, edited with an introduction and helpful notes by J. S. Atherton; the 1968 Viking Critical Library edition of text, criticism, and notes, edited by Chester G. Anderson; and the 1992 (British) Penguin edition, edited by Seamus Deane. Other annotations may be found in Don Gifford, *Joyce Annotated*, University of California Press, 1982. The only previous edited text is that prepared by Chester Anderson, first published in America in 1964 and in England by Jonathan Cape in 1968. It is also the text of the Viking Critical Library edition of 1968, as well as of the 1992 Penguin edition.

Selections of criticism on *A Portrait* include Morris Beja (ed.), *James Joyce: Dubliners and A Portrait of the Artist as a Young Man: A Casebook*, Macmillan, 1973; and Thomas F. Staley (ed.), *Approaches to Joyce's Portrait: Ten Essays*, University of Pittsburgh Press, Pittsburgh, 1976. Early reactions are collected in Robert H. Deming (ed.), *James Joyce: The Critical Heritage*, Routledge, 1970.

CRITICAL BOOKS AND ESSAYS

Derek Attridge (ed.), *The Cambridge Companion to James Joyce*, Cambridge University Press, 1990.

Wayne Booth, *The Rhetoric of Fiction*, University of Chicago Press, Chicago, 1969, pp. 323–36.

Kenneth Burke, "Fact, Inference and Proof in the Analysis of Literary Symbolism," in *Terms for Order*, ed. Stanley Hyman, Indiana University Press, Bloomington, 1964, pp. 145–72.

Christopher Butler, "A Portrait of the Artist as Displaced Author," in *James Joyce and Modern Literature*, eds. W. J. McCormick and A. Stead, Routledge, 1984.

Joseph A. Buttigieg, *A Portrait of the Artist in Different Perspective*, Illinois University Press, Ohio, 1987.

Terry Eagleton, *Exiles and Emigrés*, Chatto, 1965.

—, *Literary Theory*, Blackwell, 1983.

—, *The Ideology of the Aesthetic*, Blackwell, 1990.

Maud Ellmann, "Polytropic Man," in *James Joyce: New Perspectives*, ed. Colin MacCabe, Harvester, 1982, pp. 73–103.

—, "Disremembering Dedalus," in *Untying the Text*, ed. Robert Young, Routledge, 1986.

Richard Ellmann, *James Joyce*, Oxford University Press, 1982.

Edmund Epstein, *The Ordeal of Stephen Dedalus*, Southern Illinois University Press, Carbondale, 1971.

Hans Walter Gabler, "The Seven Lost Years of *A Portrait of the Artist as a Young Man*," in *Approaches to Joyce's Portrait*, eds. Bernard Benstock and Thomas F. Staley, University of Pittsburgh Press, Pittsburgh, 1976, pp. 25–60.

—, "The Christmas Dinner Scene, Parnell's Death, and the Genesis of *A Portrait* ...," in *James Joyce Quarterly* 13 (1976), pp. 27–38.

Hugh Kenner, *Dublin's Joyce*, Indiana University Press, Bloomington, 1956.

—, *Joyce's Voices*, University of California Press and Faber, 1978.

Karen Lawrence, "Gender and Narrative Voice in *Jacob's Room* and *A Portrait of the Artist as a Young Man*," in *James Joyce: The Centennial Symposium*, ed. Beja *et al.*, University of Illinois Press, Urbana, 1986.

Vicki Mahaffey, *Reauthorising Joyce*, Cambridge University Press, 1988.

Colin MacCabe, *James Joyce and the Revolution of the Word*, Macmillan, 1978.

Dominic Manganiello, *Joyce's Politics*, Routledge, 1980.

Roy Pascal, "The Autobiographical Novel and Autobiography," *Essays in Criticism* 9, 1959, pp. 134–50.

Jean-Michel Rabaté, *James Joyce: Portrait de L'Auteur en Autre Lecteur*, Cistre, Petit-Roeulx, 1984.

John Paul Riquelme, "A Portrait of the Artist as a Young Man," in *The Cambridge Companion to James Joyce*, ed. D. Attridge, Cambridge University Press, 1990.

Dorothy van Ghent, *Form and Function in the English Novel*, Viking, New York, 1959, pp.263–76.

CHRONOLOGY

DATE	AUTHOR'S LIFE	LITERARY CONTEXT
1882	Joyce born, 2 February, Rathgar, Dublin.	Virginia Woolf born.
1884		
1886		
1888	Joyce starts at Clongowes Wood College.	
1890		Newman dies.
1891		Shaw: *Quintessence of Ibsenism*.
1893	Joyce goes to Belvedere College.	
1895		Wilde's trial and imprisonment.
1897		James: *What Maisie Knew*.
1899	Joyce goes to University College, Dublin.	
1900	Joyce's "Ibsen's New Drama" published in *Fortnightly Review*.	Conrad's *Lord Jim*.
1901	"The Day of the Rabblement."	
1902	"James Clarence Mangan." Joyce's first Paris trip and reviews.	
1903	Begins *Stephen Hero*. Mary Jane Joyce (Joyce's mother) dies.	
1904	Joyce writes *Portrait* sketch. Publishes earliest *Dubliners* stories. Elopement with Nora to Pola (Austro-Hungary).	Opening of Abbey Theatre in Dublin.
1905	Moves to Trieste. Son Giorgio born, 27 July. Suspends *Stephen Hero*.	
1906	Brief residence in Rome. First abortive attempt to publish *Dubliners*.	Samuel Beckett born. Ibsen dies.
1907	Moves back to Trieste. *Chamber Music* published. Daughter Lucia born, 26 July. Writes *The Dead*. Begins *A Portrait*. Essays on Irish politics in Trieste papers.	"Playboy" riots (Abbey Theatre).
1909	August and October–December, trips to Dublin. Letters to Nora written.	
1910	Second abortive attempt to publish *Dubliners*.	H. G. Wells: *The History of Mr. Polly*.
1911	Joyce lectures on Shakespeare in Trieste.	

Oxford Chair of English.
lstone's First Home Rule Bill defeated.

rnell dies.

Queen Victoria's Diamond Jubilee.
Second Boer War.

Founding of British Labour Party.

Queen Victoria dies.
Balfour's Education Act.

Further educational and social reform in Britain.

DATE	AUTHOR'S LIFE	LITERARY CONTEXT
1912	Last visit to Dublin.	Charlie Chaplin's first film.
1913		D. H. Lawrence: *Sons and Lo*
1914	*A Portrait* serialized in *The Egoist. Dubliners* published by Grant Richards. *Giacomo Joyce* written. *Exiles* composed.	*Des Imagistes: An Anthology.*
1915	Joyce moves to Zürich. Work on *Ulysses* resumed, 16 June. *Exiles* revised.	
1916	*A Portrait* published in America.	
1917	*A Portrait* published in Britain. *Ulysses* fair copy begun.	Yeats: *Wild Swans at Coole.* T. S. Eliot: *Prufrock and other Observations.*
1918	*Ulysses* serialization begins in *Little Review. Exiles* published.	
1920	Joyce moves to Paris. *Ulysses* serialization halted.	
1921		
1922	*Ulysses* published in Paris (February).	T. S. Eliot, *The Waste Land.*
1924	First section of *Work in Progress* ("Mamalujo") published in *Transatlantic Review* I.	
1925		G. B. Shaw awarded Nobel Prize. Yeats: *A Vision.* Eisenstein: *Battleship Potemkin.*
1926		
1927	*Pomes Penyeach* published.	Woolf: *To the Lighthouse.*
1928		
1929	*Our Examination* essays on *Work in Progress* published.	
1932	Lucia diagnosed "hebephrenic."	
1933		Leavis attacks *Work in Progress* in *Scrutiny.*
1934	*Ulysses* published in US.	
1936	*Ulysses* published in UK.	
1937		
1938		Beckett's *Murphy* published.
1939	*Finnegans Wake* published. Joyce moves to Zürich.	Brendan Behan arrested. Seamus Heaney born. W. B. Yeats dies.
1941	Joyce dies in Zürich at age fifty-nine.	Virginia Woolf dies.

World War I breaks out. Irish Home Rule passed but shelved.

Easter Rising in Dublin.

Conclusion of World War I. Partial franchise for women in Great Britain. Irish rebel Con Markiewitz elected first British woman MP.

Irish Free State (excluding six counties) founded (December).

Baird demonstrates television picture.
Cinema "talkies."
Full suffrage for women in Great Britain.
Wall Street Crash.

De Valera's Fianna Fail takes office in Ireland.

Hitler becomes German *Führer*.
Abdication of Edward VIII.
New Irish constitution established.

Outbreak of World War II.